It was to be an enormously grand party, and even though she was only four, Rose was still going. It was the Victory Party to celebrate the end of the war. Everyone was going.

Dressed in a rose and green velvet party frock, she danced with Uncle Joe and then with Mr Laben, and then she went to look for her mother. Mummy was in bed, even though it was in the middle of a party. It was a big bed, and she was being cuddled by a man. She was smiling and she looked happy and relaxed.

'Mummy is resting now, darling,' she said. 'Go and have some Victory cake. It's almost midnight.'

'Can't I stay with you?' asked Rose.

'Not now, darling.' The man raised his head and looked at Rose in puzzlement. Then he turned away. It was as though Rose wasn't there at all.

Later, and for years afterwards, Rose blocked the memory from her mind. By the time Jon was grown-up Rose had all but forgotten it and it wasn't until everything began to explode about them that she had to dig the memory out from the past.

Also by Susan Sallis

A SCATTERING OF DAISIES
THE DAFFODILS OF NEWENT
BLUEBELL WINDOWS
ROSEMARY FOR REMEMBRANCE
SUMMER VISITORS
BY SUN AND CANDLELIGHT

and published by Corgi Books

AN ORDINARY WOMAN

Susan Sallis

CORGI BOOKS

AN ORDINARY WOMAN
A CORGI BOOK 0 552 13756 1

Originally published in Great Britain by Bantam Press,
a division of Transworld Publishers Ltd

PRINTING HISTORY
Bantam Press edition published 1991
Corgi edition published 1991

This book is set in 10/11pt Plantin by
Chippendale Type Ltd., Otley, West Yorkshire.

Corgi Books are published by Transworld Publishers Ltd., 61–63
Uxbridge Road, Ealing, London W5 5SA, in Australia by Transworld
Publishers (Australia) Pty. Ltd., 15–23 Helles Avenue, Moorebank,
NSW 2170, and in New Zealand by Transworld Publishers (N.Z.)
Ltd., Cnr. Moselle and Waipareira Avenues, Henderson, Auckland.

Printed and bound in Great Britain by
Cox & Wyman Ltd, Reading

To my family

One

From a four-year-old viewpoint, the house looked like a palace. For one thing it had marble pillars and a staircase that arched up one side of the enormous Cinderella ballroom, and down the other. A real chandelier with real candles dominated the upper atmosphere – Rose had been there when a man had lowered the entire iced-cake contraption and cleaned out the sconces and stuck in about two hundred million candles. And she'd screamed a bit when an hour ago someone else had lit the whole lot with a kind of flame-thrower. She stood just under the stairs and looked at it and wondered what would happen if it all came crashing down. There was no carpet to burn. Not much furniture either. The chairs and tables and carpets and sideboards and cocktail cabinets and china cabinets and everything else were all in side rooms. Later on, people were going to dance under the chandelier and did not want to bump into things. But if the chandelier bumped into them they'd know it. That's what Aunt Mabe's factotum said – 'If you don't look where you're going, girl, you'll know it!' Often and often Rose wanted to argue with him on that point, but she loved him too much to hurt his feelings. She always smiled at him sweetly and said, 'I know, Fack. I know now.' His name wasn't Fack of course. Aunt Mabe and Uncle Joe called him Tom, like in *Uncle Tom's Cabin*, but Rose had looked at the pictures in a copy of that book and couldn't bear to think of him as Tom. He was a factotum which was a long and important word and took him right out of the servant or servile class. She would remind him of it daily. She called him Fack.

He was here tonight. He'd driven them there in the Chrysler which looked as if it was blown up with a bicycle pump, it was so puffy and rounded. They only lived down the block and had been back and forth all day helping with tonight's preparations. But they'd had to come in the car because it was cloudy and might rain and they'd got on their best clothes.

Not that it could possibly rain on VJ night surely? Rose did not believe that God would allow it. Her mother had read bits of the last letter from home aloud to her and it had been good weather there for VE day. So if God had arranged that – when England was well-known for being constantly rainy – then it wouldn't be so much trouble to postpone any of Connecticut's famous thunderstorms.

Nevertheless it was nice to arrive in the Chrysler and sweep up to the enormous porticoed front and have Fack hand her out like a queen. No, like Cinderella. Because most of the time she ran around the farm in coveralls and a tattered straw hat, and tonight she was dressed in a long frock right down to the floor. She'd chosen the material and described the design herself. Rose-coloured satin, like her name. A green velvet sash and green velvet bows down the bodice. She did not realize that she was influenced by Disney's Snow-White until she stood before the mirror. Her hair was dark and – unusually – parted in the middle for the occasion. Her eyes were intensely blue with excitement and her mouth suddenly fuller.

She said tentatively, 'Mummy, do I look a little bit like Snow-White?'

And her mother said, 'You look the most beautiful girl I've ever seen.'

But then her mother always said things like that. Mothers did. And Aunt Mabe never noticed her. And Uncle Joe insisted on calling her his 'chickadee' all the time. And when she asked Fack what he thought he said severely, 'It's more important to be good than beautiful, girl. And if you ain't, you'll know it! One of these days, you'll know it!'

She sighed. 'Yes. I know. Now. Ackcherly.'

Because already she secretly suspected it was her fault Daddy had been torpedoed in the Atlantic. Surely if her mother hadn't been expecting her and had come to Aunt

Mabe's to get away from the bombing, Daddy wouldn't have tried to cross the sea to visit them so wouldn't have been . . .

Fack said suddenly, 'You ain't bad-looking, girl. I'll give you that.'

She flung her arms around his knees and hugged him hard and he lost his balance and fell back on her bed and Aunt Mabe came into the room when they were laughing fit to bust.

'What the hell's going on?' she asked in a voice like a lemon that had been kept in an icebox for two years.

Rose said, 'I was cuddling Fack's knees, Aunt Mabe, and he fell over and he looked so funny, we laughed.'

She was surprised Aunt Mabe needed an explanation. It was so obvious what had happened. But Fack got up, all embarrassed, and said, 'Will there be anything more, Missee Mabel?'

And Aunt Mabe said, 'I don't think so. Do you?'

And Fack was out of the room very quickly.

Mother and Aunt Mabel came through one of the doors with Mr and Mrs Laben and their two grandsons. One was called Eric and the other Lennox. They were not much older than Rose and they wore grown-up black suits and stiff white collars like the waiters. Mrs Laben said, 'She must be somewhere, girls, don't panic. Aileen, I can't tell you how lovely it is to see you looking so beautiful. The end of this dreadful war, my dear. The beginning of something new. Especially for you. Hm?'

Mother said, 'Well. England isn't new of course. But, yes, you're right. I must look forward now.'

Aunt Mabe said, 'Why don't you stay here, darling? From what I hear, England is pretty much Drab-land at the moment.'

Rose held her breath. She'd never seen England, but her mother spoke of it every day. There were nursery fires with brass fireguards around them and hot buttered scones for tea and everything was always the same. That was what Rose wanted: for everything to be always the same.

Eric shouted, 'Oh, there's Rosie-posie all the time! Hi brat!'

Mrs Laben said, 'Behave yourself, Eric. You are escorting Rose, remember. When the senator arrives I want you to present her properly. Miss Rosamund Harris. Can you remember that?'

Eric said, 'Oh Grandmother!'

Lennox said, 'I'm glad I'm escorting you, Mrs Harris. You look simply marvellous.'

Lennox always talked like that. On the whole Rose thought she preferred Eric's approach. She stood by his side in what Uncle Joe called 'the line-up', and shook hands with some of the arrivals, was picked up and admired by others. No-one said she looked like Snow-White. And Mother hadn't replied to Aunt Mabe about staying in Connecticut.

In the dining room the Victory cake was waiting on its own special table. It was as big as the sandpit at the farm, but it wasn't all cake. Only the outside was edible. In the middle there was a hole covered with white cardboard that looked like the icing. That was why the cake had its own table with a cloth going down to the floor. You could go underneath the cloth and stand up in the middle of the cake. At the appointed time an actress – a real actress from the summer theatre – was going to pop up out of the cake wearing a dress and hat made entirely of the Stars and Stripes. At first Mrs Laben had suggested Rose should be the girl. She said Rose would represent the new generation of peace. Also as Rose was sort of English, it would be kind of hands-across-the-sea. But luckily Mother had explained that Rose couldn't possibly do anything like that as she was so shy, and they had hired the actress.

As soon as the dancing started under the chandelier, Eric left Rose to her own devices and went to find Lennox. Rose looked for her mother and saw her dancing with Uncle Joe and felt fairly safe. She went back under the stairs and kept an eye on the chandelier for ten minutes and tried not to think about Aunt Mabe wanting to adopt her. Then she saw Fack walking very sedately towards the dining room

10

and knew something was up. Fack never appeared to hurry, but he never dawdled either, and this time his tread was so exactly measured that it amounted to dawdling. She followed him.

It was quiet in the dining room, but the air was tense with anxiety, condemnation, fury. Half a dozen maids and two menservants stood around the tablecloth surveying a hole in the cake. Not the proper, permitted hole through which the actress was going to explode, but a wedge-shaped jagged lump from the perimeter. Slivers of icing littered the carpeted floor, crumbs were everywhere. It was as if a giant mouse had savaged the cake. Already another maid had appeared at the far end of the room, lugging a vacuum cleaner.

One of the male servants – Mr Laben's 'man' – was saying thunderously, 'Who is responsible for this desecration!' And it was obvious he'd said those words several times. He wasn't even asking the question, but applying the words like a whip across the bowed heads of the capped and aproned girls.

Fack arrived.

'Shall we leave responsibility until later?' he said smoothly – and Rose noted that his accent had changed and he did not sound in the least like Uncle Tom.

'It needs to be cleared and – and disguised – in some way,' he went on a little less certainly. 'Move away ladies, let us at least vacuum the carpet.'

He'd said 'ladies', not 'missies'.

The vacuum went into operation. Mr Laben's man stood there like a rock, frowning massively. Fack got on his hands and knees and crawled beneath the tablecloth. The maids drew back and gazed after him uncertainly. Rose got behind a chair. She knew Fack would find a solution. And he did.

He emerged with a wedge-shaped piece of white card-board in his hand. The cleaner was switched off.

'There's a lot of this stuff underneath. I guess it's to support the funnel arrangement in the middle.' He went across to the hole. 'If we build it up around this gap

11

it will look like icing and we can take some of these garlands . . . ' he began to improvize. If you knew what had happened it wasn't much of a disguise, but if you didn't it wasn't too bad.

Mr Laben's man said, 'Rubbish!'

But the other manservant said, 'It's not at all bad. We can cut from either side of it. No-one will know.'

Mr Laben's man said, 'I intend to find out who did this. Whosoever needs to know, will know.'

Rose shivered. It sounded like the Bible. She dropped to her knees and tried to crawl beneath the sofa. Her dress hampered her; she clawed it up around her waist and ducked her head under the chintz valance. Six inches away black eyes, highlighted in very white whites, met hers. She squeaked.

'Shut *up*!' A voice hissed furiously. 'Get down and shut up, for the good Lord's sake.'

She sank to her tummy, conscious that her white socks and patent shoes were visible to anyone who looked behind the furniture.

The vacuum cleaner was switched off and the voices became more reasonable. She heard Fack say, 'Nothing to be done about it. Not really. If it was Master Eric—'

Rose wondered where Eric had got to. It was more likely to be Lennox trying to get Eric into trouble.

Mr Laben's man spoke in a different tone.

'Well of course, in that case . . . ' He cleared his throat and snapped, 'You girls stand in front of the repair for goodness sake. Mimi, you can wipe that smile off your face! Where were you half an hour ago, I'd like to know? Yes – that goes for all of you. One peep out of anyone and it'll be suspicion all around. Is that understood?'

Rose's eyes, accustomed now to the under-sofa darkness, took in the fact that there were a great deal of crumbs around the owner of the black eyes. And he was wearing a monkey suit and was probably a waiter brought in for the occasion.

Fack's voice said above her, 'And what might you be doin' down there, young missy?'

12

She backed out and stood up. Fack's eyes widened. There were crumbs on the old-rose satin bodice.

'Nothing, Fack,' she said.

He went on looking at her. Then he said, 'Then let's go back in where you kin do something, honey. I reckon there's young gennelmen out there just waitin' for you to dance before their evening is made!'

She giggled obediently and took Fack's hand. She did not even look down at the valance again. No-one must know about the waiter. Not ever.

She danced with Uncle Joe and then with Mr Laben. They picked her up and waltzed solemnly around the floor and people said 'Oh, isn't that just sweet. Isn't that the little English girl. Her father . . . yes. You remember.'

Lennox was dancing with her mother and watching her strangely as if he hadn't seen her before. She brushed the front of her dress but Fack had given her a good slap-down before they'd gone back into the chandelier room and she knew there weren't any crumbs left.

Mr Laben set her down gently in front of Eric.

'Come, grandson!' he ordered, his voice still slightly accented. 'Dance with the little lady.' He realized how similar were his words to the popular song, so he sang out of key, 'Dance, dance, dance little lady—' and laughed uproariously. Eric looked mutinous for a moment, then spotted the senator's lady approaching and took Rose's hand.

'For Pete's sake!' he lugged her against his chest. 'I'm too old to dance with you, Rose Harris! And I bet you've never had any lessons yet, have you?'

'I have so,' she panted, walking backwards as fast as she could. 'I go in to New Haven to Miss Millward's Academy.' Rose stammered the word academy and it sounded as if she had said 'mad men'. Eric snorted a laugh of derision and did something complicated with his feet and she stumbled against him.

'Jesus Christ!' he said.

She was shocked beyond words, and waited fearfully for the Lord to appear with a sword. Instead it was Lennox.

'May I cut in?' he asked in that suave voice of his. 'My turn, I think, little cousin.'

But Rose was thoroughly put out and almost forgot she was shy.

'I'm not your cousin at all,' she said. 'Uncle Joe and Mr Laben were in the old country together and you—'

He laughed and took her firmly around the waist.

'Little parrot,' he said. 'The old country. What do you know about the old country? Stand on my shoes. Go on. You won't hurt me. Then we'll show everyone a thing or two.'

Her long dress hid her patents. She appeared to be perfectly matched with Lennox Laben and didn't much like it. If it had been Eric it wouldn't have been so bad. Lennox held her clamped against him so that she could hardly breathe. She could smell him. Sort of salty talcum powder. And wine. Lennox had been stealing the wine, which was much worse than the boy who had stolen the cake.

Everyone thought it was marvellous, even Mother.

'You looked like Snow-White and the Prince,' she enthused, hugging Rose to her and smiling into her eyes. 'I had no idea you were doing so well at Miss Millward's, baby. I'll have to let Aunt Mabe send you twice a week next term.'

'But the war's over, Mummy. We can go home,' Rose bleated. 'You said we could go home when the war was over—'

'Gee, honey. Connecticut is home for you! You were born here—' her mother was talking with an exaggerated American accent. She smelled of wine too. And she kept lifting her head and laughing at the chandelier. Except that you couldn't see the chandelier because there was a man hovering there.

Rose said, 'I hate Miss Millward. She thinks I can't count and she makes me say one, two three, all the time!'

Mother seemed to think this was the funniest thing she'd heard in her life. She laughed and laughed and the man started to laugh too, and they weren't laughing at Rose at all but at some secret they shared.

Lennox said, 'Come on, baby. Let's do it again.'

'No thank you, Lennox,' Rose said primly. 'I'm going to have a lie-down until the cake is cut. Thank you all the same.'

She made for the curving stairs and went up them slowly. She could see her mother, still laughing upwards into the face of the man. She could see Lennox staring after her. And Aunt Mabe dancing with the senator and Uncle Joe pouring drinks for about six ladies. And she could see, quite suddenly, the cake-stealer, walking through the people who weren't dancing with a tray held high and expertly. She paused and willed him to look up at her. Sure enough he did. Then she lifted her skirt gently with one hand, laid the other casually on the banister, and continued to the landing. She almost kicked off one of her patents, but that was in Cinderella, not Snow-White. She went into the bedroom Mrs Laben had assigned to her, snapped on the light, and looked at herself in the picr glass.

No, she wasn't Snow-White or Cinderella or any other kind of princess in disguise. She was Rose Harris who was frightened most of the time and wanted her mother and their own home and nothing to happen to her ever again.

She went over to the bed which had its own curtains all looped up prettily. She flopped on it, not even taking off her shoes. And – rather enjoyably – she indulged in a cry.

She never knew whether she slept or not. But Lennox was there quite suddenly, leaning over her, smiling like a cat.

'Hi there, little cousin,' he whispered. 'Had your beauty sleep, have you?'

She repeated stubbornly, 'I'm not your cousin,' and made to sit up.

He put his hands on her rose-satin shoulders and held her down.

'No need to wake up yet, gorgeous. There. Is that better?'

'No. Let me up,' she demanded.

'Not yet. Listen to me first.' He went on smiling but his eyes were quite mad. 'You are my cousin. Really.

15

The English and the Americans are cousins. Didn't you know that?'

She'd heard people refer to 'our English cousins' in a condescending kind of way. She let her gaze slide away from his. His mouth was wet. He'd been drinking wine again.

He said, 'Was I a kind cousin to you downstairs tonight? When I danced you off your feet – yeah, sure, that's what I did – I danced you off your feet, little cousin!' He giggled insanely. 'Everyone looked at you. Everyone thought you were the cutest thing on two legs in that whole room! Was I a kind cousin then?'

She didn't answer at first and he pressed very hard on her shoulders. In spite of the soft mattress it hurt.

She said sullenly, 'I suppose so.'

'Suppose so?' He mimicked her very accurately. 'Serppose so? You don't guess so, do you, English cousin? You ser . . . pose so!'

She said, 'Let me up. I want my mother.'

He giggled again. 'Who doesn't? Everyone wants the ice maiden. And I reckon she's melting tonight.' He screwed up his mouth. 'I *guess* she's melting!' He threw back his head rather as Mother had done earlier. 'No guessing about it, honey! I know she's melting. I've just seen her!'

She didn't know what he was talking about, but foreboding tightened her chest nevertheless. 'I want my mother,' she said loudly.

He glanced over his shoulder at the door. It was still open but the noise from below would cover most sounds.

He said, 'No more yelling. I'm going to stop you yelling.' And he put his mouth on hers and pressed down hard.

It was horrible. The taste of wine sickened her and she twisted her head on the pillow and pummelled his chest with her fists.

He raised his head, panting.

'Don't be a little fool, Rosie. What's got into you? I've fallen for you, that's all. You should be pleased you've got a guy my age on a short string! How old are you – five? Christ, if some floozy had gone for me when I was five I'd never have stopped thanking God!' He jerked her suddenly

16

upright and dragged her off the bed. 'Come on – get on your knees and thank God for me! Thank God for Cousin Lennox from the good USA!'

He forced her down by the bed. She sobbed, 'I'm four! I'm not five till the fall. I hate you—'

'After what I've done for you? Not nice, Rosie. Not nice at all.' He had her hands behind her back, his knee was in her spine. She put her forehead on the undersheet and prayed hard.

The knee was removed and she thought God had answered her prayers. Then she felt him try to tear the skirt of her lovely dress. It gave her a new strength. She wrenched herself round to face him, screaming at the top of her voice. He put his hand over her mouth but that freed her hands and she pushed at him frantically and made for the door. She was in the upper hallway when he caught her. He held her against him very hard until her struggles died away, then he let her go. She slumped against the wall.

'I want my mother,' she whispered.

'OK. You shall have your mother.'

He frog-marched her up another flight of stairs, down another hallway, opened a door and shoved her inside. There was a bed – a bigger bed than hers – but no drapes. Her mother was in the bed. She was being cuddled by a man. She was smiling, her eyes closed.

'Mummy—' Rose approached the bed, intending to get in the other side. 'Mummy, Mummy—'

Her mother opened her eyes. She wasn't cross. She said softly, 'Mummy is resting now, darling. Go and find Eric and have some Victory cake. It's almost midnight.'

'I want to stay with you,' whispered Rose. 'Can't I stay with you?'

'No darling.' The man raised his head and looked at Rose, screwing up his eyes in puzzlement. Then he turned away and kissed her mother. It was as if Rose wasn't there at all. But she was frightened to go. Lennox was waiting.

She heard him come up behind her and opened her mouth to scream again. Then another voice said, 'Come on, kid. Time to go back to the cake.'

17

She turned round and there was the waiter again, his eyes as black as coals in their whites, his bow tie skew-whiff, but no crumbs.

She said, 'Where is Lennox?'

And the waiter said, 'I kicked his ass for him. Was that OK?'

She put her hand over her mouth and laughed through her fingers.

The waiter grinned. 'I thought it would be.' He held out his hand and she took it without fear. He said, 'Say, it was mighty nice of you not to split on me down there. Thanks a lot. You're a good kid.'

They walked back down the hallway.

'Why did you do it? Were you very hungry?'

'No. Just mad with the whole parcel of 'em. Dad included. I wish I could drop an atomic bomb on that cake.'

She didn't understand. It was such a beautiful cake.

They came to the big curved staircase.

'I have to go the back way, kid. Look out for that Lennox guy. He's bad news.'

'I want to stay with you,' Rose said, hanging on to the warm dry hand and going through the service door.

'You can't do that. You know it. Go on downstairs. The front stairs—'

Fack's voice cut across the waiter's.

'What in *hell* d'you think you're doing, boy?'

Fack was standing at the bottom of the narrow stairs, a towel over one arm, sweat glistening on his forehead.

Rose said, 'Fack. This is my friend. He kicked Lennox in the—'

The waiter said, 'Dad. No harm done. The kid was in trouble—'

Fack said, 'Miss Rose. You get back to your folks and stay there. Where you belong. And just forget you ever met Abr'am here. Don' look so upset, girl. Tidn't your fault. Why, he's more'n twice your age and should know better—'

The waiter said, 'Dad, stop talking like that. It's 1945 and we're free. Or d'you want me to say we'se free, pa!'

18

'Don't you talk to your father like that, boy. Get into the kitchens this minute! The cake's half-ruined. The actress-girl is dead drunk. If somethin' don't go right soon, we'll be free all right. Free as air, we'll be—' Fack was up the stairs by this time, holding the back of the waiter's coat, urging – no, shoving him – downstairs. Then they were both gone and there was nothing for Rose to do but return to the staircase crescent and go down to where Eric was sitting sulkily by Uncle Joe and Aunt Mabe was again dancing with the senator.

At midnight they trooped in for the cake to be cut. Everyone knew about the hollow middle and the cardboard lid and the actress, but they were going to pretend to be surprised anyway. The senator made a very sincere speech in which the words 'our boys' featured often. Then, for some reason, he kissed his wife. Then he kissed Aunt Mabe, then the lights dimmed and there was a drum roll. A spotlight leapt across the floor and hovered over the centre of the cake. The lid flipped up and out sprang the waiter.

He was stripped to the waist and apparently covered in oil because he glistened quite frighteningly. He stood there, his arms spread wide, and he looked at everyone from his superior height.

'Brothers and sisters!' he said loudly and clearly into the startled silence. 'We fought together! We died together! Let's make sure that we live together!' And then he dropped his arms and looked at everyone with a sort of quizzical smirk and said, 'Huh?'

Then the spotlight went off, the lights came on, Fack was hustling him down and apologizing to Mr Laben and the senator was saying loudly, 'How old? Fourteen? Say, I did some crazy things when I was fourteen!'

And he kissed Aunt Mabe again, which must mean he was still doing crazy things.

Rose turned round, glowing with a kind of pride, and found her mother behind her. She wanted to tell her about Lennox and Fack's boy whose name was Abram, but she was desperately tired and she knew she'd never find all the necessary words. Her mother lifted her and carried her upstairs, whispering in her ear all the time. She undressed her and hung the dress on a hanger. Then she settled Rose within her arm and waited till she went to sleep.

Some time in the night, Rose dreamed that her mother asked her a question. She half-woke and said fearfully, 'But Mummy, you can't get married to anyone. You're already married to Daddy!'

Then she went to sleep again. England was as far away as ever, but she didn't mind too much now. Abram might do dreadful things, but he was the safety and security she'd been missing for so long.

Two

But her mother did not get married and four months later they were on board the SS *Orion* bound for Southampton, and Aileen's abdomen was already beginning to press against her sloppy-joe sweater.

Rose had gathered from the sparky atmosphere of disapproval back at the farm that the new baby was not welcome by everyone. In fact Aunt Mabe had not been the same since VJ night, and had gone around the farm with tight lips between outbursts of what Mother called at first 'pure temper', and then, as the weeks went by, 'harassment'.

Eventually Uncle Joe said tiredly, 'OK. What's done is done. Christ, isn't that the truest word I've ever spoken. Sorry . . . sorry, girls. Vulgar, vulgar, vulgar. But Mab, if I have to see that expression of yours much longer . . . Christ, it looks as if you're holding a pencil in your sodding ass!'

Aunt Mabe had responded to that with a loud scream and Fack had appeared from nowhere and hustled Rose out of the room.

'Where's Abram?' she asked him, not for the first time by any means. 'What happened after the cake?'

'He's been sent away. He's gone away to a school. A real good school.'

But Fack did not look pleased about it. And Rose was not happy either. Aunt Mabe ignored her for a few weeks after the party, and that was all right because she usually did. But then she started referring to Rose as 'that poor child'. And then when Rose wouldn't go over to the Labens to play with Eric, she said, 'That poor child is positively introverted, Aileen. Leave her with me when you go back. I can do that much for you anyway.'

But unexpectedly, Mother stood up to Aunt Mabe.

'We're both going home,' she said decisively. 'I've brought disgrace to you, Mabel, but I'm not going to sponge on you any longer. I might not have a husband – I might have made a complete ass of myself – but I've got a daughter and another child on the way. I've got a family. I'm going to look after it by myself.'

Aunt Mabe said in a hard voice, 'Suit yourself.'

Uncle Joe said, 'Look here, girls. You're sisters. You're family. I look on Rose as belonging to all of us. And this new one . . . well, we shall live it down. Let's live it down together for Christ's sake.'

'What will the senator think?' Aunt Mabe paced to the window and looked out on the paddock where two horses grazed. The farm was run by a couple who kept disagreeable sights, like clucking hens and manure-streaked cows, out of sight. Aunt Mabe liked to say to visitors, 'What do I do? Why, I'm a farmer's wife, don't you know! I live on a little ole farm in Connecticut!' But she and Uncle Joe just showed people around. Uncle Joe was in insurance, and Aunt Mabe was in entertaining. It mattered to her what the senator thought.

Uncle Joe said, 'Who cares?' Which was a silly thing to say. Even Rose knew that.

'I care!' snapped Aunt Mabe. 'I care very much. I took my baby sister in when she was pregnant before. I've kept her all this time – it wasn't easy for me when Jonathan was killed, you know. A bereaved woman in the house . . . an orphan girl . . . people don't know what to say. It's very difficult.'

Uncle Joe protested. 'But everyone likes Aileen. And Rose. They like their Englishness. Their reserve—'

'Reserve! That's funny. After VJ night – yes, that's most amusing!' Aunt Mabe whirled round. 'When I think – when I remember – drunk – hopelessly drunk. You'd have had anyone, wouldn't you? You were – were – sex-crazed!'

Rose looked at the door, waiting for Fack to come in and take her away.

Uncle Joe said, 'Christ, are you surprised? Honey, don't cry. It's natural! Five years since . . . Listen, just tell me who it is. OK, so he's married and that's that. But I'll knock his teeth so far down his throat he'll . . . say, don't cry in front of the kid. It's bad for you—'

Rose hadn't realized her mother was crying and she made a dash for her. The door opened and Fack swept her up.

'Why don't you go over to the Labens and play with young Eric?' he asked, wiping her eyes and holding his handkerchief for her to blow into.

'Lennox might be there.' She looked up. 'It's all right, Fack. Really. We're going back to England. That's all that matters.'

'Yes.' He sighed from his boots. 'Reckon you'll be better off there, honey. Maybe one day you'll come and see us again, hey?'

'Yeh. Sure, Fack. And Abram too. Hey?'

Fack said with unaccustomed gloom, 'Unless he's in gaol.'

She started to laugh because it was such a joke. And after a while, he laughed too.

Although the new baby was so unpopular, Rose knew she would love it always because it was taking them home. She leaned on the rail by her mother and watched the patterns of water made by the *Orion* and knew she would never go back to America, not even to see Abram. Already she couldn't remember what he looked like. And he and Fack had to do as they were told, just as she had. Yes, America was where things happened. England was where nothing happened. She didn't want anything to happen. Not really. Not *happen*.

Mother said, 'I hope you won't find it too boring at home, darling. It won't be a bit exciting. Your Grandmother Harris asked us to live with her, but I thought we'd rather have our own little house.'

'Will it have a nursery for the baby?' Rose asked.

'Not really. I suppose the living room will be the nursery for a while.'

'And I'll be the nurse,' Rose said. 'And we'll have tea by the fire every day.'

23

'All right.' Mother was actually laughing as if she were happy again. 'I'll have it ready for when you come home from school.'

'School?'

'Yes, darling. Children go to school when they're five in England. Sooner sometimes. Actually I shall be meeting you from school, so we'll get the tea together when we get home.'

Rose hadn't envisaged school.

'Will there be millions of other children at school?'

'Not millions. But quite a few. But you'll have your very own desk. And your very own pencil case. And writing book. And reading book. And you'll have a special friend.'

'Her name will be Margaret,' said Rose dreamily. 'Together, we'll be Margaret Rose like the Princess.'

'That sounds marvellous,' said her mother placidly.

Aunt Mabe's almost-parting words had been, 'You've changed, Aileen. I've never known you like this. So confident.'

And Mother had said, 'It must be pregnancy. I feel confident.'

Aunt Mabe, who would never be pregnant now, said tartly, 'I should have said smug. Yes, you're definitely smug, little sister.'

And Mother had kissed her lightly and looked at Uncle Joe and said, 'Take care, Mab. And don't drop that pencil!'

Rose hugged her mother and thought maybe pregnancy was catching. She didn't know what confident or smug meant. But she was happy.

Amazingly, it all worked out as planned.

Grandfather Harris was Secretary to the Society of Auctioneers, and he found them a small terraced house which could be easily run on Jonathan Harris's pension. The neighbours never knew that Jonathan had been torpedoed in 1941, and they rallied round the young widow with offers of help which Aileen gently turned down. She was going to be independent from now on as far as possible.

They arrived just before Christmas and spent two weeks with the old Harrises. But the new baby did not endear Aileen to her in-laws, and what they did, they did for Rose's sake. Rose was always conscious that they were there, but once Mother and she moved to their own house they rarely saw the grandparents. Old Mr and Mrs Harris lived in Cheltenham and the terraced house was in Churchdown, a little village on a hill between Gloucester and Cheltenham, accessible to both towns by bus or rail, but far enough away not to be an embarrassment to anyone. The village consisted of the railway workers' terrace, a few farm labourers' cottages, a pub, a church and a school. There were fifteen children in the school between the ages of five and eleven. At eleven they could get a scholarship to one of the grammar schools in Gloucester or Cheltenham, or they could go to the nearest secondary modern school. The new system had only just started and people were doubtful about it, but it suited Rose. She found her special friend in a girl called Margaret Ellenbury, who was expected to pass the scholarship and go to the same grammar school attended by her mother and grandmother before her.

Meanwhile the small church school provided everything Rose needed in abundance. The education was closely linked with the seasons, and they came and went with reassuring regularity; slowly at first, then more quickly as she grew older. Mr Brooking, who took the older children, read them a poem by Wordsworth in which the phrase 'The earth's diurnal round' occurred. Rose forgot the poem but remembered the words. When she was interviewed for the grammar school and was asked what was important to her, she did not say 'skipping' or 'reading' or 'going to the pictures'. She said 'The earth's diurnal round'. She passed of course, and was in the same class as Margaret.

But before that, during the winter and spring of 1946 they settled down in their house. It was number four, Railway Villas. It had a dark brown front door, and one of the first jobs Aileen and Rose managed was to paint it white.

25

Margaret called it 'Number four with the snow-white door'. Rose gradually reduced this to the 'Snow-White house'. And so it was called.

On 3 May 1946, the midwife arrived before breakfast and said she'd got Aileen's message. Rose had no idea when her mother had sent any message, or how, but she knew that no-one would be meeting her from school that day. Margaret came back with her. They crossed the churchyard, holding hands, excited at what they might find when they got to the Snow-White house. They found Mrs Whittaker from next door, allowed to help at last, beaming and kissing everyone in sight as if the baby were hers.

'The most beautiful little girl you've ever seen!' she told Rose and Margaret as she stuffed them with lemonade and jam sandwiches in the 'nursery'. 'The spitting image of her daddy, I'll be bound.'

Rose found a photograph of her father and gave it to Mrs Whittaker. The hair was covered by his naval cap, and the eyes were intensely blue like Rose's.

'Exactly like him!' Mrs Whittaker said joyously. 'Have you finished your tea, girls? I expect Nurse will let you upstairs now. I'll just see.'

Nurse was smilingly welcoming. The baby was dark like Rose and her mother. Rose knew her father had had fair hair.

'What would you like to call her, darling?' Aileen asked.

Rose thought hard. She wanted something that sounded like 'Jonathan', only a girl's name. Margaret's mother had been reading *What Katy Did* to the girls and Rose said confidently, 'Joanna'.

Margaret was crying. 'It's so lovely,' she sobbed. 'And so sad.' Her mother had explained the whole thing to her and she thought Rose and Aileen, and now Joanna, were like people in a book.

Rose said dreamily, 'I think I shall call her Jon. For short.'

Aileen looked at her older daughter sharply. She wondered how much Rose knew or guessed. But she did not

26

protest. She had called her husband Jon. It would reinforce public assumption that the new baby belonged to him.

Jon always knew that she and Rose were quite different. Mrs Whittaker – soon known as Mrs Whittie – rubbed it in daily.

'Chalk and cheese,' she repeated monotonously. 'Chalk and cheese!'

It wasn't so much that Rose was five years older than Jon; nor that she was shy and Jon was not; nor that she was good and Jon was not always; nor that she pulled her weight in all things and Jon was lazy. It was that the sum total of all Rose's parts added up to ordinariness, whereas the sum total of Jon's added up to something that was never, ever, ordinary.

The three women lived together so peaceably that Mrs Whittie once described them as 'too good to be true'. Jon knew, from a very early age, that their three-way harmony was because Mother and Rose would always give way whenever an impasse appeared imminent. Later, she vaguely remembered their indulgent horror when they caught her eating coal from the scuttle and soil from the cabbage patch. She recalled that Rose would always take her out for a walk when the grandparents made one of their rare visits – not that Rose minded them at all, but she knew that Jon found them almost desperately boring.

It was an idyllic childhood. Jon was spoiled by her mother and sister and could easily have been insufferable. But until she was fifteen she wanted nothing that they could not give her. She was a natural tomboy and the hill with its little copses and dells was a delight to her. Their lack of social life never irked her and she put up with the church bazaars and beetle drives because they provided opportunities for what Mrs Whittie called her 'malarkying'.

When she was seven there was a big picnic for the Queen's Coronation. The choirboys and men built a bonfire on the south side of the church and there was a tea in the afternoon and fireworks in the evening. Jon was determined to stay to the very end.

Aileen was against it. The weather was typical for an English June: cold and inclined to rain. She had no wish to stand outside herself, let alone permit her baby to do so.

'Your bit is in the afternoon, darling.'

Jon stuck out her lower lip.

'Shan't be able to go to sleep with all the noise,' she pointed out. 'And Rosie is going.'

'Rose is nearly thirteen. And she'll be with Margaret and the Ellenburys'.

Jon abandoned logic. 'I want to go with Rosie!' she wailed.

As usual, Rose intervened. 'Jon can come with us, Mother. You need not come outside at all if you don't want to.'

Jon had no wish to be glued to Rose's side, but she nodded enthusiastically. 'We're sisters, after all!' she maintained.

She'd noticed before how that rallying cry practically always won the others over. Rose always smiled widely and said, 'So we are, baby.' And Mother would sigh gustily and look into the sky or the fire as the case might be.

It worked this time.

'All right then. But not too near the fire, mind, darling. And if the choir start throwing fireworks, bring her straight in, Rosie.'

'Yes, Mother.'

Jon managed to detach herself from the Ellenbury entourage quite quickly. It was a dark night and once clear of the lurid firelight, all cats were grey. She saw some interesting things. The stationmaster kissing someone who wasn't his wife. And Margaret Ellenbury's auntie without her blouse. Two of the choirboys let her smoke a cigarette when she threatened to scream if they didn't. And the choirmaster gave her a lollipop and said she could call him John.

'That's not your name,' she objected in between ecstatic licks of the lollipop. 'I've heard Mrs Vicar call you Stephen. My name is Jon.'

'That's why I chose it. So you'd remember.'

'I'm not a baby, you know. I'm seven.'

'I know. I've seen you with the Sunday school. You've got a good voice.'

'Have I?' No-one had told her that before. They told her she was pretty; and lucky to have such lovely curly hair; and bright for her age. But it was generally accepted that she could not sing.

'Yes. If I can persuade the Reverend Murchison to accept girls into the choir, would you like to join?'

'What would I wear?'

'Blue, I think. And a small blue cap.'

'I'd like that.'

'You'd have to be a very good girl. Otherwise I wouldn't have you.'

'I am good. I'm always good.'

'Can you keep a secret too?'

'Oh yes.'

'Then my name is a secret. My real name. You must call me John.'

'All right.'

'Go on then.'

It was getting silly. She intoned, 'John. John. John.'

He said, 'And you must give me a kiss.'

She did so without thinking. Entirely without thinking. And when he put his arms around her and cradled her as if she were a baby, she was surprised. He kissed her again. Then again. And she wriggled free.

'Oh dear. You're not being very co-operative.' She could hear him breathing.

'What's . . . what you said?'

'Co-operative? You're not doing what I asked you. You have to give me lots of kisses.'

She was bored and wanted to get back to the bonfire.

'I don't want to sing. I don't like singing very much.'

His face was suddenly, luridly, lit by an exploding rocket. It was white and strained.

He said, 'I'm sorry. Sorry, Jon. Forget it.'

But she was caught by the look on that face. She wanted to cry. As if the look was on her face too.

She dabbed a kiss on his nose and ran.

That night she got out of her bed and crept in with Rose.

'Is anything the matter, Jon?' Rose whispered into the curly hair.

'Don't you wish – sometimes – that we had a daddy?' Jon whispered back, keeping her head almost under the clothes as if the question were treasonable.

'We've got a daddy, silly.' Rose used her indulgent voice. The photograph which now sat on the mantelpiece was even more blurred, so it was easy to think that Jonathan Harris was as dark as Jon and Rose.

Jon said, 'Yes. But a daddy who lives with us. Not with Jesus.'

'I'm not sure.'

Margaret said that sometimes her parents 'fought'. Rose was still young enough to visualize sticks, swords; even pistols. And anyway it was hard to imagine a man in the Snow-White house.

Jon gave voice to something she had recently thought out for herself.

'Rosie. Have you noticed? When people go and live with Jesus, they don't come back again.'

'Yes.'

Rose held her small sister very close.

'So Daddy won't come back to live with us, will he?'

'No.'

There was silence in the bedroom while the two girls clung to each other. And then gradually relaxed.

Jon murmured drowsily, 'Where is heaven, Rosie? Where do they go when they live with Jesus?'

And Rose, nearly thirteen, and very ordinary, murmured back, 'I think they go to America, Jon.'

And they slept.

The following week Mrs Whittie told them that Stephen Manning, the young choirmaster, had left the village. She thought there might have been trouble with one of the choirboys.

*

When Jon was fifteen, she prevailed on her mother to buy a television set. Aileen's warning that they would get square eyes had long ago proved false – Jon had gone next door and watched Mrs Whittie's set from the age of ten. Mrs Whittaker was her godmother and Jon had informed her solemnly that to share her telly was one of her godmotherly duties.

But still she argued that her poor examination marks were because she was so behind in things like current affairs and the arts – all of which, apparently, could be absorbed from television programmes.

'Rose did not seem to feel the need for a television,' Aileen argued – hopelessly because she knew that when Jon set her heart on something, it was useless to argue.

'Rose is a swot,' Jon explained kindly. 'Don't you remember how she and Margaret Ellenbury used to sit in the kitchen for hours before their exams?'

Aileen said reasonably, 'Which enabled Margaret to go to teacher training collage, and Rose to start as a librarian.'

'Exactly!' Jon said triumphantly. 'I mean, who ever heard of anyone wanting to become a teacher or a librarian?'

'Oh Jon . . . ' As usual Aileen started to laugh and Jon knew she'd won. She asked again about a telephone but Aileen shook her head vigorously. 'Never! Our precious privacy would be gone for ever,' she said.

Jon did not quite know what she expected of the television, but she was disappointed with what she got. It made the Snow-White house more of a fortress than ever. That summer of 1961, when they might have gone with the church outing to Weston-super-Mare, made painful visits to the Harrises in Cheltenham, attended the summer picnic and shopped in Gloucester at weekends, life revolved around the new television. Unfortunately Rose actually enjoyed the kind of things Jon 'should' watch. They toured stately homes from the comfort of their armchairs in the tiny parlour; they saw fighting in Cuba and would have recognized the new leader, Fidel Castro, if they'd met him on Churchdown station. Rose was terribly excited when the books she stocked on the mobile library van were

31

mentioned during a review. Aileen copied down the recipes demonstrated by Tony Stopani. Occasionally they would watch a film, but they were always old films. Jon announced loudly that Fred Astaire was the most sexless man she had ever seen. Aileen and Rose laughed comfortably.

It was Jon who decided that Rose's twenty-first birthday warranted a party.

Rose was scoffing. 'Not on your life! I want tea here. Potted shrimps please. Margaret can come if she's home. And I suppose the grandparents. No party.'

'Everyone has a party for their coming-of-age!' Jon said dramatically. 'For heaven's sake – we shall become completely inconspicuous soon! As it is we're so well camouflaged no-one knows whether we're trees or human beings!'

'Melodrama, Jon,' commented Aileen, trying to read a knitting pattern which had fallen to the carpet.

'I shall mention it to Grandmother Harris,' Jon said unexpectedly.

Aileen looked up sharply. 'You will do no such thing!' she said.

But Jon was only temporarily silenced. Instead of coming straight home from school, she cycled into Cheltenham and bearded the Harrises in their den – actually a substantial detached house in Rodney Road.

They greeted her with surprise, then their usual remoteness. But, unexpectedly, they were on her side.

'Of course Rosamund must have a party!' Grandmother Harris did not consult Grandfather. 'We'll take the town hall. Mills can do the catering.'

Jon knew this was going too far.

'Rosie doesn't actually know enough people to fill the town hall,' she demurred. 'Besides . . . no, she would hate that.'

Grandfather smiled suddenly.

'You seem to know Rose very well. What do you suggest?'

'Well, we mustn't frighten her off.' Jon wondered why her concern for Rose endeared her to Grandfather. 'I think if we do it in the church hall . . . perhaps Mother and Mrs Vicar could do the food. And Mrs Whittie will help.'

Grandmother was disappointed. 'We can't wear evening dress to the church hall,' she objected.

Jon said simply, 'None of us possesses an evening dress anyway.'

So it was decided, and, eventually, after overriding many objections, it was arranged. Jon was much more excited than Rose. She bought material and patterns with Rose's money and they set to to make themselves suitable dresses.

And then, out of the blue, something absolutely marvellous happened to Jon. At the age of fifteen, she found out what she wanted from life. Fleetingly she recalled the long-ago choirmaster whose name had been Stephen and had asked to be called John. She knew what he had wanted from life too. It was simply . . . someone to love.

She felt guilty about it. She had Mother and Rosie. They needed no-one else. Why did she? But she did. Immediately she met Rick, she knew she did.

It was at – of all boring occasions – a *thé dansant*. Jon never stayed to anything after school; she was much too anxious to get home. But when a whole gang of girls suggested playing truant from French and going to the Cadena *thé dansant* – relic of pre-war days – she agreed without a thought.

They did what they could with their school uniforms: cinched in their waistbands, opened their shirt waister dresses to vest-level, rolled the elbow-length sleeves up to the shoulder seams and removed hated ankle socks. But they were still unmistakably schoolgirls and the older clientele gave them a wide berth. They danced with each other and pretended they were having a wonderful time, but Jon began to understand Rose's dislike of dances and parties. They were just another boring way of passing time. Worse than Tony Stopani and Fred Astaire put together.

Then the door opened and some new arrivals pushed in, all male, all in long trousers, all obviously – like the girls – looking for a lark.

They sat around two tables and ordered tea. And then, surreptitiously, began to look around them.

Jon knew immediately that the one with red hair would come over to the girls' table first. But she was not at all sure that he would ask her to dance. Sheila McConnery was very much the leader of their little group. She was blonde and blue-eyed and looked a bit like Marilyn Monroe.

Jon leaned across to her.

'Hey. She. I dare you to go and ask that dark one for a dance. Go on. I dare you. You're scared, aren't you?'

Sheila handed out one of her quelling looks and did nothing. Jon glanced over at the table and saw that the red-haired one was about to make a move. She said desperately, 'All right, if you won't, I will!' Everyone gasped and Sheila looked as if she were about to stick her tea-knife into Jon's gingham. Jon stood up and said very casually, 'I'll leave you the dark one. I'll go for poor old carrot-top!'

She reached the table just as he was pushing his chair back. His eyes were going past her but she smiled brilliantly at him and said quickly, 'I'm doing this for a dare. Will you dance with me? Just once around the floor will do.'

He was surprised. He refocused his eyes and took in her dark, impish prettiness. Everyone was laughing. Now that she was close to them she saw they were much older than boys. Older than Rosie probably.

He said, 'Sure. Come on, kid. What can you do? Three-quarter turn?'

'I think so.' They had ballroom dancing classes at school, but they were better at twisting.

They did a sedate quickstep around the room. She clung to him hard as he passed the girls' table for the second time. 'We might as well go on to the end of the number, mightn't we?' she asked.

He laughed. 'Sure. I was going to ask . . . but she's dancing with someone else anyway.'

She glanced sideways. Sheila was still sitting at the table, stony-faced. So he hadn't been going to dance with her after all.

Jon said, 'My name is Joanna Harris. We're all skiving French. Thought it would be fun to . . . you know.'

He laughed again. He had a lovely laugh. Full of fun.

'I know only too well. We all work at Prov. The insurance company, you know. We're supposed to be on the road.'

She giggled. 'I'm shocked.'

He looked down at her. 'No, you're not.'

She said, 'Well, I ought to be. I'm a well-brought up child. If my family thought I was skipping school they'd have a fit.'

'What about if they knew you were dancing with someone who was skipping work? What would they think then?' He was teasing her; humouring her. She didn't care. She wanted to dance with him like this for the rest of her life.

'They'd die!'

He laughed and she felt suddenly disloyal. 'Actually,' she went on, 'my family consists of Mother and Rosie. My sister.'

He leaned back to look at her again. 'Three women? Sounds interesting. Like a small convent.'

She nodded vigorously. 'It is like that. Very . . . self-contained. My father was killed in the war and I think Mother and Rosie went into retirement then.'

'Rosie is older than you?'

'She's twenty-one on September the twenty-first.'

'How . . . appropriate.'

'Yes. Everything about Rosie is like that. Proper.'

He was interested. Curious. 'And you're the pretty one?' He was being mock-serious.

But she answered him solemnly. She had to be just.

'Yes. But Rosie is beautiful. Rather like a nun. She's got these very blue eyes. And when she left school she folded her hair back into a bun. Mother says she looks like Snow-White. In the Disney film. Our house is called the Snow-White house.'

He was definitely intrigued. The music came to an end but he stood there with her on the edge of the dance floor, still smiling.

She said suddenly, 'Wait there. Just a minute.'

She went over to the four-piece band in the corner. Piano, double bass, violin, drums. She spoke to the pianist.

'Could you do something . . . you know, sort of jivey? We'd all like to twist.'

He looked around the room. The girls and the young men from the insurance office made up perhaps half of the dancers.

He said, 'Just one number then. Can't offend the regulars.'

She said fervently, 'Thank you so much.'

The drummer gave a roll. The pianist said in to the microphone, 'Shall we twist again, folks? Like we did last summer?' And they were away.

Rose did not look forward to 21 September, but when it came everything was so perfect, it would have been churlish to object to the party any more. The weather was halcyon, glowingly warm, the leaves beginning to blaze into magnificent old age. The postman brought a stack of cards; even Miss Marchant and Miss Smithson from the central library sent separately. Margaret, in her last year at college, delayed her return and joined Mother and the Murchisons in the village hall. 'You're not to come near the place till this evening, Rose! D'you hear me?' She was beginning to sound like a teacher already.

They lunched with the Ellenburys in their big farmhouse, then Rose and Aileen went home to rest for a hour. Jon arrived hotfoot at five, looking flushed and excited beyond reason. And after a cup of tea, they began to get ready. They all wore blue; Aileen was in a long tube dress of French navy; Rose had made a very conventional summer frock, but it was in the material chosen by Jon and the cornflower blue cotton made her eyes blaze. Jon had run hers up without a pattern; it was quite unsuitable; nylon layers with a big shawl collar that left her shoulders bare.

Aileen looked at her daughters and thought of the terrible four years in Mabel's house when she had been a nuisance, a poor relation. She said, 'We're happy, aren't we, girls? Really happy?'

Rose said immediately, 'Couldn't be happier, Mother. Don't worry about tonight. I don't actually *mind*, you know. It's just that . . . well, it would have been just as nice to take an evening picnic on to the hill.'

Aileen laughed. After a while Jon joined in.

They walked single file close to the hedgerow. There was no footpath and that hadn't mattered when they came here first, but now the motorists had discovered the charm of the village and its pub. There was plenty of traffic in the evenings and at weekends. It occurred to Aileen that perhaps their hideaway was being discovered by life, and they would be unable to sustain its pleasant uneventfulness much longer. Jon would be able to cope. She wasn't so certain about Rose.

They found Grandmother and Grandfather waiting for them in the porch. There were hugs and kisses for Rose; Grandfather hugged Aileen and Jon; Grandmother opened the inner door and went ahead of the others. Mrs Vicar had even provided a band; the church organist was on the piano and the local skiffle group backed him with a great deal of heavy percussion. Rose had to be delighted. Everyone she knew was there; her old schoolfriends, Margaret Ellenbury of course, Mr Brooking and Mrs Whittaker; her colleagues from the County Library. The band played 'Happy birthday' and the vicar asked her for a dance. There was fruit punch and a cake and lots of savoury rolls and sandwiches.

Later, Grandmother said, 'So. You've reached your majority, Rosamund. Congratulations.'

'Oh. . . . thank you, Grandmother.' Rose wondered what her options had been. Only death presumably.

Grandfather said, 'You've done well, Rose. Very well. Looked after your mother, got a good job. We're proud of you. We know it's not been easy.'

Rose was surprised. 'Well . . . it has, actually. I mean it's not been difficult. It's just . . . happened.'

Grandmother looked at her sharply, 'Nothing just happens, Rosamund. Not unless you're a fatalist, and we hope you're not that. You can make the best of things. Or the worst. You've made the best.' She looked smug.

37

'That is something you've inherited from our side of the family, of course.'

Grandfather said, 'Your father would be proud of you, my dear. I can't say more than that.'

Rose thought of the fair young man of the photographs. He hadn't been much older than she was now when he'd died. Well, that had just happened. Nothing much you could do about death.

She said again, 'Thank you.'

Grandfather cleared his throat and said jovially, 'Feel like taking me round the floor, my dear? It's a waltz. The only dance I can do.'

They gyrated sedately beneath the paper garlands which were brought out for every social. Grandfather did not hold her at arm's length like the vicar, nor too close in a way she did not like though did not know why. They could look at one another now and then and smile, yet were near enough for him to hear her when she spoke. She thought, objectively, that he was a nice man and said, 'D'you know Grandfather, I think I would have liked my father.'

'Well of course you would, Rose!' Grandfather was surprised. 'You'd have got on like a house on fire!'

'Yes. I know what you mean. But I meant – I think I would have liked him. As a person.' She smiled. 'When you're little, you don't think of your family as separate people, do you? So I must be grown-up now!'

He laughed, then said, 'What on earth made you think of your father as a person just then, Rosie?'

'Because of you,' she said simply.

She saw his Adam's apple jerk in his throat and hoped she hadn't upset him by talking about his dead son.

When the dance finished they stood on the floor, clapping gently, and then he said, 'That is the best compliment I've ever had, Rose. No-one can tell Jonathan that he takes after his father. But to be told that I take after him . . . ah, that is better still.'

She felt a rush of affection for him and took his arm. 'It was a lovely birthday present, Grandfather,' she said. 'Thank you.'

They had given her the obligatory gold watch, an exquisite Swiss watch on a bracelet. It must have cost the earth. Mother and Jon between them had given her a silver locket bought from one of the antique shops which clustered around Gloucester Cathedral. She had loved it so much, the watch had come a poor second, and her thanks had been as formal as the present itself.

'Well. Not original. But someone has to give you a gold watch!'

Grandmother came up to them, smiling.

'You're having a nice time,' she said approvingly. 'I just wish your sister would take a leaf from your book.'

Rose looked around the room in surprise. Jon was dancing with a young man she hadn't seen before. Probably a relative of one of the villagers. Tall, with fiery red hair, and a laughing, open face. They confronted each other, twisting fiercely.

Rose said, 'Oh, I think Jon is having a very good time, Grandmother.'

'She's only fifteen,' Grandmother said repressively.

'But they're not even dancing properly.'

Grandmother Harris snorted derisively. 'This new dancing reminds me of some of the animal displays seen immediately prior to cop—'

Grandfather cleared his throat. 'Absolutely. Absolutely . . . innocent.'

'Rubbish!'

Rose said, 'Jon is very athletic, you know. She was in the tennis tournaments at school in the summer. Mother and I went twice to watch the games.'

'Hmph!'

'You should come, Grandmother. You've always told me how much you enjoy Wimbledon week.'

Grandmother said nothing and Grandfather took over. 'Yes. Well . . . perhaps if Jon stays on at school we might manage to come to a match next summer. Eh, dear?'

Rose said eagerly, 'She plays hockey for the first eleven, too.'

'Winter. Bad for your Grandmother's chest.' Grandfather said diplomatically.

Rose was not at all certain that Jon would be at school next summer. She planned to do the shorthand and typing course this year which meant she would not be sitting her exams next summer and could slip out of school almost any time she wished.

It happened so gradually that Aileen and Rose barely noticed it. The red-haired young man, whose name turned out to be Rick, called the next day with a handkerchief he thought might be Jon's. Rose knew it wasn't, but Jon said it was and asked him in. The front room of the Snow-White house was small enough with the three of them; when he stood by the mantelpiece they felt they could hardly breathe. Jon's chest could plainly be seen rising and falling. Aileen and Rose went out to make some tea, and when they came back Jon was standing too, practically touching him. He was much too old for her.

'Open the window, darling,' Aileen said to Jon. 'Rick, do sit down. You're a friend of the Ellenburys, I understand?'

'Er . . . yes.' Rick gave that great big open grin that Rose had found so attractive last night. 'I'd like to be a friend of yours too. That would be a great honour actually, Mrs Harris.'

'Oh.' Aileen flushed slightly. She had always been careful to preserve their 'precious privacy' as she put it, but it was hard to resist this boy. It was his freckles. Surely someone with red freckles couldn't be devious or dangerous?

'Well, I don't see why . . . what is your full name, Rick?'

Rick glanced at Jon. 'John. Strangely enough, it's Rick John.'

Everyone laughed and the ice was broken. Late that night, Jon came into Rose's room.

'Just think. If Rick and I got married, I'd be Jon John! Wouldn't that be an absolute scream, Rosie?'

40

Rose had to smile. 'It would rather. Are you thinking that perhaps . . . later . . . ?'

'Well, he's rather dishy, isn't he?'

'I don't know what you mean by dishy,' Rose said, primming her mouth humorously. She laughed. 'He's very nice. Easy to talk to. I agree on that!'

'I'd love to get married. Early. Aren't you going to get married, Rosie. You're already twenty-one!' Jon obviously thought she was on the shelf.

Rose said soberly, 'I couldn't bear to leave home. You. Mother.'

Jon hastened to agree. 'Oh, nor me! But . . . well, it must be so nice to have a man. In the family. To see to things. You know what I mean. But . . . no, I don't want to leave you and Mother either.'

Rose was thankful that Jon had reached that conclusion. It seemed so obvious to her.

The next weekend Rick brought flowers for Aileen and a picnic hamper. The Michaelmas summer was still in its full glory and they walked up to the church and then followed a sheep trail until they could see the ribbon of the Severn and Robinswood Hill erupting from the valley floor just as Churchdown did.

Rick picked up a bunch of buttercups and insisted on holding them beneath Jon's chin to see if she liked butter. Aileen said quietly to Rose, 'My goodness, I remember your father doing that to me many years ago.'

It was as if Rick had heard her.

'Come on, Mrs Harris. Let's see if you're as much of a butterball as your daughter!'

And then it was Rose's turn and she found herself looking into very light blue eyes framed in a spider's web of laughter lines.

'Snow-White herself!' Rick said, tilting her chin and tickling her throat with the waxy flowers. His thumb felt the edge of her jaw-line. 'You've got dark hair and blue eyes. Like Snow-White.'

He was teasing of course; it was all just a silly children's game. But Rose stayed very still.

Aileen said sentimentally, 'Rose loved the film. We saw it in America. D'you remember, Rose?'

Rose put up a hand and pulled his fingers away. She sat back among the long grasses well away from him. His eyes flickered as if in pain and she felt awful. But she could not have stood that closeness a second longer.

Jon said, 'You're lucky to have been to America, Rose. I've never been anywhere, or done anything!'

Rick turned suddenly. 'Listen. I have to go to Birmingham next Friday for the firm. Come with me and I'll take you to the ice-skating rink. Have you ever ice-skated?'

'No! Gosh. I'd love to. Can I, Mother? I mean, may I? Please?'

'You'd trust her to me, wouldn't you, Mrs Harris? She could look in the shops along Corporation Street while I see our clients. Then we could have an hour on the ice. She's a natural for anything like that.'

'There's school, Jon,' Aileen reminded her.

'Mother, you just have to let me go!' Jon fell on Aileen's lap, pushing her back into the buttercups. 'Listen – it's typing on Friday and I'm brilliant at typing! And I've never seen an ice-skating rink. Mother, please. Please! Please! Please! – I'm not going to let you up till you say yes! Please! Please! Ple—'

'For goodness' sake, Jon! All right!'

'Thanks, Mrs Harris. I'll take great care of her.'

'Mother. You're an angel! I love you! Rick, it'll be such fun! What shall I wear?'

'Trousers, if you've got any. You're sure to fall down a couple of times and it will save skinning your knees.'

Jon pouted. 'I wanted to wear a skating skirt. And I haven't got any trousers.'

'I'll bring some of my sister's. You're about her size.'

'I didn't know you'd got a sister! You didn't tell me!'

'I've got a sister of eighteen. And a father of fifty. We all live together in a little cottage—'

'You're teasing!'

'It's true!' He looked at Aileen and spoke seriously. 'My mother died when I was seventeen. That's why I appreciate this so much.'

Aileen smiled and put a hand on his arm. Jon was momentarily subdued, then bounced around in the buttercups at the thought of a day off school.

Rose felt desperately left out. It was ridiculous. If Rick had asked her to go to Birmingham with him, she would have said no. And meant it. But it was her day off, and she had nothing planned.

The day in Birmingham was a great success. The trousers Rick borrowed from his sister were black nylon with a strap beneath the instep to keep them neatly to the calf. He drove a car belonging to his firm, a respectable black Riley, and wore a grey suit and white shirt. He had a zip-topped bag on the back seat which he said contained old flannels and a cricket sweater. Later, Jon told Rose that he had changed in the back of the car.

'Jon! That was a bit much, wasn't it?'

'I told him to. I said I wouldn't look or anything. But of course I did, in the mirror.' Jon sighed. 'He's dishy.'

'Jon. You're fifteen!'

'And you sound like Grandmother Harris! It's almost 1962, Rose! You're like a nun!'

'I'm not criticizing you, darling! But I think he should know better. He's much older than you, after all.'

'Women mature faster than men. I can't bear the boys at the Grammar. They're like children!'

'But Rick is older than me, isn't he? He must be twenty-three or four!'

'D'you like him too, Rose?'

'He's very pleasant. But if you mean—'

'You know what I mean all right!' Jon grinned suddenly. 'You're jealous. That's what it is. You're jealous!'

She threw herself backwards on to her bed, laughing crazily. Rose thought it best to join in.

★

43

But Rick did not call at the Snow-White house for a long time after that trip. Rose did not admit to herself that she missed him, but she did wonder what had happened in Birmingham. Jon drooped visibly and just before Christmas, Rose met her in St John's Lane when she was going to catch the bus home.

'What on earth—' she began, belatedly recognizing Jon under a street lamp.

'Oh . . . don't pretend you haven't guessed!' Jon fell into step with her and they walked towards Kings Square and the bus terminus. 'Rick John said he worked at the Providential offices, d'you remember? I hoped I'd run into him.'

Rose was annoyed. 'Honestly, Jon! It's seven o'clock—'

'Oh dearie, dearie me!' Jon mocked.

'Seriously – I don't like my late turn when it means bussing back home because of this snow!'

'And you're a middle-aged woman!' Jon went on.

They queued for ten minutes, silent because of other people. But when they climbed on to the bus, Jon said, 'I suppose it's no good asking you to take out a policy with Providential. I'm too young apparently.'

'Jon, you haven't actually been in to enquire!'

'No. It came up in business studies.' Jon grinned. 'I asked about it actually. The first intelligent question I've asked during this course!'

'Jon, you are incorrigible,' Rose said, her resignation softened by fondness.

'An enfant terrible?' Jon said the words with a deliberately atrocious accent, then with her quick penitence she hugged her sister's arm. 'I am terrible. I know that. I know it better than you. But . . . Rose, I do love you so.'

Rose was momentarily taken aback. She hugged her sister in return, but then drew back and looked at her sternly, 'But I'm still not going to take out an insurance policy!' she said.

Jon laughed. And so did she.

It was when the dreary winter was beginning to melt in February that Rick John came into the Central Library

44

when she was stacking books for the next day's run. She heard his voice behind her and whipped round much too quickly.

'By all that's holy! It's Snow-White herself!'

There he was, just as she remembered, red hair crinkling damply over his ears, freckles against his winter-pale face, but smile as wide and honest as ever.

'Oh. It's you,' she said inadequately.

'Yes. It's me.' He went on looking at her while she could have counted three. Slowly. Then all he said was, 'Hello.'

She said, 'Hello.'

Miss Marchant came between them. 'Can I help you?' she asked briskly.

'No. I'd like Snow-White to help me,' Rick said, laughing at her.

But Miss Marchant wasn't one for joking in library-time. She said repressively, 'Miss Harris is not on duty here, sir. Have you a book to change?'

He became much too solemn. 'I have. Yes indeed.' He produced a book and put it on the counter. Then waited gravely for his ticket and walked into the fiction section with a broad wink in Rose's direction.

Miss Marchant sighed, 'You'd better go and talk to him, Rose,' she said. 'But don't let Miss Smithson see you, for goodness sake!'

Rose wanted to say that she had no wish to talk to him, but she smiled her thanks and whipped to the other side of the counter immediately.

He was sitting on a stool with an open book on his knee. He said, 'Rosie! I thought she wouldn't let you out! I planned to kidnap you!'

She said formally, 'It's nice to see you again, Rick. How are you?'

He nodded. 'Sorry. I forgot I should be suitably apologetic.' But he was still grinning. 'I've been working away from home.'

'Oh.' She swallowed. So much for her suspicions about the Birmingham trip. 'Oh, I see.' He went on smiling up at her, deliberately making himself smaller, and – possibly – vulnerable.

She said, 'You could have written actually. We wondered if you were all right. Mother was concerned.'

'What about you?'

'You came to see Mother. And Jon.' She looked away from him at the shelf above his head. She pulled out two books needing repairs to their spines.

He was laughing. 'Of course I did. Yes, you're right. I came to see your mother and your little sister.'

She tucked the books under her arm and spoke with an effort. 'Well. They'll be glad to hear . . . I'll tell them you're back.' She smiled brightly. 'And looking very well, too.' She turned to go.

He stood up. 'Rosie, I have to see you.' His voice was suddenly urgent. 'You know it's you I come—'

She said briskly, 'I'm afraid I have to go now. So I must say good—'

'When can we meet?'

'You know where we live. You know you're welcome.'

She did not look behind her. The staff-room door was ahead. She made for it. Miss Marchant was there brewing tea.

'Your young man gone?' She shook her head. 'He comes in every two or three days,' she said archly. 'I wondered what he was looking for – he has obviously never opened his book. Now I know.'

Rose said, 'He's been working away for some time.'

'Not this winter. He's in too often. Unless he's working away during the daytime.'

It could have been that, of course. But for the first time Rose suspected that frank and open manner.

He called one Sunday and they all went for a walk. Jon held on to his arm and asked him if he would take her ice-skating again and he said he would one day. He asked Rose when her half-day was but she said she did not have one.

He tried to find out what her schedule was; when she collected and returned books, but she said in all honesty that she did not know what hours she would be working. She asked him about his family; what his father did.

'He's down the pit, man,' he said in a broad Welsh accent.

'Where on earth . . . in the Forest?' she asked lightly.

He was confused. 'The Forest – oh you mean Dean. No, he was in Wales. He's retired now.'

'At fifty?' she said, raising her brows.

'Ill-health,' he said shortly.

Her mother remonstrated with her later. 'You were badgering him, Rosie. He doesn't like talking about his family – surely that's obvious?'

He called about once a month. Sometimes Jon made sure she 'bumped into him' after school and then she could inveigle him to buy her tea or go for a walk with her along the river bank. She referred to him as the 'boyfriend' and when Aileen remonstrated with her she would say airily that they 'had an understanding'. They shared so many interests: all outdoor sports, dancing . . . anything energetic and slightly crazy. Jon was certain that he was merely waiting for her next birthday to propose to her. They were an ideal couple. Jon was in heaven that summer of '62. She left school without passing a single exam, and started at a secretarial college not far from St John's Lane. Rick accused her of spying on him and she thought he was teasing and laughed at him, nodding vigorously.

'If you don't like it, you can always stay away from the Snow-White house!' she taunted him.

She knew he wouldn't do that. He loved the cosiness of the house; he got on well with Rose. He really loved Mother.

That winter of '62 began early. The first fall of snow came in November.

Jon made sure she got home early most days and on his days off Rick would already be there, helping Mother make mincepies or clearing the snow from the path. When Rose was on early shift, he usually drove her from Gloucester. Jon said proudly, 'You're practically one of the family, Rick!'

47

She wished Rose would be nicer to him; if only Rose would like him everything would be perfect.

When the weather worsened he bought second-hand skis and made a run from just outside the church to the end of the garden. The crisp, freezing weather suited him. He spent Christmas Day with them, although Rose asked him several times whether his father would mind. He gave her one of the long looks which Jon knew showed he was hurt. Then he said in a low voice, 'You are more of a family to me than anyone back in the Valleys, Rose.'

Jon was thrilled. But Rose turned bright red and went into the kitchen.

After Christmas he seemed to be in Churchdown most days. Jon was nearly seventeen and beautiful in a wild, gypsyish way. Even her mother seemed to accept him as 'official' now. Only Rose still tried to keep out of the way. She did not like the cold; it was her excuse for never joining them on the hill. She could not stand on the skis, let alone move on them.

But then, one Sunday right at the end of January, Rick made a sledge and persuaded Aileen to sit behind him on the steep run from the church to the Ellenburys' farm. Unexpectedly, Aileen loved the experience. Her cheeks flamed with colour and her hair, already greying at the sides, flew around her face and made her look young again.

'Your turn now, Rose,' called Rick.

'No. Give Mother another turn,' Jon yelled back. 'Rose isn't keen.'

And by the time the sledge returned, Rose had gone, slipping away again as she so often did these days.

Rose was not happy. She kept hoping that Jon's infatuation would end; she refused to think of Rick at all. There was something wrong and she did not know what it was. For the first time since Jon's birth, she felt the outsider in the family. She went back to the house and laid the tea and wished that Rick had never appeared in their lives.

After tea, they put a tin tray of chestnuts under the fire basket, and watched the news on television. Rick was capable of being quiet, and Jon's eyelids were drooping after all the fresh air. At seven, when they opened the front door to fetch wellingtons from the porch, it was snowing hard.

Aileen said, 'Jon. You'll have to sleep with Rose. Rick can't possibly get back to Gloucester tonight.'

'Really, it's all right, Mrs Harris.' But even intrepid Rick sounded half-hearted.

Jon was overjoyed. She went straight upstairs to change the bedding.

Rick said, 'Come on. Let's go and have a snowball fight!'

Aileen laughed. 'Honestly. My dear boy! Haven't you had enough exercise for one day?'

'No. Rose – neither have you! Come on!'

He bundled her into her coat and held her wellingtons. She could have resisted but it would have meant a bit of a scene. She lingered, waiting for Jon to come back downstairs.

'Quick. Before Jon can catch us!'

He hopped into his own wellingtons, rammed his cap over his ears, and took her hand. Again she could have held back but Aileen was already closing the door against a flurry of snow and Rick was pushing her ahead so that he could tow the sledge. They ran down the lane, dragging the sledge after them and quite suddenly she belonged again. Not necessarily to Jon and Aileen . . . but she belonged. She looked round at him and saw his wide grin and the snow on his eyebrows and she laughed.

The air was full of snow. They rubbed at their faces and spat and he hooked his arm in hers to help her along. They could hear Jon shout from the house, and Rose would have hung back still, but Rick pulled her on. She forgot that there was something oddly evasive about him; that she had to fight against his attraction. She let herself be pulled and when they reached the stile and he left her to lift the sledge over, she scrambled up unaided. He swung her down, laughing at her with a sheer boyish happiness that was completely disarming.

'I was determined you should have a toboggan ride!' he said. 'Jon keeps telling you you don't like outdoor things. You believe her. It's ridiculous!'

She couldn't reply, there was no breath to spare. They trudged up the footpath and through the gate of the churchyard to the sloping fields. Reason had gone. There was just the snow and sledge and the two of them. She sat behind him. Ice found its way to the bare flesh above stocking tops. She screamed, and he lifted her legs and held them around his waist. She was forced to cling to him like a limpet or fall backwards. She clung, terribly conscious of her upper thighs, protected by a thick coat but pressed against his hips nevertheless.

They hurtled down the long slope at breakneck speed. It was bewildering and completely exhilarating. For the first time that day her blood coursed through her body warmly, though she could not feel her hands and feet. They trudged back up the hill, laughing again.

'Jon will be waiting for us, you see!' gasped Rick. But she was not. Aileen must have prevailed on her to stay indoors.

Again and again they bumped and tore down the long field of snow. And then at last she called it a day.

'I can't walk that slope again,' she puffed, hanging on to her side and gulping air like water. 'Let's walk round the road back home, Rick. Please.'

He took her hand and transferred her weight to himself. 'Say please again, and I'll do anything you want,' he said.

Jokingly she replied, 'Please again.'

They laughed as usual, and then he was quiet. The snow had almost stopped and the clouds had broken to let through some moonlight. It reflected off the snow. It was like a postcard. Black houses emerged from the wastes of white. They stared around them, breathing more normally, feeling again the intense cold beginning to deaden the heat of their bodies.

Then he said, 'Oh Rose,' and kissed her.

It was a chaste kiss at first and she did not move away. In the wild toboggan runs they had formed a physical relationship whether she liked it or not. And she did not dislike it. Her lips met his and were delighted at the gentle contact. He lifted his head and she whispered back, 'Oh Rick.'

And then he held her and pressed her against his body and she slipped her hand to the back of his head and knew that this was inevitable. It had been inevitable from the time Margaret Ellenbury had brought him to her birthday party eighteen months before. She wondered why she had fought so hard against it. It had something to do with a bedroom and a boy ripping her dress. He moved his lips to her cheek long enough to say again, 'Oh Rosie . . . darling Rosie . . . if you knew how much I've wanted – needed—' he kissed her again. And again. And then she could no longer feel his lips because the pressure was hard. He seemed to be biting her. He was asking – demanding something – she relived a moment she could not remember properly. As his tongue tried to force an entry into her mouth she screamed and pulled away.

'Rose—!'

'I – I'm sorry. I – don't like it.'

'Why? I want you, Rose. I've always wanted you. Why do you think I've put up with Jon all this time—'

'Put up with Jon? That's cruel! She – she is so fond of you!'

'And I'm fond of her too. But it's been you—'

'I'm sorry. I didn't know. Please let's go home. I'm sorry.'

She could not say anything else. He apologized. He asked her what he'd done that was so wrong. She did not know. She stumped across the field feeling ridiculous, cumbersome in her heavy clothes and wellingtons, bitterly cold. He humped the sledge behind them. At last he fell silent.

They walked along the almost indefinable road. Rose felt miserable, as if she had betrayed her sister. When they got to the house, she did not respond to all the banter about running off without Jon. As soon as she could do so without surprising her mother, she went up to bed. She got in next to the wall and squeezed up tight to make room. And when Jon

51

snapped on the light with a casual, 'Sorry Sis, but I can't see a thing!' she pretended to be asleep

She must have dropped off eventually, but almost immediately something disturbed her. She rolled into the middle of the bed, half consciously surprised to find it warm, and then she remembered. She reached for the light switch. Jon was not there. She sat up, waiting for her to return from the bathroom. And then, through the thin wall between the rooms, she heard Jon's unmistakable laugh.

She thought the next morning that she should have gone in and insisted that Jon return to bed. But she did not. And when Jon did return an hour later, she had switched off the light and was pretending to be asleep again.

Jon knew she was doing something terribly wrong and she would pay for the rest of her life. She tried to blame Rose. If Rose hadn't gone off with Rick like that, Jon would not have had to be reassured. She would not feel frightened and pushed out . . . by Rose as well as Rick.

She refused to look at the alternative, which was so simple. If she let the tears come and told Rose how she felt, Rose would hold her comfortingly and tell her she had nothing to be frightened of; not now, not ever. And if there had been anything between Rose and Rick, it would end then. Rose would stand back; she would give Jon time to grow up; she would give Rick time to fall out of love with one sister and in love with the other.

But she did not choose that alternative. She did not see it. Her body was almost bursting out of its skin for something only Rick could satisfy. She knew all about sex. That was what she wanted.

So she went to Rick's room.

At first he was horrified to see her. He sat up in bed – her bed – clutching the sheet to his chin like a Victorian miss.

She said in a thread of a whisper, 'Rick, I think I've put my shoulder out. When I fell earlier. I don't want to wake Rosie. Could you . . .' She pulled her nightie over one shoulder and stood with her back to him. He sat up in bed

– the clothes fell to his waist. He wasn't wearing anything; of course he had not expected to stay the night.

He said, 'Jon – what the hell – pull your nightdress up, for Christ's sake!'

She noticed his sudden Welsh accent; the prudishness in his tone that must come from his upbringing.

She tried to sound casual. 'Don't be silly, Rick. I just want you to massage my shoulder blade for goodness sake!'

She sat on the edge of the bed. There was a spring on the edge that always twanged when you sat on it and she could have avoided it easily. But she didn't. As it twanged, so she laughed and turned and saw him. She wasn't shocked; Sheila McConnery had loads of pictures. She was just deeply thankful to see he had an erection.

It was easy after that.

The worst part was afterwards. When he kept saying, as John the choirmaster had said, 'I'm sorry . . . so sorry. . .'

The snows went on and on and he came no more. Jon forced herself to say nothing. She knew now that Mother was right; you cheapened yourself and men didn't want you any more. And it wasn't fair because it didn't work the other way round; she wanted Rick more than ever.

And then terror struck. She missed a period. She did not know what to do. Sheila McConnery had assured her that 'it' never ever happened the first time. She waited with a sensation of holding her breath. Maybe she did actually do so, because she suffered from palpitations as well as nausea.

Aileen said, 'I wonder what has happened to Rick yet again?'

Rose said, 'Lost interest in us.'

But Aileen liked Rick. 'He had to go away before,' she reminded them. 'And he's told us he never writes letters.'

*

The snow finally cleared on 4 April and by the middle of the month the spring was on its way.

Jon met Rose as she stepped off the evening train. She had to tell someone. Rose was slightly less shockable than Mother. She watched the train draw in. Steam enveloped it from the vacuum pipes and Rose emerged within the steam, looking ethereal. For a split second Jon did not want to tell her: Rose was too good. She would never do anything . . . sinful. But before the thought registered properly, Jon was flying down the platform, arms outstretched in supplication.

'Where is Mother?' Rose asked with some alarm. Aileen sometimes met her; sometimes Aileen and Jon met her, but never Jon on her own.

'I wanted to talk to you.' Jon waited until the guard waved his green flag and boarded the brake van. She drew a deep breath; there was no way of sugar-coating this particular pill. She said bluntly, 'I think I'm having a baby, Rose. In fact I'm almost sure.'

Rose stared at her, her eyes intensely blue and wide. Then she turned and watched the train chug out of the station as if she'd never seen it before.

She spoke without looking at Jon. 'Who . . . who?' She could not bring herself to finish the question, but of course Jon knew it already.

'Well, who on earth d'you think? Rick, of course!'

Rose closed her eyes for a moment. She did not reach for Jon's hand. She seemed a million miles away, almost as if she hadn't heard Jon's words. Jon's tears overflowed.

'Oh Rosie. What am I going to do?' she wailed.

And at last Rose came out of her trance and put an arm around her.

'Come on. Let's walk home. Don't cry here, someone will see you. We'll work it out.'

And Jon wept anew. This time with sheer thankfulness. Because if Rosie said they would work it out, then they would.

Three

Rose could not believe it at first. It did not make sense to her. Rick had said he 'wanted' her that night in the snow, by which she had assumed he meant that he loved her. She remembered waking to find that Jon was not in bed with her, but though she had thought Jon's behaviour was rash and improper, she had not for one moment thought it went beyond that.

Jon's terror forced all such speculations out of her mind.

'What am I going to *do*, Rosie? He hasn't been near me since . . . that night. I don't know where he lives or anything! And in any case I can't go chasing after him! Oh my God, what will Mother do? She'll die – I know she'll die! And it'll be all my fault!' The young face looked terribly thin in the April sunshine.

Rose grasped at the only straw she could see.

'You're sure? Sometimes, if you're nervous, it's possible to miss one or even two—'

Jon said impatiently, 'I was due just after we . . . he . . . oh God, Rosie, it was that night of the snow. The one and only night he stayed in the Snow-White house! That was the beginning of February . . . I've missed three.'

Rose tried not to imagine anything. She said briskly, 'D'you want to marry him, Jon? Are you in love with him?'

'You know damn well I adore him!' Tears suddenly spouted from the brown eyes. 'Rosie, I want to marry him more than anything else in the whole world! But I'm only sixteen! And he's – gone – he's gone away – he'll never come back – !' She put her hands over her face and sobbed loudly.

Rose shepherded her into a gateway in the hedge. On the other side, grazing cows looked up, momentarily and mildly surprised by the weeping girl.

Rose said, 'Come on, Jon. This won't do. You have to look after yourself now.' She held the familiar head into her neck and stared sightlessly at the field. She had an unpleasant feeling that nothing would ever be the same. She took a deep breath. 'Listen. You're seventeen next month. Lots of people get married at seventeen. And Mother . . . she will be upset of course, but she'll cope.' The sobbing did not abate and Rose changed her tone to one of rallying indulgence. 'Listen, I'll buy you a dress. You can choose it – we'll go together. And I'll be your bridesmaid—'

Jon said furiously and wetly, 'Everyone will know! I won't be able to hold my head up!'

'They might guess, of course. But if we arrange everything by the end of May or the beginning of June—'

'Oh stop it, Rosie! He won't marry me, and you know it! It was you he was keen on!' Jon withdrew herself and stared at her sister with brimming eyes. Her face was dirt-streaked with tears; she looked younger by the minute. 'Oh Rosie, I was so jealous that night! I'm sorry . . . really sorry. But I thought he was beginning to like me best. When we went to Birmingham I kissed him and he didn't push me off or anything. I kissed him properly!' She held her breath and looked defiant. 'A French kiss! I don't expect you know what that is, do you?'

Rose flushed. 'Jon, I don't want to know all this. Rick means nothing to me in that way. I think he was despicable to take advantage of a schoolgirl, especially when he was under Mother's roof, but the damage is done and we have to think what to do next.'

'But I have to explain to you – I must! I thought – when you were such ages out in the snow and you didn't want me with you – I thought he must be asking you to marry him. It was such a relief when you came in to tea and you were all funny with him and went to bed early. I thought I'd still got a chance. And there wasn't really room in your bed, so I went to see him . . . I didn't mean . . . it was my fault.

56

I know that. I started kissing him and then I pushed down my nightie and pretended I'd hurt my shoulder—'

Rose said crisply, 'Jon. Shut up.' She put her hands in her pockets and pulled her coat down hard on her shoulders. 'Listen. It is obvious from what you've said that Rick feels a great deal for you. Otherwise, he would have – have—'

'Chucked me out? I threatened to scream if he did that.'

Rose swallowed. 'He need not have . . . Jon, I will find him. Tell him. He'll want to do the right thing. Don't worry about it any more.'

'You won't find him,' Jon prophesied gloomily. 'I bet he's left the country.'

Rose relaxed suddenly and laughed. 'Oh Jon. You're so . . .' she nearly said 'young', but changed it to ' – dramatic!'

Rose called on Mrs Ellenbury and asked if they had seen anything of Rick John lately.

'Rick John?' Mrs Ellenbury smiled. 'You mean the young man your little sister is so smitten with? Has he cooled off?' She laughed. 'Tell her that he's probably waiting for her to grow up!'

Rose shook her head. 'We were worried about him actually. And as he was a friend of yours—'

Mrs Ellenbury stopped laughing. 'A friend of ours?' She was astonished. 'We saw him at your twenty-first birthday party, my dear. But we'd never seen him before.'

Rose stammered apologies. 'I thought he'd mentioned Margaret . . . so sorry.'

She saw her superior and asked for a day off. It wasn't that easy.

'Your annual leave is scheduled for October this year, Miss Harris. Special leave without pay is very difficult for me to arrange.'

'It's a family problem.' Rose bit her lip. She did not want any enquiries, or offers of help.

'Ah. Your mother?'

Well, it was for Mother. 'Yes,' said Rose.

'I'm so sorry. I hope she'll be better soon. In that case, you may take Wednesday. It is your half-day anyway, and

57

I think I might be able to spare Miss Marchant from the Gloucester branch.'

Rose was sincerely grateful.

She cycled into Gloucester quite early on Wednesday morning, padlocked her bike in the yard at the back of the library and walked round to the front of the Providential Insurance office in St John's Lane. She had no idea when Rick's lunch hour might be, or whether he might be out collecting money or whatever insurance men did. It was all a bit of a gamble, but she was certain it was going to come off. So much effort on her part must be rewarded. She meant the effort of deceiving her mother, of arranging for the time off, of the decision to broach the problem to Rick direct; but there was a much greater effort involved. Her own pride was in the dust. Rick had professed to love her, and here she was pleading the cause of her little sister.

The weather had started out fine and sunny, but by nine-thirty it was grey and blustery and she wished she'd got more than a cardigan over her navy skirt and white blouse. She wrapped the ribbed welt closely around her waist and walked the length of St John's Lane once more. It was all hateful. Sordid and hateful. She had to force all other thoughts out of her mind and concentrate on the first task – to find Rick. After that she would think again. But she was conscious of the sheer physical weight of shame in her body, even if she would not allow any coherent thoughts to form in her mind.

She walked into Westgate Street and the sun broke through the clouds for a moment as she looked into the window of Timothy Whites. She decided to buy something for Jon. And for Mother.

She was ages in the shop. In the end she bought Jon a gigantic powder puff on a stick, and some bath salts for her mother. Then she looked at her gold watch and saw she'd probably missed Rick if he'd had an early midday break.

She ran back down the dark alley of St John's Lane and was in time to see the front door open and three young men emerge. None of them was Rick. One of them had Rick's open, keen look, and was fair. The others were shorter, brown-haired, nondescript. One of them glanced at her, then turned with his companions and made for the Northgate Street end of the lane. She had a nasty feeling he must have said something about her. The fair one looked over his shoulder, then immediately back again. She felt conspicuous and even more miserable. The long package containing the powder puff was difficult to hold. She tucked it under her arm with her handbag and began to wonder seriously what she would do if Rick did not have a lunch hour. Or if he had been sent somewhere else for the day. Or if he'd left the firm altogether.

At three o'clock she went to the Tudor Tea Rooms in College Court and ordered a pot of tea and a toasted tea cake. She would stay on till five-thirty and hope to see him when he left work, but her hopes were now very low indeed. If she had been worried about what she would say to him, she no longer cared; now she just wanted to see him.

At four the waitress said, 'Is there anything else, madam?' which meant her table was needed. She stood up with conscious dignity and walked over the uneven floor to the door. 'Excuse me, madam. You've left your brush.'

It was the wretched powder puff, now vaguely visible through its packing. She hurried off, blushing alarmingly.

She dared not walk too far from the insurance office; the ancient front door of the terraced building was just on the bend of the lane, so that a few yards either way put it out of sight. Anxious, she walked past the discreetly shabby door, turned and walked past it again.

It opened and someone came out. It was not Rick, she could see that immediately, yet the stocky figure and slicked brown hair were both vaguely familiar. Brown eyes met her blue ones. It was the young man who had glanced at her five hours ago. She turned and walked purposefully towards Northgate Street.

'Hum. Excuse me. Sorry but—'

The man was practically breathing down her neck. She stopped abruptly and he cannoned into her.

'I say. I do apologize. Are you all right?'

They were both stumbling along the red brick wall of the office.

She recovered herself.

'Of course. My fault.' She was breathing audibly. 'I'm afraid you made me jump.'

He was red-faced and looked more embarrassed than she felt, which was saying something.

'Sorry. Again.' He forced a smile. 'Look. I work in that room—' he jabbed a thumb at the window next to the office door —'can't help seeing you walking up and down. Can I do something?'

'Oh no. I was . . . waiting. For someone. Must have missed them. I think I'd better go home actually. I'm sorry if I've been a nuisance. I didn't realize anyone could actually see me.'

Suddenly he relaxed. His thickset shoulders dropped. He wore a tweed jacket and grey flannels. He looked absolutely . . . safe.

'Well. You're not invisible.' He grinned experimentally and after a moment of doubt she smiled back.

'I meant—'

'I know. And of course I wouldn't have noticed you if you'd been anybody. But . . .' he was blushing again. She rather liked him.

He coughed. 'I'm just making tea for the manager. And my room is my room. I mean, it's only a cubbyhole, but I've got it to myself. Would you like a cup of tea?'

'I've just had some. And I ought to get back now.'

'You could keep an eye on the lane from my window. Just in case your friend is late. Or something.'

Her instinct was to refuse. It was something to do with being independent, no trouble to anyone. But because of Jon none of them were independent any more. They were entirely dependent on Rick John.

She hesitated a little too long and he said, 'Not if you're in a hurry, of course.'

She heard the hurt in his voice. He wanted to do her a favour.

'I'd be very grateful actually. I wanted to hang on till five, really. Are you sure it'll be all right? Supposing someone comes to your office?'

He ushered her in through the door. They stood in a small square lobby with stairs leading off. On either side of the staircase was a door. And next to the right-hand door was an opening rather like the ticket office in a railway station.

He opened that door. 'My domain,' he said with a flourish.

It wasn't much bigger than a cupboard. There was a ledge on his side of the opening which was also his desk. A telephone and a lot of papers were on it. Under the window was a gas ring, the gas turned to a bead beneath a battered kettle. 'See? Every time I went to the kettle I could spot you. I got quite worried!'

He smiled disarmingly, turning his remark against himself. Then he drew a stool from beneath the desk/ledge.

'The guest chair. Do sit down while I make the tea. You can see the street over my head.'

He produced a teapot from an overhead cupboard and spooned tea into it, then crouched before the kettle.

She laughed. 'Please. You'll give yourself a bad back!'

'I want you to be able to see the street.'

'You're very kind.' She waited, gnawing her underlip while he made the tea and transferred it to the shelf top. Then she made up her mind. 'Actually—' she seemed to be saying actually rather a lot which Miss Marchant had told her was a sign of uncertainty bordering on deceit. 'I mean, I am actually waiting for someone who works in this office.' She laughed nervously. 'It sounds ridiculous I know. But they've no idea that I want to see them and I didn't want to embarrass them by actually asking for them—'

'Why on earth didn't you say so in the first place? I am the soul of discretion – have to be. Who is it you want to see?'

'Um. Well. The name is Richard John.' For some reason she felt bound to add quickly, 'He's a friend of the family, actually.'

'I see.' But he looked puzzled. 'Richard John. The name doesn't ring any bells for me and I thought I knew everyone.' He assembled a cup and saucer and milk jug next to the teapot. 'There are quite a few agents on the staff however. We don't see much of them of course. Let me take this upstairs, and I'll get a list from the secretary.'

'No really. Don't do anything you shouldn't—'

'No trouble at all.' He grinned. 'The secretary is my godmother.'

'Oh.'

He squeezed past her, holding the tray aloft.

'I'm David Fairbrother, by the way.'

She did not want to give her name, but could think of no reason for not doing so.

'Rosamund Harris.'

'Right. Pleased to meet you.'

He left the cubbyhole and she could hear him climbing the stairs. David Fairbrother. How marvellous it was to talk to someone, be with a member of the opposite sex, and not feel awkward or embarrassed by him. It hadn't been like that with Rick. That night in the snow she had been excited and happy in a schoolgirlish, silly sort of way. But then she had been horrified and repelled. She hoped it wouldn't be like that again. She wasn't particularly excited, so probably she wouldn't be repelled either.

She stationed herself at the window, in case Rick emerged anyway, and was still there when David reappeared, frowning slightly.

'There's no Richard John here.' He held out a sheet of paper closely covered with typed names in alphabetical order. She knew she ought not to show her this information and shook her head quickly.

'It's all right. I believe you.' She forced a very difficult smile. 'He must have given Jon the wrong name.'

'Jon?'

'My sister. Short for Joanna.'

'I see.' He put the list on the shelf and pored over it. 'We've got a Robert Jones. Might that be the one?'

'Is he tall and red-haired?'

'No. He's quite small and dark.'

'That's not Rick, I'm afraid.'

'Rick? He shortened his name to Rick? I wonder if it's Eric rather than Richard? We've got an Eric Johnson. He's been here nearly a year.' He looked up at her. 'I'm almost sure he's got red hair. It's not something I notice but . . .' He picked up the phone and waited. Then he said, 'It's David. The name I was after was Eric Johnson. But I'm still not absolutely certain. Is he that chap with the red hair. Yes?' He flashed a look at Rose and inclined his head. 'Is he in today?' The answer was obviously in the negative because he said, 'It's all right. Just a small query. Tomorrow will do. I'll bring the list back straightaway – thanks a lot.'

He replaced the receiver and looked again at Rose. He must have sensed her dismay in spite of her carefully schooled expression, because he said, 'Don't worry. I've got his address here. You can go and see him at home if you like.'

'Oh no.' She felt the heat rush to her face. 'He lives with his father. And his younger sister. No, I couldn't do that.'

David glanced at the list and shook his head. 'He's given you another false impression, I'm afraid. He lives in digs. In St James Street.'

Rose swallowed. She wondered whether it was worth pursuing Rick further. He was obviously a complete liar and philanderer.

'I don't know what to do,' she admitted. 'I did want to see him. On business. But as he has obviously tried to mislead us it seems rather pointless.'

'If it's business, I could help you,' David Fairbrother said eagerly.

'Not insurance business. But thank you. Very much. You've been most kind. At least I know . . . at least I know who he is now.'

He made room for her to get to the door and followed her into the lobby. His face was red with the effort of trying to say something.

At last he managed it. 'Look. Can't we . . . would you let me . . . do you ever go to the pictures? Cliff Richard is on at the Plaza and—'

'Oh, I don't think so.' She could not risk being repelled by this kind and pleasant young man. 'But thank you ever so much. I really must go. Goodbye.'

He tried to ask her where she lived, but she almost ran around the bend that hid him from view. He had to man his little office. He wouldn't be able to follow her.

She collected her bike. It was quite cold now. The sooner she started pedalling up London Road, the sooner she would feel warmer. It had all been a waste of time, but it was a kind of relief that she could do nothing more about it. Except that Jon was relying on her. And Mother too, though she did not know it as yet.

She cycled out of Brunswick Road, wobbled uncertainly in the traffic of Eastgate Street, and turned right instead of left. Before she knew it she was bumping over the level crossing and into Barton Street. She knew vaguely where St James Street was. If she changed her mind, she could turn left into Derby Road and go home that way. It was probably a quieter route anyway.

But she did not turn left. Barton Street leaned to the right at India House, and there was the entrance to St James Street plainly marked. She got off her bike and waited for a break in the flow of traffic.

A motorbike drew up alongside her and the rider took off goggles. It was David Fairbrother.

'I thought you might . . .' He switched off his engine and lowered his voice accordingly. 'I hope you don't mind. None of my business of course.' His face was still red. 'It's just that – I didn't give you a house number and I thought . . . and it's going cold . . . only a cardigan.' He reached behind him and pulled out of a pannier a man's sleeveless sweater. 'Perhaps you'd like—'

She was terribly touched by his consideration. 'Most kind of you, Mr Fairbrother.'

'Oh please – everyone calls me David. I'm the junior-junior-junior-tea-maker—' He stopped, smiling. He had made her laugh.

She struggled into the sweater while he held her bike. She knew it must look terribly odd over her cardigan. But it immediately cut out the cold.

'You look . . . nice,' he commented. He got off his motorbike and shoved it across the road. She followed. He said, 'I'd like to take you home.' He saw her face change and went on, 'But I won't.' He glanced up the street. 'It's number 32. And if you don't have any luck, ring the office, will you? I'll have a word with him.' He suddenly looked older than he had before. Older and quite grim.

She thanked him. They shook hands. He trod hard on his kick-start and the bike roared into noisy life. As he got under way he called, 'Don't worry about the pullover.'

But he must have known that she would.

Number 32 had seen much better days. It was large and double-fronted, soot-coloured with grey net curtains at every window. There were rusty railings around a small weed-choked front garden. A coloured man was sitting on a stool outside the door, apparently mending a piece of machinery.

'Excuse me.' Rose had no idea why, but she was drawn instinctively to all coloured people. 'I'm looking for Mr Rick – that is, Mr Eric John . . . son.' She'd almost forgotten Rick's real name. 'I wondered if you could tell me which is his room?'

The coloured man was unimpressed by her politeness. 'Six,' he said shortly. 'And mind the manifold in the hall.'

The manifold looked like part of a car. She straddled it and walked awkwardly to a door at the end of the passage. It was almost dark here, but there was a large 6 painted in white on the door panel. She knocked.

When the door opened she was bathed in the light from the window inside the room, whereas Rick was silhouett into anonymity. But of course she knew it was him; he smelt the same, and his head was aureoled pinkly.

'Rosie Harris. For God's sake. Snow-White herself!' He was actually laughing as he stood aside for her to enter the room. 'And what have you got there? A witch's broomstick? Rose, you've come to put a spell on me, haven't you? Admit it – haven't you?'

She had forgotten his infectious quality; she remembered now that whatever mood he was in, he could pass it on immediately. She tucked the powder puff firmly under her arm and marched into the room as if entering a lion's den.

That amused him too.

'Oh Rose. Rose. You are exquisitely beautiful, but that chastity belt is obviously pinching like hell!'

She went straight to the window and looked out. There was a yard crisscrossed by washing lines. She tried to imagine Jon living here. The bed had a soggy look, there were old clinkers in the grate and the wash basin in the corner was crazed with dirty cracks.

She said levelly, 'Rick, I cannot begin to understand you. Nor my sister. But . . . I've come to tell you that she is having a – a – baby.'

There was a short silence, then he said blankly. 'But . . . she can't be. She's sixteen. It was only . . . I haven't been near her since. I came out before—'

Rose kept her eyes on the clothes lines. She said, 'I don't think there's any doubt about it. And I've not come to pass any judgements. We've got to be practical about it. Jon is seventeen next month. If we can make the wedding arrangements quickly enough, it can be passed off as a premature baby. That can happen with young girls – I read about it—'

He interrupted fiercely, 'I don't want to marry Jon. I don't want to marry anybody! But Jon – she's a kid! You know it's you I want, Rosie! You know that!'

There was that word again . . . 'want'. It seemed to have little to do with love.

She said very quietly, 'Jon is frightened and very young. My mother will be . . . devastated. You must do the right thing, Rick. There's no question about that.'

'I . . . *can't*! We'll both be unhappy – is that what you want?'

Rose spoke with conviction. 'You can make your own happiness, Rick. And that's what you have to do now. For the baby's sake.' She turned and looked at him. He wore no collar, no shoes. His shoulders were bowed. She said briskly, 'Obviously you're not working today. Why don't you get dressed and drive up to Churchdown? Propose to Jon. Speak to Mother. You'll feel . . . better.'

He stared at her as if he'd never seen her before. She held his gaze with outward calm. Her legs trembled and her heart hammered at her ribcage, but she did not add to her suggestion. She was determined not to plead with him, but she did not want to sound hectoring either.

After that endless moment, he sat down suddenly on the bed and transferred his stare to his knees. He said, 'How did you find me? I thought I'd covered my tracks.'

She was momentarily confused. She did not want to mention David Fairbrother. She made her voice brisk.

'I rang your office. Luckily they realized that Rick John was Eric Johnson.'

He was startled. He said in a low voice, 'I've never seen you like this, Rosie. I thought you were soft and sweet.'

'Not when the course of action is obvious.' She wished she did not feel sorry for him. She said in a kinder voice, 'Rick, seriously, you have no option.'

He looked up then with a little laugh. 'You think not? I could disappear, Rosie. Just like that. I've done it before.' He clicked his fingers in the air. 'But it's you. I can't leave you.' He looked up again. 'Your mother . . . I've never felt part of a family since my own mother died. It was so . . . good.'

'Then it will be easier to be happy when you're married to Jon,' she came back swiftly.

He laughed again, bitterly but with resignation.

'You're like a brick wall. And I thought – I really thought you loved me a little.'

The trembling stopped and her heart slowed down; but then it was worse. She thought she might melt and fall down in front of him.

She said with a kind of formal regret, 'I'm sorry, Rick. I did not intend to mislead you. I've always thought of you as Jon's . . . friend.'

He went on looking at her; it was almost a physical contact.

She went to the door. 'I've got my bicycle outside. Probably by the time I get home you will be there already. We won't mention this . . . interview. Of course.'

She left. This time she did not notice the manifold nor the man sitting in the doorway. At almost the spot where Derby Road becomes Horton Road, she started to cry.

Amazingly, Rick was there before her. He presented Jon with the powder puff which Rose had completely forgotten, as if it were his own gift. There were flowers for Aileen.

'Nothing for you, Rosie,' he said. 'All I had left was the shirt on my back!' He laughed as if it were a joke and the other two laughed with him.

He took Jon for a walk on the hill before tea.

Aileen said, 'If Jon weren't so young, I'd think he was going to propose to her!'

Rose said, 'She'll be seventeen next month, Mother. And it's obvious she's been in love with him ever since he came to my party.'

'Puppy love, darling. It's you he comes to see.'

Rose bent over the sandwiches she was making.

'I don't think so. And as for puppy love – Jon is older than her years in many ways.'

'Yes, she is. Do you know something I don't know?' Aileen sounded jocular, then apprehensive. 'Is something wrong, darling?'

Rose held her breath. It was an opportunity to break the news of Jon's pregnancy gently. But then the back door flew open and Jon burst into the tiny kitchen.

'Guess what? You'll never guess anyway so I'll have to tell you! Rick and I are getting married!'

68

There was a silence. Behind Jon, Rick appeared, for once in his life looking discomfited. Rose glanced at her mother; Aileen was stood with her back against the gas stove, rigid and stunned and still apprehensive.

Rose said, 'Why don't we go into the dining room? Jon, carry these in, will you?' She handed over the plate of sandwiches and practically shoved Jon ahead of her. Rick and Aileen perforce followed.

They sat around the dining table. Jon bumped on her chair like a child at a party.

'Well? Isn't someone going to congratulate us? You did . . . hear, did you? We . . . are . . . getting . . . married!'

She mouthed the words idiotically and collapsed laughing against Rick's shoulder.

Aileen said repressively, 'You are sixteen years old, Jon. Rick, you know we are all fond of you, but you must realize—'

Jon's laughter vanished on the instant. She clamped a hand on Rick's wrist, to stop him from speaking. Then she leaned forward.

'You've got to let us, Ma. I mean it. I'm pregnant.'

It was as if Aileen had known it all the time. She flinched visibly, but there was no other reaction. She stared at Jon for a long instant, then looked at her plate.

Rose leaned across and took the tea cosy off the teapot.

'Let's all have a cup of tea,' she said tritely, 'and discuss the arrangements. Shall we?'

Rick laughed. It started Jon off again. Rose wondered if it was hysteria; Jon fell all over Rick, unable to control her giggles. Aileen said nothing but she accepted a cup of tea from Rose and drank it carefully. After a while, controlling herself by the simple expedient of clamping a hand over her mouth, Jon passed sandwiches and they all took one. She herself proceeded to make an enormous tea; when Rick shook his head to cake, she fed him from her own plate. If Rose had not been so anxious about her mother, she might have felt physically ill at such an infantile display. Except that she knew Jon's behaviour was a sign of her infinite relief.

Aileen managed a sandwich and a second cup of tea. She smiled tremulously when Jon said that Rose was treating her to a wedding dress. Much later she said, 'I'll see the Reverend Murchison tomorrow. Perhaps he can start calling the banns this Sunday.'

Both Jon and Rose were amazed. Rose looked searchingly at her mother. She must have put up a protective wall of some sort; Rose was terrified it might crumble at any moment. But it lasted throughout that long, long evening. It survived Jon's ridiculous, schoolgirl excitement; it outlasted Rose's own matter-of-fact approach. At ten o'clock when Rick announced he had better catch the last bus into Gloucester, Rose had had more than enough. She leapt up to fetch his coat and could have screamed with frustration when he followed her into the narrow passage. He closed the door behind them, saying something over his shoulder about the bathroom. But he did not go upstairs.

'Thanks, Rose.'

He took his topcoat from her and let it fall to the ground.

'You realize this is my present to you? No flowers. Just my life.'

For the first time, Rose saw that Jon and Rick were a good match. She said nothing.

He took her by the shoulders; she knew he was trying to break the barrier she'd put up and which was fast disappearing. She steeled herself. He kissed her angrily, pressing his mouth to hers so that it hurt. She stood quite still.

He whispered, 'You . . . you bitch!'

Then he opened the door and said, 'Right. I'm off. Coming to the bus stop with me, Jonny?'

Aileen's voice said, 'I don't think that's wise, darling. It's cold and dark and you—'

'Coming, Rickie,' Jon called and giggled insanely again.

It wasn't until her mother asked her what on earth she'd got on that Rose realized she was still wearing David Fairbrother's pullover. It gave her a sense of comfort; the thought of him restored some of her battered self-respect. He had made her feel rather special. Not cheap. Not nasty. Certainly not a bitch.

Four

If it hadn't been for Rose's insecurity, she might not have returned the pullover, and perhaps David Fairbrother would
not have called for it either, and things would have been very
different. But Rose had a sudden urge to see him again, and
anyway she felt she really ought to return the pullover. So
ten days later, when her half-day fell on a Thursday, she
went down to Gloucester and pushed her bike up St John's
Lane. Jon wanted to be met out of secretarial college, where
she was wasting the end of term away, and be taken to the
Bon Marché to choose a wedding dress; Rose told herself
she would have had to come into the city anyway.

Ironically, she had no sooner padlocked her back wheel
than the shabby door of the Providential office opened and
out stepped Rick.

His face lit up.

'Rosie! Jon said you were coming down this afternoon,
but I didn't dream you'd come to see me!'

'I . . . ' For some reason Rose did not want to disclose her
contact with David Fairbrother. She searched frantically for
a reason for being there. 'I wondered if you had any ideas
about the dress. The wedding dress, you know. We're going
to choose one this afternoon. After school.'

It all sounded odd but Rick nodded. Evidently the dress
had featured strongly in the wedding discussions. 'Oh yes.
The dress. I don't think I can get time off to come with you,
Rosie. I've got a letter here to deliver to the Shire Hall, but I
can't spin that out longer than half an hour. Let's go through
to the cathedral and sit down for a while—'

'Don't be silly, Rick.' His careless attitude to everything
was frightening. 'I just want to know what you think about
the colour.' That was something of a brainwave.

71

'Colour?' Rick looked blank. 'The colour of Jon's dress, d'you mean? You know darned well I shan't have a say in that! White, I suppose.'

Rose blushed and he laughed.

'Oh I see. She's not entitled to wear white in your book? Come off it, Rose!'

Rose bent over her bike, hiding her face as she fiddled with the padlock.

He said, 'Hang on a minute. I'm glad you popped in. You see, we need your powers of persuasion. I was wondering how to have a private word.'

The chain clattered as she put it into her bike basket. She began to walk away from the office window. Rick kept pace with her.

'It's like this, Rosie.' He had the decency to sound diffident. 'I'm rather strapped for cash. You've seen the flat. No good for Jon in her condition. I wondered . . . your grandfather is an estate agent, I understand—'

'No, Rick. You must ask Jon to do that sort of thing. I couldn't ask him.'

'You mean you wouldn't ask him!'

They emerged into Westgate Street and she prepared to turn left towards the Cross.

'I'm sorry, Rick. I have to go.'

'It's not three o'clock yet—'

'Rick. I'll see you this evening.'

She got on her bike and pedalled away. She felt hot and bothered although the weather was still overcast. Her eyes felt scratchy, as if some of the city grit was caught beneath the lids.

'I hate you, Eric Johnson,' she whispered.

She went back to the office, did not bother to lock her bike this time, and dashed through the ancient door. Rick must not find her here a second time.

David Fairbrother must have seen everything; he opened his door immediately and she went into the cubbyhole holding the bag containing the pullover well ahead of her.

'I brought this back,' she said abruptly. 'You were kind . . . it was kind of you . . . thank you.'

He took it slowly. He was different. He would not meet her eyes.

He said, 'I saw you just now. Guessed you'd be back. You don't want . . . him . . . to know about me?'

'Oh, it doesn't matter. Not really.' She made her voice deliberately offhand. It was obvious she'd been wrong about David Fairbrother too. He wasn't interested in her as a person after all. There must be something very wrong with her.

She turned to leave.

He cleared his throat elaborately. 'Umm . . . he's asked me . . . to be his best man. At the wedding.'

She was surprised out of her spurious coolness.

'But you don't know him!'

'Quite. But it seems his family lives in Wales. He's lost touch with a lot of friends. Thought I'd be suitable.' He forced a laugh. 'I think he meant dull. Respectable.'

Was that what had put him off? He did not want to be drawn into such an unrespectable affair?

She smiled. 'I suppose you declined with thanks?'

'No. I wanted to see you first. I thought . . . maybe . . . I could help. By being there. You know.'

He was looking straight at her now. She thought his eyes were the colour of milkless tea. You could look right into them. You couldn't stop looking right into them.

She said in a low voice, 'Thank you. Yes. It would be . . . nice. Actually.'

His face seemed to dissolve in sympathy. He said, 'Rosamund. I'm so sorry. I didn't guess . . . should have done, of course. I would kill the rotter only that wouldn't do any good.'

She was infinitely touched. Nobody ever called her Rosamund, and it sounded delightful. She said, 'It's not that bad, actually. I mean of course it is. She's so young. But by the time they marry she'll be seventeen. And she's so happy about it. I realize he must be . . . a bit of a rotter, actually. But she loves him. And in his way—'

He said, 'Who?'

She said, 'Who what?'

He said, 'Who are you talking about?'

She said, 'Rick and Jon. Eric I mean. And my sister, Joanna.'

'You mean, it's not you? You're not marrying Johnson? You mean you were finding him because of your sister?'

It was like seeing the sun come up. His face practically glowed.

She said, 'You thought . . .'

'Yes.'

'And you were still willing to be best man.'

'Of course.'

She gazed at him and swallowed a lump in her throat.

'Will you still be best man? Please.'

He stared back. 'Of course.'

She said with total inadequacy, 'Oh good.'

They agreed to meet after the shopping spree and go to the cinema. She took her bicycle to the library and locked it there and walked to meet Jon. Her legs did not tremble and her heart did not hammer. But she glowed, as he had, with the joy of meeting someone so completely . . . nice. She could be so natural with this man; there was no fear anywhere. She thought of his baggy flannels and tweed jacket and smiled fondly. How Mother would like him!

She said yes to the first dress Jon tried on.

'But we can't get the very first one,' Jon protested. 'When you go out to choose a dress you need to see at least two. That's what choosing means!'

'Sorry, darling. Try that pink one.'

'I'm having white, Rosie, and that's that. If I wear any other colour, everyone will think I have to get married.'

Rose did not even bother to raise her eyebrows. It didn't matter any more.

After trying on another three dresses in various shops, Jon had had enough.

'You're right. The first one was best. Let's go back there.'

'When are you meeting Rick?'

'I'm not. He's got a meeting after work. Then he'll come on up to see us.'

'He didn't say anything about a meeting.'

'You've seen him?' Jon's eyes became sharp.

It would have been so simple to tell Jon about returning the pullover; Rose wondered why she felt this need to protect David Fairbrother. To keep him a secret.

'I wondered if he had any ideas about your dress.'

Jon stared in silence for a long moment. Then she said bluntly, 'I know he likes you. Do you like him?'

Rose said, 'Jon, if you think for one moment that there is anything between us, put it out of your head. As a matter of fact, I don't like him particularly. Remember, he lied to us about his name.'

'That was nothing. Eric's a ghastly name. You can't blame him for wanting to change it. And maybe he said Johnson right at the beginning and we didn't quite catch it!'

'Well, I've heard some excuses, but that takes the biscuit.'

'If you don't like him "particularly", why did you go to see him? And don't give me that eyewash about the dress. That takes the biscuit too!'

Rose paused, wondering whether the time had come to explain about David Fairbrother and then to tell Jon that she was going to the pictures with him that evening and must not be much longer.

Then she said, 'Look. He wants me to tackle Grandfather. About a house or a flat. Have you seen his bedsit in St James Street?'

'No.'

'It's awful.'

'And are you going to try to get us something?'

'I can't, Jon. You know what the grandparents are. They've always treated us as charity cases—'

'But you're the favourite. They like you better than me. Better than Mummy even.'

'Rubbish.'

'It's not rubbish.' Jon's gaze did not waver. 'But if you're not going to do it, why go to Rick's office to see him?'

'Listen, Jon—'

'You must be thinking about it. Please try, Rosie. Please.'

Rose smiled and shook her head helplessly. 'You're incorrigible, aren't you? I'll have a word. But I'm not going on my hands and knees.'

'Oh, you're a darling! I don't know why you're so good to me – I don't deserve it!' Suddenly, unexpectedly, the brown eyes filled with tears. 'Rosie, I love you so much. As long as I know you're on my side, I can face anything. Anything at all.'

'Less of the dramatics, little Sis.'

But Rose, too, felt the tie between them. She had assumed it was a one-way tie, based on the fact that Jon's birth had brought them back to the safety of England. It was good to know Jon felt it too.

But then she spoiled everything by saying, 'I'm not being dramatic, Rosie. You must see that if I can give Rick something, he's bound to love me!' And suddenly she giggled. 'Something besides the baby, I mean!'

The film was called *Summer Holiday*. Rose was worried for a while that David Fairbrother would try to put his arm along the back of the seat, but he did not, and after a tense first half, she relaxed and began to enjoy everything. He produced a box of chocolates and when the lights went up they discussed deeply their preferences among the soft centres.

'Not strawberry,' David said earnestly. 'Too sickly.'

'And Turkish delight – yuk,' responded Rose.

'What about lemon cream?'

'Sort of. Coffee is best. Or plain.'

'Oh yes. And marzipan.'

'We like all the same ones!' Rose discovered, amazed. 'I mean, that is unusual. If you don't like strawberry cream, most people don't like marzipan either. But I like marzipan too. And I don't like strawberry cream.'

They gazed at each other, smiling their pleasure. Then David fumbled inside his jacket and produced a penknife.

With infinite care he halved the marzipan and coffee creams. Rose laughed delightedly. His fingers were sticky and she wiped them on her scrap of handkerchief and told him he could keep it. He folded it carefully and put it in his inside pocket.

'There. I've got a bit of you. You should have kept my pullover, then we'd really know each other, Rosamund.'

He was going too fast. She sucked some coffee cream away from a suspect tooth and said quickly, 'A nice idea. But not very realistic. For instance you don't know that I am never ever called Rosamund.'

He said, 'I'm sorry. You don't like it?'

'Oh yes. It's much nicer than Rose. Or Rosie. But I meant that . . . we don't know each other at all. Not really.' Her face was getting hot. She wasn't putting things well.

He said, 'Let's make a start. I'm always called David. My father works at Providential, of course. My mother sews.'

'Sews?'

'Loose covers. Curtains. For people.'

'My mother knits a bit. But she doesn't actually do anything.'

'But she's had to stand in for your father, hasn't she? He was killed in the war.'

'Yes. How did you know that?'

In the semi-darkness she could see he too was getting warm. 'I asked Johnson. I felt if I was going to be his best man I should know something about—'

'Yes. Of course.'

He said doggedly, 'I have a brother too. Martin. He's quite a bit older than me. He's in an accountancy office. He's married. To a girl called June who doesn't like us very much. And they have two little boys. One is called Charles and the baby is called Arnold after my father. We call him Arney.'

She wondered how to reciprocate. She said, 'We were in America in the war. Then we came home and Jon was born.' And after that nothing had happened.

The cinema darkened and the newsreel started. He whispered, 'Now we know everything.'

She thought about life's diurnal round on Churchdown hill, then of the snow; then of Rick. David knew nothing of her. The news finished and the film began. A double-decker bus rolled across the screen and Cliff Richard sang through his nose while Hank Marvin played his guitar and flashed his spectacles happily. Rose settled back in her seat, confident by now that no intruding arm would be there. It really was a very good film.

She waited until the day after Jon's seventeenth birthday to call on the Harrises in Cheltenham. Jon had her usual card and a cheque for twenty pounds which was four times as much as usual, so they assumed it was a wedding present. It was the only acknowledgement they had to their invitation. Aileen merely rolled her eyes; Jon said petulantly, 'Well, if they come there will be no food for them! You'd think they'd have the courtesy to RSVP, wouldn't you?'

'I'll go and see them,' Rose promised. 'Find out what is happening.'

Jon perked up immediately. 'You're wonderful, Rosie,' she said fulsomely.

Rose had forgotten that Grandmother hated unexpected callers. It was very hot and both grandparents were in the old walled garden behind the house awaiting guests for tea. The maid – Jon had named her the dragon when she was very small – showed Rose through the house hurriedly. She was making scones and cutting cucumber sandwiches and disliked unexpected callers even more than Grandmother did.

'Rose!' Grandmother got out of her garden chair with difficulty. 'My dear child! If only you'd let us know! Never mind, I don't suppose you can stay long. Come and sit down for half an hour and talk to us before the McIntyres arrive.'

The McIntyres were both solicitors, both retired. Mrs McIntyre wore black with white collar and cuffs and was very severe.

Grandfather fetched another chair. He looked delighted. Nevertheless Rose knew she'd blotted her copybook with Grandmother.

'Thank you so much. I didn't mean to interrupt anything—'

'Not at all, Rose. Take your time.' Grandfather shot a look at his wife. 'Edith. Perhaps Rose would care for a cup of tea.'

'No. Really.'

But Grandmother was already up and making for the house, where she could check on the dragon with impunity. Rose settled herself next to her grandfather. It was now or never.

He said, 'You wanted to ask me something, child?'

'Oh. Yes, I did. Actually.' Rose smiled tentatively. 'Was it so obvious?'

'Only to me, don't worry. Something to do with Joanna's wedding? It's difficult for you, I realize that. But Edith insists we keep away – none of our business, all that kind of thing. But if there is something I can do . . . quietly, you know—'

Rose was surprised. 'But surely it is your business? We understand that you disapprove, of course. Jon is so very young.'

'We try not to approve or disapprove. It would be different if it were you.'

Rose frowned. 'Why? Is there something wrong with me, Grandfather?'

'No, child. Of course not. Now come on. Ask away. How can I help?'

Rose said flatly, 'They need somewhere to live.'

'Ah.' He nodded judiciously. 'Of course. But you know I've been retired for a long time now, Rose?'

'Yes. But you might hear of something to rent? Something like ours? Mother often says how good you were to get the Snow-White house for us.'

'Does she?'

'Yes.' Rose had never actually heard her mother utter those words but was certain she must have said something like that at some time. 'I've seen Rick's bedsitting-room.

It's in St James Street in Gloucester. It's not very nice.'

'Don't you think it would do Jon good to make a home from unpromising material?'

'I suppose so.' She glanced at her grandfather quickly. 'It's just that . . . '

'There's a child on the way,' he supplied quietly.

'We thought you must guess.' Rose could not look at him.

'We guessed . . .'

'Oh Grandfather, I'm sorry. She is so young—'

'But he is not all that young, I understand?'

'Twenty-three,' she murmured.

'Quite.'

'You see, I feel sort of responsible. I should have kept an eye on her. Or talked to him.'

'Joanna has therefore suggested it would salve your conscience to ask me for help?'

'Not . . . not at all . . . here's Grandmother.'

He said swiftly, 'I'll do what I can. Tell her it might not be until next year. Leases fall vacant in March and September.'

'Oh Grandfather—'

'Don't thank me. Not yet. I might not be able to do anything at all. It's not easy these days. Property prices are going sky-high and immediately a lease is up, the owners tend to sell. You can't blame them. With controlled rents—'

Grandmother arrived, smoothed her skirt and sat down gracefully.

'Doreen suggests you stay and have tea with the McIntyres, my dear.' She was flushed; Doreen the Dragon had probably won their most recent bout. 'I should have thought of it myself. Emily was always very fond of you as a child and she loves reading.'

'Reading?'

'Books, child. You'll be able to talk to her about the library.'

'Oh. Yes. How nice.'

Grandfather said jovially, 'I found an old snap of Jonathan the other day, Rose. Bit younger than you. Playing cricket on the College ground. Remind me to show it to you when we go indoors.'

'Oh. Yes. That would be . . . nice,' said Rose.

They both looked disappointed and she wished she could find something else to say about her father. But she had never known him. Unless . . . there was a vague and faraway memory of a man with her mother. When, later on, her grandfather showed her the fuzzy photograph of a boy in cricket flannels, she looked up, bright-eyed.

'I think . . . I sort of recognize him,' she said.

Grandfather smiled sadly. 'I don't think you ever saw him, child. But you're so like him that I expect his face is familiar to you.' He put a hand on Grandmother's shoulder. 'She is very like Jonathan, isn't she, Edith?'

Grandmother said briskly, 'In her ways too. Far too diffident.'

Rose sighed. Sometimes she felt sorry for her father and glad that he had married someone as soft and gentle as her mother.

Five

The wedding was on the last day of May and was very quiet indeed. The grandparents did not turn up and Jon was given away by Mr Brooking, the schoolmaster. In spite of her confidence, there was a definite bulge beneath her pristine wedding dress, hidden discreetly by the veil as she went down the aisle, but revealed on the return journey when she had thrown the net back. She clung to her new husband with an odd mixture of defiance, triumph and smugness.

Her schoolfriends were in the church in great numbers, but not one of them had been invited to the reception. Aileen had maintained quite definitely that she could not afford to entertain more than twenty people, and Jon had said that if she couldn't have them all she didn't want any. If she had thought to get her own way over this, she was disappointed. Aileen was adamant. She was not going to ask the Harrises for help, and her carefully hoarded nest-egg was for the baby as well as Jon. Rose had bought the two dresses and the flowers. Rick was always 'strapped for cash'. The reception had to be tailored accordingly.

Aileen did a buffet in the church hall, where, so recently, they had had Rose's party. Mrs Whittaker from next door, who was Jon's godmother, was there with her husband, and Rose's friend Margaret Ellenbury came with her brand-new fiancé, who was a teacher at a Worcester primary school. Rick's rather disreputable father turned up with his daughter, Trudie, and seemed to think the occasion was something of a joke. 'Your turn next, girl,' he said in a loud voice, poking at Trudie's abdomen so that no-one could mistake his meaning. Trudie laughed loudly at this. Rose glanced at Rick and understood for the first time why he had lied about his name and his background.

Rick had found someone to take photographs; and David, his face set in lines of concentration, arranged groups, read cards, pointed out the presents which Aileen and Rose had arranged in the middle of the room, and generally did his duty with determination.

Jon was popular in the village and at school, and had a great many tablecloths and napkins, saucepans and crockery, cushion covers, bed linen and handwoven rugs. Aunt Mabe had sent a satin bedspread. Mother and Rose had bought an armchair each, upholstered in pale green velvet. The newly-weds would have somewhere to sleep, and to sit down in comfort, but no table for the many cloths, no cooker for the pots and pans. Jon had already informed Rose and Aileen that until Grandfather 'coughed up' she and Rick would have to come to Churchdown for all their meals.

David was introduced; he had shaken hands with Rose in the vestry and walked sedately by her side down the aisle, but they had exchanged no words.

Now he said, 'I'm so pleased to meet you at last.'

Rick laughed. 'I've told David about you. All of you.'

'Nice things, I hope.' Jon said pertly, fluttering her lashes at David.

There was a moment of horseplay, Rick pretending to be madly jealous, Jon pouting and protesting in a baby voice. David said, 'Only nice things. Of course.'

Rose did not dare meet his eyes. Aileen said, 'We haven't had time to meet any of Rick's family and friends, did you go to school together?'

David said, 'No. We work in the same office.'

'How nice.'

Mr Johnson growled, 'Rick 'ad friends at school. Plenty of 'em. Not good enough now. None of us no good to 'im now.' His Welsh accent was heavy with condemnation. He did not mind that his son had got a seventeen-year-old girl pregnant, but he minded very much that he had cut away from his roots.

Rick said, 'Now then, Da. None of that valley talk!' He grinned at David. 'I've been away from home for seven

83

years! Time to make other friends, wouldn't you say?'

'Of course.' David nodded at Mr Johnson. 'I'm honoured that he chose one of his new friends above his old ones, Mr Johnson.'

Rose heard Jon say sotto voce to Rick, '. . . but why him – he's so terribly ordinary.' And Rick's reply, 'Don't be an idiot, buttercup. He's the son of the branch manager!'

Rose transferred a startled gaze to David. He was dealing with Aileen's salmon mousse and talking to the vicar's wife at the same time. Rose felt almost let down. This was a secret he had not shared with her.

Unexpectedly, Aileen was terribly depressed that evening and the next day.

'It's anti-climax, Mother,' Rose consoled her, making tea and laying the trolley with a lace cloth. 'And Sundays are sometimes a bit much. It seems very Sundayish today.'

'Perhaps if we'd gone to Evensong . . .' Aileen glanced at the clock. 'It's too late now. I hope the Reverend Murchison will understand. He was so good yesterday. He must have known. Everyone must have known. Oh dear . . .'

Rose hugged her. 'Do stop it, darling. Of course everyone knew. But it happens all the time—' Aileen wailed loudly as if Rose had stabbed her. Rose said, 'Hush, Mother. It's 1963, after all.'

'The worst winter for years,' Aileen interpolated inconsequentially. 'That's what did it. Being cut off – isolated – it's a kind of euphoria—'

Rose said soothingly, 'And it brought a lovely spring, didn't it? The weather was grand today. I just hope the photographs—'

'Though of course it's in the blood,' Aileen went on, pursuing her own line of thought. 'Bad blood.'

'Mother. Darling Mother. Jon will be home in two weeks' time. Bournemouth isn't far. And once she's home—'

'I know. Of course I know all that, Rose. It's just—' she looked up with a watery smile. 'It's intimations of mortality,' she misquoted.

Rose could offer no comfort. She knelt by Aileen's chair and held her, while her mother talked uncharacteristically of her past.

'In a way, Rose, I've been a selfish woman. Oh I know you've romanticized me, darling. Young widow with two daughters to bring up on her own. But there's another side to it.' She wiped her eyes and leaned back, exhausted by her own tears. 'My parents married late. Both second marriages. Your Aunt Mabe was my father's child by his first marriage. She was fifteen when I was born. How she must have resented me. But my parents . . . they doted, absolutely doted on me. Father called me his little princess. Things like that. I dreamed I really was a princess. The war started and Jonathan was billeted on us. We lived at Plymouth and he was a young naval officer . . . you can imagine. Then we went to London. Mummy and Daddy and me. A show, I think. Jessie Matthews. Daddy's favourite. We were staying near Paddington. The next morning I went for a walk in Hyde Park and the sirens sounded. A warden got me into a shelter somewhere. But the boarding-house was flattened. They couldn't have known a thing. I came home and married Jonathan. I loved him, but in any case . . . there was nothing else to do. And you were on the way and he was in the Atlantic somewhere and Mabs said we'd be safer over there. You know the rest.' She sighed deeply.

Rose said, 'If my father hadn't been trying to get to the States to see us—'

'Oh no, darling. Nothing like that. He was on convoy duty and his destroyer was torpedoed.'

Rose sat back on her heels and gazed at her mother, eyes intensely blue.

'Of course! How silly of me. All these years I've felt somehow guilty!'

Aileen was conscience-stricken. 'Was it something I said, darling? I used to be terribly fraught at Mab's place. I mean, it wasn't really a farm, was it? More like a country house.'

'It was frightening,' Rose said soberly. 'I felt it was . . . dangerous. I was sure we'd be safe in England. And we have been.' She did not answer her mother's question; she wasn't certain why she had felt responsible for her father's death. It was so long ago and she never thought about that time at all now.

'Yes, we have been.' Aileen smiled. 'It's worked out exactly as I hoped. I always knew that Jon would be wild. Well, she's settled now. And if only Grandfather can find her something next autumn, everything will be fine.'

Rose kissed the top of her mother's head. Aileen was only in her mid-forties, but already her hair felt thin against her scalp. Rose shivered.

She had a note from David during the week. It was the first letter he had written to her.

Aileen said, 'I thought it was from Margaret Ellenbury at first. But it's a Gloucester postmark.'

Rose said, 'It's from David Fairbrother.'

Aileen waggled her eyebrows significantly. 'He met you on Saturday and he's writing to you four days later? He must be smitten!'

'Mother, what an old-fashioned word. Of course he's not smitten. He simply says that if I'm working in Gloucester some time, would I like to have high tea at Lawrence's.'

Aileen was thrilled, 'Darling. Did you know his father is the manager of Providential? And he seemed so quiet and respectable.'

'His father is the branch manager, Mother!'

'Well, it's all the same.'

'Mother,' Rose scanned the letter again. 'Don't . . . get any ideas about this. Please. I – Mother – I'm not the marrying kind. Really.'

Aileen looked about to protest, but then she said, 'Who said anything about marriage? He's just a nice young man. Perhaps a friend for you, darling.'

Rose re-read David's letter when she got to bed.

'Dear Rosamund,' it said. 'Did you say you were collecting books from Gloucester library on Thursday? Would you like to meet me in Lawrence's for tea at six? I'll be there. Love David.'

It was so simple and direct and honest. Like David himself. She felt a little ache of affection in her chest. Nothing like the terrible fear and attraction she'd felt that night in the snow for Rick. A kind of protective fondness. Rather like she felt for Mother.

He was already in Lawrence's at a table by the window where he could wave as she walked along the pavement. He was wearing his tweed jacket and flannels, and his carefully brushed hair was falling over one eye which made him look very young.

'Ros!' His face lit up as she went inside, and he stood up, rocking the table perilously. 'You look . . . good!'

It had been her exact thought about him. They shook hands, smiling at each other like old, old friends.

'Have you heard from your sister?' he asked when they were settled.

'Oh no. She won't write. What about Rick?'

'Same applies, I imagine. I don't know him well enough for a personal card, and he's never sent anything to the office before.'

They ordered boiled eggs and toast. The silver teapot was old and heavy with a rickety hinged lid that slopped tea into the saucers. David held a napkin beneath the spout and managed to burn his fingers. She always had a tube of aquaflavine in her bag, and produced it. He called her a girl scout and she laughed again.

After tea, relaxed and comfortable, she said suddenly, 'You didn't tell me you worked with your father.'

He looked surprised. 'I thought I did. The old man's hardly ever in the office anyway. Meetings and so forth.'

She said with difficulty, 'Yes. But I didn't realize he was . . . the manager.'

'Perhaps I didn't . . .' he looked apologetic. 'It's difficult to say – "my father is the branch manager of Providential Insurance" – if you see what I mean.' He grinned. 'It was awful at first. Everyone thought I was going to get special treatment. I've lived that down now.'

Again he was surprised. 'Surely he's not green enough to think it will do him any good? He knows I'm the glorified office boy!'

She said quickly, 'You're not that, I'm sure! But yes, I rather think he hoped you would help him. In future. I'm sorry, David. I feel very embarrassed about it.'

'Don't give it another thought. It won't be like that, anyway.' He smiled and looked at her with those clear eyes of his. 'I'm glad you know. Even a little thing like that might come between us. I want you to know everything there is to know about me.' He must have sensed the faint withdrawal in her, because he said quickly, 'I've got a wart on my elbow! I've had it since I was eight!'

They both laughed. They got on so well. She had never felt at ease like this with anyone else, not even Margaret. Not even Mother or Jon.

They walked down towards the library cycle shed. David bought a *Citizen* from the paperboy on the corner of Brunswick Road, and the headlines were all about a government minister called John Profumo. He started to read it to Rose, then stopped, embarrassed.

She said, 'What is it? Has something awful happened?'

'A political scandal seems to be brewing.'

'It's all in London. Nothing like that could happen here,' she said comfortably, then thought of Rick. 'It's been a lovely day, hasn't it? So warm.'

He met her eyes and laughed suddenly. She thought he was laughing at her, but he wasn't. The June evening had turned brassy and sultry. 'You might carry a first-aid kit around with you, but you're certainly never prepared for the weather,' he said.

And she replied, thankful that the subject was well and truly changed, 'It so happens I have a cycle cape in my saddlebag!'

Again they laughed, then he suddenly sobered and said, 'Oh Ros. I think . . . I love you.'

but perhaps that was what he meant. And she would not have meant that.

She said firmly, 'I feel we might be good friends too.'

He said, 'Ros. Will you come to tea on Sunday and meet the parents? Please?'

She hesitated and he followed up quickly, 'Please, Ros. No need to feel you're . . . sort of committing yourself to anything. I want you to meet them. They're OK.'

She said, 'Well, if you're sure it'll be all right. It's just that I'm not sure we can reciprocate. I mean, I don't know how Mother . . .' her voice trailed off. He had met her mother, he knew she wasn't an ogre or anything.

He said quickly, 'Ros. Just this once. Really.'

Still she procrastinated. 'I don't know where you live.'

'Stroud Road. I'll meet you here.' They were in the bike shed which was locked on a Sunday, but she nodded. She could wait outside.

'Thank you, David. It's very kind of your mother.'

'Three o'clock?'

'Make it four. Mother and I usually have a walk after lunch.'

She knew she was using Aileen as an excuse. She was frightened and she wasn't entirely certain why.

Aileen was very happy about it.

'Darling, I was right – he really is nice. You must see that he won't do anything improper. Nothing to frighten you off.' She touched Rose's hand. 'You are frightened, aren't you, Rosie?'

'Of course not. Nothing to be frightened of. Sunday afternoon tea . . .'

'Quite. He sounds just right for you.'

Rose thought of that frightful day waiting outside the Providential office; of the sheer consolation of David's instant help.

'Mother. There's nothing . . . like that between us. We're friends, and that is all. He is a very pleasant, nice friend. No more, no less.'

'I *know*, darling! Isn't that just what I've been saying?' And Aileen smiled. Almost smugly.

Rose got to the library bicycle shed at ten to four. The weather had broken with a thunderstorm the previous Thursday night, and it was as grey as November with a slight drizzle now and then. She struggled out of her hot cycling cape and locked her bike against the wall. Her hair was already wet and she stood inside the porch of the library, raking it with her fingers. She had a comb in her bag, but ladies did not comb their hair in the street, especially on Sunday afternoons.

At five past four she crossed the empty road and surveyed herself in the windows of the Co-op. The hem of her dress was bedraggled and damp and her dark hair was plastered unbecomingly to her head from its centre parting. She pushed at it futilely and shook her skirt. Then she turned and glanced back at the library, sure that David would have arrived while she wasn't looking. He wasn't there.

She began to walk up and down beneath the Co-op's awning. It kept her warm, passed the time, and he would be sure to have arrived after twenty turns. After thirty he was still not there.

She looked at her gold watch. It was only twenty past four; but if she knew anything about David Fairbrother it was that he'd never be late for an appointment.

By half-past four she was certain she was being stood up. Reason went overboard; David was no longer a kind and considerate friend, he was a typical male trying to humiliate her just as Rick had done. All right, so he wouldn't touch her physically and make her feel like a tramp. He would keep her hanging about until she was almost in tears. It did not occur to her that her tears were a sign of her concern for him. She determined that she would never have another thing to do with him. Even if he had a good reason for being late, he should have let her know.

But she did not go home.

It was nearly five when David rounded the corner from Eastgate Street and ran towards her. He looked terrible; his face was red from running and he was panting painfully, but there was something holding his features in a state of immobility. A kind of disbelief. Shock. Something.

She did not give herself time to register anything, or to let him speak.

'I've been here for an hour! I didn't know what had happened to you – how could you – oh I can see you've been running but surely – what on *earth* has happened!'

Even the question sounded like an accusation. He stood before her, not meeting her eyes, trying to catch his breath, staring at the pavement as if he expected answers to be written there.

At last he said, 'My father . . . my father is dead.'

It was as if he had punched her solar plexus. The breath left her lungs in a whine of distress. She put a hand to her mouth, staring at the top of his head where his brown hair swirled in a double crown. Then she bundled her bicycle unceremoniously behind the library wall and came back to him.

'Oh . . . David! Oh . . . poor David . . . I'm so, so—'

'Don't say anything, Ros.' His voice was stern, abrupt. He went on standing before her, breathing badly, his body rigid. She was dumb, frightened to move or speak.

After what seemed an age, he took her arm and turned her towards the park. They began to walk. She had never been so conscious before of putting each foot in a certain place on the pavement. It seemed vital that she should measure her steps exactly with his; it was the only sign of empathy she could give. He maintained the grip on her elbow when she wanted to take his hand; he did not speak and she wanted to find words of comfort; he did not weep so that she could weep with him. But their steps matched perfectly; down kerbs, across roads, through the empty Sunday afternoon silence they walked. Past the marble war memorial ablaze with flowers, and under the blotched plane trees.

'We'll sit on the next vacant seat,' said the unfamiliar hoarse voice at her side. She did not reply, but kept her

91

eyes ahead, searching for a seat that could offer at least temporary privacy.

They came to it at last, right out in the open, away from any protection the trees might have offered against the sporadic drizzle. A nasty little wind blew around it; it did not welcome them.

They sat down.

David said, 'I can't take it in. I had to see you. It's insane. And you are my sanity. But I shouldn't have come. My mother is distraught.'

Still Rose did not speak. She took his hand in both of hers and held it sandwiched.

David said, 'He went for a nap. A Sunday afternoon nap. Mother said he should stay and help her, as you were coming to tea, but he must have felt ill because . . . he always helps her, they're so close.' He looked up, his face raw with sudden agony. 'She can't live without him, Ros! What will happen to her?'

She met his gaze; then suddenly she released his hand and put her arms right round his shoulders. He collapsed against her; she could feel his tears warm through her cotton dress. She made sounds against his ear with her lips, and she wept too. She thought; I'll never see David's father now.

David kept his head down, his hands tight around her waist, but gradually he stopped crying. She whispered in his ear, 'I want to help you. I don't know what to do.'

His voice was thick with tears when he replied, 'You are helping. You are here. If only you could always be here.'

And she said the obvious thing. 'I'll always be here. Don't worry.'

His hands tightened yet again; she could hardly breathe.

He said, 'Ros. It's what I want. More than anything in the world. And now . . . oh Ros.' He lifted his swollen face. His eyes were clear brown; she felt she could see into his soul. 'Ros, will you marry me?'

Her heart thumped once, hard, apparently in her throat. Then she said, 'Yes. Of course I will, David.'

He wept again, holding her fiercely, murmuring things like 'my saviour', 'my precious girl' in her ear, but thankfully he did not try to kiss her.

She wondered what she had done, but there was no drawing back. She thought that perhaps in a week or two she could ease out of the situation, but she knew that at that moment she could have answered him no other way.

They parted outside the library again. He shook her hand as if sealing a bargain, and then watched her pedal to the corner.

It seemed to take a long time to get home. She cycled past the gate of the house and on to the hill and left her bike at the stile. She walked to the top of the 'sledge run' and looked down on Gloucester.

Her mind felt very clear and calm. She knew she wasn't in love with David Fairbrother, yet she loved him very much. In a sense he had rescued her from Rick. Perhaps it was right to marry him.

She told herself it was a logical and sensible decision she was making; yet as she stared at the familiar view in front of her, the moment became almost sacramental. Standing there, in the shadow of the ancient church, she pledged herself to him. And felt a surge of strength, and a great peace.

Six

Rose saw nothing of David for two weeks. She began to wonder if the scene in the park had been mostly her imagination. She felt a kind of relief. And a kind of disappointment.

Rick and Jon came back from Bournemouth and took up what Rick jokingly called 'temporary tenure' in the St James Street bedsit. The new wedding presents looked incongruous down there, but once Rick was back at work Jon was hardly at home, so it did not matter. Rose was on a late shift that first week and did not leave for work till midday. Jon was always at the Snow-White house before she left. Sometimes she was still there when Rose returned in the evening; more often than not Rick was with her.

He was as charming as ever, but of course Rose knew him properly now; she told herself he was despicable. But then again she wondered if her sudden friendship with David Fairbrother had blossomed because she needed to prove something to Rick. Or to herself.

But, to do him justice, he did not try to speak to her alone; he rarely even met her eyes. He seemed to be putting everything into his marriage. He had always been perfectly at home in the small cramped house; now it was as if he'd been there always. He enjoyed being the only man among three women. He borrowed the firm's Riley and took them out for a meal. He cooked spaghetti for them one evening and served it with a towel over one arm and an execrable Italian accent.

Rose could see it was a happy time for Jon and Aileen, but for her it was uncomfortable to say the very least. She began to feel that if Jon and Rick did not find their own place and stay in it, she would have to move herself.

After that first intolerable week, she went to see her grandfather and found him in bed with bronchitis.

Grandmother said, 'Don't stay long, Rose. He'll love to see you but he doesn't know his own weakness and I'm terrified this will turn to pneumonia.'

Rose sat with him and held his hand. She did not intend to mention the possibility of a house for Jon; the old man brought up the subject himself.

'I've been to most of the house agents, Rose,' he said, speaking in short phrases to match his breathing. 'It's not going to be easy. Evictions are unknown these days.'

'Please don't worry about it. I wish I'd never mentioned it.' Rose was distressed. It was natural for Grandmother to be over-anxious to the point of pessimism, but Rose had found Doreen the Dragon weeping outside the bedroom door.

The old man moved his head. 'I want to help, Rose. But I would suggest they put their names on the council list.'

'Yes. All right, Grandfather. Thank you.' Rose forced a smile. 'Would you like me to read to you? The evening paper is here.'

'The cricket scores, Rose. Back page. Gloucestershire has been playing on the College ground today.'

She picked up the paper. She would visit him often, she would close the inexplicable gap between the families. She turned the pages and saw the announcement of Arnold Fairbrother's funeral. It was the next day. At Gloucester Crematorium.

Rose sat right at the back of the small chapel and knew she stuck out like a sore thumb among relatives and friends. She hardly knew why she went; she hoped it was for David's sake.

She watched them file in. Mrs Fairbrother was tall and bony, her back ramrod stiff. She maintained her self-control until the curtains of the crematorium began to open and the coffin slid through. And then, with a strangled cry, she collapsed in a heap on the floor, and had to be lifted and supported between David and his older brother. Rose,

95

screened by several rows of stalwart backs, felt her own eyes fill with tears. She wondered if her mother had been spared something after all. She had known nothing of her husband's end; there had obviously been no funeral to attend. And Rose thought: I couldn't stand it . . . I couldn't go through this.

Martin's wife was small and very pale. Rose knew that somewhere there were two small boys named for their grandfathers: Arnold and Charles. She identified David's brother, Martin; taller than David, darker too. Rose had another maverick thought: if David and I have children they won't know what the word grandfather means. Not that David's proposal had meant anything more than a cry for help; not that she would ever have children; not that she would ever marry. And then she remembered Grandfather Harris and half-smiled. If only he could be around – how he would love great-grandchildren. They would heal any silly breach.

Martin's wife looked round and saw the smile and looked away quickly. Rose straightened her face with a sinking feeling that she had made a bad impression. She held right back in her corner as everyone went out, but when she finally emerged into the brilliant sunshine the family was still there, looking at the flowers. David's eyes met hers across several bowed heads and she knew that he was glad to see her. But as they got into the cars at last, she felt that condemning face turned towards her again. Rose waited until the cortège had gone, then walked through an archway into the garden of remembrance. The banked flowers were everywhere. 'To a respected colleague.' 'Grandad Fairbrother, with our love.' 'To my dear Arney. With my love. Maudie.' 'A wonderful Dad . . .' 'Uncle Arney . . .' 'Friend and comrade . . .' 'Brother-in-arms . . .' She stood there quietly, trying to find suitable thoughts for such an occasion, and nothing occurred to her. Then she walked through the garden to the back of the little chapel where her bike leaned against the rough stone wall. From the basket she took a bunch of asters buried in a cushion of forget-me-nots. She went back and laid them at the end of the pile. The card read, 'For David's father.'

It was even more galling than usual to get home and find Rick there in Mother's armchair, one long leg dangling over the arm.

For the first time he spoke to her directly.

'You've been to old Fairbrother's funeral, haven't you?'

Rose said almost defiantly, 'Yes. I have.'

Jon came in from the kitchen carrying a tray with four sherry glasses on it. This was something that had not happened before Rick; now it was a regular feature of their evenings. She edged around the sofa sideways; she was getting much bigger quite suddenly.

'How on earth did you guess, Mr Holmes?' she asked curiously. '*I* didn't know. And Mother hasn't said anything.'

'She's in that grey suit. Wearing a hat and gloves in spite of the heat. And the whole damned office were off today – everyone wanted to go.' He shrugged. 'Aileen said David has taken her out a couple of times, so I assumed the obvious. Elementary, my dear Watson.'

Rose was terribly conscious that he had not used her name. Jon did not seem to notice it. 'Hey, what's all this? Mother hasn't said a word to me! I didn't notice anything at the wedding.' Jon was all agog. Not only was she uninterested in the fact that David's father had died, she then said, 'You're crafty, Sis – turning up at the funeral was a good idea. Did you take flowers?'

Rose said curtly, 'Shut up, Jon.'

'Sorry. Bad taste. You look a bit peaky too. Here, drink up.' She poured an extra large glass and passed it to Rose with her usual instant contrition. 'It's salad tonight. Let's eat and go out on the hill.'

It sounded a good idea. Rose walked with her mother and thought that as Grandfather could not help Rick and Jon to find somewhere to live now, she had better get used to living with them. After all, once the baby arrived there just wouldn't be room for them any more.

As if following her thought, Aileen said, 'I only hope Grandfather Harris can fix something for the children before the baby arrives.'

Rose had to think for a moment about 'the children'. Jon, yes. But Rick?

She said, 'I went to see him on Wednesday, Mother. He's ill. I don't think he can do much for them. He thinks they should get their names down on the council list.'

Aileen was not surprised. 'I thought he'd give poor Jon the thumbs-down.'

'He's really ill,' Rose protested. 'Bronchitis.'

'I'm sorry. Of course. But he'd have turned her down anyway.' Aileen smiled up at her elder daughter; she barely reached Rose's shoulder. 'Not to worry. If they move in with us, they will stand a jolly good chance of a council house. Overcrowding.'

Rose swallowed. 'Do you mean with the baby?'

'Yes. You wouldn't mind too much, would you darling? Rick is such a dear boy. And it would be for a short time only.'

'No. No, of course I wouldn't mind.'

Jon turned a flushed face towards them. 'Let's stop here, loves. I can't drag all this extra weight any further!' She perched on a molehill, pulling Rick down to her. 'Listen, Rick's had a wonderful idea. Why don't we invite David Fairbrother up here? To a meal? Rick says he'll do the cooking and the washing-up!' She laughed. 'Frankly, it's an offer we shouldn't refuse!'

Aileen was delighted. 'Would you like that, Rose?'

Rose was appalled. 'I think – in the circumstances – his mother only just widowed—'

Rick said quickly, 'Leave it a couple of weeks then. I'll be able to tell how he is. I'll let you know.'

'I don't want him to think I – I—'

'You're keen?' Jon laughed uproariously. 'Knowing you, Sis, I can imagine that is highly unlikely! Your idea of encouraging a chap would be to talk about the weather!'

Rick too laughed. He said, 'Don't worry, Rosie. The invitation will come from me. He was my best man after all.'

It was the first time he had used her name since his marriage. She glanced sideways at her mother, expecting her to have registered it too; it had sounded so . . . tender . . . so fond. But Aileen merely smiled encouragingly. It seemed Rose's acquiescence was taken for granted. They wandered back down to the Snow-White house just as the sun was setting.

Jon said, 'I'm dead beat. We might as well stay the night, mightn't we?'

'Can you manage in the single bed?' Aileen asked in all innocence.

Jon laughed. 'Well, we did before, didn't we Rickie?'

He was silent for a moment, then he laughed too.

Jon cuddled his arm possessively, 'I say, it's rather great that my sister is going out with the manager of Providential Insurance, isn't it?'

Rose looked across at Rick, startled.

His voice was unexpectedly apologetic. 'Well, hang on, baby. He's not manager just yet, you know!'

But for Rose it was one more betrayal in a long line of them.

It meant she had to see David before Rick said anything.

She dared not leave it until Monday. On Saturday morning before Rick and Jon had appeared for breakfast, she went to the telephone box in the village and thumbed through the tattered directory. She could not find an entry at all. Surely the branch manager of an insurance company would have a phone at home? She ran a finger down a column of Fabers, Faddenhursts and Fagins – were there really Fagins living in Gloucester? – and went on to the facing page. Gough and Goring met her eye. She examined the book carefully; a page had been torn out.

She bit her lip and began to turn to the front for the number of Directory Enquiries. And there it was, the torn page, folded and jammed in at the beginning of the book. A. Fairbrother, 7 Stroud Road, was listed as Gloucester 2244. Thankfully she dialled the operator and asked for the number. She was even more relieved to hear David's voice greeting her when she pressed button A.

'Hello. Gloucester double—'

She said quickly, 'David. It's me. Rosamund Harris. How are you?'

'Rosamund!' He sounded overjoyed. And incredulous too. 'Rosamund, it's wonderful to hear you! How are you?'

'I asked first.'

'Oh. . .' there was a smile in his voice. 'I'm all right. Yes. All right.'

'Your mother?'

'Amazing. I can't say more. Listen. Can I see you? In an hour? Lawrence's?'

'It's only nine o'clock.'

'Would this afternoon be better? Tea?'

'I'm working this afternoon.'

'Then this morning,' he said doggedly. 'Please, Rosamund.'

'Yes. All right. Thank you. Lawrence's. Ten o'clock.'

They were among the first to sit down for coffee. The city was packed with Saturday shoppers but inside the old-fashioned café it was quiet; the bottle-glass windows framed the milling crowds as if they were in a fish tank. Not that David and Rose looked outside much. They looked alternately at each other and the tablecloth and they smiled all the time.

David said, 'I can't get over your combination of dark hair and blue eyes. Are you sure you have no Irish blood?'

'Almost sure.'

She glanced up at him for reassurance yet again. And there it was. Ordinary brown hair inclined to flop over his forehead. White shirt, dark tie, sports jacket. And his eyes were pretty amazing too. If she looked at them for too long she might easily walk into his head.

He leaned back so that the waitress could put the coffee pot on to the table.

'May we have scones? Or biscuits or something?' he asked. And when she'd gone he smiled again. 'I haven't had breakfast yet.'

She thought back. 'Nor me. Mother nearly had a fit when I told her I was coming down here immediately.'

His grin became wide enough to crack his face. 'I wondered . . . I couldn't believe it had happened. Not seeing you . . . you know.'

She nodded. The scones arrived. She unfolded her paper napkin with great care.

He said, 'When I saw you at the funeral I hoped I hadn't dreamt it. I was going to come up to your house today.'

'How did you know where I lived . . . oh Rick, of course.' Her disgusted tone made him laugh.

'D'you mind me knowing? Don't you want me to come to your house? I thought your mother quite liked me. At the wedding.'

'It's why I telephoned you actually.' She stopped smiling. 'You're going to get an invitation. From Rick. On Monday. To supper. Or tea. Or something.'

'And you don't want me to come?' He too stopped smiling. 'What is it, Rosamund? Are you regretting . . . what you said?'

She could not answer that. She said, 'I like you calling me Rosamund. But it's so formal.'

He nodded. 'You prefer Rose? Or Rosie?'

'No!' She shook her head vehemently. 'But Ros. Ros would be all right.'

He nodded and looked at the tablecloth again.

She said, 'I'll pour, shall I? D'you take it white?'

'Half and half,' he said levelly. 'And you might as well be honest with me, Ros. It's off, is it? Our engagement?'

She was startled. 'Engagement? I didn't know we were engaged.'

He was suddenly grim. 'I asked you to marry me and you said yes. We were then engaged to be married. I am asking you if that is off.'

'No. I mean, I don't know. I didn't think of it as an engagement exactly.' She put the heavy silver pot down.

'Oh David, I just don't know. It's too soon. We've only just met.'

'But you didn't come here to say you'd changed your mind?'

'No. I came to warn you that Rick is going to—'

'And you don't want me to accept his invitation when it is given?'

'I thought you'd be horrified. Your father . . . and anyway Rick is only keen to ask you because he thinks you'll be the new manager!'

She looked at him wide-eyed, aghast at her bluntness. But he stared right back and started smiling all over again.

'Oh Ros. Did you tell them that we're . . . you know.'

'Of course not!'

'They're matchmaking!' He looked delighted. 'They think I'll be suitable!' He started to laugh.

She was suddenly annoyed with him. 'I'm glad you find it funny. That my family are so – so self-seeking and insensitive, and – and—'

'And on my side!' he concluded.

She met his translucent eyes again. And smiled unwillingly.

But then he said, suddenly not so intrepid, 'Ros. It won't happen, you know. Me being manager. I'm still learning the ropes. I'm really only a glorified office boy.'

She sighed deeply. 'Oh thank goodness! I don't mind you knowing that Rick and Jon are – what's the word – self-seeking. But I'd hate you to think I – I – liked – you for your prospects!'

They both started to laugh and having started could not stop.

He brought his mother with him. Rick explained that in the circumstances he thought it would be a good idea. It threw Aileen.

'We'll never get round the table!' she exclaimed. 'And afterwards – the sitting room is so small! Oh my God – I expect she gives proper dinner parties!'

102

Rick was stage-managing the whole thing. 'We shall eat outside. On the hill. Don't give it another thought.'

But Aileen said, 'What if the weather breaks?'

'It won't.'

He was right. It was August Bank Holiday; the village strangely deserted because the Sunday school treat was at Weston-super-Mare. Rick carried rugs, baskets, the old paste table and six chairs, down the garden and on to the hill and arranged them all among the buttercups. David brought his mother in the family car, a pre-war Lagonda, and they parked outside the railway terrace and came slowly up the path exclaiming over the flowers. Aileen and Rose went out to greet them; Rick and Jon were in the kitchen.

Maud Fairbrother looked bonier than before. She was very obviously older than Aileen and in her blue linen frock and cream hat, both apparently too big for her, she looked very much a product of the nineteen-twenties. Her hair was at first invisible, but when she swept off her hat with a strangely girlish gesture it was still almost unnoticeable. Pepper and salt, dry and inclined to frizz, it seemed to come from a centre parting and be cut short with a fringe. But she had dignity; and what was more she had David's smile and light brown eyes.

Aileen took her hand.

'We're so glad you felt able to come, Mrs Fairbrother.'

Maud Fairbrother looked down at the pretty dark woman and shook her hand formally.

'I couldn't have managed anywhere else. But I know you will understand. We're in the same boat, aren't we? Besides, I want to meet David's friends. Thank you for asking me.'

Aileen smiled her relief. For the first time in her life she felt like a woman who had been loved, been married, and lost her husband. She and Maud Fairbrother were part of the great sisterhood of widows.

The evening was an unqualified success. When everyone was introduced Mrs Fairbrother held Rose's hand longer than anyone else's, so Rose knew David had told her about their 'engagement'. Rick was even more open and frank

103

than usual; Jon was sweet and girlish. After the sherry, Jon led them through the kitchen and the garden – Mrs Fairbrother loved flowers – and on to the hill where Rick had erected the wallpaper table and covered it with a quiet green cloth, easy on the eyes. They started with chilled grapefruit, followed by chicken in aspic with salad, and finished with biscuits and cheese.

'It's all Rick's doing,' Jon said proudly to their admiring guests.

'And I understand that if it hadn't been for you, David would not have met Rose?' Mrs Fairbrother said happily.

Rick wasn't in the least embarrassed.

'Probably not,' he said.

But Jon was not going to let him get away with it. She kissed him lightly. 'I think if it hadn't been for *me* Rose wouldn't have met David,' she corrected.

David said, 'Oh, I think we would have met. Somehow.' He carried Rose's hand to his lips. She tried to pull away. She hadn't meant it to happen like this, so quickly, so inevitably. But Mrs Fairbrother was looking happy and Mother was grinning like a Cheshire cat. And only Rick was suddenly serious. Well, it served him right. He'd precipitated the whole thing by this evening. So she stopped trying to withdraw her hand, and simply said, 'Oh, David.'

It was as if she'd accepted a public proposal of marriage. Everyone clapped delightedly and Mrs Fairbrother said, 'This is the best thing that has happened since . . . for a long time.'

That night the television news was all of the robbery on the Glasgow to London mail train.

'Two and a half million!' Rick said, whistling through his teeth. 'It's been a special day for some people!'

Rose had not been listening to the news, but she nodded with the others. It had.

So the official courtship began. They met two or three times during the week she was on early shift; usually at Lawrence's. She was glad to get out of the house. She felt she was proving something to Rick. But she did not want to go any faster. David asked her several times to set a date for their wedding and she would reply, 'I'd rather wait until my grandfather is better. To give me away, you know.' But when Grandfather was – thankfully – better, she said, 'I'd like to wait until Jon's baby is born. So that she can be my bridesmaid.'

'Matron of honour,' he corrected.

'Matron. At seventeen. It's ridiculous.'

'Let's look at furniture. Shall we? Instead of going to the pictures?'

'But David, we can't afford new stuff.'

'I know. But let's look anyway.'

*

When she heard of the great negro freedom march on Washington, Rose wrote to Aunt Mabe. She had had presents from America and had written dutiful thank-you letters each time. Indeed she had written on Jon's behalf not long since, thanking Aunt Mabe for the beautiful bedspread. She had never written this kind of letter before.

' . . . I have a vague memory of a kind of butler you had at the farm. I cannot remember his name. I think I called him Jack. Anyway, Aunt, the news sounds rather desperate this week, and I am wondering how he is and what has happened to him . . .'

She never had a reply.

It was arranged that they would pay a return visit to the Fairbrothers' house on Michaelmas day.

Maud wrote to Aileen, 'I have never forgotten that day eight weeks ago. I have wanted to see you again, but there has been so much to do. I know you have been through my experiences so will understand. September 25th seems a good time to meet again. We cannot eat al fresco I am afraid, but if the weather is good, I can open the doors to the garden. I am looking forward to showing you the garden . . .'

Aileen was delighted.

'It's ages since I went to Gloucester, Rosie! We'll go early and do some shopping, shall we? I know you and David want to wait until you've saved some money, but I thought I might look for a winter outfit that would be suitable. It's sure to be some time this winter, isn't it?'

'Mother, I don't know. David's mother will be all alone, remember, when we do get married. And it's early days for that.'

Aileen said, 'Well, I should still like to go shopping.'

'Jon won't want to shop, Mother. She gets tired quickly these days.'

'We'll go on our own, darling. We'll pick Jon and Rick up at the flat. We'll have a cup of tea with them and go on down to Stroud Road in the early evening.'

So they caught the ten-twenty to Gloucester and had a delightful shop-fuddle. Aileen bought a rose-coloured two-piece in fine wool.

'Does it remind you of something, Rosie?'

'I don't think so. You had a pleated skirt once—'

'No. It's the colour. Exactly the same as the dress you wore for VJ night.'

'As if I'd remember that! I was about two!'

'You were nearly five actually.' Aileen held her arm as they walked through the foyer of the shop. 'You were so sweet.' She stopped. 'Oh my God.'

Rose looked past the bright lights of the showroom. Outside it was almost dark. A jagged line of light split the sky, immediately followed by a clap of thunder that shook the building.

The two women huddled on the pavement under the awning. Rain descended in a solid wall of water. They were dressed for summer.

A taxi drew up hopefully.

'Come on Rosie,' Aileen said. They scrambled inside. 'Thank goodness for that.' She raised her voice above the drumming rain. 'St James Street, please. Oh if only we had an umbrella!'

'Jon will have one.'

'I doubt it,' Aileen said gloomily.

When they reached St James Street, the tiny brook which was culverted under roads and pavements and appeared unexpectedly now and then between houses, had burst its confines. The narrow side street was flooded. The water lay, clear and still, the road beneath it making a ford of about knee-depth. Two of the men from the nearby coal yard were laying tyres for the pedestrians. People were standing around waiting to cross, laughing good-naturedly for the most part. The rain had stopped. There was a Noah's Ark feeling to the scene.

The taxi driver surveyed it unhappily.

'Can't get through that lot, missis. Flood me engine,' he said over his shoulder. 'That'll be five bob.'

They got out and stood looking down the small side street.

'It goes right up to number 32,' Rose said anxiously. 'The house is damp enough as it is.'

'Don't worry. They can come back with us tonight,' Aileen said.

That was exactly what was worrying Rose. 'You know Jon hasn't put their name down on the council list yet?' she asked.

'I know, darling. But if you and David are getting married, it won't be necessary for them to bother with a council house, will it?'

Rose looked at her mother incredulously.

'But we haven't got anywhere to live either!' she protested.

'Oh, you'll find somewhere.'

The coalmen approached and put an end to the appalling conversation.

'Coming across, ladies?' said one. 'Reckon you'll need an arm apiece. Them tyres wobble when you least expect it!'

They did too. Rose felt her shoe fill with water and envied the woman the other side who had borrowed her husband's wellingtons and shuffled across under her own steam, shoes held head-high. Aileen came off worst. One of her high heels got stuck in the tread of a tyre and she was forced to lift out her foot while the coalman released the shoe. The other shoe was then stuck. Finally she walked over in her stockinged feet.

They hurried on to number 32, already shivering in the rain-chilled air.

Aileen said, 'There's nowhere to dry off. I'm absolutely soaked.'

'I think there's an oil-stove. We'll manage something.'

But wet feet were forgotten when they went into the bedsitting room. Jon lay in a tight semi-circle on the unmade bed, still wearing her nightdress. Rick was throwing things into a suitcase.

'We think it's the baby!' he said, eyeing his wife without a lot of sympathy. 'She's been like this for ages.'

Aileen went to the bed. 'Oh my poor baby. How are you? Mother's here now.'

Jon replied with a moan. Then she said tensely, 'You didn't tell me it was like this. I don't want it. Get someone to take it away. Quickly.'

Rick said, 'That's what she keeps saying. I'm going to find a taxi and—'

Aileen said, 'A taxi won't get through. There's a flood.'

Jon screamed at that. 'I need a doctor! Get me a doctor!'

Rose went to the bed and slid an arm beneath the sweat-tangled hair.

'Come on, Sis. Don't waste your strength like this. Remember that book we were reading? Try to relax—'

'You don't know what you're talking about! You can't relax when you're—' she gave a great shriek and threw her arms around Rose's neck. 'Oh God, oh God, oh God—'

'It's all right Jon . . . all right,' Rose said.

Aileen squeaked. 'The waters! They've broken – oh darling – it must be nearer than—'

Rick put his head in his hands and moaned almost as loudly as Jon.

Rose said, 'It'll be easier now, Jon. Breathe properly. Come on now. In and out. In and out.'

Rick said, 'I've had enough of this. I'll get an ambulance.' He shot through the door, slamming it behind him with unnecessary force.

Jon screamed again and straightened convulsively, flinging her hands to the bedhead to grip and pull herself up and away from the pain. Her stomach contracted visibly.

Rose said in a low voice, 'She's nearly there, Mother. She should be pushing now.'

'Well, stop her!' Aileen was suddenly frightened. 'It's too soon, Rosie! Don't let her push for goodness sake!'

'Let's make her comfier. Can you get some newspaper? And a clean sheet.'

'Rosie! Help me!' Jon's eyes looked black with pupil. 'Help me Rosie. Please.'

'Of course, darling. Let's just get this nightie up. And a nice dry . . . '

She worked beneath Jon's buttocks. Aileen said, 'The ambulance will be here in a moment. Try to hang on, Jon.'

'It's not you lying here, is it?' Jon sobbed helplessly. 'It couldn't have been like this for you, Ma. You'd never have bothered to have me if – oh God it's coming again! Rosie!'

This pain was worse than the others. They stood either side of her, holding her writhing body. Her stomach moved with a life of its own. She tore at her nightdress. 'I've got to . . . I must . . . ' she shouted.

Aileen said, 'Stay with her, Rose. I'll be two minutes. The ambulance should be here and we need Rick to carry her down to it.'

Rose took her mother's place and held Jon's hands. The girl sobbed. 'I'm frightened, Rosie. I don't know what to do.'

Rose said gently but loudly, 'Listen, Jon. Next time you get a pain, push down. Hang on to my hands and push as hard as you can.'

'But Mother said to hang on. It might not be time—'

Jon's face was shining with sweat. Rose wondered if all was well. The baby was not due for another two or three weeks. She made the decision.

'It's time, darling. Don't worry.'

She could tell, from Jon's suddenly tense fingers, that another enormous pain was on its way. She braced herself and the next instant her arms nearly left their sockets. Jon's feet were scrabbling for purchase on the sheet. Rose moved her body and braced her sister's legs. Below her, in the gaping chasm of the vagina, miraculously, something appeared.

Jon flopped, whimpering.

Rose said urgently, 'It's coming, Jon. I can see the head. Can you push again?'

Jon made a mewing sound, exactly like a kitten. 'Too tired . . . ' she murmured.

Rose released the flaccid hands and lifted Jon's feet to her shoulders. She knelt between the crooked legs and grabbed the hands again.

'Come on, little sister! Come on. Push. Shove!'

Before her eyes the distended abdomen went into another spasm and Jon gave a thin scream. Hand tightened on hand, heels dug into shoulders. When they'd been small girls they had done 'acrobats' in the garden and it hadn't been unlike this. And there had been diagrams in Jon's ante-natal book . . . Rose pulled hard; felt Jon respond; watched as the vagina was filled to overflowing with a hairy spherical . . . object. And then the head was born and Jon collapsed again.

Rose cleared the mucus from the face. The eyes were closed. She was terrified the child would die then and there in front of her.

'Jon – again—'

But Jon had given her all.

Rose slid her fingers behind the sticky ears; there were slippery ledges. Shoulders. She worked one finger beneath an invisible armpit. Very gently she began to turn the shoulder. It lifted definably in a tiny shrug. With very little help from its aunt, the baby slithered itself free. And was born between the mingled legs of the two sisters. It took a breath and expelled it on a thin scream. It was a boy.

Everything seemed to have happened very quickly up to that moment. Afterwards things slowed to a crawl. Aileen came in at a run gasping, 'I can't find Rick! But the ambulance is here—' then 'Oh my *God*—'

Rose got off the bed in slow motion and looked for a shawl, while Aileen said, 'It's a boy! Oh Jon—'

And Jon wept with relief and said, 'I couldn't have done it without Rosie. Oh Sis—'

And Rose said, 'The cord. What shall we do about—'

And Aileen said, 'They're qualified. The ambulancemen. Don't worry about a thing.'

And there was no more worrying. Two men in uniform brought in a case and saw to everything. Everyone was laughing. Aileen made tea and Rose said it was nectar, and everyone laughed again. Then at last Rick came in and Jon had to tell him that Rose had done it all and they'd got a perfect little boy and where the hell had he been.

'I rang the ambulance, then waited about—'

'Oh it doesn't *matter*. Come and sit here and tell me how clever I am!'

But they were already cocooning her in blankets and lifting her on to the stretcher. Aileen carried the baby. Everyone filed into the passage.

Rose stared around the deserted room, bemused. The stove was off all right. She stripped the bed and rolled the soiled sheets in a bundle. The whole place needed a damn good clean; Jon couldn't have done a thing for ages.

The door opened again and Rick came in.

'She won't go till she's seen you,' he said breathlessly. 'What the hell are you doing?'

'Trying to clean up a bit.'

'Leave it, for Christ's sake.' Suddenly his eyes filled with tears. 'Oh Rosie. You delivered my son. If I hadn't loved you before, I would love you now. Oh my darling.'

It was the first time he had used that word. Love.

She said, 'Don't be ridiculous, Rick. I was simply there.' There was whisky on his breath. He must have been away longer than she'd thought. He'd had time to go to the India House for a drink.

'Should have been yours, Rosie. It's you I love. Will always love. You know that.'

He lurched forward suddenly and grabbed her by the shoulders. She twisted round and felt for the doorknob, but he simply leaned against her and she was trapped.

111

She said, 'Stop it, Rick! You're drunk. Let me go this minute—'

He kissed her.

She tried to push him off but she couldn't and he just stayed there, his mouth on hers, not trying to force an entry as he had before. She felt his tears and knew that they were maudlin. Then through the door she could hear Aileen calling her.

'Rose! Where are you? Jon wants you—'

And they both moved and turned at the same time.

He whispered, 'Rose. Please—'

And she whispered. 'No. Never.'

And then she was in the passage and moving towards the light and sanity.

'They're waiting for Rick too,' Aileen said, frowning at Rose's mottled face. 'Ah. There you are, Rick. You haven't been drinking, have you?'

'Had to wait for the ambulance . . . India House . . . ' panted Rick as if he'd been rushing around the flat tidying up.

'Listen.' Aileen sounded amazingly composed now. Rose had a nightmare sensation; none of it had happened, she had dreamt it all. 'We'll go on to the Fairbrothers by ourselves, my dear. They've got a phone and you'll be able to get in touch with us there if necessary. We shall be leaving about sevenish I expect, and we'll call into the hospital on our way to the station.'

It was hard to know whether Rick understood any of this. He sprinted to catch up with the ambulanceman, and ploughed through the water regardless of his trousers. Aileen and Rose walked down to the flood and watched as the ambulance drove away.

Aileen said inadequately, 'Well. What an afternoon!'

'Yes,' said Rose.

'First a cloudburst, then—'

'Yes.'

'And you delivered that baby. You do realize that, Rose dear?'

'Not really. Jon delivered it.'

'Rubbish. You took that child from its mother. That is important, Rose, dear. There will always be a special link between the two of you.'

Rose, still horrified and bewildered by her own reaction to Rick's drunken embrace, looked at her mother without comprehension. Aileen said slowly, 'Darling. We both know that the baby will need you.' She tried to smile lightly. 'Jon is so . . . young.'

Rose forced herself to push Rick's image away.

'Of course. But she'll learn.'

She sounded more robust than she felt. Somehow Jon had always been her responsibility, and still was in spite of being married. Might it be that the dependency could continue to the next generation?

She linked her arm through her mother's.

'Come on. Let's get along to Stroud Road.' She glanced at her watch. 'Good Lord. It's only five o'clock. Can you believe it? We must have been in the dress shop at two—'

Rose helped her mother across the diminished flood. 'It'll be good to see David,' she said. But Aileen made no comment, so perhaps she had spoken only to herself.

Maud and David Fairbrother couldn't get over it.

'You mean it happened while you were there?'

'While Rose was there.' Aileen was proud of everything now. 'She is solely responsible for—'

'Mother, do stop it!' Rose's exhaustion was making the feeling of unreality very strong.

'We can't help being proud of our children, Rosamund.' Maud smiled happily. 'And we've certainly got children we can be proud of!'

Aileen smiled too. The fantasy which Maud cultivated of their being two respectable widows was very strong by this time. Maud had given Aileen the confidence she had lost in America.

They had tea on the lawn. David took Rose around the garden. It was a riot of colour with little secret paths behind the rhododendron bushes and a lovely wild area behind the summerhouse, where the piled bonfire smelled of the roses deadheaded on to its summit.

'You're tired, Ros. Would you like me to cancel dinner and run you and your mother home?'

'No. Really. We're going to see Jon afterwards, anyway.' Rose smiled mechanically. 'I'm fine.'

'It's wonderful that we all get on so well, isn't it?' David was looking back at the two women in the deckchairs, their nodding heads proclaiming great enjoyment. 'They're talking babies, I bet.'

'Probably.'

David cleared his throat. 'Shall we have a child one day, Rose?'

Rose said, 'I don't know. I'm not very . . . that way inclined.' She saw David's face and went on quickly, 'Anyway I wouldn't want just one. And they'd have to be close together. The gap between Jon and me is too big.'

David laughed. 'I'll have to remember that!'

Rose shuddered; it was the kind of remark Rick might have made.

David said, 'Cold, Ros? Are you sure about a lift home? I'd take you in the Lagonda.' She shook her head vehemently and he went on, 'I sold the motorbike today, Ros. I thought . . . it would pay for one or two things. For us.'

She felt awful and did not know why. 'You shouldn't. You loved the motorbike. Oh David—'

He took her arm. 'Come on. You need something. A glass of sherry.'

They returned to their mothers and David fetched a tray of drinks. It was so much nicer without Jon and Rick. Rose wanted badly to cry at the traitorous thought.

Maud said, 'Good. You're looking better, Rosamund. Would you like your conducted tour now or after dinner?'

Unexpectedly, Aileen spoke up. 'Now, I think. Then we can talk about . . . things . . . during dinner.'

'Good idea, Aileen.' Maud stood up. 'David, why don't you put the chairs away now? We'll see you in about ten minutes.'

114

It was so obvious he was being dismissed that even Rose in her zombie state wondered what was afoot. However the tour of the house proceeded normally enough, even if it was a little too detailed for mere formality.

It was a rambling Edwardian residence, probably ideal when the two Fairbrother boys were young and had friends coming and going, but quite unsuitable for two people.

Maud Fairbrother acknowledged this immediately.

'You see the extent of my problem, Rosamund. Yes, my home is my problem. It's rather sad. I love it, yet of course I cannot stay in it. David and Martin tell me to wait a year. But the longer I wait the less I want to move.'

She led the way through the big arched hallway to the dining room which was solid and square, with French windows on to the walled garden. The table was laid for six people.

'This was ideal for the sort of entertaining we used to do,' she said, moving plates to the sideboard. 'We could get twelve round the table. French doors open in the summer. So pleasant. Now . . . just look at the dust on that bookcase.'

Rose glanced at it, suddenly sure it had been left there deliberately. But why?

They went back into the hall. There was a potted palm and an escritoire in the recess beneath the stairs. 'A sort of writing room,' explained Mrs Fairbrother as she led the way into the breakfast room. And beyond that, the scullery which was twice the size of the kitchen in the Snow-White house.

Reading her mind, Maud said. 'So cosy and compact in your house, my dear. I fell in love with it. Aptly named too.'

'Very crowded when Rick and Jon are there,' Rose murmured, glancing at her mother who was smiling and silent.

'Quite,' Maud said and also glanced at Aileen.

They went upstairs. Four large bedrooms and a bathroom. A bath with claw feet and a mahogany lid on the lavatory.

'We won't go further. But there are good attics above. David had his train set up there.'

Rose said inadequately, 'A lovely family house, Mrs Fairbrother. Such a pity to have to move.'

'Call me Maud, Rosamund. Please. Your mother and I are already on first name terms.'

They went downstairs and into the big drawing room. Maud Fairbrother stood in the bay window. 'My roots are here. I know my husband will be with me wherever I go, yet here is where we were.'

Rose did not know what to say. Even Mother's smile had disappeared. After a while they trailed into the dining room and David poured them some fruit juice. And while they were eating Maud spoke of her idea; and everything became very clear.

'You have no savings, and flats and houses are unobtainable to rent.' She spread her hands. 'This house is owned by the firm and if David continues to live here the lease will be renewable. We could have it converted into two flats if you think you could bear—'

David's face lit up. 'Mother! It would be—' he checked himself and turned to Rose. She had her spoon halfway to her mouth. She put it down on her plate and he took her hand. 'Ros. What do you say? It's up to you, of course. But it would mean we could get married . . . immediately!' He laughed. 'Next week! The week after! And Mother would be able to stay in her house!'

Rose was trapped. She looked at her mother and saw that she had already accepted the suggestion; her eyes were brightly encouraging. She looked at Maud, for whom it would be perfect. Of course, it *was* perfect. Jon and Rick could come to the Snow-White house with their baby. And down here, with David, she herself would have room to breathe. No buses to catch to get to the library. It was all . . . perfect. Except that once again, Rose had the feeling events were pushing her into something much too quickly.

David said, 'Not if you're in the least bit—'

She looked into his clear eyes. He was all the things she wanted most. He was the absolute opposite of Rick. He was safety.

She said, 'It's wonderful. Just wonderful. I feel as if I'm dreaming. Will someone pinch me, please?'

David obliged very gently. Aileen clapped her hands. 'You lucky, lucky pair.' Maud said, 'I am the lucky one.' David said, 'No. I am.'

Obediently she responded. 'We both are.'

She pressed David's hand gently. She was quite certain that after a good night's sleep she would believe all of it.

Seven

On the way round to the hospital from Stroud Road that evening, Aileen could not stop marvelling at 'the way things have turned out'.

'I really can't get over it, Rosie. We were only talking about it this afternoon if you remember – you said to me that you and David had nowhere to live. D'you remember?'

'Yes, Mother.'

'The next thing that happens is dear Maud—'

'So Jon will bring the baby to the Snow-White house when she comes out of hospital?'

'Well, I'm not sure. If we're having another wedding—'

'No fuss, please Mother.'

'Jon's was a no-fuss wedding. Surely yours can be a bit more—'

'No. David would probably prefer a registry office do anyway.'

'I doubt it. They often go to the cathedral. As a family.'

'Mother, you're surely not thinking the cathedral—'

'Of course not. Old Murchison would be cut to the quick!' Aileen smiled. 'And though it's going to be soon, he'll know that you and David don't have to get married.'

Rose felt sick. She said, 'It won't be that soon. We'll think about it after Christmas.'

Aileen took her daughter's arm. 'It would be so nice if we could all be settled for Christmas. Jon and the baby at home. You in your own place.'

Rose was beleaguered. She made one last stand. 'Mother, I don't think you're strong enough to take on this new baby.'

It was doubtful whether Aileen even heard her. She was wondering what they were going to call the child, and whether there was time to decorate Jon's old room in nursery paper.

Rose said no more. It was already dark and they went on to the Midland station and used the bridge to get across to the Great Western. The long length of the lamp-lit bridge was eerie and lonely. Rose shivered.

But Jon was on top of the world. She was the youngest mother in the maternity ward and her baby was the bonniest. They'd both been asleep most of the afternoon and when they woke up there was 'Daddy' – Jon actually called him that – with a big bunch of flowers and a silver tankard for 'George' and grapes and real blackcurrant juice and a lacy nightie.

Even Aileen had soon had enough of this. 'Are you really calling the baby George?' she asked. 'It's not very fashionable.'

Jon grinned. 'It was Rick's idea, of course! Grandfather's name. In fact Rick wanted George Harris Johnson, but I thought that was a bit much.'

'It certainly is,' Aileen agreed.

Rose peered into the cot. The baby's hair was like apricot down. He was going to be a redhead.

'What if it had been a girl?' she asked, smiling in spite of herself. 'Would you have called it Edith after Grandmother?'

Jon grimaced. 'Depends. If they promised to put us in the will . . . '

'Jon. You can't go on being the enfant terrible all your life!' But Aileen was laughing. 'You're a mother now!'

'I know.' Jon sounded mock gloomy. 'It's pretty depressing, isn't it? How on earth am I going to manage?'

'We'll talk about that later.' Aileen rolled her eyes mysteriously and took Jon's hand. 'Don't worry, darling. You've got us behind you!'

Jon squeaked. 'Grandfather has been in touch?' she hazarded. 'Aunt Mabe has sent some money? What then?'

Aileen told her. Jon looked at Rose and saw only her smile. She thought it sounded marvellous.

'I thought you'd want Rose to stay in the Snow-White

119

house with you,' she said and there was a wistful note in her voice. 'I've always felt sort of odd one out.' She shook her head as the other two protested. 'No, of course you never showed Rose any favouritism, Mummy. But you had five years together without me.'

It was pathetic. She was overjoyed about everything.

Aileen said, 'Where's Rick, darling?'

Jon made a face. 'Wetting the baby's head! He was going to call for David. Didn't you see him?'

'No. But we walked down and it took some time.'

Rose said, 'He's not drunk is he, Jon?'

'No, of course not. Well, only a bit. You think he might upset your David?'

Rose did not dare think how easily he might upset David. She shook her head.

Jon said, 'David might be a bit stuffy, but Rick thinks a lot of him. Honestly. He won't queer your pitch.'

'David isn't a bit—' Rose began.

Jon said, 'Oh never mind all that. Tell me exactly what David's mother said. Tell me all. I liked her that day in the summer.' She lent half an ear to the plans, then said with sincerity, 'I'm so . . . glad!'

She sounded relieved too. She hugged her sister and went into transports about being matron of honour. The baby, disturbed at last by his mother's high-pitched chatter, started to cry.

Rose and David fixed on the first Saturday in November for their wedding date. Rose was already spending an occasional night at the Stroud Road house, looking at plans with Maud for adding a kitchen to the middle floor and a bathroom to the ground floor. The quiet, secluded life she had been used to had disappeared with the advent of Rick and Jon, but already the Edwardian house promised a new kind of peace and security. She was no longer devastated at moving out of the Snow-White house; but she was still frightened of other things.

At half-term they spent a day in Weston with Martin, June and the two boys. Martin's wife, June, was still rather stiff and unfriendly, but Charles took to Rose immediately and wanted to sit on her lap in the Lagonda and build sandcastles with her on the beach.

'You don't want me to be a pageboy like Nigel Tredworth?' he asked several times.

'Not if you don't want to,' Rose said.

'And you'll tell Mummy so?'

'Of course. If you want me to.'

He loved her passionately and built sandcastles for her to admire. Arney staggered over them, flattening them before they were finished, and Rose comforted the infuriated Charles and took him down to the tide where Arney couldn't reach them.

'My sister is four years younger than me, too,' she told him consolingly. 'In fact five years. It won't be long before you can play together.'

'But I'm always going to be the eldest! I'm always going to have to look after him!' spat Charles indignantly.

Rose could not deny that. She waited for David to catch them up.

'Are you too old to be swung down to the sea?' she asked Charles.

He was not. David took one hand, she took the other. They dunked Charles and then watched him run through the mud back to the others, good temper restored.

'You'll be a wonderful mother one day,' David said.

She said, 'David, I want to talk to you about that. Would you – how would you feel if we didn't have children at all?'

He looked at her. 'That's the second time you've said something like that. You know what my answer is. You are enough for me. You are all I want in this world.'

She felt her eyes fill with tears. She said, 'June is telling Charles off for being muddy. And it was my fault.'

He grinned. 'June is like that,' he said.

Grandmother insisted on doing the reception at the house in Rodney Road. It was select but informal, a buffet put on by Doreen the Dragon with help from two elderly cousins. The walled garden was still warm enough to take the overspill and Grandfather had even put out the chairs.

Maud Fairbrother helped make Rose's dress: slipper satin cut on the cross. Jon said, 'Talk about figure-hugging! You're determined no-one will think *you're* pregnant!' The dress was not fashionable, but it suited Rose very well. She had always worn full skirts; the swathed effect of the satin revealed her figure for the first time.

Rick wanted to give her away, but it was settled that Grandfather would do that. And Martin was David's best man. On the wedding morning, Rick lingered in the house after Aileen had settled herself in the taxi with Georgie on her lap. Jon, still plump but very pretty in blue muslin flounces, leaned through the window.

'If he cries, take him straight out, Mother. Have you got that bottle? Shove it in his mouth as soon as you get inside the church.'

'I shall do no such thing!' Aileen said indignantly. 'You do that too often, Jon. He's got perpetual wind, poor little lambkin. Who is Nanny's little lambkin, then?'

In the house, with about one minute's spurious privacy, Rick said urgently, 'Are you all right, Rosie?'

'Of course.' She was not nervous about the wedding at all.

He said, 'It should be me giving you away. I feel as if I'm doing just that.'

'Please, Rick.'

'It's true. And there's part of you that knows it's true.'

'Grandfather is in the kitchen, Rick.'

'He won't have to put himself about to find us somewhere to live now, will he?' Rick commented bitterly.

He saw her face and took her hand contritely.

'Rose. I know what you think of me. But I'm not such a bad chap. If I can't have you, then I'm glad it's David Fairbrother. There. I can't say more that that, can I?'

'Rick. Be kind to Jon. Please.'

'I am kind to her. I'm fond of her. And of your mother. Of everything. But I'm in love with you.'

She turned and went into the kitchen. Grandfather was

gargling with TCP and looked up from the sink guiltily.

'Just coming, Rose.'

She heard Jon call Rick to get in the car. She said, 'Is something wrong? Don't you feel well?'

'Bit of a sore throat. Left over from before. Nothing to worry about.'

Jon burst in. 'Rosie, I'm just off. Let's look at you . . . yes, you're fine. Don't cry. Whatever you do, don't cry. You'll ruin that Max Factor not to mention the mascara. And don't *dare* wash it off! It took too long to talk you into it and then get you to sit still long enough . . . Are you all right, darling?'

Rose looked at her sister. She knew that Jon was feckless, but she loved her. She said, 'Did you feel like this? Calm as a cucumber while you watch everything you've ever known rush away from you?'

'Of course not! You idiot! Where do you think we're rushing to? I shall be around – so will Mother – ' she grinned at Grandfather, who was wiping his mouth on a snowy handkerchief – 'so will Grandmother and Grandfather and Georgie . . . ' She hugged Rose through the veil. 'Darling, you and David are perfect for one another. Stop worrying. Enjoy it all!'

It was one piece of advice that Rose could actually take. Immediately she saw David waiting for her at the chancel steps, she knew everything would be all right. A great sense of partnership descended on her with the wedding service. The niggling worry that her love for David wasn't the right sort of love disappeared. To be married was to be joined in a partnership. And that was how she felt about David. He was her partner. It was so simple, so obvious; yet she hadn't quite seen it.

Photographs were taken from the west door overlooking the patchwork of fields that descended to Cheltenham. Aileen held out Georgie's podgy fist clutching a cardboard horseshoe. Margaret Ellenbury, engaged to someone completely different now, caught yet another bouquet. The McIntyres thoroughly approved of David and his mother and shepherded Maud into the Rodney Road house as if it were their own.

Doreen made sure that everyone ate and drank all the time. Grandmother said without intentional immodesty, 'I don't think I've ever been to such a nice wedding in my life!' Charles held Rose's hand and said fervently, 'Thank you so much for not asking me to be a page-thing.' And, for once, Arney met his match in Georgie, and fell in love with someone as plump and noisy as himself and insisted on holding the baby precariously on his knee, which effectively anchored him in one spot.

David said, 'Ros, I'm so happy. Thank you, my darling.'

Rose held his hand as if she might be going to shake it. 'I think we've done the right thing, David.'

It was a strange thing for a bride to say to her groom on their wedding day, but neither of them realized that. David retained her hand and drew her towards him for a kiss. Jon shrieked and Rick looked away. But it was the kind of handhold, the kind of kiss, that sealed bargains.

They honeymooned in Paris in an hotel quite close to the Place de la Concorde from where they could walk to places of interest. They had worked out their finances carefully; David had already warned her that without his father, promotion in Providential might be slow.

'I didn't like to think I had a special pull because of Dad, but he would have kept his ear to the ground for me – he'd built up a good reputation there.' David made a face. 'I don't know how I shall fare now.'

'You've built up a good reputation too!' Rose declared stoutly. 'Miss Westlake told me so at our wedding reception.'

'If I'd gone out on the road . . . I've always stayed in the office.' He smiled wryly and apologetically at her. 'Can you imagine me touting for business?'

'No. I wouldn't like you if you "touted for business" as you put it! We shall manage very well. Five pounds rent. Hardly any furniture or household stuff to buy. And between us, we're earning nearly fifteen hundred a year! Honestly, David, we're rich!'

So they'd decided that Paris wasn't an extravagance, as long as they did not go over thirty pounds.

They spent the first night in London. Rose had been fitted with a Dutch cap and had a miserable time inserting it. The female doctor, to whom she had applied privately, had taken her through the procedure several times, and it had been easy in clinical surroundings. Crammed into a tiny toilet which backed on to an airshaft smelling of cabbage, it became sordid and horrible. She was red-eyed when she emerged, and David held her close and comforted her and told her they could wait if she preferred. But she was determined. She said in a high-pitched voice, 'We certainly can't wait now I've gone to all that trouble!' And he held her away from him and looked at her and forced her to smile at him. But it didn't help.

She had assumed that the membrane had been broken by the cap; it must have been, but the pain was intense as David entered her, and she clenched her fists on his shoulder blades and squeezed her eyes shut against crying out. He knew something was wrong. He would have stopped then and there, but she held him to her with a kind of anger, wanting him to make her shake and tremble like Rick had done. She did neither. And as he went on, the whole miserable business seemed to come between them. He sobbed with exertion; he seemed to forget it was she beneath him; he wanted to get it over with quickly and he pounded away like an automaton. It was no longer David. It was someone taken over by the demon sex. She tried not to think like that, but it was awful . . . hateful. Afterwards, it was a relief to find David still inhabited that sweaty body. He kissed her gently and she kissed him back.

'I'm sorry, darling,' he whispered.

'No. It's me. I'm sorry. I'll get better at it, I expect.'

In Paris, Rose suggested that they put the Dutch cap away – 'just for our honeymoon'. That night there was no pain, but no ecstasy either. She hated herself and purposely wandered around the room nude though it made her feel nasty. However, when she saw he was being aroused again, she was into her dressing-gown in a flash. And hated herself again.

Sheer weariness beat them the second night and they fell asleep in each other's arms with only a kiss to mark the occasion. There were two more days of sightseeing, then David fell victim to a bilious attack that confined him to bed for the rest of the week. Rose ventured down a side street off the Avenue Georges-Cinq, and found a chemist. '*Mon mari . . .*' she faltered in execrable schoolgirl French. '*Il est malade—*' she made graphic gestures with her hands – '*à l'estomac!*' She was given a packet of Alka-Seltzer and hurried back to the hotel trying to work out how far they had eaten into their thirty pounds budget.

It was good to get back to the big quiet house in Stroud Road, where they took over Maud's double bed with its mahogany head and foot and its feather mattress that puffed the covers up high during the day and sank like a cloud each night. After the smallness of the Snow-White house, there was a spaciousness here that Rose had only felt standing on the top of Churchdown hill. She loved going shopping and coming in to the warmth and the big table in the breakfast room where she could drop everything and leave it while she had a cup of tea. Sometimes she would come in from work before David and walk around her new domain, savouring the ticking clocks, the murmur of the coke in the Aga, the gentle creak of the timbers expanding and contracting.

Maud rarely intruded; if she was going out or coming in, she would call from the hall to let them know what she was doing, and they invariably asked her into the big front room, or went out to her. When Rose was on late duty, they might share their elevenses and Maud might confide her anxieties about Charles's schooling or June's lack of control where Arney was concerned. Usually her sympathy was for June; Arney was definitely a 'handful'. But once when she had described with much laughter Arney's come-uppance after an escapade, she commented with a sigh, 'June has such big hands.' Rose looked at them when they next met and decided they were average-sized. And then June leaned down and whacked Arney's small tight backside. And Rose knew what Maud had meant.

The only drawback to her new life was her husband.

126

She wanted a friend and partner but knew there was more to marriage than that. David would have let it stay at friendship; it was Rose herself who religiously inserted her cap and crept into the feather bed without her nightie.

David went so far as to say, 'Ros, I'm so tired . . . '

She would have none of it.

At one point, her eyes wide, she straddled him. 'I need to get used to it!' she said, fumbling and gasping and hating every moment.

By the end of November she was feeling ill.

She did not admit it for a long time. She hardly knew how to get out of bed each morning and drag herself to work. When David said, 'Darling, when you go to bed, you are going to sleep!' she accepted it at last. She hoped the whole thing was psychosomatic and would then go away; but it did not. Her head ached perpetually, she had shooting pains in her legs, her arms each weighed a ton.

Aileen was too busy to notice. Now that Georgie was teething, she was up with him most nights so that Jon and Rick could have their sleep. Jon often popped in to see her sister, but it was usually to tell her that Rick was a total swine and had been seen in Cheltenham with a much older woman.

At any other time that bit of news might have caused Rose some concern, but she was entirely absorbed with getting through each day. The one person who might have helped her was Maud. But how could she tell David's mother that she was ill because she couldn't stand sex with David? She tried to take more interest in world affairs. But when President Kennedy was assassinated, she could not stop crying. And she had liked Harold Macmillan, whereas Sir Alec Douglas-Home seemed cold and unyielding.

David said, 'He's a good statesman, Ros. Lots of experience.'

She said helplessly, 'It's his mouth. I can't bear his mouth.'

He said, 'That's the trouble with television. We're almost encouraged to judge by appearances.'

She was unaccountably angry with him. 'Don't be so condescending, David! There were newspaper photographs

127

before television! And anyway you can tell a lot from a person's facial expressions!'

He said soothingly, 'Yes. Of course, Ros.'

But even when he agreed with her she didn't like it. Christmas came. And went. There were the usual get-togethers. Martin and June and the boys came to lunch. They went back there to tea. Aileen, Jon and Georgie came down for Boxing Day. Thankfully Rick was tactful enough to stay away. Even so it wasn't a success. Georgie yelled lustily the entire day.

January dragged itself to a close and in desperation, Rose took a week off work. She told David and Maud she thought it was flu.

'I'm not surprised. Nasty dreary weather.' Maud brought down her little television for David to install in the bedroom. When David went to work she made tempting meals and brought them in on a tray. Rose felt so guilty after the first day she thought she would have to get up.

'Just one more day,' David said. 'Then if you're no better, darling, I'm coming with you to see Dr Boardman.'

Dr Boardman 'belonged' to the Fairbrothers, and Rose wasn't keen on the sound of him. He was too practical; he would know nothing of guilt-illnesses, probably would not believe in them.

As if to reinforce her lie about flu, June went down with the real thing and Maud moved in to their house to look after the two boys. She felt terrible about it. Rose practically pushed her out.

'Listen. I can get to the kitchen. I can make my own meals. Those children *need* you.'

But she missed her mother-in-law. It meant she was alone in the house with David. It was wicked to feel like that. But she did. And she missed the meals too. If she'd wanted anything she could have got it herself with ease; but she did not want anything. Maud had not asked; she had simply come in with trays. Rose knew she was in a trough of self-pity, but she could not do anything about it.

On the second afternoon of Maud's absence, she lay in

bed and listened to the house around her and tried to find the energy to read her book. She switched on the radio and switched it off. She looked out of the window and saw that the sleet was turning into snow and did not care. She thought of the two new tweed sofas they'd bought in the January sales and tried to be thrilled about them, and could not. She wondered if she was going mad. She closed her eyes and turned her head into the pillow, holding a determined smile until it became a grimace.

Then she heard a sound that had nothing to do with the house. It came from the kitchen. Maud must have popped in to pick something up.

But nothing happened.

She called weakly, 'Maud? Is that you?'

The door opened, and Rick stood there.

Rose screamed and tried to sit up and he came to the bed and made shushing movements with his hands.

'It's all right. It's only me. Sorry. Sorry, my darling. My love. Lie back. Are you ill? What has happened? Why are you home? I thought you'd be at work and I was going to wait for you. Tried the back door. I'm sorry. There. Easy. Don't cry.'

He sat on the edge of the bed and produced a handkerchief. She had not realized she was crying. His handkerchief dried her eyes and his hand cupped her cheek. She moved away from it and the room spun.

'You shouldn't be here! Why are you here?' She looked at him. 'Oh my God – is it Jon? Is it Mother?'

'No. They're all right.' Snow still clung to his eyebrows. He said urgently, 'What is wrong with you?'

'Nothing. A bit of flu. Nothing.'

'Your mother is always boasting that you and Jon are never ill. Toothache . . . nothing more.'

'I'm all right. Don't mention it. Back home.'

He took a deep and shuddering breath. 'You don't know then? I thought Jon would be down to tell you. I've left.'

'You—' She recalled he hadn't been with them at Christmas. Jon had said something about an older woman. In Cheltenham. She hadn't listened properly. 'You can't have left Jon. Not already! You've only been married six months.'

'Eight months all but four days. You must have guessed it wouldn't work, Rosie.'

'I thought – you were doing so well.' There was genuine regret in her voice.

'I did try. She's such a . . . child.'

'She'll get older.'

'Yes. I know. So will I.'

She felt awful. It was something else she'd done wrong. She said, 'Oh Rick. I'm sorry.'

He looked at her. She thought he was going to touch her and she did not move away. Her body began to feel alive again.

But he did not touch her. He said, 'I have got some bad news, Rosie. I had to come and see you. Tell you myself.' He bit his bottom lip. His teeth were very white. He seemed to be growing a beard and it was ginger like his hair. Or perhaps he simply hadn't shaved today. He said, 'I'm living in Cheltenham. I was in the High Street half an hour ago and recognized that maid of your grandparents. Doreen something.'

She hardly heard him. She was fascinated by his hands on the sheet, the golden hairs, even on the backs of his fingers.

He said, 'Are you listening, Rosie? Look at me.'

She looked at him. Deep inside herself she began to tremble.

He said slowly, 'She came over to me. She remembered me from the wedding – your wedding.'

'Who?' she whispered stupidly.

'Doreen. Your grandmother's maid. She told me. She told me that . . . Rosie, your grandfather died two hours ago.'

Her head jerked up and she met his eyes. She said, 'Oh *no*!' Her hands covered her mouth. She was shaking all over now.

He said, 'Oh God. Rosie, I'm sorry. I know you were close. I had to come and tell you. I had to see you. Darling

– please—' He encircled her with his arms, tentatively, expecting her to pull away. She put her head on his shoulder and began to weep.

He stroked her hair.

'It was in his sleep. No pain . . . how he would want it.'

She turned her face into his neck. Turned it again, finding comfort in the feel of his skin against her mouth. His hands tightened, suddenly aware of what was happening. Her aching body relaxed against his damp raincoat; it was as if he were drawing the malaise out of her.

She said, 'I can't bear it! I'm only just getting to know him and now he's dead!'

He murmured something incoherent but infinitely comforting in her ear. His one hand ran the length of her spine and massaged her back.

Her grief was sublimated into a sudden knowledge of her desire for him. She drew away and gave him a startled look, and then his mouth was on hers and he was pressing her back into the pillows which, a moment before, had seemed so uncomfortable.

She was no longer the frightened girl. She knew what to do; she knew about the mechanics of sex. She helped him to undress, pulling at his clothes crazily and throwing them to the floor.

She panted hysterically, 'He loved me. He was like my father. I never knew my father. But we couldn't be close. I don't know why. We couldn't be close. Not ever.'

Rick translated her words accurately. She wanted closeness. Now.

He whispered, 'Rosie – I love you – Rosie—'

But she did not reply. She turned her head again and again in the pillow so that she would not have to look at him. She wanted him to be someone else. She wanted him to be David.

He slid his hands to her breasts and then her waist. He looked down at her. He was as bewildered as she was, but he was an opportunist to the core.

They made love with a fierce abandon. They were in

a no-man's-land where guilt made their passion more intense. Rose continued to weep for her grandfather . . . like a flickering, silent movie, she saw him gargling in the kitchen of the Snow-White house; giving her the gold watch on her birthday; dancing with her. She clutched Rick closer as if to shut out the movie. And then at last everything was forgotten except the moment.

Afterwards they lay side by side on their backs, each staring at the ceiling. She knew what she had done; she did not try to rationalize it or justify it in any way. She had betrayed David and she hated herself. She wished Rick would disappear; she could think of nothing to say to him. She lay waiting for illness to descend again, to be even worse now. She wanted it to be worse. She wanted to be punished for what she had done.

But, incredibly, she felt well. She felt hungry. She wanted a cup of tea.

Rick said, 'Rosie? Are you all right?'

She forced herself to answer him.

'Yes. I'm all right.'

Guilt would come soon and she would be ill again; but now she was all right. How could she be?

He said, 'Rosie. You must leave David. We'll go away. France. Spain. Australia.'

She said practically, 'I haven't got a passport, Rick. And we couldn't live together. You know that as well as I do. Jon is the one for you.'

'How can you say that after we've just been together like that! I always knew you felt like this for me—'

She forced herself to speak about it. 'Rick. I can't explain what has just happened. Perhaps I've had some fantasy in my mind about you. But now it's gone. I'm sorry, but that's the way it is – I have to be honest with you.' She sat up and pulled on her dressing-gown. He tried to put his arms around her, but gently she pushed him away.

'Listen Rick, I hate myself for what has happened—'

'Rosie – please – my fault—'

'No. I could have stopped you.'

'It was grief! It was grief for your grandfather—' he was

132

scrabbling over the bed, kneeling in front of her, ridiculous without his trousers.

She stood up. 'Rick, stop it. It doesn't really matter why it happened, does it? It happened. And I really don't think I can bear it.' Her voice was very calm.

He babbled, 'Rosie – don't send me away! I must see you again!'

'It's over. Finished. Please go now. And don't ever—'

'You're doing it! Sending me away!' He held her around the knees desperately. 'Let me see you sometimes. Just sometimes!'

'No. We must never meet again, Rick.' She leaned down and disengaged his hands firmly. 'Get dressed and go away now.'

'I love you, Rosie! You cannot be so cruel—'

'Rick. You do not love me. And I do not love you. We wanted each other. And now we've had each other.'

'You're so cold. So clinical. I never thought you were like this.'

She said, 'I can only say this. I am glad it was you who told me about Grandfather. If it had been anyone else, I think . . . ' She retied the cord of her dressing-gown. She really did feel amazingly strong. 'I think I might have died.' She smiled. 'Perhaps not.' She glanced at him. He was scrabbling into his trousers. 'Let yourself out of the front door, please. I'm going to the bathroom.'

He stood up. 'Rosie, I'll do anything—'

'Then go back to Jon,' she said quickly. 'Tell her about Grandfather and she will instantly forgive you. Please.'

He said, 'If I go back to Jon, you'll have to see me! I shall be there when you come to the Snow-White house. And I shall visit here with Jon and Aileen!'

She paused by the door; she had not thought of that.

She said slowly, 'Rick, perhaps . . . perhaps we can be friends. Just within the family circle, you understand.'

'Yes. Yes, I understand that,' he said eagerly.

'Jon and David must never – *never* – know what has happened. Do you understand that too?'

'Of course! Did you think – it's our secret, Rosie. Our special, wonderful—'

'All right.' She did not want to think of it as something shared with him. She wanted no more intimacy with him. She knew that she would never tremble again when he came close.

The phone rang urgently in the hall, and she closed the door on him and answered it. It was Emily McIntyre, Grandmother's friend.

'Poor Edith is lying down, dear, but she wanted you to be the first to know. After me.'

Rose said something, then promised she would send a message to the Snow-White house.

She went into the kitchen and watched the gas under the kettle. She looked at the snow falling softly against the kitchen window. After a while she heard the front door close and relaxed thankfully against the window ledge. Somehow she would get through life with this knowledge deep inside her. Buried. Almost forgotten. Just as she had almost forgotten so many things before. The kettle began to whistle and she turned to make tea. It was the first time she'd enjoyed a cup of tea for weeks. She sipped slowly, relishing the steam rising into her face. The house creaked around her. She sat at the kitchen table and wept again for Grandfather Harris whom she would never know fully now. But even as she wept she was aware of her body belonging to her again, free of pain.

That was it. She was free.

Eight

At first, Rose was appalled at how easily she lived with her guilt. Perhaps it was because she suddenly felt so well; perhaps it was because the sense of freedom stayed with her. She was free to love David.

It did not happen immediately. It might easily have done, but something fastidious in her nature prevented her from turning from Rick to David quite so rapidly. David could sense the change in her when he came home that night, but he had no idea that her renewed health was more than a sudden recovery from the lingering virus that had haunted her since the first month of their marriage.

She told him quietly that Rick had brought her news of Grandfather's death and they got the Lagonda out of the garage and through the snowed-up drive to the road, and drove carefully over to Cheltenham. Grandmother was stony-faced, rigid as a ramrod, Victorian in her grief. She accepted their condolences stoically, then said quietly, 'I never really felt for your mother before this, Rose. I'm sorry.' She took David's hand. 'Your mother too, young man.' She shivered suddenly. 'It's a terrible world when two go back to being one.'

That night Rose wept tears on to David's shoulder and did not know for whom she wept. When Jon rang from the phone box in Churchdown to tell her that Rick had been away but was back home now and had some sad news, Rose whispered, 'Thank God.'

Jon said. 'Sorry? This line is awful, Rosie. It must be the snow. Did you hear me say that poor old Grandpops is dead?'

Flippancy was Jon's way of dealing with it. Rose smiled down the hall to where David was wheeling the tea trolley into the back room.

'Yes,' she said. 'We went to see Grandmother earlier this evening. She's amazing.'

'She would be,' Jon said unsympathetically. 'Anyway, I can't be too unhappy, Rosie. Rickie is back home. All's well with the world.'

Rose nearly thanked God again, but she managed a simple 'Good.'

So Rick had gone home as she asked. He hadn't mentioned seeing her. The whole . . . incident . . . could be folded up with the loss of Grandfather, and tucked into her subconscious.

That night she tried to tell David that things were going to be different, but of course he hardly believed in her good health let alone her good intentions. He kissed her and told her to go to sleep. Miraculously, she did.

And her wellbeing continued; the guilt was cocooned successfully; she did not weep at Grandfather's funeral. She knew that one day fate would make her pay for what she had done. But it wouldn't be yet. Not yet.

Before Maud came back home, she and David consummated their marriage properly. This time, it was he who needed reassurance.

'Darling, are you sure you're better? You know how happy we are without bothering—'

She stopped his words with a kiss. And then another. She took a long time over those kisses, cradling his head as it lay on the pillow, tracing lines along his cheekbone with her free hand. The light in his clear eyes filled her with remorse. She whispered, 'Darling, I love you. Oh my God, I do love you.'

She kissed him again and still he did not move. She was terrified she'd left it too late. She sat up in bed abruptly and peeled off her nightie. She said bluntly, 'David. Please . . . let us make love.'

He smiled slightly and raised himself on an elbow to shrug out of his pyjamas. He thought this was going to be the usual thing. 'You never cease to surprise me, Ros,' he said. 'You're so honest. So straightforward.'

For a moment the guilt almost took over. Then she thrust it from her as he took her by the shoulders. She had wanted him desperately for over a week now and abstinence had stoked her passion until she was on fire for him. Nothing else in the world mattered. She made no comparisons with Rick, she knew quite simply that this was the real thing. The swift and inevitable coupling with Rick had been physical only. David and she were already familiar with each other's bodies; they were familiar with each other's minds. The two came together as one. He could not believe it. Occasionally he would gasp her name on a question, afraid he was hurting her. She would hold him fiercely to her, answering the question without words. And afterwards they lay awake, staring at each other's dark faces until they fell asleep without a word.

The next morning David woke early and went to the scullery to make tea. It was still dark with snow piled almost to the window ledges, and they felt cut off from the world.

'If only we lived in the country,' Rose said, 'you wouldn't be able to get into work today.'

He sipped his tea. 'I won't go,' he said, suddenly defiant. 'I'll ring Miss Westlake and tell her we need to be together all day. We can't spare each other.'

She started to laugh, then, out of the blue, was swept with nausea. She just got to the bathroom in time. The tea came back and some of her supper. And, just as startlingly, she was well again.

David was frantic.

'It was last night! I shouldn't have—'

She said, 'David. I am all right. Look at me!' She did a crazy dance around the bedroom, lifting her nightie and finishing with the can-can.

But he refused to be reassured.

'I'm definitely not going to work. We're going to see Dr Boardman. Should have done it ages ago – before Christmas—'

There was no gainsaying him. Even in the waiting room when she mourned that it was a waste of a day off, he said she was talking through her hat and the sooner she started looking after herself the better he'd be pleased. Last night might never have happened. She clung to his arm. 'This is a waste of time. Let's go home,' she repeated.

'Shut up,' he came back at her. And when it was her turn he stood up and practically shoved her through the surgery door.

Dr Boardman was as she had imagined, even to the glasses on the end of his nose. He looked over them. He could have welcomed her on to his list or said he'd been looking after Fairbrothers for longer than he could remember, but all he said was, 'Sickness? Missed any periods?'

'No.' She felt her face flame. How could she have missed any periods after the fiasco in Paris?

He said, 'I shall have to examine your wife, Mr Fairbrother. Perhaps you would wait outside and send nurse in.'

Neither of them could believe it. When David returned they sat side by side, holding hands and expecting the worst.

Dr Boardman said without much enthusiasm, 'You're having a baby. Nothing wrong, everything absolutely normal. I'll make an appointment for you at the hospital.'

Rose looked at David, then back to the glasses. 'How can I be pregnant when I haven't missed one solitary period?'

'It happens,' he said without interest.

'My wife uses a Dutch cap,' David explained politely.

'No contraceptive can be one hundred per cent safe. You are over three months pregnant, Mrs Fairbrother. I'll send the health visitor round to discuss the arrangements.' He stood up to show that the consultation was at an end and had been rather a waste of his time anyway.

Back at the house, David said, 'You didn't put that thing in properly. D'you remember how it hurt? It shouldn't have hurt. Oh darling, do you mind? How do you feel?'

'Wonderful. But I can't believe it. David, will your mother mind? Noise . . . bad nights?'

'Don't be silly. Do you *think* she'll mind?'

'No.'

'Well then.'

She did not want to ask if he minded. They'd hardly spoken a word in the car coming home. He obviously did mind. They stared at each other. They hadn't taken off their outdoor things and snow clung to every indentation of clothing.

'David?' Rose said.

'Ros!' David said. And she knew it was all right.

She leapt at him and he caught her and they swung wildly down the big hallway and crashed into the escritoire beneath the stairs. Snow flew everywhere.

'I love you – I love you – I love you—' chanted David.

And Rose thought: if it hadn't been for last night we wouldn't have been so happy – not like this – it's as if the baby was really conceived last night – oh, please God, no retribution yet – please.

She did her best to placate Him through the following months. She visited her grandmother; had Georgie when Jon and Aileen had had enough; spent long afternoons with June and Arney, knitting and sewing; grew to love her mother-in-law deeply. Life was very good. When Prince Edward was born she wondered how it would be to have a boy. When Princess Margaret gave birth to a girl, she had to admit deep inside her that she would like a girl. Not that it mattered, she said quickly inside her head. Just let it be all right; it doesn't matter whether it's a boy or girl. She continued to feel very well right up until June. Then, after the South African leader, Mandela, was imprisoned, she began to go downhill. She said nothing. June struggled to its thirtieth day, then it was July. The last month.

It was the hottest July Rose could remember. Day after day the sun shone out of a cloudless sky and as the house warmed up for the somnolent, baking afternoon, so Rose's legs swelled. David removed the feather bed and she lay on top of the horsehair mattress, her feet lifted on a pillow so that they were higher than her head. But then her abdomen was so uncomfortable, she eventually had to move.

Everyone told her that she had been terribly lucky to be so fit all through the winter and spring; as if that were a sort of compensation for this last month of enormity.

June, who had envied her her energy and glowing health, said with satisfaction, 'Well. I suppose you had to pay for it some time. Pregnancy is never a picnic.' Maud and Aileen were worried; but mothers always worried. It was unfortunate that David was away during the week on a new-fangled management course. And Rose could not face casual Dr Boardman; she simply felt too ill to walk along to his surgery. In any case, the baby was due at the end of August; not long now.

Perhaps it was lucky that on 16 August, Jon and Rick had one of their frequent rows and Jon banged out of the house in a temper and came down to Gloucester to see her sister.

She surveyed her in undisguised horror.

'What has happened?' she asked unequivocally.

Rose knew what she meant and chose to misunderstand. 'I don't know until you tell me.' She led the way into the old dining room. The French doors stood open to the garden. 'Where is Georgie? D'you think you should leave him with Mother so much? She's not strong, you know.'

'If you're going to be crabby . . . ' Jon flung herself down on one of the tweed sofas. 'My God, it's hot! Georgie is better at home. Mother sits in a deckchair and he poddles around her.' Jon grinned. 'Poddles is a mixture of toddles and paddles, and is done on the stomach! Rick's bought him one of those inflatable pools. You should see him.'

'I will soon.' Rose lowered herself on to a straight-backed chair with some difficulty. 'Well. I take it from the way you stormed through the door that you and Rick have had another bust-up. What is it this time?'

But for once Jon was reticent. Perhaps Rick's infidelities were now too regular for discussion, even with her sister. Instead she asked again, 'Never mind us. What is the matter with you? You look absolutely awful, Rosie. The last time I saw you, you were bouncing about like a beach ball. Now look at you.'

'It's the weather. And it's not long now.'

'Sis, something is not right.' Jon was unusually concerned. 'Sorry. I don't want to sound all doomish, but

140

look at your legs! I think you should be in hospital.'

Unexpectedly, Rose's eyes flooded. She was as shocked as Jon.

'Sorry. Sorry. I don't know why I'm crying! Good Lord, I should be so *happy*! It's just . . . I feel rotten again. Like I did at the beginning. I know everyone does at the end. And it's so hot. And I've been lucky up till now.' She mopped at her eyes and turned and rubbed her face against Jon's consoling arm. It smelled of sour milk. It was the first time that Jon had ever comforted her older sister. Rose forced a smile, sniffing dramatically. 'Funny. The first three months were awful – I really thought I'd got some ghastly disease! Then . . . ' she remembered when she had started to feel so well, and bit her lip ' . . . after Grandfather . . . it was as if he was giving me strength. Now I feel the same again. My head . . . and my legs . . . ' She had told no-one how ill she felt. She rested her head on Jon's shoulder and wept again.

It worried Jon more than Rose's appearance had done.

'Look. I know you'll say no to old Boardman. Don't blame you. But I'm going to get in touch with that health visitor. You liked her. Let's get an outside opinion. How would that be?'

Rose said, 'I don't mind . . . I really don't care. Oh Jon, I'd forgotten how . . . I do love you.'

Jon cried too at that and Maud, coming in from the garden gate, saw them through the windows and hurried in, aghast.

So the three women waited together for Miss Jenkins, the health visitor. And one hour after she arrived, Rose was in hospital. She had toxaemia.

She was allowed to see no-one except David, but flowers and cards arrived all the time. She was in a single-bedded ward which soon became a bower. David said the phone never stopped ringing at home and even in the office. He passed on all the messages, brought the flowers, read out the cards; his face was white, the skin stretched over the bones, but his voice did not falter and his hand was warm and steady when it held hers. She wanted so much to tell him that she wasn't going to die; that this was all happening because of her infidelity with Rick. But she knew she mustn't. Instead she whispered, 'I love you, David. I love you so much.' And he stroked back her sticky hair and whispered his own words of love that she would treasure always.

After three days she was strong enough to be examined. She knew something was wrong, though everyone kept smiling. When David arrived, he was taken straight into the Sister's office. She waited with a kind of fatalistic calm for him to tell her about it.

They stood by the bedside together; Mr Campion the gynaecologist, and her husband. Perhaps they expected her to faint. Or to have a fit. She knew that women with advanced oedema sometimes had fits. She did so hope she wasn't one of them.

David sat on the bed with difficulty; there wasn't much room. He smiled directly at her with those tea-brown eyes of his.

'Mr Campion thinks a Caesarean would be a good idea, Ros,' he said. 'He has just discovered something that makes it . . . necessary.' His face smiled. 'Darling. There are two babies there. Twins.' He took her hands and held them tightly. 'D'you remember saying to me that we wouldn't wait long between babies? Well, there won't be any space between them, sweetheart. Can you imagine that?'

She knew his pleasure was feigned. They didn't expect the babies to live.

She said very quietly, without any surprise in her voice, 'I should have thought . . . I had regular examinations.'

Mr Campion leaned forward. 'I understand you have been in such wonderful health, Mrs Fairbrother . . . just a routine examination made each time . . . '

'Yes.' There was no point in going on about it. If the babies were dead and had to be taken away, then there was no point in anything. Just a waste of time.

David whispered, 'Are you all right, Ros?'

'Of course. I don't mind about the Caesarean. Really, David. It will get it over with.'

He kissed her gently. It was only when she felt his lips, warm against hers, that she realized she was cold. For the first time this month she was cold. She was sweating with the cold.

It must have been a bad sign because almost immediately they brought the pre-med injection. She had already been shaved. They washed her while she drifted into the no-man's-land of drugs, then someone helped her on to a trolley. And then she woke up and felt sick and sore and knew that it was over.

David was there. She knew he would be there. He held a kidney dish while she was sick. He laid her back down gently when her stitches pulled agonizingly. He wiped her face with a damp cloth and lifted her pillow into her neck.

She said, 'I'm sorry, David. I'm so sorry.'

But his face, bright with tears, smiled genuinely. It was close to hers.

'You're going to be all right, darling. And the babies are all right. Everything . . . everything is fine. We're all safe, Ros.' He began to cry in earnest, huge racking sobs that shuddered through his hands into her own body. 'Darling, we've got two daughters. They're all right. And you're all right. Oh Ros . . . Ros . . . '

She held his head into her neck. He cried for them both. She was still drugged and very tired and her back and abdomen hurt with each breath she took. But it hadn't been a waste of time after all. Retribution was still to come. She kissed the top of David's ear and knew that he would never let this happen again. So she was doubly thankful that it had not been a waste of time.

*

They called the little girls Elizabeth because of the Queen, and Ellen which was a version of Aileen. Rose and the babies stayed 'in' for six weeks until Rose's blood pressure was back to normal. She was kept very quiet and though Aileen and Maud and even Jon visited her occasionally, they mentioned nothing of the outside world. She and David talked of nothing but the twins.

David bathed Elizabeth and Rose, Ellen.

143

'Little Betty Blue, has lost her best red shoe,' David chanted, more to reassure himself than the baby who yelled lustily as the water touched her bottom. He dabbed at the tiny wizened scrap. 'She's getting fatter every day,' he said dotingly. 'Look at that waistline!'

And Rose, finding her pleasure through David, said, 'But this little Ellie's got the biggest fat belly!'

He laughed at such unaccustomed vulgarity, knowing it was a kind of bravado on her part. For some time he continued the joke, referring to the babies as Ellie Belly and Betty Blue. Then, when the rest of the family were there, or others, the girls came to be known as Ellie and Blue. Strangely, Ellie was fat and content; Blue was solemn and serious.

Through that autumn and winter, Rose gradually regained her strength. Maud was a great help, and once a week Aileen would come down and take the girls for a walk. Rick, returned to the fold, put in an appearance at the christening and came to family teas once a month. His days of organizing the Harrises, of being head of the little household, were over. Jon confided that he still 'had the Cheltenham woman' and that she didn't much mind as long as he turned up each night and pretended to be a good husband and father.

Rose found herself defending him.

'You don't know he's still seeing that woman, Jon.'

'Quite. And so long as I don't know, I don't mind.'

It didn't make sense, but Rose had to leave it at that. She was surprised when Jon suddenly flung her arms around her neck and hugged her hard.

'What was that for?' she asked, bewildered.

'I know it was you who sent Rick back to me.' Jon's eyes were filled with tears. 'Everyone thinks it was because of Grandfather dying. But he told me he'd come to you first and you persuaded him to come home.' She butted Rose with her forehead. 'I don't know what you did or said, Sis, but I do thank you for that.' She moved away, blowing her nose, embarrassed, then before Rose could say anything, she said laughingly, 'Funny. You're the quiet one, but it's you

144

who seems to be holding everything together, doesn't it?'

The terrible irony of it all was too much. Rose turned away. 'I'm just stuck here. With Ellie and Blue,' she said.

'Yes. But you and David . . . you make your ma-in-law happy. Mother loves coming down. You fixed things for Rick and me and delivered Georgie. I don't know what we'd do without you.'

'You make me sound awful. Pi and awful.' Rose tried to laugh. 'You know very well I'm the most ordinary person in the world.'

'Exactly. That's what makes you extraordinary. Doesn't it, Georgie-Porgie?' Jon tapped the baby on his bottom as he crawled past.

Rose changed the subject determinedly. 'You wanted another baby at one time, Jon. Georgie is just the right age for a baby brother or sister.'

Jon shrugged. 'I don't think I can manage one on my own, Sis.' She glanced at Rose, saw her expression, and hurried on. 'Besides, I don't want any more. Not now. I'm eighteen. I should be having some fun.'

Rose made a face. Rick and Jon were so alike; perhaps too alike.

Exactly a year after Grandfather's death, Winston Churchill died.

It was a snowy afternoon as Maud and Rose sat nursing a baby each and watched the funeral cortège on the television. Richard Dimbleby talked them sonorously through the proceedings. Maud said, 'He'll do him proud.'

Rose nodded. 'Life's diurnal round,' she quoted from long ago and for no particular reason.

Maud nodded too, on the same wavelength. 'It's comforting. Life rolling on. That song – "Let the great big world keep turning" – so unstoppable really.'

'You're wonderful, Maud,' Rose said. 'I don't think I've ever thanked you properly for giving us this home—'

'My dear girl, you pay rent for it!' But Maud's face was hot from the fire. She held the baby close. 'I'm happy,

Ros. I never thought I could be again. But I am. I hope you are too.'

'I am. Oh yes, I am.'

They watched as the coffin was put on a barge. The public display of grief seemed to intensify their own content.

Jon observed her sister's total contentment with very mixed feelings.

In many ways she felt sorry for Rosie. She had been staid – old even – before her time, and marrying David had launched her into middle age immediately. But something had happened when the twins were born, something that cemented David and Rosie into a whole. Jon was impatient with their calm and uneventful existence and told herself she would infinitely prefer the old high peaks of her own married life even if they were inevitably followed by troughs. But they did not happen anyway these days. The few times Rick made love to her, it was almost like a duty. He took infinite care with his 'precautions' and told her most definitely that he did not want any more children.

Probably it was just the same for Rosie. For most married couples these days. After all, who wanted to bring children into a world haunted by hydrogen bombs? But if it *was* the same for Rosie, then she had something else which compensated. Jon could not work out what it was. Contentment was something absolutely foreign to her nature.

Meanwhile she chose to believe that Rick still had his fancy woman in Cheltenham, though she had no evidence of this. When she accused him of unfaithfulness he never bothered to deny it, which in one way was proof enough, but in another, more subtle way, meant there really was no-one.

When Rose sent out invitations to the twins' first birthday party, Jon wasn't keen. Martin and June would be there and they were both incredibly boring. Arney and Charles weren't much better. Grandmother would be in a state of constant disapproval; Maud and Aileen would get together in a duet of adoration for the twins. Rick would be totally preoccupied with keeping Georgie in order.

146

But when Rick's reaction was, 'Well, I'm not going to that!' she about faced very rapidly.

'What d'you mean? We can't possibly not go to Blue and Ellie's first birthday party! My God, we don't go anywhere together, surely you're not going to—'

'You go, Jon. I don't want to stop you – of course I don't.' He sounded so damned reasonable. She couldn't even provoke a row-reconciliation out of this! 'David will fetch you.' He smiled peaceably and just for a moment she felt a pang of sheer tenderness. 'Aileen will want to go so you'll have company.'

She squashed the tenderness – it had nothing to do with their relationship – and said stubbornly, 'I am not going without you and that is that.'

And instead of taking up the flung glove, he suddenly lost interest and said, 'Well. It's up to you really, isn't it?'

They were in the bedroom that had been Rose's. Georgie had Jon's old room because it was furthest from Mrs Whittie's house and she was a light sleeper. Rick was already in the trendy 1960s nightshirt she had bought him last Christmas; he riffled the pages of his book, dismissing the subject.

Jon stood in front of the dressing table, still wearing her petticoat. There was a time when she would have stripped off and continued the argument in the buff, but it was humiliating to stand about in Rick's presence when he completely ignored her. And the petticoat hid the fact that she wasn't quite the sylph-like schoolgirl he'd married.

She used a different tone. Not wheedling exactly; persuasive.

'Rick. I can't possibly go without you. Everyone would think it so odd.'

'Hm?' He kept his place with his thumb and looked over his book. 'Oh come on, Jon. It's just an excuse for the family to get together. The twins are too young to know what's happening.'

'Well, you're family! When we were married first you practically took us over!'

'Did I?' He looked past her, remembering. 'Yes. It was the idea of your family that was so attractive.' He did not smile. 'But really, we're not talking about the Harrises any more. Rose has got a much bigger family now. David, Maud, that ghastly Martin and June. Rose belongs to them now.'

'No she doesn't.' Jon hated the thought of Rose belonging to anyone else. Rose was very specially hers. 'She's still my sister and I want to go to her party!'

He repeated tiredly, 'Fine. I'm not going, Jon.'

She suddenly pulled her petticoat over her head.

'Listen,' she commanded. 'I'm not having the Fair-brothers gossiping about our marriage going down the drain. This is important to me. It's vital to me.' She sat on the bed, took away his book and kissed him firmly. After a while she felt his response and smiled. 'Oh darling,' she murmured into his neck.

He said, 'Wait. I have to . . . ' He scrambled out of bed and went to the chest of drawers. She could have wept with frustration.

'Rick, don't. Please. I'd love another baby. It wouldn't worry me two hoots.'

He said, 'No. Because Aileen would look after it.'

He came back to her and they made love passionately. But somehow without heart. She thought afterwards that it was impossible to make love passionately without heart. Yet it happened.

And then he said, as if paying her for a favour, 'All right. I'll come with you to the party.'

She had won. But as with so many of her little victories, she got no satisfaction from it. Quite the reverse. She felt angry with him; resentful. And her own self-respect was in the dust. She said that to her reflection in the bathroom mirror the next morning. And added, half-humorously, 'As per-bloody-usual!'

She tried to blame him for what happened at the Stroud Road house. She told herself if she didn't have to work so hard to keep him interested, it simply would not have

148

occurred to her to behave so badly. But it was much more than that. She had to prove something to herself. It was as if her womanhood was at stake.

It was a beautiful day and she wore the dress she'd made for Rosie's twenty-first and backcombed her hair until it was a dark aureole around her head. Aileen told her she looked stunning. Rick said nothing.

David was picking up Grandmother from Cheltenham, then coming on to Churchdown for them. Jon primed Georgie to run down the garden path and give Grandmother one of his sloppy kisses. Georgie looked angelic in a cotton pinstriped romper suit and he could say all kinds of words now. When he was lifted into the back of the creaking old Lagonda next to Grandmother, he took one look at her hat and said 'Foony.' She pretended not to understand and said, 'Yes dear. It's called a feather. Not foony. Feather.' Aileen, settling herself on the other side of the child, remarked diplomatically, 'So nice to see a hat again.' And then hastily, in case Grandmother thought she meant hats were out of date, 'And what a lovely day Ellie and Blue have got for their first birthday!'

'Yes,' Grandmother said repressively. 'Let's hope they can behave themselves!'

Jon tried to catch Rick's eye and failed. Such a short time ago they would have had the giggles at an incident like this. Not any more.

David turned round.

'Are you all right squashed up in the back? Jon, there's room between Rick and me, if you prefer.'

Jon started to get out again, but Grandmother said, 'We're quite all right, dear. And we're rather late as it is.'

So of course they drove on and Jon missed the chance of being pressed close to her own husband. Discontent was like bile inside her. She made no effort to join in the stilted conversation; instead she fixed her eyes on the back of David's neck and wondered if she had been wrong all the time about his dullness.

Everything was chaotic at Stroud Road, yet, paradoxically, everything was also under control. Jon could not understand that either. Charles and Arney were hovering in the bedroom with Maud, waiting for the girls to wake from their nap. Martin was putting up sunshade and deckchairs in the garden. June was helping Rosie to lay the table. There were balloons and jellies and a cake shaped like a house.

Jon said, 'Can I do anything?'

June said, 'You'd better keep an eye on your son!' She slapped Georgie's hand away from one of the high chairs where he had been picking at something spilt down the legs. Then she fetched a cloth and ostentatiously began to wash the chairs.

Jon glanced at Rosie who smiled easily.

'Arney will be down in a minute, Jon. He'll amuse Georgie. Is Grandmother all right?'

Jon nodded briefly. Georgie tugged at the flimsy net of her skirt and she lifted him to her hip.

'And Mother?'

'Yes. We're all fine.'

She drifted into the garden. Rick and David had joined Martin. She put Georgie down.

'Go see Daddy,' she said. He ran off and she smiled at Martin. 'You're almost as awkward as I am!' He'd got a deckchair upside down. 'Here, let me.' She took it from him and upended it next to another. 'Come on. Let's test them!'

He laughed and sat down next to her. She turned and studied him openly. He looked like David.

She said, 'You know, Martin Fairbrother, you're a very attractive man!'

He coloured slightly. Poor lamb, if David was dull, Martin was duller. He simply wasn't up to badinage of any kind.

And then he said, 'And you . . . you are the most beautiful thing I've seen for ages!'

She almost felt her jaw drop. But she recovered and let her open mouth laugh, tilting her head so that the long line of neck disappearing into the shawl collar was completely exposed.

150

June called from the kitchen door, 'Martin! Don't just sit there! Those boys are making a nuisance of themselves – go and sort them out!'

He stood up as if the deckchair canvas was on fire, but then he could look down into her tilted face. She went on laughing and closed one eye. After a moment, he winked right back.

It would serve June right. What a cow the woman was.

It went on being very predictable: a messy tea, screeches, screams, tears, laughter; the grandmothers running round like scalded cats after the children, Ellie and Blue in their new baby-walkers. But Jon was no longer bored. She felt as if she were sizzling with life even though she spoke far less than usual. It was as if she could see herself: nineteen, her face small in its big halo of dark curls, her gauzy dress . . . and then she saw the others: all much older, set in their ways. And one of them was seeing her. Really seeing her. The fact that Martin was over thirty made the whole thing even more exciting. He passed a dish. 'Jelly, Jon?' She could not meet his eyes. His words were deliberately childish and hilarious. Arney picked them up, of course. 'Jelly-jon? Jelly-jon!' he giggled. And everyone laughed and did not know that for her and Martin it was funnier than funny. She got up to take Georgie to the bathroom and brushed Martin's shoulder in passing. His neck was like David's. She remembered it from the car this afternoon. Briefly she laid her fingertips just above his collar. She felt a nerve leap.

They played cricket. Martin was positioned just outside the summerhouse. She sidled up to him. Charles drove the soft tennis ball down the garden and it disappeared in the bushes. They searched together.

Aileen said, behind them, 'Whatever are you two up to?'

'Looking for the ball, Mother – can't you see?'

Aileen's face was set with disapproval.

'It's right here. You'd better have your turn now, Martin.'

He took the bat. Jon said, 'Honestly, Mother. A harmless flirtation—'

'June wouldn't see it like that!'

That was what made it so exciting, of course. And the fact that Rick too might be jealous. Not that Rick had noticed a thing. He was enjoying the damned game, actually enjoying it.

She murmured something about the heat and went inside. She could feel her old mood of discontent settling somewhere just above her head again. She walked the length of the hall and envied Rose its spaciousness. She sat in the cubbyhole beneath the stairs where old Mr Fairbrother's desk still held an old-fashioned telephone. There was a stack of unopened birthday cards still there. Rosie seemed to know no-one, yet on occasions like this – and when she was in hospital – people surrounded her with their concern. Jon's sudden marriage to an older man, and the birth of Georgie, had somehow cut her off from her old schoolfriends. She hadn't had time to make any new contacts since.

She shook herself fiercely; she had come near to envying Rosie then! Yet she knew very well she couldn't stand Rosie's life.

Someone came into the kitchen. She peered out of the alcove. It was Martin. In an instant, discontent was gone.

She breathed, 'Peep-bo!' And his face turned towards her, suddenly full of . . . joy. Was she really capable of making anyone joyful?

She laughed and emerged and he came down the hall to her.

'You didn't have a very long innings,' she commented, literally sparkling at him.

He stopped short and took a breath.

'I put my leg in front of the wicket,' he said. 'I knew Charles would spot that instantly.'

He moved forward two paces and stood so close her skirt brushed his legs. He did not know what to say or do next. She would have to make all the running. It was up to her.

She was conscious of having a moment when she could make a decision.

She said conversationally, 'I'm desperate to go to bed with you, Martin Fairbrother.' She did not recognize the words as being decisive; in her book they were merely a gambit. She waited for a suitable reaction.

He did actually flinch. And then he said, 'Oh my God . . . you wonderful girl. You crazy, wonderful girl.'

She laughed. 'It's all your fault. You're incredibly . . . ' she dallied over saying 'sexy' or 'male'. Either could put him off. She whispered, 'Could you just kiss me?'

He kissed her. He had been trained by June and it was not a satisfying or wholehearted kiss. She worked on his technique until he was nearly crazy for her. She still did not realize that the decision had been made.

He opened the door to the old sitting room which was now David and Rosie's bedroom. The bed was piled with cardigans . . . someone's hat – not Grandmother's thank God – gloves and handbags.

He said hoarsely, 'Oh my God . . . '

Jon laughed and cleared them all by the simple expedient of dragging off the bedspread. Then she jumped into the middle of the bed. It was a feather bed – in this weather – and she sank into it like a bird in a nest. She had intended to bounce provocatively, but her first effort served merely to embed her more firmly in feathers.

Martin had gone far past any preliminaries. He put one knee next to her and unzipped himself at the same time. He was sobbing. She held his head and said, 'It's all right.' And she kissed him and he was on her.

She was suddenly frightened. But she could only stop events now by hurting him terribly. And she did not want to do that because after all he was nice. He had made her feel wonderful. The least she could do . . . fear was replaced by a sense of resignation. It meant nothing, after all. Passion without heart . . . she knew about that already. It would be a quick coupling; hardly time for her to realize she was being unfaithful to Rick – who after all deserved everything he got after his philanderings with the Cheltenham woman.

153

But it was not quick. Martin was afraid he might hurt her, and then when it was all too obvious he would not, he was filled with a kind of religious ecstasy for her that brought him to tears again. She tried to reassure him by pretending she was desperate for him; she squirmed and groaned and sank her teeth into his neck just above that white collar. The collar and the neck that had started the whole thing at the beginning of the afternoon. She tried to tell herself that it was ironically funny that here she was making love to Rosie's brother-in-law on Rosie's bed in Rosie's house during Rosie's daughters' birthday party. But when Martin rolled off her and lay, panting, by her side, she was weeping though she did not know why.

He said, 'Jon. Oh my dear. What is it?'

She scrubbed her eyes like a child. 'I don't know. I never cry. I'm sorry.'

'This isn't . . . you know . . . a one-night stand. Whatever they call it.'

'Oh Martin . . . ' she laughed shakily. 'It's not even night!'

'We'll get married, Jon. I've never felt like this. Really.'

He tried to take her in his arms but she did not want that. The sense of power, of being able to manipulate her own fate, had gone. She drew herself up in the bed. Her lovely dress was rucked sordidly around her waist. Martin had taken no precautions. There was a mess on the bed. She began to feel frightened again.

He said urgently, 'Listen. Darling. I love you. You make me feel . . . wonderful. I could – ' he laughed – 'I could conquer the world, Jon! I mean it!'

'I know.' It was how she had felt once.

'It'll be a nasty business, my love. Rick . . . June . . . they'll kick up a stink. But we'll survive. We'll get married. We'll make a home for the boys – all of them.' He laughed; he thought he could cope with anything. 'We'll have a family of our own, Jon. Won't that be marvellous?'

She shivered with terror and horror. She did not want any of this. She wanted to put time back to when they were kissing in the hall and she was in charge of her own destiny.

She said, 'They'll take Georgie away from me.'

'We'll fight for him, Jon. And June won't want Charles and Arney. She's forever smacking them.'

She did not want them either.

'Rick—' it was a cry for help but he did not hear it.

'Darling, stop worrying. He'll be all right. Eventually. So will June.'

That was the trouble. Rick would be all right, and quite soon too. He'd probably go and live in Cheltenham with whoever it was.

She bleated, 'Rosie . . . David . . . '

'I know they'll be hurt. And my mother too. But we'll make it up to them. We'll live it down.'

He had an answer for everything. She could almost hate him. She closed her eyes and sent up an urgent prayer for help and instantly the door opened and Mother stood there like an avenging angel.

She took in the situation without difficulty, which was hardly surprising as Jon had not even pulled down her dress. Martin scrambled off the bed more or less intact and started to make a speech. Aileen ignored him. Jon ignored him.

Aileen said, 'Get up and go to the bathroom. I'll see to the bed.'

Jon said, 'Mother. I'm sorry. I didn't mean—'

But Mother was taking it all as if it happened every day. She glanced at Martin who had just got to . . . 'we are very much in love . . . ' and snapped, 'Nobody has missed you as yet. Go on outside.'

But he was unstoppable. Heaven knows how long he would have pontificated if Rosie hadn't appeared in the open doorway. She was less quick than Mother and might never have realized the true position if Martin had shut up. But when she did, her face opened wide with a kind of horror. She over-reacted as Jon might have expected. It was as if she had come upon them while they were actually in bed. Her skin turned a kind of ashy-grey and her mouth twitched frighteningly.

Aileen moved to her side and at long last Martin stopped for breath.

Into the silence Jon began again. 'I didn't mean . . . '
She looked at Martin who turned and stared at her. She
finished, 'I didn't mean it to go this far. I'm sorry.'

He couldn't believe it. He stammered something like 'Jon
– darling—' and hung on to the bedpost.

Aileen said, 'Are you all right, darling?' And she was
talking to Rose.

Jon said, 'I love Rick. I'm sorry, Martin.'

Aileen said, 'It's a mistake. That's all. Jon has made a
mistake.' She had her arm around Rose's waist and was
talking to her. As if Jon wasn't even there.

Martin said, 'You can't mean it, Jon. Just now . . . you
said you loved me . . . '

'No. I didn't say that.'

'But what we did – it must mean—'

'In a way. Perhaps. But Rick . . . '

Aileen said, suddenly stern, 'Jon is too young to know her
own mind, Martin. Too selfish to consider other people's
feelings. She wanted a flirtation. Nothing more.'

Martin looked sick. He tried once more. 'Jon?'

She simply stood there, and hung her head. She could
not meet his eyes. If Mother had given her the role of silly
schoolgirl then she would behave like one.

When she looked up he had gone.

Aileen and Rose moved to the bed and began to strip
it. Rose had herself in hand now. She did not speak
but her colour was almost back to normal. Mother was
marvellous. Anyone would think she had coped with this
kind of thing before.

They remade the bed and replaced everything on it.

And at last Rose spoke. She said in a low voice, 'No-one
must know about this. Martin will be able to forget it quite
quickly if it's a secret. Is that understood?'

Aileen said, 'Of course. Everyone makes mistakes. It's
much better not to mention them.'

Jon could not believe the two of them. It was as if they
were holding up the edge of the carpet for her to sweep
the last hour beneath it. Aileen picked up her discarded
pants and handed them to her and went on kindly, 'You'd

better clean yourself up, darling, and get properly dressed. I'll make us a nice cup of tea.'

And the two of them left her standing there.

*

She half expected Martin to try to get her alone again. But when she emerged from the bathroom he was herding the boys outside and into the car. They had got into a fight over the cricket and were being taken home in disgrace.

June's voice, strident with anger, came from the bedroom. 'I had a cardigan. I can't find it anywhere now.'

Martin caught Jon's eye and looked quickly away. She wondered why she had wanted him in the first place. Ordinary people were so . . . ordinary. He reached into the car for something and her teeth marks were revealed on his neck. Perhaps, just for an hour or two, he hadn't been that ordinary. She looked around for Rick. He was still in the garden giving Blue and Ellie encouragement with their baby-walkers. The sun, low over the summerhouse, made his red hair flame and sent little glinting lights along the backs of his hands and his arms. She remembered the first time she had seen him at the Cadena four years ago. She had known then that he was the one for her. But he had never really taken her seriously. She wondered what he would say when she told him about Martin. If she told him about Martin. It was something to think about . . . after all, she'd made no promises to keep it a secret.

Nine

Jon saw nothing of Martin during the long month of August. Her mother never referred to what had happened at the birthday party and they saw very little of Rose. That was Jon's fault of course; Rose was tied hand and foot by the twins and it was always up to Jon and Aileen to visit her. Aileen made no such suggestion, and Jon gradually stopped going altogether.

She grew resentful. All right, so she had sinned. That much was obvious. But no-one had been hurt by it. And Aileen seemed to find it easy to pretend nothing had happened. But anyone would think Rose had been physically injured by her sister's . . . misdemeanour. It took Jon a very short time to change the word 'sin' into 'misdemeanour'. They were midway through the swinging sixties when there was no such word as sin.

As for Martin . . . if he'd been smitten that much, surely he would have tried to get in touch with her. She forgot the moment of terror when she had thought he was so committed he would accost Rick and wreck her marriage for ever. She thought now he was under June's thumb. He was so wet.

Georgie was almost two, and a handful. She left him with her mother more and more and joined a tennis club in Cheltenham. She flirted with the men during mixed doubles and told Rick about it, but he was unaffected. One day he picked her up from the courts, and she kissed her partner goodbye before running to the Riley. Rick made no comment at all.

'He's my special,' she said, stowing her stuff on the back seat. 'We're dynamite together.'

Rick ignored the double entendre and said, 'I've got a couple of calls to make on the way home.'

'D'you have to? Mother's had Georgie since nine this morning.'

'That's rather up to you, Jon. I'm supposed to be working. That's why I've got the Riley.'

'All right, all right.' She relapsed against the hot leather. 'I don't see why you can't have it all the time. We need a car.'

'You mean you need a car.'

'Well, it's not easy living out at Churchdown with Georgie so small.'

'You leave him with Mother anyway. He won't know you soon.'

'My God, you sound crabby! Is anything the matter?'

'No.' He was silent, negotiating into Winchcombe Street to get to the Evesham road. They drove in silence for a while, then he said, 'David's been made manager. The youngest branch manager Prov's ever had apparently. Quite a feather in his cap.'

'Rick!' Jon slewed in the seat and stared at him. 'We'll be all right now! David will let you have the car! He'll give you a rise! Rick, this is wonderful!'

'I don't quite see it like that, Jon. If you think I'm going cap in hand to my brother-in-law—'

'Don't be silly, darling! It won't be like that! If you like I'll fix it! Oh Rick, this is great news—'

'Don't you dare – ever – ask favours of David Fairbrother! Is that clear?'

He did not take his eyes off the road but she could feel his anger beaming on her. His hands on the wheel were white.

She laughed. 'Darling, I shan't have to ask even. Martin will do it for me. For us.'

He was silent; still angry. He could put up a wall between them so that she had a physical sense of stretching, as if to look over it.

He said at last, 'Martin Fairbrother hardly knows us. Anyway he and his wife are a pair of snobs. They even look down on David and Rose.'

'Who of course are the very best,' Jon said, suddenly back to being resentful.

'Better than those two any day.' Rick drove past the cemetery and pulled up at a semi-detached villa. He turned to look at her. 'What's going on? Why do you think you've got some kind of pull with Martin Fairbrother?'

She tried pouting. He used to love her pout.

'He's got a thing about me. You know. Lolita. Sort of.'

His reaction was absolutely wrong. He stared for a moment and she thought he might explode into a rage and shake her – maybe even hit her. Which would have been fine. She could have taken it from there. But instead, he suddenly started to laugh.

She said, 'What's funny? Why are you laughing?'

But he couldn't stop laughing for ages, and when he did he had no real explanation.

'Martin Fairbrother . . . dirty old man!' was all he spluttered.

She couldn't let that go; after all Martin might be dull as ditchwater, but he wasn't a dirty old man. She said, 'No. It's more than . . . that, Rick. He loves me.' She tried to get the conversation back to the main point. 'He'll do anything for me. I know. He'll bring it up quite casually – David won't even know I've mentioned it. Honestly. I can work it. Promise.'

The last of his laughter disappeared. He said slowly, 'He loves you. He told you that, did he?'

'Umm . . . yes.'

'And you believed him.'

'Oh yes. He was . . . yes. I believed him.'

'The day of the birthday party. Yes?'

She did not know why, but she began to feel frightened again. As if things were galloping past her control.

'Umm. Yes. I think it was then.'

'You know damned well it was then. You and he disappeared. After tea. Then he left.'

'The boys had been playing up. June—'

'He left. And Rose looked sick. And Aileen's back was as stiff as a ramrod.'

'I didn't notice. But Martin will definitely—'

'You and he went to bed. David and Rose's bed?'

160

As if that mattered. 'Listen. Rickie. Darling. I can explain. It wasn't as bad as it sounds. And it made me realize just how much I love you.'

He started to laugh again. He said, 'You and Martin Fairbrother. In Rose's feather bed. Oh God!'

'Why are you *laughing?*'

'It's just . . . *déjà vu.*'

'But . . . it's not funny, Rickie!' Now that he knew, she wanted him to be angry; to be furiously jealous. She said flatly, 'We made love. Don't you understand that? We went the whole way, Rickie. I was sorry after – I admit it – but it happened!'

He nodded, still laughing. 'Oh I get the message, Jon. No wonder Rose looked sick. No bloody wonder!'

He got out of the car, reached for his case on the back seat, went up the path to the house. She watched him, frustration making her throat ache. Why on earth was he laughing? Did he really not care two hoots whether she went to bed with another man or not? What was so amusing about it being Martin? About Rose being so sick at her sister and brother-in-law . . . unless Rose fancied Martin? But no, Rose and David were practically one person; welded together.

Someone came to the door and then went again, leaving Rick standing on the step. What a lousy job: selling insurance. A doorstep man. The woman reappeared, money changed hands, a book was signed. Transaction over. Why couldn't he see that if she pulled a few strings he could now have the car permanently and some more money. And maybe a job in the office too.

He came back. The laughter had all gone. He got in, started up, slammed the door and did a tight U-turn in the road.

'I thought you had another call to make?' she said.

'It doesn't matter now.'

That was hopeful. Perhaps they were going home to make mad passionate love after all.

She said, 'After supper we could have a walk over the hill if you like. Up the old ski slope.'

161

She'd said the wrong thing again. 'By the time Georgie's in bed you'll be too tired. All that tennis.'

'Oh Rickie. Mother will put him to bed anyway if we ask nicely.'

'Aileen is doing too much. If you won't put our son to bed, I will.'

'OK, OK. I'll do it. Mother's only just fifty, you know. Not decrepit or anything.'

He said nothing and she let him drive through the town to Staverton before speaking again.

'Rickie. Let's go for a walk. I'll put Georgie to bed and read him a story. I won't be tired. Let's go for a walk.'

'I'm tired.'

'Please. Please, Rickie.'

'Don't you ever give up?'

'Not on something that's important. No.'

He changed down with a horrid grinding of gears. She exclaimed, 'Careful darling! If the car's going to be ours we don't want to ruin the gearbox!'

He glanced sideways and started to laugh again.

She might just as well have stayed in and watched the film on television because he was at his most determinedly non-committal all evening. She asked him why he had laughed at her and he said he didn't know. She asked why he wouldn't let her talk to Martin and he just reiterated that he forbade it absolutely.

'I shan't have to do him any favours,' she said with her usual brand of brazen innocence. 'If I threaten to tell his precious brother, he'll do anything for me!'

He looked at her curiously. 'Is there nothing you won't do to get your own way, Jon?' he asked.

'Not much. And I'd be doing it for you anyway, Rickie Johnson!'

He actually smiled. 'Oh yes. I'd forgotten that,' he said agreeably. And then she realized he was smiling too widely and his voice was too agreeable. 'You went to bed with Martin Fairbrother for my sake, did you?'

Her heart lifted slightly. He was jealous after all.

She said, 'He swept me off my feet if you must know.'

'I'll bet.'

'You haven't done that very often for some time, darling.'
She tried to speak lightly. 'It's all rather businesslike with
you. At least where I'm concerned. Perhaps the lady friend
you have in Cheltenham might be a different story.'

He stopped and looked at the view through narrowed
eyes. They were on the Gloucester side of the hill. It was
as if he were looking for the Stroud Road house in the city
jumble beneath them.

He said quietly, 'I haven't seen . . . anyone . . . for
eighteen months now, Jon. That time . . . when Rose sent
me back to you . . . I've been faithful since then.'

She swallowed but still said defiantly, 'You don't spend
much time at home then!'

'I'm trying to build up my commission. I thought we
might get away from here.'

'Away? From the Snow-White house?'

'Yes.'

She stared at him. He had changed so much since she
had first met him. Then he had been as crazy as she was
herself. Now . . . of course, he *was* twenty-six.

She said, 'I thought you liked it here? I thought you liked
living with Mother.'

'I do. But I hate working at the Prov. And now that
David is the manager . . . I'm more of a practical man. I
thought I'd like to do something with my hands.'

Something stopped her from making a flip remark about
what he could do with his hands. She sat down suddenly
on a molehill. She could not imagine life away from the
Snow-White house. The few months she had spent in St
James Street had been terrible.

He squatted by her and put a hand on her arm.

'We'd take Aileen. Of course. But I'd like it to be our house.
I'd like Aileen to live with us instead of us living with her.'

'There's no difference,' she said, her mouth dry.

'There's all the difference in the world.'

'Did you . . . ' she forced a sarcastic note into her voice.
'Did you have anywhere in mind?'

163

'Newcastle. They need riveters in the shipyard. I did some riveting in Wales.'

'Rick!' She was appalled. 'Everyone we know – they're all white-collar workers!'

He stood up, laughing again. 'You're a snob too, Jon!'

'I'm not! I'm not – really!' But again she felt helpless. Things were going all wrong somehow and she did not seem to be able to stop them. She said stubbornly, 'Mother would never go to Newcastle.'

'Then you'd have quite a decision on your hands, wouldn't you?'

He spoke banteringly, but she had a feeling he wasn't joking.

Somehow she couldn't tell Mother what Rick had said, but she wanted to talk it over with someone. She asked Aileen to go with her to see Rosie.

Aileen said, 'It's rather hot, darling. Leave Georgie with me and pop down on the bus.'

But Jon wanted the bastion of her mother's presence.

'We all need to go. We can buy a congratulations card for David. Rosie must be delighted about it. And Maud of course.'

Aileen nodded. 'Sorry. I'd forgotten their wonderful news. Isn't it marvellous, Jon? They'll be all right now. Not that they weren't all right before, of course. But this makes everything . . . perfect!'

Jon said, 'Yes. Perfect.'

Aileen went to the post office and bought some cards and held Georgie's hand while he did a shaky kiss on his. They went down to Gloucester the next day.

It really was hot and the low-lying city was airless. The big old house in its bower of trees was a haven. The twins were naked, crawling over the inflated lip of their paddling pool and splashing into the three inches of water with great glee. Georgie joined them joyously. Everything seemed normal again. The four women watched them and laughed together. Rose put an arm across Jon's shoulder just as she'd done when they were children. Jon knew she

164

was being conciliatory. It gave her the courage to say in a low voice, 'I want to talk to you, Rosie. Privately.'

Rose withdrew the arm and looked slightly alarmed. Jon said hastily, 'Nothing about . . . not what you're thinking. Something to do with the house.'

'The Snow-White house?'

'Where else?'

'Come and help me make us some lunch.'

They went back into the dim coolness of the kitchen and began to get stuff out of the fridge. Jon told Rose flatly that Rick wanted to go to Newcastle to work. Rose did not seem particularly surprised.

'What about Mother?' she said immediately.

'That's it. I'm sure she wouldn't be keen on going.'

'She could come here. I know Maud wouldn't mind.'

Jon spread cream cheese on crackers. She said slowly, 'That's good of you, Rose. But . . . Mother loves the Snow-White house.'

'Well, she could stay there. It would be up to her really, wouldn't it?'

Jon was surprised. 'That sounds rather tough.'

Rose laid plates around the table as if she were dealing cards.

'I didn't mean to be tough, Jon. But we've no right to order Mother's life for her. She might be jolly pleased to have the Snow-White house to herself.'

Jon was silent. Somehow Rose was not giving her the answers she wanted. Though, as she did not know what she wanted, it was all difficult.

She waited until the kettle was boiling for tea, then said, 'Actually, Rosie, I'm not that keen on going myself.'

Rose poured the water carefully into the teapot. Steam engulfed her. Just as it had the day she stepped from the train when Jon had been waiting to tell her about Georgie's existence.

'Why ever not?' she asked.

Jon said sharply, 'Well, it's the only home I've known for one thing. And for another I don't want to be separated from my family!'

'Rick and Georgie are your family, Jon.' Rose spoke slowly. 'And it might be a good thing to go right away. A fresh start.'

Jon was cut to the quick. 'You want to get rid of me. Of course I know I'm a nuisance. I don't melt into the background like you do. I'm not quite so conventional and—'

'You know it's not that, darling.' Rose brought the teapot to the table. Her face was strained. 'I shall miss you terribly. We shall all miss you – the twins love Georgie. And you're their favourite aunt. You know all that!'

'I haven't got much competition there, have I? June's never going to be favourite anything!'

Rose was silent.

Jon said, 'Oh, I see. You want me away from Martin.'

'Jon. Be sensible. It might be . . . better. Mightn't it?'

'For whom? Him? Or me?'

'Both of you, I imagine.'

'It was a fling, Rosie! For goodness sake! Haven't you ever done anything on impulse?'

Rose had been going to pour tea. She put the teapot down suddenly. Jon laughed.

'Of course you haven't! You had to weigh up the pros and cons for marrying David, even!'

Rose said evenly, 'It wasn't a fling for Martin, actually. He has fallen in love with you, Jon.'

Jon was not displeased with this piece of news.

'He's talked to you?' she asked.

'Yes. He's very unhappy. It would be easier for him if you were . . . away.'

'My God. You do want to get rid of me!'

'I want you and Rick to be happy. It was me who arranged your marriage, Jon. I want it to work well, for your sake. For Rick's sake. Especially for Georgie's sake.'

'Yes, yes, yes!' Jon was impatient. 'And for Martin's sake too now, it would seem. Oh, and don't forget Mother! And Maud and David. In fact . . . the whole bloody world!'

Rose said gently, 'Jon . . . you're still only nineteen.

It's important for you to make a go of your marriage. You love Rick.'

Jon sat down suddenly. 'Yes.' She gave a rueful laugh. 'In some ways it would be easier if I didn't. I don't think he loves me.'

'Don't say that.'

'He knows about Martin. He wasn't jealous. Or even particularly angry.'

Rose too sat down. 'You told him?' She stared at the tablecloth for a long moment. Jon had a feeling she might be going to say something marvellous; something that would put everything right. And she did.

'Jon. Don't you see? If he knows – about you and Martin – and he still wants to make a new life together . . . he must love you, darling.'

Somehow they were looking at the same thing from different places. And Rose knew nothing of the complicated relationship Jon had with Rick. But on the other hand, Rose was older and much wiser.

Jon said hopefully, 'D'you think so? Really?'

'It's obvious to me.'

'Well . . . it might be interesting to have a change.' She brought up an old grouse. 'After all, I've never been anywhere. You've lived in America!'

Rose laughed and hugged Jon suddenly.

And Jon said, 'Oh Rosie. I shall miss you. You're the one . . . normal thing in my life.'

'Rubbish!' Rose withdrew, almost guiltily. 'You've got Mother.'

'What's normal about Mother?' Jon was joking. Then she added soberly, 'Mother is the loneliest person I've ever met.'

Rose looked horrified for a moment. Then Aileen came in from the garden, blinking in the sudden cool gloom of the kitchen. She smiled widely at her daughters and started to tell them what Georgie and the twins were up to. It was so ridiculous to think of her as lonely that both girls laughed inordinately.

*

Plans were made.

Aileen decided to stay on at the Snow-White house, at least for a year. She said she wanted to be independent, but both girls knew that not only did she think Rick and Jon should be on their own for the first time, but she was also worried that Grandmother might well sell the little cottage if it were empty.

Rick went up to Newcastle and found a flat on the heights above the river. He was lucky enough to get temporary work at the dockyard too. The keel of a new Scandinavian ferry was being laid; the men envisaged a year's work. Rick planned to move his family up at the end of September. Jon cancelled the tennis club; she packed; she drew pictures for Georgie of 'Daddy's ship'. She was excited but nervous too. She lost weight and her hair drooped out of its natural curl. Aileen insisted she went for a check-up. Rick would be home later that day and they were leaving on the nine-fifteen in the morning.

'The doctors up there might not be quite so . . . good,' Aileen said unfairly. 'Besides, I can come with you this morning and look after Georgie.'

Luckily, Jon declined the first offer. 'No need to bring him, Ma. I'll go early and be back long before Rick's train is in.'

She could not believe what the doctor told her.

'I haven't missed a single period! And I'm losing weight, not putting it on!'

'That can happen, Joanna. Now stop worrying. I can give you a letter which you will take to your new doctor. He will put you in touch with the local ante-natal clinic. You're in perfect health. Still in your teens – a brother or sister for young George. Couldn't be better!'

She stared at him. In all her life she'd hardly needed a doctor. She'd brought Georgie for injections and things, and that was all. How could she tell him what a ghastly catastrophe this was?

All the way home she rehearsed how she would tell Rick. Then she decided she wouldn't tell Rick. Surely when they were in their new home he would forget his usual

168

precautionary measures and she could pass the baby off as premature?

It did not help to find that Rick had taken a train at the crack of dawn, a taxi from Cheltenham, and was already in the house. He greeted her almost gladly; Georgie was on his lap. She flung herself on them both; she was nearly weeping.

Aileen said, 'Jon? Are you all right? What did the doctor say?'

'Of course I'm all right!' She was sweating profusely but then it was very hot for September. 'He says I've been getting too excited about the move. I'll be fine once we're settled.'

There was a knock on the door. It was Mrs Whittaker. Aileen showed her in and went to make coffee.

'I saw Rick arrive. Have you told him yet?' Mrs Whittaker was all agog.

'Told him?' Jon hugged Rick's arm to her side. Everything was going to be fine. She was cross with herself for getting into such a state.

'About the baby!' The old neighbour looked coy. 'That's what it is, isn't it? I knew it over a month ago! Of course I've always been able to diagnose pregnancies. Funny, as I've never had a baby of my own. When's it due? Let me guess . . . April? April the first?'

Jon laughed loudly.

'Honestly! Mrs Whittie! You'd be ducked for a witch a hundred years ago! Yes. April the first. All Fools' Day!' She tried to take the shrillness out of the next laugh. 'The doctor says nothing the matter with me that Newcastle won't put right! I've been getting keyed up about the move apparently.'

Mrs Whittie looked disappointed. 'Oh. Oh, what a shame. Never mind, you're both young yet. Plenty of time. Where's your mother, dear? I'll keep an eye on her for you, don't worry.'

'She's still in the kitchen.' Jon felt Rick try to withdraw his arm. She hung on. 'I think she wanted to give Rick and me a bit of time to say hello.'

169

But Mrs Whittaker could not be offended. She chuckled. 'Hint taken, dear. I'll join her.'

Rick stood up and took Georgie's hand. 'Daddy's been on a big train for a long, long time, Georgie. Let's have some fresh air, shall we?'

Jon sat alone in the tiny sitting room. It wouldn't be natural to chase after Rick; that might show that she was guilty. Or would it? What would she have done if Mrs Whittie's words had been just figments . . . ? She shook her head angrily. Damn and blast Mrs Whittie! Mother would never have said anything even if she'd had proof positive. Nor Rose. Mrs Whittie was about the only one who didn't know all about the bloody Martin business. If only . . . if only . . . damn and blast Martin too. Or – before that – Rick, for goading her into it. Yes . . . basically, it was Rick's own fault.

She stood up and fiddled with the box of spills on the mantelpiece. Should she be doing something – taking the initiative in some way? She could hear them outside going round the flower beds with Georgie, Mother trying to get him to say 'rose'. Georgie said stubbornly, 'Nannie Rose.' Meaning Aunty Rose. He and Rick were so close. Rick adored the child. He certainly wouldn't risk losing him.

The spills tumbled to the floor and she knelt to thrust them back into their container. For the first time, she felt sick and knew that the doctor had been right. The sheer enormity of it hit her again. Martin's child. A Fairbrother. She was carrying a Fairbrother baby. It wasn't so incredible after all; she had conceived that first time with Rick; and now with Martin. God. What was she going to do? How was she going to cope? The unfairness of it hit her again. She had wanted another baby and Rick hadn't. And now she was having one. Wasn't that his fault too?

They came in from the garden. Aileen looked surprised to find Jon sitting on the sofa still; so it hadn't been the natural thing to do.

Mrs Whittie wished them well and, thankfully, mercifully, left. Aileen said she was going to the village to buy chops for lunch.

Rick said, 'Are you going with Grandma, old chap?'

Georgie shook his head. 'Daddy,' he replied simply.

Rick found half-a-crown in his pocket. 'You can spend that in the post office.' He squatted in front of the small boy. 'Buy a little car. Yes?'

Georgie already knew the significance of big silver discs. His fist closed on the half-crown and he trotted after Aileen. Jon watched them go down the garden path, and she felt sick again.

She said brightly, 'It's his birthday next week, darling. He should wait for his presents till then.'

He sat down opposite her, put his elbows on his knees and looked at the carpet. There was a finality about his attitude that terrified her. This was the man who had danced with her at the Cadena; who had skated with her in Birmingham; skied with her during the awful winter of '62. She had to remind herself of that. She had known he had changed, but only now did she see how much.

She said tentatively, 'Rick? Is anything wrong?'

He looked up as if surprised. 'Wrong? Oh Lord, Jon. What is wrong? What is right? You're having Martin Fairbrother's child. That's right for you. Probably right for him.' He actually smiled. 'Now we've come to the end of the road – well, it wasn't a very long road, but it's come to an end anyway – there's a certain relief. Do you feel it?'

She was appalled. She pushed herself off the sofa and landed on her knees in front of him.

'Rick – darling – what are you talking about? You heard what I said to Mrs Whittie—'

'Get up, Jon!' He spoke curtly now. And when she did not move he jumped up and moved away from her. 'For God's sake, let's be honest for once! You're pregnant and it can't be my baby, so if it's not Martin's—'

'Rick! Stop it! Please!' She was sobbing tearlessly. 'Don't talk like this – as if it's . . . it's someone else! It's me! And I'm your wife!'

He came back to her and pulled her to her feet.

'I know. But Jon . . . it's no good laying on the histrionics any more. Can't you see that? Can't you spare us both? It's over—'

171

'Don't say that – don't say it!' She tried to cling to him, but he held her at arm's length. 'Rick – I love you – I told you all about Martin and how I knew then that it was you I loved! I explained everything – I was honest enough then, surely?'

'Yes. In a way. Sit down. You shouldn't be getting overwrought like this.' He pushed her back on to the sofa, but quite gently. He said, 'After all, Jon, that's how it happened with us. And now it's happened with someone else.' He smiled. 'Are you going to get Rose to plead your cause again?'

She was angry then and caught his hands, digging her nails into the backs of them as hard as she could.

'You swine! It wasn't the same – not a bit the same! And you know it! You'd lied to me and my family and Rose was the only one who could track you down and make you do the right thing!'

Suddenly he was angry too. 'You're right there!' He pulled his hands away and sucked the knuckles furiously. 'She was the only one in the world who could have persuaded me to sacrifice myself! She knew I'd do anything for her! My God – both of you – you're as bad as one another! Rose is more subtle but just as determined!'

'What d'you mean? You loved Rose better than me – is that what you're saying? I knew you had a crush on her – but it was me you loved! Me who gave you a son!' She scrabbled up again and tried to hold him. 'Rick – you know there's something special between us – you know it! Rose would never have looked at you – she and David, they haven't got what we've got. Rose is such a cold fish—'

He hit her. She fell back on to the sofa again, not so much hurt as shocked beyond speech. She put a hand to her cheek.

He said, 'Rose is not cold. And she and David have got the whole world more than we've got. Don't ever speak like that again, d'you hear me?'

She stared at him. They were both breathing heavily.

172

She whispered, 'You've . . . you've been with her. With Rosie.'

He seemed to slump into his clothes. He said, 'I'm going. Don't try to get in touch with me. You can have Georgie.'

He turned. She screamed, 'Rick! You can't!' But he kept on going. She got up and ran after him.

He paused at the gate and said in a low voice, 'What has been said today, Jon, is between us. If you try to wreck Rose's marriage, I shall hear of it. And I'll come back and take Georgie away from you.'

'Rick – listen – I don't care about any of that – don't go!'

He opened the gate and started down the road. Mrs Whittie's curtains twitched. Jon went back indoors.

She had never felt so lonely in her life.

Ten

Aileen wanted to send for Rose but Jon would not hear of it.

'I don't want to see Rose,' she said adamantly, sitting on the sofa in the front room, refusing even to cuddle Georgie, just gazing into space.

Aileen made the mistake of trying to joke about it.

'Not ever again?' she said, as if Jon were still a baby and she was jollying her out of a bad mood.

Jon said woodenly, 'Not ever again.'

That shocked Aileen. She hardly knew what to say. She had come back from the village with a tired, fractious Georgie, to find that Rick had gone and Jon was in this peculiar state – almost a trance. She had to get lunch for Georgie – the chops went into the fridge because it was obvious Jon would not eat and Rick, for whom they had been bought, was not going to be there.

She put Georgie to bed for his nap and came back down to try again to find out what was wrong.

'Darling. Rose has always been able to sort out your troubles for you! Why don't you give her a chance now?'

Jon said, 'She is the last person . . . Ma, if you breathe a word of this to Rose, I'll – I'll – kill myself!'

Aileen ignored this. It was a threat Jon had used before and meant nothing.

'Rose could talk to Rick. She's done it before.'

'I know.' There was a wealth of bitterness in Jon's voice.

'I don't see why you speak like that, Jon. It worked, didn't it?'

'Yes. It worked. But not this time, Ma. Rick has gone for good. You missed Mrs Whittie's announcement, didn't you? I'm having a baby and Rick knows it's not his. So he's gone. It's quite simple. Rick . . . has . . . gone.'

'You're having a baby?' Aileen sat down suddenly. 'Oh Jon – my poor girl! Is there no end to it! Oh my dear . . . ' She put her head in her hands and rocked back and forth.

Jon managed to pull herself up and touched Aileen's hair briefly.

'I'm sorry, Ma. It's a mess, isn't it?'

Aileen's distress was much worse than Jon had anticipated. She had relied on her mother to find a silver lining; to say they would pull together. In the wilderness of Rose's betrayal and Rick's desertion, Aileen had been her one sanctuary. But suddenly all Aileen's quiet reassurance and strength had gone. She keened like a Jewish woman at the Wailing Wall. It was horrible.

Jon said, 'Ma! Stop it! We'll manage! If the worst comes to the worst I'll see Martin Fairbrother!'

Aileen looked up. Her face was wet and her eyes drowned. She said, 'You don't understand, Jon. It's my fault. It's been bred in you. Hasn't Rose ever told you? Haven't you worked it out for yourself?'

Jon said flatly, 'I don't know what you're talking about.'

'You! Me! Jonathan was drowned in the Battle of the Atlantic, Jon! In 1942! You were born in 1946!'

Jon stared at the mottled face as if she'd never seen it before. There was silence in the room except for Aileen's indrawn sobs.

At last she said, 'Did Rose know this?'

'Yes. Of course. She was five. We came home together and talked about the new baby.'

Jon dropped her head. It was yet another betrayal.

She said in a low voice, 'Who is my father?'

'I didn't even know his full name. He was a naval lieutenant. Married. We . . . fell in love.'

'Why didn't he get a divorce – if he loved you—?'

'I wouldn't tell him. I wouldn't have let him, Jon. He had a child. A son.'

'Did you talk about it?'

175

Aileen's voice thinned to a thread. 'I only knew him for eight hours. It was VJ night. A big party. I went with Mabe and Joe. And Rose.'

There was another long pause. Then Jon said, 'A one-night stand?'

Aileen sobbed but said, 'Yes. Yes, I suppose . . . I think we were properly in love. But . . . yes, that's all it was.'

'Well, I wasn't properly in love with Martin Fairbrother. That's for sure. So we've both been . . . ' Jon stood up and tried to laugh. It sounded like a croak. 'We've both been taken for a ride! Eh Ma? In every sense of the phrase!'

Aileen said, 'Jon – please—'

Jon said, 'Ma. I have to be by myself. D'you mind if I go on to the hill?'

Aileen collapsed on to the chair again. She looked beaten. 'All right, darling,' she said in a low voice.

Jon had never felt lonely before. Not like this. This brought home the true meaning of the word. Alone. Solitary. Isolated. All the people she had relied on were gone. Rick, Rosie, and now Mother. She walked down the back garden and through the gate on to the hill. The heat was heavy; humid. She began to walk up the 'ski slope' and felt as if she would burst out of her skin. That was what she wanted to do. Burst out of her skin. Be nothing. Soak into the summer-hard surface of the hill. Belong to something. Properly belong.

She whispered to her moving feet, 'Bastard.' That's what she was. A bastard. She had never associated loneliness with the word before. Now, its full implication hit her between the eyes. Unwanted. An embarrassment. In the end, just a dirty word.

She reached the top of the slope and stared across at the church. She had never felt the reality of God; now quite suddenly she saw that there must be something in all that stuff. A jealous God. Visiting the sins of the fathers unto the . . . she lost track of the quotation and said again – louder this time – 'Bastard!'

She went into the church and sat in one of the pews at the back. The place was empty. Its silence bit into her

176

preoccupation. The heat was sucked from her and she started to shiver. She was so filled with hatred that again she wondered if she might burst. She hated everyone who had brought her to this place. Her mother; her unknown lecher of a father; her sister who was no longer her sister, who was a betrayer, a female Judas. Rick, who was another traitor. Martin Fairbrother because he had mistaken a flirtation for something else. Even David who was Martin's brother and so besottedly in love with Rose. But mostly, she hated herself. And what was inside her.

Without conscious thought she got up and walked the length of the nave to the tiny door of the bell tower. Inside was the vertical ladder to the belfry. She began to climb.

She'd done this before; three or four times. It had been an act of rebellion, of sheer devilment; another time it was done for a dare; another, more romantically, to see the view. This time there was a reason; she did not let the reason become conscious until she fought her way past the single bell and out on to the parapet. And then suddenly it was obvious. She was going to burst her skin herself. She was going to become one with the only thing that had not betrayed her. The earth itself.

She stood there, holding the head of a gargoyle in her left arm, staring down. Childishly she thought: 'They'll all be sorry. They'll wish they'd told me the truth. Been kinder to me. Understood . . . ' And she began to count to ten.

She had reached seven and closed her eyes because that way the vision of her nineteen-year-old body plummeting to earth was not quite so horrific. But as she murmured 'Seven,' she felt a tiny jerky movement in the crook of her left elbow. She opened her eyes and looked at the gargoyle, startled. There was a crack in its neck. She said aloud, 'Eight.' And the head dropped off.

Without volition her right arm reached back and grabbed at the arrow slit through which she'd emerged with such difficulty. It was so quick that she was able to watch the head bounce off the chancel roof and crunch on to the pavement. She hung on, her left arm waving in the air, her eyes now wide. That could have been her. She hadn't realized the chancel roof would break her fall. She would not have reached the earth probably. She might have broken her back on the apex of that roof and lain there for weeks till someone found her.

Again she closed her eyes, fighting nausea. And after several very long seconds, she began to worm her way back through the tiny aperture and on to the ladder. And halfway down the ladder she began to weep. She couldn't even finish her own useless life. She didn't have the guts to do that. She had blamed everyone for her ghastly predicament; and all the time, it was her own fault.

She sobbed aloud and the sound rushed up the tower and back again, gathering a tinny echo from the bell on the way. She took a hand from the rung above her to scrub at her eyes, and her foot slipped, the weight of her body jerked on to the remaining arm, for a moment she swung still thinking she was all right, she could regain her footing and go on down the ladder, but then the sweaty palm slipped off the rung, and she fell.

Aileen went to see Rose. The weather had broken and a dreary rain fell; beneath her plastic mack Aileen sweated profusely. She should have worn a coat and carried an umbrella, but it was so difficult to manage a pushchair and an umbrella.

She sat in the breakfast room, convinced that Rose must blame her for everything. After all the girl had seen her with Philip; of all people in the world, Rose knew what her mother really was. Aileen knew full well why Rose had been so shocked to find Jon and Martin Fairbrother together. It must have been a nightmare for the poor child: history repeating itself.

She said, 'I can't think what to do, Rosie. My brain is addled.'

Rose put her arm across her mother's bowed shoulders and squeezed gently.

'I'm not surprised. It's such a mess. I feel responsible in a way. After all I was the one who persuaded Rick to marry poor Jon in the first place.'

'The thing is, she still loves him. It's because he rejected her that she tried to commit suicide.'

'Darling. She didn't try—'

'Face facts, Rosie! You keep saying it was an accident – but why on earth would she climb the church tower if—'

'*She* says that, darling! We don't know why she went up the tower, she doesn't know herself. But she does know it was an accident. She'd tell us if she'd deliberately done something foolish. You know how brutally honest she can be.'

'There's something you don't know, Rose.' Aileen looked out of the window. Maud had just come around the side of the house wheeling the high twin pram with Georgie sitting on the apron, almost invisible in his sou'wester. They had been shopping. Maud had risen splendidly to this occasion; she looked indefatigable in her aristocratic Burberry with a scarf hiding her sparse hair.

Aileen said hurriedly, 'Jon was expecting a baby. Martin's. That's why Rick left—'

She stopped, expecting Rose to react strongly to her words, but Rose was strangely calm about it. She looked her shock, then she said, 'Poor Jon. It's not fair, is it?'

Aileen knew this was some reference to her own past: to that history being repeated. But there was no time to say more. The door opened and Georgie, lifted from the pram, ran in brandishing one of the American flags that were being sold everywhere in honour of Major White's walk in space.

Maud was such a comfort. Aileen let herself be taken off to the upstairs flat while Rose put the twins down for their nap and bribed Georgie to lie down too in the spare cot. Maud was strong and eminently respectable; very like Rose. Aileen relaxed in her presence, allowed herself to drink a medium dry sherry; watched her while she prepared a snack lunch for the three of them.

They sat over coffee, waiting for the babies to wake again. Rose had planned to visit Jon that afternoon, but Aileen had to tell her that Jon had insisted on no more visitors.

179

'She does blame me,' Rose said steadily. 'I knew it when I went in yesterday. The nurse told me she did not want to see me, but I went anyway. She was so odd. As if there was a wall between us.'

Maud was kindly impatient. 'Rosamund, dear. How could she possibly blame you? Rick was always very . . . volatile. She can't blame you for that.'

Maud knew that Rick had left Jon; no more.

Aileen nodded. 'Jon is ill, darling. Whatever you say, she tried to . . . she is mentally ill. That is not your fault.'

Rose said, 'We must get this news to Rick. Somehow. If he came to see her—'

Aileen shot her a look over Maud's head. 'You know he won't do that, Rosie.'

'It's the only way,' Rose said stubbornly. 'You cannot cope with this, Mother. And Georgie.'

'Of course I can!' Aileen interrupted quickly and robustly. 'Another year and he can go to nursery school and Jon can get a job.'

But Maud agreed with Rose.

'It won't do,' she said worriedly. 'You've been doing too much as it is, Aileen. There must be some other way.'

Rose said slowly, 'There is. Jon must go to Newcastle. Be with her husband.'

'Well, obviously.' Maud tried to smile. 'But I gather that is not what he wants. Do you think this . . . accident . . . will make him change his mind?' She swallowed, embarrassed; after all this was not, strictly speaking, her business. 'Forgive me, but it might seem to him that Joanna is trying to blackmail him. Emotionally, I mean.'

Rose said, 'I must talk to David. There is a way.'

She would say no more. After a while, Aileen put on her mack again and went to visit Jon, and Rose took the children for a damp walk to the park.

Rose wished so much she could be absolutely straight with David. Not only did it go terribly against the grain to deceive him – as she must do – but she needed his considered judgement of her plan. She no longer trusted

180

herself. It seemed that the only way to help Jon, and her mother and Georgie, was to reunite Jon and Rick. But it was a solution she wanted for herself as well; it would be such an enormous relief to have Jon and Rick and all their problems right away from Gloucester – it would be so *convenient* that she suspected her own motives. She wanted the whole problem a long way off where she could possibly forget its existence. She wanted to expiate her own guilt. Jon's situation was unfair, grossly unfair. Rose herself had committed adultery – she forced herself to speak the words. But her husband had never found out and she had been able to sweep the whole ghastly incident under the carpet. If David had known – would he have left her?

Rose would not allow herself to continue that line of thought. She had done a terrible thing; she had always known she must pay for it. Perhaps now was the time.

But of course David did not know the enormous intricacies of this present situation. He said, 'Why you? I should have thought you were the last person to go traipsing all up there on a wild-goose chase!'

They had eaten their evening meal in the dining room; the candles were still on the table with the cheese. She began to stack the place mats.

'I was able to talk him round before.'

'Perhaps he realizes that was a mistake.'

David frowned into the fire. His new job was arduous and he was anxious to do well for his father's sake. It was unfortunate that within a week of taking over he had lost one of his agents, and now his sister-in-law was in hospital after what looked like a suicide bid.

Rose said, 'The thing is, David, I don't quite know what will happen if Jon doesn't go back to Rick.'

David sighed. 'That is the main worry, of course. Aileen will take the brunt of it. Is Jon having a full-blown nervous breakdown, d'you think?'

'I don't know. She won't see me. I barged into the ward yesterday, but she wouldn't talk to me properly.'

David said, 'Oh hell.'

181

'Quite.'

'I don't want you going all up there, Ros. You've got enough on your plate. And anyway, we don't know where he is, so it's all a bit hypothetical.'

'I wondered if you could find out.' Rose used Maud's old-fashioned crumb tray.

'How?'

'Well. This new ship. It's bound to be insured. Lloyds? You've got contacts there.'

'For Pete's sake, Ros!'

'You did a spot of detective work for me before,' she reminded him gently, smiling, trying to make it sound reasonable.

But it wasn't reasonable any more. She was a wife and a mother now and had other responsibilities.

'I'll see,' he said noncommittally.

If it had been any other man, Rose would have assumed that was that. But she knew David would take it a step further.

She did not consider that the step might be to visit Jon in hospital.

He went the next day, in the morning. He took the precaution of telephoning ahead and asking permission to make a special visit. When he went into the ward another man was sitting with Jon. It was the Reverend Murchison from Churchdown. He stood up with alacrity, relieved to be leaving such a recalcitrant patient. Jon looked past both men, her expression dark and sullen.

'Well . . . ' the priest shook David's hand warmly. Rose had always been his favourite. Little Joanna was unpredictable, to say the least. 'Joanna is doing well for visitors today. And it's only ten-thirty.'

David smiled at the face on the pillow.

'Ros and I have to come separately because of the children.' He allowed himself to be blessed with Jon, said goodbye to Murchison and sat on the edge of the bed. 'How are you, Jon?'

'Fed up,' she said.

'You're lucky to be alive. You must have fallen at least twenty feet.'

She shrugged. 'Lucky?'

'Oh come on. It's not as bad as that. You and Rick have fallen out before.'

'He's left me. Surely you know that?' Jon looked up from the bedcover. 'Haven't they told you anything?'

'They've told me. I don't believe it's permanent.'

She said flatly, 'They haven't told you. God. I was pregnant. It wasn't Rick's. Now d'you believe it's permanent?' She hunched a shoulder. 'That's the only good thing about falling off that bloody ladder – the baby's gone for a burton!'

He looked at first shocked, then appalled at the crude brutality of her words. For the first time in three days she smiled.

'Don't look so pi. It was your brother, actually.'

This was another shock; Martin was almost eight years older than David; he was the wise and careful brother. David found the whole thing ludicrous, impossible to take in. He looked away from the aggressive figure in the bed and down at the honeycomb blanket, rucked and twisted hopelessly in spite of the recent bed-making. He thought of Aileen, beaten and defeated; and Rose trying desperately to resolve this frightful tangle. He said quietly, 'Ah. The birthday party.'

'Ah,' she said as if congratulating him.

He looked at her. She was so pretty, so outrageous; at her best she was such fun. He could not blame Martin. But he could not blame her either.

For her part she felt only his disapproval.

'I've done it now, haven't I? You've finally put me outside the boundary! If it had been anyone but your brother, would you have felt a bit of sympathy?'

He was suddenly exasperated. 'For God's sake, Jon! Do you expect me to apportion blame or something? You're Rose's sister. I want to help if I can!'

She was filled with envy. She met his very clear eyes for an instant. She thought how bloody lucky Rose was. How

183

very easy it must be to be good and conventional if you had a father and a husband.

She looked away; it was all so hopeless.

'Lucky old me, being Rose's sister. We're not alike, are we? Oh, we're both dark . . . we've both got webbed toes – did you know that? But we're not alike. What if I'm a changeling. Would you help me then?'

He said quietly, 'Jon. What do you want to do? Do you love Martin? He would be here if he knew.'

'I don't love Martin.'

'You love Rick.'

'Ten out of ten.'

'Jon, I don't know what to say. Have you told Rick you love him?'

'Of course. That's hardly the point, is it?'

'It's the only point.'

'You see – ' she spoke as if to a backward child – 'he doesn't love me. That's the trouble.' She glanced at him again and hated him with Rose. She said deliberately, 'He loves your wife.'

He said automatically, 'Don't be silly, Jon.'

'Silly? Who is silly? Think about it, David! Why was it she could talk him into marrying me in the first place? He did it for her!' She flung herself back in the bed petulantly. 'She could patch it up now if she wanted to! He'd do anything for her.'

He was suddenly stiff, formal, his objectivity gone. He had held out against the barrage of facts; he could not hold out against Rose's implication in this sordid business.

'I hardly think Rose would go to Rick again on your behalf—' He remembered that that was why he was here; Rose wanted to go to Newcastle and intercede with Rick. He swallowed. 'Of course she has no idea of his feelings.'

Jon spoke almost wearily, 'You don't get it, do you? She can talk him round because they're lovers! It's her fault that he doesn't love me any more! She led him on – if she hadn't been pregnant with Ellie and Blue she might well have had his child! He'll do anything for her if she asks nicely enough!' She stopped for a breath, and then put her knuckles in her mouth. She stared at him, her dark eyes enormous. He said nothing. Nothing at all. His face said nothing either.

At last she put her clenched hand on the sheet and said, 'Go away, David. It's all too difficult. Too awful. Just go away.'

And after another pause, he did.

Rose never knew why he agreed to her Newcastle visit. Aileen had the address of the flat Rick had taken and David wrote to Rick himself and enclosed a stamped addressed envelope. A reply came by return and at the beginning of the next week Rose was on her way north, one night's bed and breakfast booked at an address in Jesmond recommended by the manager of the Newcastle Provident Society. Aileen had moved into the Stroud Road house with Georgie so that she could visit Jon daily. They weren't going to say anything to Jon herself until Rose's return.

The journey was long and became tedious very quickly. The fifty miles north of Birmingham seemed like a wasteland full of pylons and power stations. Burton-on-Trent, a town given over entirely as far as she could see from the station to brewing, resembled something out of an Arnold Bennett story. Chesterfield, with its leaning spire, was interesting; York and Durham exquisite. But when the train trundled slowly over the Tyne bridge and into the very mouth of Newcastle, she felt nothing but terror.

Rick did not know exactly when she was coming; it occurred to Rose belatedly that David had never told her the contents of the letter he had written. He had arranged for her to be met by his counterpart in Newcastle, who turned out to be substantial and fiftyish with an enormous moustache.

He surged forward at the ticket barrier and held out a hand for her case.

'Mrs Fairbrother? I'd have known you anywhere from your husband's description.' He held out his free hand. 'Ward. Albert Ward. At your service.'

She was glad to see him – everything looked so vast and strange. He led the way across the concourse to the taxi rank and gave an address. As she watched him, she was reminded that David was the youngest branch manager in the country. Somehow all this business with Jon had completely stolen that particular clap of thunder. Perhaps that was the reason for his preoccupation over the past week.

'You'll like it in Jesmond, pet,' he said to her as they started up Newgate Street. 'Select, but it's kept a feeling of community. If you've got time tomorrow, the wife would be delighted to run you around a bit.'

Rose smiled gratefully. 'I'm hoping I can catch the first train home. We've got twins, you know.'

'So I understand!' he grinned broadly. 'David had a job to spare you, I'll be bound!'

'My mother and mother-in-law are there.' She wondered what David had told this man.

He said, 'Ah. David said it was an errand of mercy you're on.'

She smiled and said nothing. Perhaps Maud had put it to him like that. Perhaps that was why he had so suddenly changed his tune.

They said goodbye in the porch of a cottagey-looking house in a street of tiny houses. Rose liked what she saw of Newcastle; it reminded her of Gloucester and Cheltenham before modernization. Mrs Kingsway, who ran the tiny bed and breakfast house, was as old-fashioned too. The aspidistra in her front room window, the sparkling cleanliness of inaccessible places like chair legs and skirting boards, spoke volumes. She called Rose 'pet' as had Mr Ward and, though unable to provide 'proper dinner', she plied her with tea and scones and assured her there would be cocoa and biscuits before bed.

'And if you care to stay in your room till midday, it's all right with me, pet. I'm not like some who want to be polishing straight after breakfast. I let three-thirty till three-thirty.'

'I'm rather early then,' Rose said, dismayed. It was not yet three o'clock.

'Nay pet, I've no-one in at all this week. Come and go as you please.'

It was Mrs Kingsway who directed her to Topps Green and told her about buses.

'It would be easier to walk to Eldon Square, pet. But if you'd rather, I'll call a taxi for you.'

But Rose wanted to see just what Jon might have to cope with up here.

'I'll walk down to . . . where you said. Eldon Square. And I'll go soon, before it gets dark.'

'Will you be home late? You can have a key, you know.'

'Oh no. I might be very quick. But I'll be back by nine. Definitely.'

'That's fine then, pet. Button your coat now. It's going to be cold tonight.'

It was. The temperature was surprisingly lower than at home. It was only October, but autumn had gone up here; the trees were black against a blood-red frosty sunset. She went slowly through tree-lined roads to Newgate Street and crossed the road to look in the bookshops and admire the golden cupola of the university. By the time she had found the proper bus stop, she had missed at least two buses, but people assured her another would be along at any moment, and it was. She thought of the difficulties of public transport at home, and decided Jon would appreciate this. They went past the Newcastle football ground and climbed high above the city. Rose could not always understand what was being said, but the various tones were friendly. Jon would like that, too. Far below them the dark ribbon of the Tyne cut a swathe through newly-lit lamps. She identified the railway bridge and possibly the castle. They must be driving along the site of Hadrian's Wall. She peered through the windows with unaccustomed excitement. She had always maintained she would not want to travel; suddenly she was not so sure.

She got off the bus outside a cinema. It was dusk. The conductor, coloured and therefore somehow familiar, leaned out of the platform.

'Topps Green there, lady. Big park. See? The road runs along the end. You can't miss it.'

For once that was true, too. She skirted the dark, tree-lined city park. Jon could take Georgie there in the afternoons. The road was a solid phalanx of Edwardian villas, red-brick with yellow inserts making patterns over the doorways. She counted to sixteen then went close to the front door to check. Number 16. Wonders would never cease. She knocked.

The door was opened by an Indian woman in a sari. Rose asked for Rick and was ushered in immediately. The long hallway was bare but the small room at the back was warm with a fire in the grate, and old-fashioned, over-stuffed furniture.

'He will be back very shortly from his work,' said the Indian woman in a lilting sing-song. 'I am Mrs Raschid. Mr Johnson has this room and two bedrooms upstairs.' She kept her palms together as if praying. 'We share the kitchen and the bathroom.'

'You are the landlady? The owner?' asked Rose.

'No. I have the front rooms downstairs and upstairs. The landlord is elsewhere.'

'I see. It's just . . . the fire,' Rose indicated the grate.

'I light this for Mr Johnson when he works on late shift. When he is early, he does it for me.' Mrs Raschid smiled. So did Rose. It sounded the perfect arrangement. Jon would like Mrs Raschid.

Rose said diffidently, 'I am Mr Johnson's sister-in-law. Rose Fairbrother. Mr Johnson knows I am coming. I have to see him – family business.'

Mrs Raschid smiled; she had wonderful teeth.

'He has said this. But he did not know when you would be here. We are very sorry about his wife.'

'Oh. Um. Yes.' Rick had doubtless lied again. 'Well. Do you know when he finishes work?'

'When the daylight goes. He will be home soon. Will you be with me in the kitchen? I can make tea while I cook the meal.'

Rose felt at ease. Suddenly in this impossible situation, about to see a man she wished only to avoid, she felt at home. Mrs Raschid ensconced her in a Windsor chair in the corner of the small kitchen, covered her sari with a large butcher's apron, and went to work at a chopping board with a very foreign-looking knife. Rose was reminded of something . . . someone. She reached back into her memory but could not resurrect exactly what it was.

'There is very little meat at home,' the lilting voice explained. 'And we are *Vaisya*.' She glanced up from her work. 'That is our caste, you understand. Our food therefore is nearly all from the land.'

Rose said, 'I imagined Indian women were . . . secluded.'

'You think of purdah.' Mrs Raschid smiled again. 'My caste are workers and the women work alongside the men.' She straightened, looking suddenly proud. 'We are respected.'

Rose wished she could feel the same. Her feelings about this whole trip were so ambivalent; she no longer knew whether she was doing it for Jon's sake, Georgie's . . . her mother's . . . her own.

Mrs Raschid put down the knife.

'Mr Johnson tells us about your sister being ill. We all hope she will be better soon and bring his son here.' She poured the chopped vegetables into a pot and lit the gas. 'I can help her to look after him. I work some days, you understand. We are here to help our son through the medical school. But I am here in the afternoons and evenings.'

'Most kind,' Rose murmured.

The front door opened and a draught swept down the passage into the kitchen. Rose tensed, expecting Rick, but a young Indian man appeared in the doorway, bare-headed, darkly handsome.

'Ah, Ali!' Mrs Raschid beamed. 'This is my son, Mrs Fairbrother. The cleverest boy in the Punjab!'

Rose shook hands, smiling. She would guess that Ali was in his early twenties. His smile was as wide as his mother's.

'My parents are not as objective as I would wish,' he said happily.

'Parents are not meant to be objective,' Rose replied.

They were getting along like old friends when Rick finally appeared. This time, because Ali stood with his back against the kitchen door, there was no telltale draught and they all jumped when Ali was pushed against the kitchen table and suddenly there was Rick.

He was dressed in overalls covered by an ancient raincoat; his red hair sprouted from beneath a cap – not a smart cap – old and pulled down to his ears. Rose knew instantly that it wasn't simply his clothes that had changed.

The others were startled and their laughter covered the initial embarrassment. He was staring at her with that terrible awareness she remembered so well. After the first shock, she let her gaze go to the Raschids and laughed with them.

Mrs Raschid spoke first.

'You are surprised and we are surprised, Mr Johnson!' She smoothed her apron. 'Mrs Fairbrother arrived not long ago. We talk together most pleasantly.'

Rick said, 'Oh . . . good.' He cleared his throat. 'Hello Rosie. You came, then. When I got David's letter . . . I didn't really think . . . ' He belatedly removed his cap and his hair sprang up. 'Look. We'll go out for a meal. I'll change and – wash—'

She shook her head definitely. 'I have to be back at the boarding-house by nine, Rick.'

'Have you had anything to eat?'

'On the train. And tea at Mrs Kingsway's. Where I'm staying.'

Mrs Raschid beamed happily. 'I have made curry for many people! Mr Johnson enjoys Punjabi curry and I hope that you will also, Mrs Fairbrother.'

'Really, we cannot put you to the trouble—'

But Rick was saying, 'How kind. Mrs Raschid is a wonderful neighbour, Rosie.'

Perhaps it would be easier to share a meal with the Raschids. She accepted as gracefully as she knew how. This whole meeting was going to be difficult. She had deliberately not allowed herself to think of it.

Mrs Raschid tactfully ushered them back into Rick's living room and left them to discuss their 'business'. Rose made for one of the chairs at the side of the hearth and sat down. She was still wearing her coat and it was warm in the room, but she didn't want to stand up and take it off. It looked too . . . familiar.

Rick stood by the door.

'I'd better wash.' He did not move. 'Rosie. Why you? Why didn't David come? Or Aileen?'

'I thought . . . David thought . . . ' She knew exactly why she had come; but why hadn't David insisted on coming? It hadn't occurred to her before. She said, honestly, 'I thought you might listen to me.'

'You knew I would. But . . . I still never imagined . . . you've been so defensive since . . . that time.'

She said nothing; she could not even meet his eyes.

He said, 'I wondered if you would be thankful that I had gone.'

She spoke with difficulty. 'Rick. I am deeply ashamed of that day. But . . . I cannot explain it . . . David and I have been . . . we are . . . very close. Since then. But I still wish it had never happened.' She lifted her head. 'At the back of my mind, always, there is . . . guilt.'

'Ah . . . Rosie. Don't say that.'

'More so than ever now. None of this would have happened if it hadn't been for that day, would it? You and Jon – you had something mad and crazy. But something. Then it went. And she looked elsewhere.'

He pulled out a dining chair and sat down abruptly.

'Listen, Rosie. Those words sum Jon up. She is looking. For something – someone – somewhere.' He made a wide gesture with his arm. 'All right. That afternoon changed me, I admit that. But it made me more determined than ever to make my marriage work. So that we could be one family – that's what I've always wanted. To be part of a family.' He shook his head. 'Jon hated my new attitude. She doesn't want to settle down and work at anything. She wants to try new things all the time. The tennis club. More money. Your mother caring for Georgie . . . I can't explain, Rosie. You simply wouldn't understand anyway—'

'We've spoiled her. Mother and I. We know that. But underneath, she is so sweet, Rick.'

191

He nodded. 'I know.'

'She loves you quite desperately.' She leaned forward on to her knees. At least they were talking properly, without embarrassment. 'Rick, she has lost the baby. Yes, I know about the baby—'

He was tense; he was actually worried about Jon.

'What happened? Is she all right?'

'Yes. Physically she is all right. But . . . she fell down a ladder. That's all I know. She is very . . . ' she searched for a word to describe Jon's devastation. 'Upset,' she said inadequately.

He said, 'Oh God. You mean she chucked herself off a ladder?'

'She says she fell.'

He was angry. He moved from the door and held on to the back of a chair. 'Why go up a ladder in the first place? If she thinks she can force me home like this, she's got another think coming!'

'I think she's given up hope of a reconciliation.' Rose looked into the fire, suddenly in touch with Jon's feelings. 'I think she wishes she had died.' That's how she would feel if David rejected her.

His sudden anger left him. He came round the chair and sat on it. Rose looked at him again and saw that he had indeed changed. He had lost that carelessness; he had matured in some way. She wondered very fleetingly whether anything would have been different if he'd always been like this.

He said in a low voice, 'You must blame me for this. I've brought Jon to this. Wishing she was dead.'

She almost laughed. 'Rick! Don't be ridiculous! Jon has brought herself to this pass.' She leaned forward and made up the fire. Sparks flew up the chimney. 'But . . . oh I know you can't forget what happened between her and Martin, but could you – possibly – go back to how things were? Could she join you up here?'

'Is that what you want?'

'Rick, it's nothing to do with me—'

'But you have come up here to try to sort things out.'

'I came because I felt responsible. Guilty. Yes, guilty. It's all to do with . . . that.'

He stood up quickly and leaned on the mantelpiece. There was a long silence. He said levelly, 'If she still wants to come, we could try again.'

She sat back in her relief and closed her eyes.

'Thank you, Rick.'

'You don't know that she will come up here, Rosie.'

'Of course she will. It's the only thing she wants.'

'There are other things . . . perhaps you don't fully understand.'

She said confidently, 'I know my sister.' She felt almost light-headed now that it was all settled; all over. She hadn't realized how tense she had been. She could catch that nine-thirty tomorrow. Be home in time for tea.

He pushed himself off the mantelpiece and made for the door. 'You were right, Rosie. You and I wouldn't have done together. You're much too . . . reasonable.'

She did manage a small laugh at that. 'You mean, you need someone unreasonable?'

He kept his back to her but she could see his shrug. 'What's reasonable about love?' he asked. Then he said, 'I'll wash and change. Mrs Raschid does not like anyone to be late for supper.'

Afterwards she was to remember that supper with great pleasure. It seemed as though she and Rick had come to some agreement; their peculiar awareness had been merely a passing attraction and meant very little. He was really in love with Jon, and now he intended to make their marriage work well. It was good that she had been able to contribute to that. And the supper became a sort of celebration of such a neat ending. Mrs Raschid without her apron, her sari gauzy and floating; young Ali, unbelievably handsome and talented and adored; Mr Raschid, a porter at the hospital where his son was training, proud and determined; they all made a suitably exotic background to the evening. Rose knew that Jon would love these people and would be happy here. She visualized Georgie playing in the park and Jon and Rick watching him with the same pride she could see on the faces of the older Raschids.

It would all work out. They would live happily ever after.

Eleven

In the next few years Rose could judge Jon's happiness only by the fact that Jon stayed in Newcastle and so did Rick. It was a big step in their marriage; they were on their own, because Aileen opted to stay in Churchdown. And Jon rarely came to visit, except on the few occasions she brought Georgie down. He chattered happily about days in Whitley Bay and Tynemouth; and then about the Magpies – Newcastle's football team – of which he and his father were ardent supporters. It sounded an entirely different life from the secluded rural existence they had shared in Churchdown, but there were no indications that it was not suiting any of them. Mrs Whittie complained that Georgie was 'getting out of hand', but she herself was now in her seventies and young children not the unadulterated joy they had been.

It was just before Georgie started school that he told them Jon was going out to work. It seemed she had done a beautician's course during the evenings, and Mrs Raschid got her into the hairdressing salon where she swept up hair clippings. The owner of the salon liked Jon and employed her in his other shops. Aileen said hopefully, 'Jon is really settled now. Don't you think so, Rosie?' And Rose nodded thankfully.

Rose herself was, indeed, very happy. She enjoyed the kind of deep contentment that promises to go on 'ever after' simply because it asks for so little. The knowledge that Jon, Rick and Georgie were 'all right' up in Newcastle was a kind of propitiation to fate. So long as they were happy she had earned her own undoubted good fortune.

And good fortune was everywhere in her busy life. The twins started school and got measles, but not badly. Madcap Ellie fell downstairs and was not even bruised. During Georgie's visits Blue usually managed a fist fight, but so far had escaped with a cut lip.

Maud too blossomed. She took up her needlework again and made new curtains and covers for the Snow-White house, which delighted Aileen. She rediscovered old friends and had supper parties in the upstairs flat and invited David and Rose.

As for Aileen, she made an art out of living alone. She had good friends in Mrs Whittie and the Murchisons, but she chose to detach herself for long periods. She would walk on the hill, write letters, work in the garden. She created again the kind of atmosphere she'd done when they first arrived in the Snow-White house. It was her special talent. Just as then she had made a secure haven for Rose and Jon, cocooning them in love and respectability and convention, so now she made for herself a genteel retirement. The girls loved visiting her; in the summer they picnicked outside, gathered wild flowers, pressed them between the pages of *The Wonderland of Knowledge*. In the winter there were muffins on long toasting forks by the fire, snakes and ladders, photograph albums to be pasted and labelled. Even Georgie responded to the domestic routine and apart from having to kick a ball daily down the ski slope – and one time through Mrs Whittie's kitchen window – he made the best of a dull job and restrained his outbursts to scathing comments on the television programmes.

But for Rose, the most contented member of her family was David. She loved to watch him take a positive joy in everything he did. He became an expert with the roses and each spring would prune them to mere stumps which flowered riotously in the summer. Each morning when he woke, he would smile as if it were Christmas. At night he would pillow Rose's head into his shoulder and breathe into her hair and they would talk about what had happened during the day: the twins, the office, Charles and Arney. He rarely mentioned Martin; June had improved since the

196

boys went to boarding school. 'She never really liked them,' David commented acutely.

David was good at his job; Rose knew that because Miss Westlake told her so and Miss Westlake was obsessively truthful. One Sunday on her return from church, she said, 'He runs a happy ship at the office, does your husband.' And Rose said, 'He does that here, too.'

Miss Westlake was a pillar of the Methodist church and took the girls to Sunday school there. They were at the age when they collected illustrated texts for their Bibles; Ellie's were dog-eared and often nibbled at the corners. Blue's were immaculate.

Miss Westlake watched Rose smooth out the Sea of Galilee and said, 'I think *you* run this ship, Rosamund. And very well too.'

This was praise indeed from Miss Westlake. Rose smiled and just hoped Blue would not seize the creased bookmark and hurl it into the fire – or at least not until Miss Westlake had departed.

'It runs itself,' she demurred. 'Just good luck.'

'We make our own luck.' Miss Westlake stood up and dusted off her best coat. 'A lot of young women might be bored with what you have here – ' she lengthened her top lip over her teeth with difficulty. 'But the secret of—'

Blue's hand shot out, the illustration of the Sea of Galilee went sailing over the nursery guard into the fire, Ellie howled, and they never knew just what secret Miss Westlake referred to. But Rose had already guessed who might be among the other 'young women'. Miss Westlake had been dragged willy-nilly into Jon's marital troubles twice, and made no secret of her disapproval of Rose's sister.

Rose took her to the door and tried to reassure her. 'Jon has a job now, you know. She works as a beautician in a chain of hairdressing shops.'

'So I hear,' Miss Westlake said in a voice of foreboding.

When the girls started school, Rose and David bought another car. Ostensibly it was a birthday present for Blue and Ellie. It was an old banger and they were allowed to decorate it as they wished. They called it their Fairy Coach, and by the time Georgie came down for the summer holidays it sported lace curtains and minuscule teasets on the rear window ledge. He was frankly jealous.

'It's not fair,' he stated. 'We haven't got a car and Uncle Stan won't even let me take my football in his!'

'Uncle Stan?' Rose tucked in his shirt as he clambered into the back seat – with great difficulty as Blue and Ellie had filled it with their dolls.

'Mum's boss,' he said briefly and with the same tone of casual offhandedness that was Jon all over again.

'Oh.'

Blue yelled, 'Leave Miranda alone, Georgie! You'll break her arm!'

Ellie said soothingly, 'You can sit next to Teddy if you like, Georgie.'

Georgie snapped, 'Her arm is digging into my—'

Blue snatched Miranda away, realized that Georgie had been deliberately twisting the plastic arm, and dealt with him summarily. He retaliated. Rose ordered Blue to behave herself.

Ellie said righteously, 'I don't like fighting. Georgie, you won't fight with me, will you?'

Georgie did not deign a reply, but he put a protective arm around his cousin's shoulders. Blue simmered, furiously.

Rose waved to Maud and rolled her eyes. They chugged out of the gate and made for the Bristol Road and the Severn Wildfowl Trust which was their outing for the day.

'Do you see much of Uncle Stan?' she asked casually as soon as they were out of the traffic.

Georgie laughed. 'Too much, Daddy says.' He leaned forward. 'Uncle Stan used to play for Newcastle.' Blue made a sound of disdain and he added defiantly, '*I* like him!'

Rose was filled with Miss Westlake's foreboding.

Jon came down to take Georgie home for his second year at school. It was one of her rare and always flying visits. She looked different. Somehow brittle. Her hair was a deep auburn, her brows plucked to thin and elegant arches, her eyes outlined as was the fashion, with false lashes almost sweeping her cheeks. She could stay just one night.

'Ma can't put up with me for longer than that!' she joked, darting Rose a series of glances from beneath the eyelashes as if looking for something.

'Anyway, how are you, Rose? How's Maud? How's David? I can see Blue and Ellie are as gorgeous as ever!'

She had brought them tiny satchels printed with their names. They shrieked their delight; they loved Jon and the aura of excitement and glamour she brought with her.

Rose nodded in reply to the barrage of enquiry and said, 'What about you? You look very professional somehow!'

'Well, I'm my own advertisement!' Jon made a face. 'It seems to work. I'm rushed off my feet.'

'Is everything . . . all right?' Rose had never asked outright about Jon's marriage. Jon had never told her anything. She had gone up to Newcastle with Georgie four years ago as if nothing had ever happened.

'Fine. Absolutely fine.' Another darting glance. 'And you? Is everything all right with you?'

'Yes. But then we're so . . . ' Rose did not know what to say to describe their happiness. 'We're so ordinary.'

Jon laughed as if relieved. 'You can say that again!' She sobered and added sincerely, 'Listen Rosie, now the girls are at school, you could work again.'

Rose nodded. 'There are part-time posts in the library service of course. But sometimes the hours are difficult. With a family.'

'You've got Maud on tap! More than I've got!' Jon pouted childishly.

Rose said, 'I thought perhaps Mrs Raschid would help out with Georgie. She was such a nice woman.'

'She's a saint.' Jon laughed. 'And therein is the rub! Because I'm not. Still—' she shrugged. 'Ali's wonderful. He brings his books into our room and listens out for Georgie some nights.'

Rose wanted to ask a lot of questions. Where was Rick in the evenings? Did he go out with Jon or was she alone? Or with someone else?

But if Jon told her the truth – unlikely – it might be unpalatable, so instead she said, 'I wouldn't want to put on Maud. She does such a lot for us as it is.'

'Ma would always come down. You should get out, Rosie. You're . . . you'll become . . . narrow.'

Rose said pacifically, 'We'll see.'

The girls enjoyed school. They were popular – the two of them seemed to offer a double security to anyone in need of friendship – but they were self-sufficient and never wanted anyone to come home to tea or to explore the interior of the Coach. Rose was also self-contained; she had been too busy to make friends or socialize since the twins were born, and now quite suddenly she found herself with time on her hands.

It was as if David had anticipated this.

'I've had a word with your mother – and mine of course – and we're going off by ourselves now and then, Ros. Would you like that?'

They were cutting off the early chrysanthemums which had crisped in the first frost of the year. David had arrived home unexpectedly for lunch and announced he was going to take an occasional half-day. Rose was delighted.

She said now, holding secateurs awkwardly in her gloved hand, 'Well, yes. I suppose so. But . . . why?'

He picked up a sack full of dead flowers and laughed. 'Oh Ros! What a reaction! Do we have to have a reason to spend time together?'

She was honestly bewildered. 'But we are together. Now. Here.'

He went behind the shed to dump the flowers in the compost bin; she followed almost anxiously.

'Yes.' He shook the sack vigorously. 'And in one hour's time you will be getting the Coach out to pick the girls up from school and then—' he paused to give the sack a last shake and she said, 'And then we'll all be together!'

He laughed again and came to her. His arms went round her gently and she looked into his face and saw her own love mirrored there. She thought suddenly: if I hadn't met

David I'd never have married – there is no-one else in the whole world for me.

He said quietly, 'I'd like to have you to myself, darling. Just a long weekend now and then. Perhaps one before the winter sets in, and then next spring . . . we'll see.'

She said in the same voice, 'Thank you, darling.'

He kissed her very gently and when he drew back she stared into those clear brown eyes and for the first time in their marriage, could not read them.

She said quickly, 'David, are you all right?'

He smiled. 'Of course.'

'You're sure?'

'Listen, Ros. So long as I have you, I shall be all right.'

She pulled off her glove and put her hand to his cheek. He felt very cold. But, after all, it was a cold day.

'Then you'll always be all right. Because you won't get rid of me!'

She smiled and he smiled back. She pulled his head down and kissed him.

He whispered, 'Sure?'

She said very solemnly, 'Absolutely sure.'

They went to Lynmouth, staying at the Lobster Pot almost on the jetty. They walked to the lighthouse with its brazier perched on the top and looked back at the land mass facing the sea.

'We'll go up to Lynton on the rack railway,' David said enthusiastically. 'Isn't this terrific, Ros?'

'It is,' she agreed contentedly. Then, suddenly fervent, 'We're so lucky, David. Everything goes well for us.'

He squeezed her hand. 'We shall have problems, I expect,' he said as if reassuring her. 'Ellie will fall for rotters. Blue will want to be the first woman prime minister.'

'Mother might win the pools,' Rose went on – Aileen had started doing Littlewoods last week. 'And she'll take Maud on a world cruise—'

'Where they will meet two ageing film stars who'll marry them for their money!'

They laughed helplessly and a wave hit the side of the pier and soaked them. They ran back to the inn shaking themselves like dogs, and in the lee of the public bar he kissed her.

Later they went up to Lynton on the water-weighted rack railway, browsed through the shops, descended again to dinner laid on a table close to a log fire in the lounge. The season was over and they were the only guests in the inn. Somehow, ridiculously, it made them feel conspiratorial. They giggled and held hands and drew apart when the landlord's wife brought in their steak and kidney pudding.

David said, 'D'you know, Ros, we missed out on this. Being young. Being silly.'

She thought about it and nodded. 'There were times . . . when we went to the cinema—'

'We both liked coffee creams—'

'And having tea at Lawrence's.'

'But when Dad died—'

'And the business with Rick and Jon. They were so young and foolish I suppose we reacted the other way.'

'Perhaps.' He grinned. 'We might make that our project now – to make up for it!'

It sounded crazy and very attractive.

When they got back, very late on Sunday evening, still with the feeling that they had played truant, they were unbearably touched by the note propped on the stairs which read: 'Sleep well. Blue and Ellie have been angels.'

They had a weekend in London in November and 'did' a show. Then it was Christmas and Jon brought Georgie down to stay with Aileen. The two families got together on Christmas Day and Rose could have imagined it was like the old days, except that her mother had very little to say and Jon had too much. Rose had suggested that Martin and June and the boys could come to them on Boxing Day as usual. She was careful never to risk a meeting between Jon and Martin and was thankful that David never queried this.

202

Charles and Arney were a much easier option than Georgie. Blue said, 'I think Arney is going to be a nice boy. I love him better than Georgie.' And unexpectedly Ellie rushed to Georgie's defence. 'Arney doesn't like us as much as Georgie likes us. Georgie is . . . ' she searched for the right words. 'Georgie is ours. He b'longs to us. Doesn't he, Mummy?'

It was David who replied. 'Mummy was there when he was born, so in a way he is rather special.' He smiled. 'Charles is solemn, Georgie is mad and Arney is in between!'

Both girls giggled. Blue said, 'Charles and Arney are going to boarding school now and we don't see them much. Auntie June said she couldn't stand them any more!'

Rose did not dare to meet David's clear gaze. Blue was a natural mimic; June would not have appreciated it.

Jon travelled back home the next day and Georgie stayed in the Snow-White house. Rose took the girls to Churchdown in the Coach, negotiating the hill with some difficulty; there was no snow as yet but the steep roads were dangerous with black ice.

Aileen looked pale and was still quiet.

'Is anything the matter, Mother? Are we too much for you? I'll take all the children for a walk on the hill – get rid of some of their energy.'

'We'll all go. There's nothing wrong with me. I'd like a word though.'

Rose supposed it was something to do with Jon. The sense of foreboding was very strong.

They made for the church from where many paths were open to them. The grass was slippery with frost and Georgie had taken a tea tray. They had a fine old time sliding genteelly down the old ski run and trudging back. Rose and her mother took the Hucclecote path and walked down to a clump of trees.

'Is David all right?' Aileen asked, leaning against a silver birch and surveying the children in the distance.

'Fine. He's gone back to work today. But he'll have extra time off in February. Why do you ask?'

'Something Jon told me.'

Rose was alarmed. 'What? He seems fine. He didn't eat all his Christmas lunch, but—'

Aileen shook her head. 'Nothing important. She wondered if . . . if . . . does he know about Jon and Martin?'

'No.'

Aileen pushed away from the birch. 'That was all.' She started to walk back up the hill, then stopped. 'Rosie. Jon is on her own again. Rick has left.' She turned and looked at Rose's startled face. 'I wondered if you knew.'

'Left? Oh no – I thought – everything seemed so settled!' She joined her mother and took her arm. 'You must have had an awful Christmas. Poor Mother. And poor Jon. I didn't think he'd do this again. I thought he intended to work at things now.'

'So he's not been in touch?'

'With me? No, of course not.' Rose drew away slightly. 'Why on earth would he?'

'Well . . . you are the family . . . diplomat. I just wondered . . . hoped . . . '

'I think I made it clear – in Newcastle – that I was bowing out of their affairs.' Rose wondered if her mother was about to relay some kind of request from Jon. Not again. It wouldn't happen a third time, surely?

Aileen said simply, 'I'm going up there, Rosie. To live with Jon. She can't manage Georgie on her own.'

'She what?' Rose was suddenly furious. 'She has asked you to give up your home and your independence and go up there to be an unpaid—'

'No!' Aileen pulled away abruptly. 'Don't say any more, Rose, you'll only be sorry! She didn't ask me. I suggested it. I can't leave her up there on her own. She's – she's my baby!'

'She's an adult now, Mother! We've both spoiled her – let her think of herself as an outrageous child! You won't be doing her a favour if you go up there and look after her.'

Aileen walked on, leaving Rose standing. She said over her shoulder, 'You know why I have to go, Rosie. We won't talk about it any more if you don't mind.'

'But—' Rose scrambled after her mother. 'Hang on, Mother! When – what is going to happen to the Snow-White house? Oh – you can't go – you're happy here—'

'I shall be happy with Jon, too.' Aileen waited and managed a wan smile. 'But the house – that *is* worrying me. I'm afraid your grandmother might want to sell it once I'm out of it. And it would be good to know it's there. In case we decide to come back home.' Her smile widened. 'It's all right, darling, I'm not going to ask you to see her and intercede. You've done your bit, I know. But if she does ask you about it, can you put in a word?'

'Oh Mother . . . ' Rose wanted to weep. It was all so sudden, so unexpected, so unnecessary! She voiced her thoughts. 'Rick will be back. Basically they get on well – they quarrel – I know all that, but they can't live without each other.'

Aileen said sadly, 'It wasn't Rick's doing this time, any more than last time. It's Jon. She had a – a fling – with that young Indian chap—'

Rose groaned. 'Not Ali Raschid?' She recalled the clean-cut young Pakistani doing his four years at medical school. She could cheerfully have throttled Jon at that moment.

'Yes. And the Raschids moved out. And it's rather unpleasant for Jon.'

'Oh . . . ' Rose looked at the children screaming and shrieking on their tin tray. She looked up at the grey sky, full of snow. She closed her eyes. 'Oh . . . *damn*!' she said. First Martin made unhappy. And now the Raschids.

She took her mother's arm and squeezed it comfortingly. 'The Snow-White house will be waiting for you. Don't worry,' she said. 'In fact don't worry about a thing. You'll all be back by the spring. In time to see the cowslips on the hill.'

Aileen gave her small smile again but she did not respond to Rose's rallying. Rose took her and Georgie to the station the next day. She leaned out of the train window as it was pulling out of Cheltenham station, and said, 'Rose . . . I'm sorry. Try to forgive me, darling.'

Rose had no idea what she meant.

*

The trouble was, Jon had never been as happy as Rose had hoped. She had gone up to Newcastle in a curious mood: half of her deeply thankful to be going back to Rick, the other half defiant and unrepentant. After all, if Rick had allowed her to have another baby, she would never have been tempted to flirt with Martin. If Martin hadn't taken her so seriously, it would never have gone so far. And how dared Rick leave her for sleeping with another man, when he had actually slept with her sister? And then had come the awful realization that Rose was not completely her sister anyway.

Also she hated herself for spilling all the beans to David; but even that had had no effect whatsoever. David had apparently agreed to let Rose go up to Newcastle, knowing full well that she had special influence with Rick. Perhaps they had slept together again while she was there? Perhaps David didn't mind?

On subsequent visits to Gloucester, Jon tried to sound out the situation as delicately as possible; but it was obvious that everything was all right. David and Rose, against all odds, were as happy as sandboys. They were dull and conventional, but they were happy. It didn't make sense.

And Rick had changed. She realized now his change dated from Rose and that did not help. He talked to her like a Dutch uncle about trying to make things 'work'.

She said, 'That's why I'm here, Rick. I wanted to make it work before. You couldn't do that because I was pregnant. Now I'm not pregnant. So shall we take it as said?'

He looked at her for a long moment, then nodded. And they took Georgie to the swings on Topps Green and later met the Raschids. And – like Rose before her – she took to Newcastle and its bracing air and friendly people and thought things might work out.

It was Mina Raschid who got her the job at the salon. Jon called herself a receptionist but she dealt with most of the organization as well as cleaning the premises before they opened each morning. When she met the owner she told him that she was a qualified beautician. He knew she was lying but he asked to see her diploma, and she spent two evenings with mapping pens and Indian ink and invested her precious wages on having it professionally framed. He accepted it without question and told her to 'bring her tools' and take one of the cubicles one day a week.

Rick said, 'You're a fool, Jon. He knows you're lying. It's just a game you're both playing. I don't like the man.'

She was genuinely surprised. 'I thought you did! When he said he'd take you and Georgie to the match, you were really pleased!'

'He got us into the stand. Sure. But this . . . '

'Not so long ago you'd have thought it was terrific. Getting by on a forged diploma! Come on, Rick – it doesn't hurt anyone! And I'll do well – you know I will.'

'Probably.'

She did too. Before long Stan McKee was running her to his other shops, even as far as Cullercoats. He was an ex-footballer and his mother had owned the small hairdressing shop in Topps Green. When his footballing career came to an end he was still in his twenties, and had a decent nest-egg, but no job. His mother took the nest-egg and gave him a job supervising the two new shops she bought. And unexpectedly he became interested in managing them; he liked the staff – mostly young, attractive girls; his name still meant something and business boomed. He liked Jon the moment he met her; later he liked Rick and Georgie too. He would have taken them all under his wing if Rick had allowed it. As it was, he made do with Jon.

For the first time in her life, Jon had her own money. It was a marvellous feeling. Their overheads were low, and Rick was earning well; she could spend her money on herself. She bought new clothes and had a proper hair-tinting job and went dancing with Stan. There was nothing in it, but of course Rick made a fuss and retaliated by going to the pub.

This didn't matter too much; Mina Raschid was better with Georgie than she was herself. But then suddenly, Mina thinned her lips and told her no more baby-sitting. And that was when Ali came into his own.

Jon knew Ali doted on her. He was just a year older than she was and had studied all his life; to him Jon was the epitome of the Western world. She was beautiful, not rich but with money to spend; she was careless and pleasure-seeking. And she loved the feeling of power she had over Ali. She did not have it with Rick. Nor Stan. But Ali looked at her with his huge dark eyes and if she smiled, so did he, and if she looked sad, he did too. It was something completely new. Like the money.

Stan did not want her to go south that Christmas.

'What's the point? You don't enjoy it – you've told me so often enough.'

She shrugged. 'I don't enjoy it, but I have to go.'

'Why for Christ's sake?'

'I belong to them.'

'You don't belong to anyone. Them. Nor Rick.'

She laughed. 'You don't know me, Stan. I belong to Mother and Rose. And I can't live without Rick and Georgie.' They were going to a dinner dance at an hotel in Whitley Bay where Stan hoped to open what he now called a 'body boutique'. Jon would not have missed it for anything but she was not going to admit that to Stan.

He said, reasonably enough, 'You're not with them now. You had the choice and you came out with me.'

She said shortly, 'Rick's not home. And Georgie is in bed. So I might as well be here.' She shrugged again. 'Anyway I'm going home for Christmas, and that's that.'

'Rick not going with you again?'

She was not enjoying this conversation; one of the things she liked about Stan was that he never asked questions.

'Probably not.'

'Who's looking after the kid tonight?'

'Ali Raschid.'

'Bet Rick enjoys that too!' He laughed at her. 'I rest my case.'

208

'Oh shut up, Stan! Rick won't take me dancing and you will! And Ali writes up his notes when he's in our flat. Neither of them mind.'

'Ali doesn't. Rick does.'

She wished she could tell him to mind his own business; but he was a good employer and she liked her job. She said nothing and he took her silence for agreement and laughed. And she accepted that the interrogation was over. He wasn't the sort to get intense. Thank God.

They had a good evening; he introduced her to the manager of the smart hotel where the dance was held, and suggested that it might be to everyone's advantage if McKee's opened a shop there. Jon shook the manager's hand, smiling with the right mixture of friendliness and confidence.

'Mrs Johnson would be managing it?' he asked.

'Mrs Johnson is our beautician,' Stan said smoothly. 'She would be taking appointments on a set day.'

The manager nodded and asked Stan what sort of financial arrangements he had in mind. Stan knew better than to sound too eager.

'We could talk about it later if you're interested,' he said. 'It was simply a suggestion. This is a social occasion for Mrs Johnson and myself.' He smiled. 'Celebration of our latest success.'

When they were dancing he gloated, 'He's hooked. It's almost too easy, isn't it? Better than dashing up and down a muddy football pitch any day of the week!'

'You don't mean that,' Jon replied.

'Any more than you mean that you have your husband's blessing on our evenings out,' he came back.

She was late home. It was almost three when she waved to Stan from the door of the Topps Green house and inserted her key into the lock as quietly as possible.

She crept down the hall and into the back room. She would sleep downstairs and pretend to Rick that she had been home by midnight and had not wanted to disturb him.

209

She snapped on the light and immediately put her hand to her mouth. Ali was struggling out of the armchair, blinking like an owl.

He smiled. 'I have been asleep, Jon. I am sorry. But if Georgie had woken I would have heard him.'

'You mean your mother would have heard him and come to tell you!' She smiled. 'It's so silly the way she refuses to listen for Georgie – obviously he would wake her first!'

He shrugged, not wishing to discuss his mother. 'What is the time?'

'Very late. I do apologize, Ali. I thought Rick would be home when the pubs shut. Obviously he's found a bed for the night.'

She tried to keep the bitterness from her voice, but he picked it up and lowered his enormous, liquid eyes.

She said again, 'I'm really sorry. You get on upstairs now. Oh dear, you've only got another four hours of sleep. Your mother will kill me!'

'I have been asleep – you saw I was asleep.' He looked up again and added defiantly, 'I am a grown man. If I choose to stay up all night it is no concern of anyone's.'

He was older than she was, yet there was something boyish about him. His adoration of her was just a schoolboy crush.

'I'm going to make myself some tea. Would you like some?'

'I will do it—' he was scrambling to his feet. 'Sit here, Jon – you're cold—'

'Hush, you'll wake up the house. You brighten the fire. I won't be long.'

She went into the kitchen. Mina kept it as neat as a pin, all her cooking pots shining on one shelf. Jon's were stacked on the draining board from yesterday. She sorted out cups and piled them on a tray. It was bitterly cold; she leaned over the gas jet and peered out of the window expecting to see snow, but it was as black as a hat outside. She huddled inside her short fur jacket while she made the tea. But Ali had thrown some wood on the fire and it was warm in the back room. She put the tray on the hearth rug, flung her coat over the back of a chair and sat on the floor.

'Milk? Sugar?' she asked.

'You know I have it clear.' He looked at her bare shoulders, then went back to the fire to sweep up some ash.

'Sorry, so I do.'

She poured and passed him a cup. He sat back in his chair, holding it between both hands. She settled herself with her back against the arm. It meant he could look down on her newly hennaed hair and probably into her cleavage too. She had no intention of repeating the Martin experience ever again, but she was angry with Rick for staying out overnight and thought it might do Ali good too.

There was a breathing silence for a long time. She stared into the snapping fire and told herself how well she was doing these days. Of course she had got this far because Stan 'liked' her. No doubt about that. But at least this time she was keeping a firm hand on things. So long as she maintained the deception that Rick did not mind her social life with Stan, she could use her assets to full advantage. Everything would be all right eventually.

Ali said violently, 'Your husband is a fool!'

She was surprised. She had thought Ali was simply taking pleasure in this time together. She glanced up into his angry face and smiled. It was rather comforting to have someone so thoroughly on her side.

'Why?' she asked naively.

'He does not appreciate you! He should not let you go out with Mr McKee in the first place! But if it is . . . politic to do so . . . then he should be here to look after you when you come home!'

He was so direct and succinct she could no longer pretend. She leaned back again and said sadly, 'All that depends on something, Ali. It depends on him caring for me. Loving me. Which he does not.'

He said nothing to this, so she supposed he knew it already. It must be obvious anyway.

211

She wanted to go on talking, being honest for once. She said thoughtfully, 'It's not his fault. Not entirely. I loved him and I thought that was enough – he would have to love me in return. But it wasn't like that.'

He said softly, 'Ah. Jon. I am sorry.'

'Don't be. I think – now that I am earning my own living – and a good one too – he will at least respect me. And from that . . . ' She glanced up again. His eyes were so bright she could have thought he had tears in them. She looked away and went on talking. 'There has to be respect in marriage, you see. Like your parents, Ali. Like my sister and her husband. Rick has not respected me.'

There was a pause then he said chokingly, 'I do not understand that.'

She sighed. 'No. But it is so.' She thought back and said, 'There have been . . . faults . . . on both sides.'

'In that case . . . ' he was trying so hard to understand. 'In that case, there has also been forgiveness on both sides.'

'I suppose there has.' She was suddenly unbearably tired. She said, 'Perhaps if I had had a father. Yes, that might have been the trouble.'

'Oh Jon.' He tried to laugh and failed. 'Everyone has a father. Rick himself told me that yours died in the war.'

'No. He thinks so, but I don't know who my father was. Is.' She nodded. 'That is it, Ali. I do not know who I am any more. I have no respect for myself. That is why Rick has no respect for me. I did not see it before. But that is why it is.' She looked round at him. Her dark eyes shone into his.

He said, 'I respect you, Jon.'

'Oh, Ali.' He had said the absolutely right thing. She went on looking into his eyes, almost drinking the worship she saw there.

Then he put one of his pale palms on top of her head as if in a blessing. She closed her eyes, smiled dreamily. He slid off the armchair on to his knees and pulled her against him. She kept her eyes closed, wondering, tipsily, if they were praying together. And then, with a suddenness that took her completely by surprise, also with the expertise that she might have expected from a doctor, he pulled her dress from her shoulders and his lips were at her throat and between her breasts. It was exactly the same as Martin; one minute she had been in control, the next she had not. He was consumed by his own adoration of her; if she had screamed or hit at him she could have stopped him. There was no other way and she actually opened her mouth to scream and lifted her hand to strike and the door opened.

Mina screamed instead. And then stifled it with a hand across her mouth and turned to face the wall.

Ali scrambled to his feet with no dignity at all. Jon merely subsided to the hearth rug and hung her head in a kind of despair. Her dress was somewhere around waist level, her hair all over the place. The word respect was laughable.

Ali gabbled – as Martin had gabbled – 'I love Joanna, Mother. I want to marry her and look after her for the rest of our lives.'

Mina replied to him in their own language and he was silenced. She then looked at Jon's bare back, and spoke in English.

'Do you wish to marry my son?' And when Jon did not answer she spoke again to Ali. And then they left.

Rick did not turn up until the following afternoon. She had telephoned direct to Stan to plead illness. He had not believed her any more than he had believed the beautician's certificate, but he had been forced to accept her absence with ill grace.

'Don't mess me about too much, pet, will you?' he said. She chose to hear a menacing nuance in his voice and was not surprised. He was lying in wait; if Rick did not come home again, he would close the gap between them without any difficulty at all. She had at last recognized her own glaring fault.

She managed to crawl up to bed before Georgie woke and she boiled an egg for him and nagged him into washing and dressing as if everything was as usual.

'Where's Dad?' he asked. 'He's not on early shift, is he?'

Jon could not remember which shift Rick was on. She said, 'Well, he left before you were awake so I suppose he must be.'

Georgie was so like Rick in appearance. His red hair was a dry mat of curls and his pale blue eyes had the same hypnotic quality.

He said, 'When are we going down to see Ellie and Blue?'

'When you break up for Christmas. If you behave yourself.'

'Is Dad coming with us?'

'You know he's not.'

'Why not?'

'He doesn't get long enough off from work.'

'What will he do all by himself up here?'

She felt like telling him. 'He will spend Christmas Day with those friends of his. And he'll sleep a lot of the time.'

'Will he go to watch football without me?'

'You'd better ask him.'

She walked across the park with him and watched him tear down the road and through the school gates. She had no reason to think Rick had left home for good, but her morale was at such a low ebb she felt she could not bank on anything.

She intended to go back to bed, but the Raschids were coming down the stairs in force lugging mattresses with them. She went swiftly down the hall and into the living room. There was a great deal of thumping and bumping. She needed more wood and coal for the fire, but had no wish to meet them in the kitchen, so she shivered the morning away in her top coat. About midday there was a tap at the door. It was Mina.

'I have to come to tell you that we are moving into a different flat.' She handed over a slip of paper. 'In case any mail arrives for us.'

Jon felt herself going to pieces.

'Mina, you can't go. Nothing happened. I wouldn't have let it happen.'

'I saw that,' Mina said woodenly.

'It's true! If you hadn't come in—'

214

'My son is besotted with you. It is better that we remove ourselves from your presence. We shall miss your husband. And your son.'

She turned and Jon began to weep.

'Mina, please. I cannot manage without you – don't go – you've been so close—'

Mina looked through the side of her head veil. She said, 'You hurt people who help you, Mrs Johnson. That I have noticed of you. You must take more care.' She adjusted the veil. 'Goodbye.'

She walked down the hall. There was no sign of Ali or Mr Raschid. Jon followed and saw that the front room was completely empty. Outside a van waited. Mina got into it and it drove away. Jon clung to the door lintel and wept helplessly.

Rick came home at three after the first shift. He looked exactly as usual, overalled, capped, tired.

She said accusingly, 'Where have you been? I had to tell Georgie you'd gone before he woke up—'

He interrupted wearily. 'Which I would have done if I'd been here, so that's not the end of the world.' He flung his cap and raincoat over the banisters and then looked at her properly. 'What's up?'

'Isn't it enough that you've been out all night and I didn't know if you were alive or dead?' she blustered. 'I'll have to go for Georgie now and there's nothing for tea—'

'Why aren't you at work? Are you ill?'

'No. Yes.' She calmed somewhat. 'As a matter of fact I feel rotten.'

He followed her into their back room and surveyed the ash-filled grate.

'No wonder. Have you been sitting here without any heat all day? My God, Jon, snow is forecast! If you don't want a fire, you might consider Georgie.'

He went out again immediately and through the kitchen into the coal house. She heard him fill a bucket and come back. Then he paused. She shivered and wrapped her arms around her shoulders.

215

He appeared in the doorway.

'Mina Raschid's pots have gone.' He put down the bucket and went next door. When he returned his face was set. 'They've left, haven't they? I can guess why.' She started to speak but he cut across her words, not hearing them. 'Don't think I don't know what's been going on. Ali is your slave. I wondered when you would grant him favours. Mina found you, did she?'

It was so staggeringly near the truth, Jon gasped. Had it all been so obvious? Right from the beginning?

He picked up the bucket and went past her; knelt in front of the grate, reached for the box of kindling.

She said, 'Rick, I want to tell you what happened. Properly. Will you listen?'

He took a deep breath and let it go in a sigh.

'No. Sorry, Jon. I don't want to hear. Just forget it, will you? I take it there is no risk of a baby?'

She gasped again, then blurted angrily, 'It didn't come to that! I tried to tell Mina! It wouldn't have either! I was going to yell – hit him—'

'OK. That's all I need to know. Now shut up.'

She did so, gasping again. Then realized she was sobbing. She sat down and watched him lay the fire with infinite care, reach to the mantelpiece for a match, light the paper. She seemed to be doing a lot of watching today, as if her power for action had gone.

He sat back on his heels.

'That'll be OK by the time Georgie gets home.' He glanced at her. 'Stop looking like that, Jon. This isn't a movie and you're not much of an actress anyway.' He sat in his chair. 'As a matter of fact, I haven't been to work today either.'

'What?' She stopped hugging her own shoulders and put her hands on the arms of the chair. 'Why didn't you come home then? My God – all this need not have happened if you'd been here.'

He smiled bleakly. 'Murder might have happened instead!' He looked at his watch. 'Get your coat on. We'll go for Georgie together.'

216

'Oh God. I can't. I'm so cold—'

He stood up. 'I'll go then. And while I'm gone, think this over. I've been accepted as an emigrant by the Canadian authorities. I applied some time ago for all of us. But I had to have a job. One of the blokes who used to work in the yard is out there lumberjacking. He got me a job. I'll have to work in a camp but I can get to Calgary most weekends. You and Georgie could settle there.'

'What?' It was too sudden, too surprising for her to take in. 'Georgie . . . me . . . on our own in a foreign country?'

'Hardly foreign, in that sense. Think about it.'

'You've done all this – not discussed it—'

'My plans are definite, Jon. I shall go. It's up to you whether you come with me.'

'You mean – but if I stay – Georgie—'

'I shouldn't contest anything. I love Georgie. But until he's grown-up he'll be better with you and your family. He loves his cousins—'

'Oh my God. You mean it.'

It was his turn to be surprised. He'd thought about it for so long, it seemed quite simple to him.

He said, 'You'll get used to the idea, quite quickly. You don't have to let me know for a few days.'

He made for the door. She said wildly, 'Don't go. Rick – are you asking me to come with you? Do you want me to come? Really?'

He said woodenly, 'Yes. I want you to come with me.'

Then he left.

It was totally unconvincing.

When he returned with Georgie she had stirred herself to make tea and toast, comb her hair, wash her face. He had said nothing to the boy and she assumed this was because he did not really want them to go with him. She caught herself watching again; watching for any sign of affection towards her.

When Georgie was sitting in front of the television set, Rick came into the kitchen and started drying the dishes.

He rarely did this and she guessed he was giving her the chance to discuss his bombshell.

Instead she said, 'Rick, when I began to work – first of all – with Mina – you were quite pleased, weren't you?'

He polished a glass with care and put it on the shelf where Mina had kept her pots.

'Yes. Yes, I was.'

'Would you say you respected me for doing that?'

He looked at her, frowning. 'Respected you? Perhaps. I don't know. I thought it was better than joining the tennis club!' He tried to laugh and for a moment her heart lifted. But she pursued her line of questioning.

'When Stan decided to take me on as a beautician . . . you weren't so keen. Were you?'

'No. I don't trust Stan. He's a get-rich-quick merchant.'

'So when I began to do well, you no longer respected me?'

'It was nothing to do with your doing well, Jon.' He took a handful of cutlery from the draining board. 'It was the way you entered into Stan's conniving. That certificate you did—'

'But you would have thought that was terrific at one time.'

'Yes, I would. But we were going to start afresh up here, don't you remember? All that sort of thing—'

She turned blindly to reach for some washing-up liquid and knocked the cutlery from his hand. They both waited for the clatter to die down. Georgie yelled, 'What's happened?' Rick called back, 'Dropped the forks and knives. Nothing serious.'

Jon said, 'I don't know where I am with you, Rick. I try to be what you want me to be. It never works.' She looked at him. 'I can't go on.'

He stared at her. 'Is that how you see it? Oh Lord, Jon. What a mess. My fault. I see that.'

'I'm willing to take my share of the blame – but I don't know what to do to make things all right.'

He bent slowly and began to gather up the cutlery. She looked down at the top of his head. She thought: I can't

218

live without him. But underneath that she knew she could no longer live with him.

He kept his eyes down and said, 'If you decide to stay here, how will you manage?'

'I don't know.'

'Will your mother come up? Or will you go back there?'

'I don't know that either.'

'But one or the other?'

'I suppose so. Yes.'

'That's what I was banking on. Otherwise . . .'

She crouched down so that their eyes were level. Even then it might have resolved itself into another of their reconciliations. Except that he continued speaking.

'I'd prefer it if you went back to Churchdown. So that Georgie could see something of Rose and David.'

Before, he'd spoken of Blue and Ellie. Now, it was just Rose and David.

She said, 'I would prefer Mother to come here. So that I can go on working.'

And she stood up and continued to wash the dishes. It was the end.

Twelve

They missed Aileen; of course they did. But their lives rolled comfortably on without any break in the pleasant routine. Rose felt guilty because she was relieved there seemed to be no possibility of Jon moving back to the Snow-White house. And Grandmother was unexpectedly accommodating about the house too.

'Might as well let it furnished on a short lease,' she said glumly when Rose broached the subject. 'The way Joanna conducts her life it is more than likely that poor Aileen will need a roof over her head one of these days.'

Rose was encouraged to say tentatively, 'It might be nice for them to come down for their holidays now and then.'

'In other words you want me to forgo any possible income from it and hold it open just for holidays?' Grandmother looked grim most of the time, but she looked even grimmer at that moment.

'Perhaps you could let it as a holiday cottage? It's a good centre for the Cotswolds.'

'Who on earth would want to spend a holiday in a little terraced house like that?' Grandmother saw Rose's expression and went on, 'And who would supervise it for me? I'm not up to cleaning a house any more. And neither is Doreen.'

'I would clean it. I should enjoy that. And Mrs Whittaker would keep an eye on the guests.'

'You've thought it all through, haven't you, Rosamund?' But the disapproval had gone from the old lady's voice and she managed a wintry smile. 'All right. I'll leave it all in your hands. We'll open an account at the bank and you can pay the rents straight in to it.' She added sharply, 'And I shall want proper bills and accounts!'

'Yes Grandmother,' Rose said meekly. And she wondered why she could always talk her grandmother round.

The Snow-White cottage became a great interest to her. She would drive the Coach very slowly up the steep hill and go through the inventory after each batch of visitors had left. She arranged the bookings carefully so that it was always free when Jon and Georgie and her mother came down for their holidays. It was like playing house. But it was time-consuming, too, and she did not take up Miss Marchant's offer of a part-time post with the County Library. It would have meant she and David could not always get away for their 'escapes', and she would have hated that.

On the twins' eighth birthday, they held a grand picnic on the hill. Jon had run out of holidays, so Aileen and Georgie were on their own in the Snow-White house; it meant that Rose could invite Martin, June and the boys. Georgie ran wild with Arney and bragged loudly all through tea-time about 'Stan' getting him a Kevin Keegan shirt.

Charles said, 'We're keener on Rugby at school. There is an Association football team of course, but—'

Georgie laughed raucously, 'Association football! What are you – some kind of nancy boy? Soccer – that's what it's called – soccer!'

Georgie had no idea what the term nancy boy meant, but Charles turned deep red and was silent. Blue put her sandwich carefully on to her plate, turned and dealt Georgie a blow to the stomach. He doubled over with a yell.

David said, 'Blue – what on earth d'you think you're doing?'

And Aileen said, 'It's her birthday, David. And Georgie *was* rude.'

Georgie recovered enough breath to protest.

'I weren't rude, Granny! It's not called Association football. It's called soccer.'

Ellie said, 'Oh poor Georgie. Would you like a drink? It might stop you coughing.'

221

Above the babble of noise, Rose met David's clear brown gaze. She closed one eye deliberately and waited for him to do the same. He did not. He looked down at his plate where his sandwich lay, untouched. Instead, somehow, she caught Martin's eye and he smiled faintly. She looked away.

The fracas abated and Martin and Charles organized a complicated game of hide-and-seek.

Aileen said, 'David. Would you like to take me back to the house and have a proper cup of tea? The sun is rather hot.'

Rose stopped packing up the sandwiches and stood, ready to offer an arm to her mother. But David was there ahead of her and she could not very well simply walk away from June and Maud.

She said, 'Does my mother look all right to you, Maud? It's not like her to want to go indoors on a day like this.'

'Perhaps she wants a quiet talk with David,' Maud suggested.

'Yes. Possibly.'

Rose felt a definite qualm. Any private word with David could only be about Jon. She did not want David worried any more about her family.

June voiced her thoughts. 'Hope Jon's erstwhile husband hasn't rolled up again.' She spoke with obvious relish. 'That's all we need.'

Maud said sharply, 'We have a very pleasant and easy life down here, June. You speak as if we're on the verge of complete breakdown.'

June got to her knees and shaded her eyes with one hand. 'I wish Martin would remember he's not as young as he was,' she replied obliquely as Charles followed his father into a distant copse.

Rose returned to packing the sandwiches. She wondered sometimes if she were getting smug. Deep within herself there came a stirring of the old guilt. She broke David's untouched sandwich into pieces and scattered it for the birds.

'I wish David would eat more. He's getting as skinny as his father.'

Maud spoke without expression. Rose looked at her sharply but said nothing. She had not noticed David's lack of appetite or his skinniness. The guilt stirred itself again.

That night she tackled him direct.

'Who was it who needed to get out of the sun? Mother? Or you?'

He was sitting on the edge of the bed taking off his shoes. His ordinary brown hair was dry and floppy, but she thought that too much of his scalp was showing through. He was thirty-four. It was still young.

He glanced up and smiled. 'You don't miss much, do you?' He removed his socks. 'Aileen wanted to ask if we'd have Georgie for the last two weeks of the school hols. She thinks she should get back to Jon.'

'Why?' Rose looked up at him blankly. 'Surely she's only up there to see to Georgie. And if Georgie is here—'

'It's not quite like that apparently.' He grinned. 'She sees herself as a bit of a chaperone, I gather. This chap Stan threatens to take advantage at any minute!'

Rose snorted inelegantly. 'Jon is quite capable of dealing with him, I imagine.'

'Is she?'

She went to the window, opened the sash from the bottom and hung out into the garden. The air outside was as sultry as inside. She thought of Jon's vulnerability where Martin was concerned. But then, David did not know about that. She withdrew her head and adjusted the curtains.

'Most people know how to keep those kind of men at arm's length.'

'Do they?'

'I wasn't being literal.' She was alarmed. 'Does Mother think this Stan might get violent?'

'I don't know. I said we'd have Georgie. Was that all right?'

'Of course.'

She undressed quickly and slid into bed. She had removed the feather bed last month and it was good to lie on the hard, cold mattress. David's arm pillowed her neck but he made no attempt to kiss her.

223

She whispered, 'What is it, darling? Is something wrong?'

He said, 'No. The bed's a bit lumpy, isn't it?'

'I suppose it is.' She sat up. 'Let me hold you, David. Come on. Head on shoulder.' She put her other arm around him and massaged the small of his back. Maud was right. He was skinny.

She said, 'You didn't eat any of the picnic. Nor supper.'

'I had a milk shake.'

'A *milk* shake?'

He always wrinkled his nose at the twins' favourite beverage.

'Sometimes bread and stuff is hard going down. You know how it is. Sometimes.'

'How long is sometimes?'

'Oh I don't know, Ros. Coupla days.' He sounded sleepy already. Unless he was trying to get out of her questions.

'You know you're losing weight?'

'Not me. Georgie is shooting up. Getting skinny. Not me.'

She stared down at his face. In the dim summer twilight she saw his eyes were closed. She kissed him gently.

'We'll talk about it in the morning.'

It took less persuasion than she'd imagined to get him to Dr Boardman's surgery. But then he had to wait a week for a barium meal X-ray.

'Probably an ulcer,' said the doctor with his usual air of indifference. 'Easily treated with diet. Keep on the liquids and milk drinks as you are at present.'

She collected Georgie and his clothes and took her mother to the station. She did not mention the X-ray; if Aileen was leaving Georgie to return to Jon, there were problems up there and Rose had no wish to add to them. But Aileen seemed completely relaxed that August afternoon. She stood very upright watching a London train pull out, hands in the pockets of her cardigan, the grey streaks in her hair hidden by a straw hat. She winced humorously at the scream of the diesel engine and talked about the steam trains that had stopped at Churchdown.

The station there was closed now, the stationmaster's house up for sale.

'Pity the Snow-White house isn't bigger. You could have moved there then. You always loved it and it would be good for David to get away from the Gloucester fogs.' She glanced up at Rose from beneath her hat. 'Has Grandmother given the house to you, darling?'

'Good Lord, no. I wouldn't have expected it anyway.'

'Why not? You love it up on the hill.'

'Yes, but if she gave it to anyone it would have to be you. It's your home, Mother!'

Aileen laughed. 'Come off it, Rosie. You know she'd never give it to me. But I'm surprised you haven't got it now. Doesn't seem much point in making you wait till she turns up her toes!'

'Mother, you're becoming so – so—' Rose laughed, searching for a word. 'Irreverent! Must be living with Jon.' She hugged her mother's arm. 'Grandmother is keeping the house in trust for you, darling. Really. She thinks one of these days you'll want to come home. With or without Jon.'

'I don't think Jon would want to live there again.'

'One day you might come back.'

Aileen shrugged slightly. 'Maybe. I don't think so. Anyway my place is with Jon. I should have gone to Newcastle in the first place.'

'Why?'

The tannoy blared above their heads. 'The next train on Platform One is the two fifty-five for Edinburgh. Calling at . . . '

Aileen was answering Rose's question. Rose could see her mouthing words exaggeratedly. The tannoy cut off and Aileen said very loudly, 'Jon and I are the same, you see.' She lowered her voice. 'I had you. And a driving ambition to make a home and dig into it.'

'But . . . ' Rose was bewildered. 'I was only five, Mother.'

'You gave me stability. I can't explain.'

The Edinburgh train ground into the station and was alongside them. Vacuum brakes hissed. Doors opened and announcements were made.

225

Rose lifted her mother's luggage on to the overhead rack and found her a seat facing front. She fought a feeling of sudden exclusion.

'Mother, when you come again, we must talk. Properly.'

'Of course, Rosie.' Aileen took off her hat. 'You'd better get out, darling. I'm always terrified the train will start while you're still aboard.'

'They're loading parcels.'

But Rose got out and stood on the platform. Aileen closed the door and hung out of the window.

'Be firm with Georgie,' she said. 'I'll see you in three weeks. Or Jon will. One of us.'

But the following Thursday, David's X-ray revealed a blockage in his oesophagus and he was admitted to hospital for tests and to have his throat stretched so that he could take nourishment. There would have to be an operation and he needed building up for it. The whole family were shocked; Rose cold with terror. Martin offered to take Georgie back home immediately.

'I don't think you can cope with him, Ros. And if you can then Mother can't. She can manage the twins when you visit David, but not Georgie as well.'

Rose said faintly, 'Not you. You mustn't go up there.'

'There's no-one else.' He did not pretend to misunderstand. 'I probably won't see Jon anyway. She'll be at work.'

He spoke Jon's name with difficulty. Rose protested no more. Such a short time ago she had been sure of herself, mistress of her fate. Now suddenly everything was taken out of her hands. David was going into hospital; Maud was looking after the twins; Martin was taking Georgie back to Newcastle. She felt as if she might be physically breaking up into small pieces.

David was still going in to work as if nothing had happened and when he came home that night Martin broached his plan again.

'Jolly good idea. Thanks very much, Brud. Good of Martin, don't you think, Ros?'

She looked at the dear face which she now saw as bone-thin.

'Marvellous,' she agreed, nodding and smiling as if they were discussing another of their 'escapes'.

That night when David was asleep she propped herself on an elbow and looked at him, trying to photograph him on to her brain. For ever.

He spent a day in the infirmary. Rose fetched him at five o'clock. He was dressed, and grinning from ear to ear.

'I've had a ham sandwich! No problem!' he announced.

'What have they found out? What is happening?' Rose kissed his cheek. He smelt peculiar. 'Should I see anyone? Sister? A doctor?'

'My doctor is actually a professor!' David said boastfully.

'Well?'

'Well. He's one up on a doctor!'

'Well, do I see him?' she asked with exaggerated patience.

'No. No results yet.'

'Why not?'

'They took some snippets. They have to be looked at.' He saw her face and kissed her quickly. 'Ros, I was under – didn't know a thing. And if it had been obvious, they wouldn't let me go home, would they?'

She did not reply. A man within earshot called out, 'Nothing much wrong with him, missis! You should have heard what he was saying when he was coming round!'

Several other men laughed. Some of them were hitched up to drips. Rose shivered in the heat of the ward.

David said, 'Come on. Let's get going. This lot will get me into trouble.'

Unexpectedly he took her arm as they went into the corridor. She told herself he was still groggy from the anaesthetic.

'I wanted to get a celebration tea, but I was worried you wouldn't feel like it,' she said brightly, manoeuvring him out to the car park.

'I'd love some salad stuff. Out of the garden.' He was short of breath and leaned on the roof of the Coach,

227

breathing deeply. 'Those lettuce – I know they're going to seed, but would there be enough leaves to make a salad?'

He hadn't been able to manage raw food for weeks.

She said joyfully, 'Of course. And your mother has some ripe tomatoes in the kitchen window.'

David smiled, 'Oh. How . . . lovely.'

She leaned across to lock his door and to hide sudden tears. He caught her and kissed her gently.

'Thank you, my Ros. My beautiful Rosamund,' he said.

She swallowed frantically. 'It's my pleasure.' She cleared her throat. 'My pleasure,' she repeated emphatically.

It was a wonderful evening. They were almost hysterical with relief at seeing David eat again. He had little enough, insisting the anaesthetic had to 'work its way out' before he could really tuck in, but he ate more than Blue, if less than Ellie. Ellie said, 'I wish Georgie was still here to see this.' Blue, trying to remove seeds and skin from a tomato and ending up with nothing, did not refute her sister's words. David raised his brows and said, 'Love-hate relationship, would you say?'

Maud nodded. 'Blue misses him more than Ellie.'

Blue fired up at last. 'I do *not!*'

David hugged her. 'There's no-one you can hit when he's not around,' he teased.

Rose removed the plates and produced a magnificent trifle.

'Ooh Mummy!' breathed Ellie reverently.

'Grandma made it,' Rose said.

Rose had done nothing but walk from room to room and stare at the garden. Maud had taken the girls out and somehow found time to make a trifle.

The phone rang then and it was Maud who answered it. It was June enquiring about David. Then it rang again and it was Aileen. Then it was Miss Westlake. Then it was the Murchisons from Churchdown. And Mrs Whittaker. Rose answered them, hearing her own voice, bright and rather higher than usual. She wondered how this could be happening. She wondered what *was* happening.

228

*

Two weeks passed, superficially normally. David went to work and the twins started school again. They were in Miss Baldwyn's class and emerged each evening clutching homework books, full of importance. Rose was still disorientated, but allowed herself to believe in this spurious normality. After the peculiar lethargy of David's day in hospital, she filled every minute of every day. David could no longer manage the heavy Lagonda, so she would take him to work each morning, then drop the girls off at school. She would plan meals carefully, minimum bulk, maximum nourishment. David put on half a pound and she was overjoyed.

Maud said tentatively, 'It must be all right, Ros. Two whole weeks. If it had been . . . you know . . . we'd have heard by now.'

'He's looking better. Don't you think?'

'Yes,' Maud said.

It was her birthday; she was thirty-two. There were cards and presents and phone calls from Newcastle. Georgie said, 'Kevin Keegan is in the England team, Aunt Rose!' Blue, sharing the receiver with her mother, said scornfully, 'Who cares!' and Georgie blew a raspberry that nearly exploded their eardrums. Rose could actually laugh about it. She could actually say that night, 'It's been a wonderful birthday, David. Thank you for everything.'

The next day a letter came from the infirmary. She took it up to David with a tray of tea. She did not sleep these nights and made her wakefulness an excuse for bringing him breakfast in bed.

He read it and passed it over. It was like a formal dinner invitation. Would Mr and Mrs Fairbrother meet with the consultant the next day at two o'clock.

David went to the bathroom. She drew back the curtains vigorously and flung up the window. But she could still hear him vomiting. It was nerves of course. She felt sick herself.

David telephoned Miss Westlake and asked her to arrange for him to have two weeks off. He did not give explanations either to her or to Rose.

She organized the children into the Coach and drove them to school. When she got back, Maud had also read the letter and was on her hands and knees polishing the hall floor as if her life depended on it. She said, 'David is in the garden.' And Rose went through the house without a word.

He was looking behind the summerhouse where the dahlia heads still awaited incineration. The leaves were coming off the beech trees already and one had settled on his head. He looked at her as she rounded the shed, and held out one arm. She stood by him, her hands clasped loosely around him, taking some of his weight on her. He was quiet for a long time; she felt as if she were entering his body, sensing his physical malaise. Gentle nausea surrounded her, a gnawing hunger too, a desperate thirst.

He said, 'It doesn't worry me, you know.'

She wanted to ask him what there was to worry about. The consultant was surely going to give them good news. But she did not. She wished they could die then. Together.

They left much too early the next day. It was suddenly chilly and Rose could not find her gloves. She fussed about them, though it did not matter. Maud said, 'Borrow mine,' and thrust a pair of black kid ones into the pocket of her coat. David said, 'We'll go in the Coach, darling. Easier to park.' He got into the passenger seat as she was walking round to it. She went back to the driver's side and got in. Her hands trembled visibly on the steering wheel and she felt for Maud's gloves and tugged them on. Then they were chugging sedately towards Southgate Street, and David said, 'It's busy for a Wednesday.'

'Early closing tomorrow,' she replied, pulling up at the lights.

He said, 'Let's go to Lawrence's for a cup of tea afterwards, shall we?'

'That would be nice.'

The sister's office was strangely homely with a strip of carpet around her desk and two armchairs. David sat in one, Rose sat in the other. Professor Carter sat on a corner of the desk, holding papers in his hand. A nurse stood nearby.

The professor said, 'The news is bad, Mr Fairbrother. I have to be brutally direct about this because you need to know. You have a large malignant carcinoma – growth – in your oesophagus. It is making it difficult for you to eat and drink. It can be removed by surgery, and hopefully that will be the end of the matter. But it is a very big operation, and until I see the extent of the growth I can make no promises.'

Some time during this speech, which was delivered woodenly, in a low voice, Rose heard a moan and felt David's hand on hers. She took it, assuming the moan came from him. The nurse at her elbow, comforting arm on her shoulders, told her that the moan had been hers. She dropped her chin to her chest, so that her mouth could not open. Her overriding concern was for self-control. She heard David's voice say levelly, 'What happens if there is no operation? Is there any other treatment? Radium?'

'I'm sorry. This growth is too large for radium treatment to be successful. Afterwards we shall recommend a course of chemotherapy to make certain the whole area is clear. Chemotherapy is a drug treatment.'

David said, 'Yes. I understand.' He was looking straight at Professor Carter. He repeated slowly, 'And so . . . what will happen if there is no surgery?'

There was a short pause, then the older man said very quietly, 'I would estimate you will live for another six weeks.'

Rose felt herself slipping from the chair. The nurse and sister hauled her up and pinned her there. Sister said, 'A glass of water please, nurse.' And Rose said, 'No.' And everything was still again.

David said, 'Then of course I will have the operation.'

Rose felt tears of relief run warm on her face. 'Thank you, darling,' she said.

Professor Carter went to the business side of the desk and said briskly, 'Then I will see you on Monday morning, Mr Fairbrother. The anaesthetist will be with me. If you are fit we will operate on Tuesday morning.' He glanced up. 'You will spend two or three days in the Intensive Care Unit immediately after the operation. Then you will be back in the ward for a week to ten days and we will feed you up.' He smiled. 'And then I suggest you and your wife take a holiday.' His smile widened. 'How does that sound?'

After the horror of his diagnosis, it sounded blessedly normal. Feeding up. A holiday. Incredibly, Rose felt herself smiling and looked at David to see he was smiling too.

The relief was short-lived but it got them as far as Lawrence's and the first cup of tea. When David could not drink it, the euphoria disappeared. Rose felt almost angry with him.

'It's liquid. Thin liquid.'

'I could get it down. I don't want it really.'

'Try to tell me . . . please. We've got to share this . . . this whole thing. Tell me why you can't drink the tea.'

'It's rather hot.' He stirred it with a kind of helplessness that was infuriating.

'You sound like Blue! It will cool!'

'Perhaps I'll have something fizzy. Yes. I'll order a glass of pop. Or something.'

'I'll get it for you.' She couldn't bear him to summon the waitress and watch his dear face as he asked for what he did not really want at all.

'No. Ros. Let me—'

But she was at the kitchen door, saying in a low voice to the girl who was emerging, 'Could you bring us a small bottle of lemonade, please?' not waiting for an answer, going back to him, smiling brightly.

He said, 'You shouldn't, Ros. I'm not sure that I can manage—'

'You need to drink, at least.' She felt he wasn't trying hard enough. 'And this is a kind of celebration.'

He poured the little bottle of Corona into a glass and raised it to his lips several times, but she could see that the contents of the glass did not diminish.

He said, 'Where shall we go?'

'Home, I suppose. No hurry though. Your mother is picking up Ellie and Blue.'

'I meant for our holiday. Afterwards.'

'Oh. Well, I don't know. We'll have to wait and see—'

'Let's plan it. Now, Ros. Like one of our escapes. Let's go abroad.'

'Abroad? France, d'you mean?'

'No. Somewhere hot. Really hot. Spain. Or an island. A Greek island.'

'Such a long way, David.'

'We'd fly. Four or five hours. And they look after you these days. Meals and things.'

She tried hard to go along with him; she knew he needed this.

'Tell me what you feel are our priorities, and I'll fix it,' she said grandly.

He smiled, grateful. 'Sun. Hot sun. No wind. No rain. No sightseeing. Four-star hotel. Beach or pool. Those long deckchair things with umbrellas over them.'

'One of the Caribbean islands?'

'Yes please.'

'Done. We'll go after Christmas.'

'No. Before Christmas. We'll go into the travel agents on our way home and get some brochures.' He drew out a pen from inside his jacket and started scribbling on the paper napkin. 'September 25th is the op day.'

'24th, isn't it?'

'That's Monday, when I go in. Tuesday I have the op. Two weeks later, home. That's 9th October. We could go the following Saturday.'

She swallowed, wondering how serious he was.

'Why the rush?'

He gave her a wolfish smile and quoted, 'Gather ye rosebuds while ye may . . . '

'All right.' She did not smile. 'I'll go along with that. If you'll drink your lemonade.'

His expression changed to one of apologetic little boy.

'Let me off. This once.'

'That's the bargain,' she said crisply.

He made a face, picked up the glass and downed it. She was triumphant.

'You see? You can if you try.' She leaned across the table. 'Darling, you must try. You have to be strong for this operation. Don't tease me – I'm serious. You've got to fight, David. You've got to fight.' She was gripping his wrist, her eyes enormous.

He nodded. 'I know.'

But before they reached the travel agents, he was terribly sick into the plastic bag they always kept for the children. She pulled into a bus-stop, almost weeping with remorse.

'Darling, I'm so sorry . . . so terribly sorry.'

He was exhausted by the retching.

'It's all right, Ros.' He leaned back, eyes closed. She dealt with the bag and wiped his mouth tenderly with her handkerchief.

They did not go to the travel agents.

Miss Westlake called with a large flower pot so full of golden chrysanthemums it was difficult to see her behind them.

'We all knew something was really wrong, David,' she said severely. 'But we couldn't help you until you allowed us to.'

David smiled and told Rose later that he was always 'Mr Fairbrother' in the office and 'David' outside.

'How could it have helped to tell you what was happening?'

Miss Westlake said simply, 'We could have prayed for you, David.'

He did not know what to say. He lifted his shoulders. 'My dear . . . it could have been nothing. Just a blockage or something.'

'No difference. We would have prayed anyway.' Miss Westlake's strong simple faith was suddenly what they wanted.

Maud said, 'It's so good of you, Enid. Perhaps I could come with you on Sunday evening?'

'You know you are always welcome. I will keep a seat for you. It gets very crowded.' She spoke proudly; not many churches could say as much.

Ellie entered the room at that moment and heard the last words.

'I want to come to church with you and Miss Westlake, Granny,' she said. 'I want to say a prayer for my daddy.'

Everyone looked at David except Miss Westlake. And she said matter-of-factly, 'Of course you must come, Blue.'

Ellie said, 'Oh Miss Westlake. I'm Ellie. You always get us mixed up.'

Miss Westlake, with a perfectly straight face, said, 'Don't you mean "muxed ip", Ellie?'

Ellie doubled over with laughter and Blue, following her sister into the sitting room, demanded to know what was funny. Ellie told her. The two, standing side by side, brown heads close, did look identical. Rose registered them fully for the first time in weeks. She was so thankful they had both inherited David's transparent brown eyes.

'Will you have a cup of tea, Miss Westlake?' she asked, smiling warmly. People were so good and kind; she and David must learn to lean on them more.

She stayed in the ward with him nearly the whole of Monday. When Professor Carter and the anaesthetist arrived, she went to the toilet and washed her face. It was so hot in the infirmary; her eyes felt gummed up. David was allowed no food even if he had wanted it, so she disappeared twice more to get herself tea and sandwiches from the WVS stall. At four o'clock, the arrival of the barber was heralded by ribald yells from the other men. 'Sweeney Todd!' 'Here he comes – the Demon Barber!'

She went away again while he dealt with David.

'I've got a bald tummy!' David whispered on her return.

They kept on joking and when it was time to leave she was in a panic that she hadn't said something she should have.

'I shall be with you all the time. In my head,' she murmured as he walked with her to the corridor. 'Just talk to me. Close your eyes and talk to me. You will, won't you?'

'Of course.' They got to the head of the stairs and he held the banisters and looked at her. 'Know that I am with you too, darling. Go about things as normally as you can.'

'I will. I will.'

'I'll see you the day after. Wednesday morning. All right?'

'Yes. It's going to be all right, David. I feel it.'

'So do I.'

She walked downstairs, turning to wave at every other step. It was dark in the car park outside the pools of lamplight. No stars, no moon. It had been raining too and she had not noticed. Released from rigidity, she shivered uncontrollably, hearing her teeth clacking, hardly able to control her limbs. She unlocked the Coach and looked back at the windows. On the second floor, a line of light showed the corridor where she had so recently stood with David. And there he was, waving, though he couldn't possibly have seen her. She switched on and flashed the headlights. He waved both arms ecstatically and blew kisses. She flashed again, started the car and drove away. She wanted him to go back to bed and sleep.

She gripped the wheel and leaned over it, peering through the night.

'Oh God,' she ground out through clenched teeth. 'I believe in You. I know You can save him. Do it. Just do it.'

By the time she let herself in through the front door, she was smiling and cheerful. Maud had not put the girls to bed.

'How is Daddy?' they clamoured. 'We've made him cards at school! And Miss Baldwyn said a prayer for him in the hall.'

'He's fine. All sorts of exciting things have happened. The doctors came to see him. Yes, two. And lots of nurses. And one of them used to know me when I was at school . . . ' She had hardly registered any of this throughout the day; now suddenly it was important.

'Can you read us a hospital story in bed, Mummy?'

'Mummy's tired,' Maud intervened. But Rose said, 'I feel fine. I've had such a lazy day. Let's have a drink together by the fire – tell me all your news – then we'll have your hospital book.'

Maud was looking exhausted. Rose made the drinks and took them in. It felt cold in the hall and there was the slightly sulphuric smell that heralded the first of the fogs coming up from the river. She said in an assumed falsetto, 'Actually, I think you'd better start calling me "nurse". I'll have to look after Daddy when he comes home, just like a proper nurse. And perhaps take him somewhere warm to get better. Could you three manage if I did that?'

The twins looked baffled, but Maud nodded vigorously for them as she distributed cocoa.

'Sit down, Nurse Fairbrother,' she said formally. 'Would you like a biscuit with your cocoa?'

Ellie giggled, but Blue played along immediately.

'Tomorrow, we'll make you a proper cap, nurse,' she said. 'And *I* would like a biscuit. Very much.'

Ellie said swiftly, 'I too.' It did not sound right and she tried again, 'I as well.'

Rose hugged them and wished she could keep them home tomorrow. They made normality easy.

She need not have worried. Normality was impossible because a constant stream of visitors went through the house most of the day. The insurance agents from the office included Stroud Road in their list of calls, and brought humorous cards for David and flowers and fruit for the family. Mr Murchison telephoned and asked if he could visit David later. Rose gave him the ward number and promised to get in touch when she knew more. And then, at three o'clock, when she was counting the minutes until she could phone the infirmary, a face appeared at the kitchen window. It was Jon.

Rose flew to open the door and hurled herself at her younger sister. Maud had gone to get the girls and the house was momentarily empty. Rose wept uncontrollably and it was some time before Jon could discover what had happened.

'Why didn't you let us know!' she said furiously.

Rose sobbed, 'We thought – hoped – we didn't want to worry you—'

237

'And he's actually had his operation today?'

'Yes. No. I don't know. I have to phone at three-thirty.'

'Thank Christ for that!' Jon pulled Rose's hands away from her face and used a handkerchief with surprising expertise. 'I thought for a ghastly moment—' She lowered her head and peered humorously into her sister's drowning eyes. 'Come on now, Rosie-posie. This isn't like you. David's going to be fine.'

'I haven't told you everything.' Rose fought for control. 'It's cancer. Bad. But yes, he is going to be all right.' She managed a smile. 'It's just that the house has been like a railway station all day! Phone going. People in and out. Just look at those flowers!'

'They're beautiful,' Jon agreed, giving them a cursory glance. 'Look, don't worry any more. I'll deal with the callers – it's my forte, dealing with people!' She pushed the handkerchief into Rose's hand. 'Now. Blow. I take it the girls will be home at any moment. You won't want them to see you like this.'

'No.' Rose blew obediently. 'Where's Georgie? What made you come? You didn't phone or anything.'

'Georgie is with Mother, of course.' She pushed Rose gently into a chair and knelt in front of her. 'Darling, it's Georgie's birthday today. When we had no card this morning we knew something was terribly wrong. Mother wanted to come down. But I got in first.'

Rose was appalled. 'Georgie's birthday. Oh God. I'm sorry, Jon! I completely forgot—'

'Darling, shut up,' Jon said gently. 'Georgie is old enough to understand. He wanted me to come down.' She leaned back on her heels. 'Is it all right, Rosie? D'you mind me being here?'

Rose wept anew. 'I'm so pleased to see you,' she sobbed. 'So pleased.'

Jon closed her eyes for a moment above her sister's dark hair. It was going to be all right again.

She said, 'Tea. Let's have some tea.'

Rose said, 'The crockery is all used. It's in the sink.'

'That many visitors, eh?' Jon went to the door. 'Look. Why don't you phone the infirmary? I'll find my way around.'

'Thank you, Jon,' Rose said humbly, and made for the phone.

The voice on the other end of the line was cheerful.

'Yes. Mr Fairbrother is out of theatre. The operation was successful. Yes, by all means, Mrs Fairbrother. Leave it till this evening – we're still settling him into the intensive care unit. About seven?'

Rose sat in the tiny area beneath the stairs where Arnold Fairbrother – whom she had never known – had had his desk. She lowered her head and fumbled the receiver back on to its rest. For the first time today she allowed herself to imagine David's vulnerable body, inert and helpless, laid on a table like meat, like a carcass, surrounded by gloved fingers, swabs, forceps, lights. And now they were settling him in. What did that mean? More tubes . . . a catheter to his bladder . . . a drip? She wondered whether they had done the right thing. The other option – six weeks of slow starvation, but with a whole body and perhaps a retained dignity – did not now seem so impossible.

There was a scuffle at the front door. The twins leapt past her to where Jon waited at the breakfast-room door with outspread arms. Maud's face hovered above the desk.

'What did they say?' Her face was raw with anxiety.

Rose whispered, 'It's all right. It's been a success.'

Jon heard the words above the heads of her nieces.

'Yippeeee!' she yelled at the top of her voice.

The girls did not know what it was all about, but they loved the injection of energy brought by their crazy aunt from the north. They shouted too and started running around the hall with Jon chasing them. Maud crouched by Rose and held her hand.

Rose said quietly, 'Everything is going to be all right, Mother.'

Maud nodded.

They went into the breakfast room where Jon had failed to find anything beyond a tablecloth and the breadboard. Merrily they started getting tea. During it the phone rang and more people called. But it did not erode Rose any more. She felt her spirits rising to near hysteria. David was safe.

Thirteen

They showed her into a high, airy ward with beds inclining at all angles, surrounded by modern technology. David was propped at an angle of forty-five degrees, his eyes were closed, an oxygen mask attached loosely to his face. That was a shock. She had imagined the other equipment, but not the mask. It distanced him from her.

If she sat on the proffered chair he was above her line of vision, so she stood up, leaning slightly over him, watching him breathe, noticing eye movement beneath his closed lids.

Then, without warning, he suddenly opened his eyes. She lowered her face so that he could focus on her. There was no drugged clouding of his irises. It was like looking into a cup of milkless tea. She smiled and said in a low voice, 'Hello, my darling. You're safe.'

There was another moment, then his face gradually lifted in a smile. It was the most wonderful sight Rose could remember seeing. It brought him back from his shadowland into reality, it proclaimed that his reality was his heaven. Then he reached up and pulled the mask away.

'Oh Ros.' His voice was strong. 'Ros. Give me a kiss.'

She touched her lips to his quickly.

'Let me put the mask back—'

'No. I don't want anything between us.'

A nurse arrived. 'He can leave it off if he feels able to, Mrs Fairbrother. We'll keep an eye. Don't worry.'

It was a wonderful feeling. All care lifted. Responsibility was somebody else's. She kissed him again, tiny butterfly kisses that could not interfere with his breathing. Then she said, 'How do you feel?'

241

His reply was amazing. 'Wonderful. On top of the world. I could . . . I could do anything. Climb a mountain.'

'Shush, darling. Don't talk too much. Don't overdo it.'

'The marvellous thing is that what I want to do most is to live with you. And I can do that.'

'Dearest David. I love you. You're going to be all right.'

'I am. I'm going to be all right.'

She hovered over him, smiling into his eyes, and he smiled back. For five or ten minutes they swapped phrases meaninglessly. Ecstasy was in the very air. Then the nurse approached again.

'That's really enough for a first visit, I'm afraid.' But she was smiling too. 'Can you bear to wait till tomorrow, Mr Fairbrother?'

'I want to sleep,' David said. 'If I go to sleep will you be there when I wake up?'

Rose hesitated, unwilling to make a promise she might not be able to keep. The nurse made it for her. 'She will be here when you wake up,' she said solemnly.

David's eyes closed almost immediately. His smile was still there. 'Good,' he murmured. And was asleep almost straightaway. The nurse waited a moment, then slid the oxygen mask back over his face.

'He's sedated, of course. He won't remember this tomorrow.' She looked at Rose and her smile had gone. 'But you can come any time after nine-thirty, Mrs Fairbrother.'

Rose must have caught some of David's drugged euphoria because she said formally, 'How nice of you.' She turned to look a farewell at David, and the light caught the front of the mask and reflected his face at her. His smile hung, disembodied, like the Cheshire Cat's.

She would tell the girls about that.

It was as if she were drunk. She could not stop talking and laughing.

'I'm longing for you all to see him!' She accepted the sherry poured by Jon. 'He looks so marvellous! He smiled immediately – his beautiful smile – well, you know what his

242

smile is like – it's just . . . David! His eyes were clear and his skin looked lovely, sort of translucent. No, I don't mean like that, Mother. Glowing. Sort of glowing.' She giggled insanely. 'It was like seeing him for the first time! I mean, the first time! Not as I'd seen him when I met him first – I don't mean that. The very . . . first . . . time.' She emphasized her words carefully. It seemed an important point she was making.

Jon said, 'I've never seen you like this. Even when you knew him first – fell in love—'

'I am falling in love now!' Rose drank her sherry in a gulp. 'Both of us! We're falling in love!' She looked at Maud. 'Mother. I'm so happy. I want you to see him. You will be happy too.'

'But they said he could only see you for the first three days, Ros.' Maud was smiling herself, but anxiously.

'I know. But as soon as . . . at the weekend perhaps. Perhaps sooner. I'll see what they say. He's so with it. So himself!' She pushed back her hair, suddenly hot. 'The nurse said he wouldn't remember what he said, but that's ridiculous. He'll know.'

Jon said firmly, 'I think you'd better go to bed, Sis. If you've got to be there by half-past nine tomorrow morning, you'll need your beauty sleep.'

'Yes, all right. Did you ring Mother?'

'Yes. And she's fine. And Georgie is fine. They both send love to David – mad with you for not telling us, but still . . . I'll wait to have a look at David at the weekend, then I'll go home. OK? Can you put up with me till then?'

'Oh Jon. Silly girl.'

She went to bed and dreamed of David. They were making love. It was so real. She said to him, 'Your tummy is still smooth and hairless. How long before all that hair grows back?' And he kept smiling and smiling and moving within her, until, just before her orgasm, she awoke. For a long moment she could have wept with disappointment. Then the thought of him came back to her warmly and she put her hand out to his side of the bed and fell asleep again contentedly. There were no more dreams. She woke to a dark, chill morning. She was half ashamed of her erotic dream, but cherished it too to tell him when he was home. She toyed with the idea that they had met somewhere, been together. But then Blue stuck her head round the door and said that Ellie was playing with Auntie Jon's lipstick.

'Tell Auntie Jon, not me,' Rose said, sliding unwillingly out of bed.

'She won't wake up, Mummy. She just says to go away and play.'

Rose dragged on her dressing-gown and went to sort them out. She looked with amusement at the crumpled figure of her sister lying in the middle of the spare bed. She had been a godsend yesterday, arriving unexpectedly, bringing her own sense of excitement with her.

In the cold electric light of this November morning, she knew that Jon had had her own selfish reasons for turning up unannounced: maybe one of them was a desire to see Martin. Rose took the lipstick away from Ellie and put a warning finger to her lips as she herded her daughters out of the room. They all washed and dressed quietly together and crept downstairs. She made tea and gave a mugful to Ellie.

'Take this to Auntie Jon. Make sure she's awake before you leave it. Say you're sorry for messing about with her dressing table.'

She grinned as she and Blue settled to their cornflakes and toast. Jon might be terribly concerned about David, but it did not stop her from enjoying her sleep. It would serve her right to be thoroughly wakened by the insistent Ellie.

David was not awake when she arrived on the dot of nine-thirty. He lay in exactly the same position, but the quality of his skin had changed. It had somehow fallen back against the bone; it was waxy white, the hollows well defined.

A different nurse, vivid auburn hair pushing her cap high, said, 'I haven't woken him, Mrs Fairbrother. Denise told me you would do it.'

'Denise?'

'The nurse you saw yesterday. My name is Jean.'

'Oh.' Rose flashed a smile. 'How . . . nice.' It seemed marvellous that a Jean and a Denise should be caring for David; both of them bursting with vitality and health.

Jean removed the oxygen mask and whispered, 'Why don't you wake him with a kiss?'

Rose re-registered the illness of him, so obvious now, and brushed her lips to his. His eyes opened very slowly and he stared at her, for a dreadful moment, without recognition. Then came the smile.

'Ah. Ros.'

She kissed him again and took his hand. 'You still all right?' she asked.

He did not reply immediately. His eyes searched her face drowsily, his smile coming and going as if he could not hold it for long. Then he said with an effort, 'It seems five minutes since I waved to you from the corridor.'

Her disappointment was out of all proportion. She had so firmly believed that he would remember their ecstasy of yesterday.

She said, 'Are you comfortable, my love?'

'Yes. Absholu . . . yes.'

'Good.' That was inadequate. 'Thank God.'

His eyes still roved her face. He was silent, while she held his hand and smiled at him. Then he said, 'Well?'

'What? What is it, David?'

'The op. Did I have it? Did it work?'

'Oh, darling. Of course. I'm sorry, I should have told you right away. It worked. It was successful. You've done wonderfully.'

His eyes closed, then opened. His smile returned and stayed in place.

'I love you,' he whispered.

'David . . . ' it seemed imperative to tell him now. 'I dreamed of us last night. Together. And you were strong.'

For a moment he did not understand. And then he did. His smile widened.

Jean approached.

245

'Post has just arrived, Mrs Fairbrother. Cards galore for our star patient. Would you like to open them?'

At first it seemed a complete waste of their time together. But then she noticed a little flush of pleasure appearing on David's white face. She opened a pencilled effort.

'This looks like Blue's writing,' she said, puzzled. Ellie and Blue had not suggested writing cards.

It was a gaudy collage card, signed by all the children at the girls' school. Rose swallowed tears and showed David the list of signatures – Deborah, Samantha, Alexandra, Dominic, Andrew; then 'Ellen' and 'Elizabeth'; finally 'Sarah Baldwyn, with best wishes from all the class at Stroud Road Primary.'

David said hoarsely, 'I'm a lucky man.'

There was a card from Charles at boarding school in Wales. She was glad that June and Martin had told him. There was a beauty from Grandmother and a discreetly religious one from the McIntyres. Jean hung them over the curtain rail where David could see them.

'Professor Carter is on his way now, Mrs Fairbrother. Would you like to come back in about an hour?'

Rose wandered down corridors that were already familiar. She stood where David had stood the night before last and looked down at the Coach, parked below. Some of the girls' efforts with the paintbrush looked garish in the quiet grey light and she could understand why David had preferred to struggle with the old Lagonda for so long.

At some point she saw Professor Carter. He told her rather briskly that the growth had been entirely removed. He had investigated the liver and found no trace of further 'contamination'. Mr Fairbrother would be moved back into his ward tomorrow or the next day. He would continue to be fed intravenously for another week. Then there would be a 'swallow test'. If that proved successful, he would be discharged within two or three days. Within two or three weeks he would be given an appointment for commencing chemotherapy treatment. It was all so routine it sounded mundane. The crisis was over.

She came and went all day. Already the drip was working and hydration lifted his face away from the bone. He could turn his head. There was no pain – one of the many tubes saw to that – but a soreness in his arm where the needle was taped.

He smiled at himself. 'It makes me feel fretful. Like a baby. Perhaps I'm reverting.'

The next day he complained again of his arm. And his bottom was numb.

'I shall be glad to get back to the ward tomorrow,' he said. 'They're wonderful here. But I'd like to see the others. There was a chap – Bill Masters – two beds down. He'd had the same thing a week before. I'd like to talk to him.'

It was a familiar pattern for hospital patients to turn their interests inwards, but Rose had not expected it of David. She had imagined that she provided the only company he could want. Denise – Jean had a day off – walked with her to the door.

'That's a good sign,' she said conversationally. 'When a patient wants to see only his nearest and dearest, we get worried.'

Rose smiled, 'Thanks,' she said.

David returned to the ward as planned and normal visiting times resumed. Everyone wanted to see him. She had to keep a careful rota. If Mr Murchison went in with the carte-blanche of his dog-collar during the morning, David could not take an afternoon visitor. If more than two people called in the afternoon, then strict limits had to be imposed in the evening. He tired so easily. His face could flush hectically, his eyes burn fever-bright after a long succession of ill-assorted couples. He asked to see Martin and June separately; she came with Maud, and he – unwisely – came with Jon. Rose never discovered how this was engineered; Jon declared David had requested it. All that had ceased to matter to Rose anyway; Maud and the twins were certainly real, but had receded into the background of her life. She felt as if all her energies, all her thoughts, were directed towards David. She had been delighted to see Jon, but she was also relieved to see her go; she needed to concentrate exclusively on David.

On the day of the swallow test, she could eat nothing. It had become the first hurdle since the operation: for David to get off the drip. The night before, the bottle had not emptied properly and the needle was found to be out of place. The doctor on duty, young and nervous, had spent nearly an hour trying to replace it. David's arm was dark blue from inside elbow to pulse-point at the wrist.

She arrived at two o'clock and waited outside the ward doors for the visitors' bell to ring. Occasionally she would approach the portholes and try to see through. David's curtains were closed.

The door opened and Bill Masters came slowly through, pushing his drip holder ahead of him. He should have had his swallow test a week ago; Rose had been frightened to ask what had happened.

He grinned at her.

'Don't worry, lass. He's fine. Drank half a pint of soup. Anyone would think he'd done a marathon!'

'Really? A whole half-pint?'

'Really. He'll be out by the weekend. You see.'

'It won't be a fortnight till next Tuesday.'

'They'll kick him out. Need the beds.'

The bell rang. He grinned and went on down towards the phone. She did not give him a second glance; she was through the doors and almost to the curtains when they opened and a nurse came out.

'Hang on just a minute, Mrs F.' A young nurse, with none of Jean's or Denise's glow, was on her way to the next closed cubicle. 'Bedpan,' she explained over her shoulder. 'Won't be a tick.'

She was ten soul-searing minutes. Then she pushed back the curtains while she was still tucking clothes around David. 'Nothing,' she said disgustedly, dashing off with the pan under a towel.

David was drawn again. The effort of the last ten minutes showed even in his neck.

She said, 'To see you without that damned drip . . . '

248

They kissed. He hung on to her hand, patting the side of the bed.

'Stay by me for a while. Close. Closer.'

She moved. 'What is it, David? D'you feel rotten? Bill Masters said you'd had some soup.'

'It's just . . . you know . . . how do they put it – no bowel movement.' He smiled wryly. 'Sorry, darling.'

'Don't sorry me. Not me.' She kissed his forehead; it was damp and cold. 'Is this because you've had your first solid food?'

'Don't know. I've got a sore tail.'

'Is it a bedsore?'

'Don't know.'

She said, 'Darling. Bill reckons they'll send you home at the weekend. Once you're in your own bed, we'll get rid of bedsores. And we'll feed you up. And your arm will get better. You'll be all right. I'll make you all right. I promise.'

'I know. Once I'm home . . . But I have to walk first. Maybe they'll let me have a bath tonight. That would be nice.'

'Dear love. You're a hero. I wish there was some . . . some award. Or something.' She smiled against tears. 'You deserve the Victoria Cross, darling.'

He didn't want visitors that night. 'Just you. Don't bring anyone else, darling. Please.'

She remembered Denise's words just a week ago and said, 'What about Mother? She will be so disappointed.'

'I know. But I don't think I can face anyone.'

'Then that's how it shall be,' she said.

He did not mention the soup. If he had been cockahoop about it such a short while ago, she wondered what had happened since. But he was not sick. And when the teas came round, he ate a slice of bread and butter and sipped a cup of tea.

They bathed him, and got him walking slowly down the ward. He was sitting out the next afternoon and she took his clothes in that evening and helped him to dress. It was her first sight of the bedsore which was making it difficult for him to sit down. It was a gaping, open wound. She asked to see Professor Carter, but he was not in the infirmary until next week. Sister was in conference. She spoke to the small, active nurse, keeping pace with her as she swooped down the ward. Yes, they were aware of the sore, and it would heal in time.

She fetched him home on Sunday, less than a fortnight since she had taken him in. She had bought him a rubber ring which she put on the car seat; even so he gasped when they went over bumps. She slowed right down to cross the old tramrails by the park, holding up outraged traffic. She did not even wave apologetically to any drivers who managed to pass her.

David ate a small piece of fish under the admiring eyes of his daughters, then thought he would go to bed.

'You don't know how I'm looking forward to your old feather bed,' he told Maud, trying to grin about it.

Her smile trembled for a moment. 'Martin has fixed a little television in your room,' she said. 'He did it this morning. A surprise.'

'What a great idea,' Rose enthused for David.

David nodded without much interest. 'Right. Up the wooden hill to Bedfordshire, I think.'

The girls laughed uproariously. The last time their father had said that, it had been to them.

'Good old Dad!' Ellie said robustly, sounding exactly like Georgie.

Rose took most of David's weight on her shoulder as they went upstairs. She was glad of it. It was real.

She glanced over her shoulder at the trailing twins.

'Could you bring the *Radio Times* upstairs for Nurse Fairbrother?' she said in her high voice. 'She wants to watch her favourite programme!'

By the time the girls had giggled their way back downstairs, found the *Radio Times* and the paper nurse-hat they had made for their mother, David was pillowed deep in the feather bed, a look of bliss on his thin face. He was asleep long before the end of *Coronation Street*. Maud herded

250

the girls into the bathroom and there were hushed sounds of them going to bed themselves. Rose switched off the television and got between the sheets very carefully, fully clothed. She wanted to be ready for any possible emergency. She covered the lamp with a scarf, leaving just enough light to see the dim outlines of the room and David's face. But he slept exhaustedly all night long, his breathing so shallow she had to put her ear to his mouth several times to check he was still alive. And when he awoke he announced immediately that he was 'better'.

'That was all I needed. A good night's sleep. Once this damned sore has gone, I'm going to be fighting fit!'

She stared at him, amazed. He had the healthy look he'd had that day of the operation; his eyes were clear and alert.

She went to the bathroom to do something about her frowsy hair and the awful taste in her mouth. And she sat on the lavatory and put her hands to her face. It was going to be all right.

'Thank you, God,' she whispered. 'Thank you.'

Fourteen

David made a set of dominoes for Martin and June. He became completely absorbed in the task.

'They need a decent box. Tailor-made for them,' he said, lining up the neat rectangles of wood. 'Then they'll make quite a good present.'

'Perhaps I could do a box.' Rose thought of the million and one things to be done before Christmas and nodded. 'Yes. I reckon I could make you a box. I remember doing pasteboard work on a library course.'

'It will need to be a fraction over-size. So that the dominoes fit in easily. And make that nice clicking noise when you pick them up.'

Rose knew the dominoes were an important stage in David's recovery. The bedsore did not worry him so much now, and his arm was fading to a pale violet colour. Dr Boardman had sent along a nurse called Sister Gordon who seemed to have lifted all their worries and packed them in her black bag. She sat on the tweed sofa and drew diagrams to show what David's inside now looked like. She examined his bedsore with Rose in attendance and explained that for the moment it must be kept open so that it could heal from inside out, instead of the other way around. She showed Rose how to dress it expertly. She left painkilling tablets that actually worked. She suggested menus. She gave them a phone number for emergencies. And finally she suggested that David should 'take something up'.

'Do you paint?' she asked him. 'Or knit? Or sew – don't smile, lots of men do and are much better at it than women! How about a spot of woodwork? Have you got a fretsaw? You could make a set of dominoes for Christmas.'

'Thank you, sister.' Rose had gone to the door with her. 'I can't tell you how much better we feel about things since you came.'

The nurse had smiled. She was younger than Rose. She said, 'Call me Mary. I'd like to call you Ros and David if I may.'

It seemed such a suitable name. Mary.

Rose cut her thumb making the domino box, and, privately in the bathroom, she wept about it. But no trace of tears showed on her face when she emerged.

'A little nick,' she scoffed at David's concern. 'It's my potato-peeling thumb – it always gets in the way of knives!'

'But it's my fault,' he mourned. 'Fussing about these stupid dominoes!'

'They're not stupid. They're your banner - the one you keep flying.' She kissed him, closing her eyes and thinking that she hoped everything in life could be David's fault . . . just as long as he was here.

That night he wanted to make love to her and could not. She pillowed his head and kissed him and told him - truthfully - that it did not matter.

He whispered, 'I won't always be an invalid, Ros. I can feel myself getting stronger all the time.'

'Yes. I can see it happening. Of course you won't be an invalid. You're no invalid now!'

He said, 'I wanted to . . . make love to you. Like in your dream.'

She had a job to hold back her tears then. She propped herself on an elbow and kissed him again.

'Darling. Don't you think we're closer now than we have ever been?' She cupped his cheek with her hand. 'Listen. Most of what we do is – is – a sort of symbolism. Isn't it? I mean – the basic things, eating, sleeping . . . they're to keep us alive. But words – speech – signs of affection . . . they just symbolize something else.'

He turned his head and kissed her hand. 'You're getting too deep for me, Ros.'

'No, I'm not. I only mean that lovemaking is to show closeness. And we – oh David – we're making love all the time. As we breathe.'

He reached up and touched her hair. In the darkness they could barely see each other's faces. He whispered, 'Breath of love. Dear Ros.'

She knew he was weeping. She pulled his head on to her shoulder and held him. It was like the time in the park.

When she felt him stir, she said, 'Thank you, David. How was it for you?'

He was startled into stillness for an instant. Then he laughed. Then he pulled himself up on the pillow and said, 'Perfect. You were right. We've just made love, and it was perfect.'

They slept.

The first injection of drugs was given just after Guy Fawkes Day. The chemotherapy department was already hung with paper lanterns and bunches of holly. They waited, as they might have done at the dentist's, with half a dozen others, some of whom talked as if they were there for an afternoon out, others who were grimly silent. One man kept his hat on. A woman proudly announced she was wearing a wig and could anyone notice the difference. When David went into a cubicle, a nurse sat by Rose and explained that there might be after-effects. Sickness. Exhaustion. And later, maybe after the third or fourth injection, the hair-loss.

'We can supply a wig on the National Health if your husband would like one,' she said. 'And of course it will all grow back.' She smiled. 'Sometimes it grows back quite curly.'

Rose shook her head. 'That doesn't matter. But the other symptoms. How long will they last?'

'About a week. Might well be less.'

'But he's having these injections every three weeks.'

'Yes. He will feel fine the week before each appointment – don't worry. He will be able to get here.'

'Yes. I was only thinking—'

'Take it as it comes,' the nurse advised. 'Some people have no after-effects at all.'

Rose prayed David would be one of those.

For a time she thought he was. He drove home. Had tea with all of them in the breakfast room. Talked to Martin on the phone. Even got the wood ready for his next set of dominoes. But in the night he was violently sick again and again. By the next day he was weak, almost delirious. She phoned Sister Mary who came within ten minutes.

'Ah, David.' She sat on the edge of the bed and did the kind of things that reassure. With a thermometer in his mouth and her cool fingers on his wrist, he managed a lopsided smile.

She said, 'It must sound ridiculous to talk of "normal symptoms" at a time like this. But what you have to hang on to is the thought that if the drugs are having such a strong effect on your normal cells, what are they doing to anything that's not normal!' She smiled warmly. 'This will last only a few hours. The more violent, the sooner it is over.' She removed the thermometer, looked at it, and shook it back down without comment. 'You must drink as much as you can to avoid dehydration. Anything – ordinary fruit squash is fine – don't bother about body-building foods at this stage.' She stood up. 'We'll wash you now and make your bed.'

It was amazing that David accepted these proposals – Rose had tried to sponge him and been unable to do more than hands and face. Mary gave him a bed bath, then helped him into the chair while she stripped and remade the bed. She talked gently all the time and it seemed to take his mind off his sickness.

On the landing she said to Rose, 'Call me again if you need me. But I think he's over the worst.'

The sickness returned later that day, but it was mild compared with previous bouts. And then, for three days, he lay like a dead thing, sleeping and waking through day and night and not knowing the difference. On the fifth day after the treatment, he began to revive.

'He's a textbook patient,' Mary congratulated him, changing the dressing on his bedsore. 'Look how beautifully this is healing!'

Rose obediently looked. She could see no difference, except that the angry flush around the wound had quietened.

Mary rolled him back.

'Now, I think today an effort must be made.' She smiled to take any sting from her words. 'Downstairs for lunch. Soup. Or an egg. Stewed fruit after, perhaps. And wear a lot of loose clothing. You'll feel cold.'

It was difficult to keep his temperature just right. He would sit in front of the fire shivering uncontrollably, then suddenly flush and begin to sweat. But at the end of two weeks he was almost better and starting on his second set of dominoes.

'As soon as I've finished the treatment, we'll have that holiday. Somewhere hot,' he said. 'I've never felt the cold like this.'

'Next time I go shopping, I'll get some brochures.'

But it was difficult to find time to go shopping. Maud and June brought in everything they needed, and she did not want to leave David if she did not have to.

They dreaded the next appointment at the chemotherapy department. David ate as much as he could to build himself up against the debilitating vomiting. Rose changed the bed linen and stockpiled clean towels surreptitiously.

This time it was worse. He was barely back inside the house before the terrible sickness began. Mary came and sat with him while Rose ate a meal. Maud took her turn but was so upset that Rose spared her when she could. The girls and their school life receded into the background. They were subdued and white-faced; they must have heard the ghastly human sounds at night and in the early mornings. Rose wondered if she should be concerned for them, but she was not. There were days when she did not see them. She thanked Maud with a brief kiss as she passed through the kitchen. And she registered that Maud looked terrible.

With only a week to go before the next dosage, she asked Mary if it was necessary.

256

'He cannot go through this again so soon.' She clasped her hands in front of her as if praying. 'He's not been able to go to the bathroom yet. How can he get into the car next week and go through all this again?'

Mary hesitated. Then she said, 'Look. I really don't know if it is wise to postpone the treatment. Why don't you make an appointment to see the therapist yourself? Without David?'

Rose seized on the suggestion gladly. 'Would it be all right?'

'Of course. Any time, Ros. We're all here to help you.'

'I feel you're a friend. But there are so many others.' She let Mary reassure her, but it was as if she had to make objections. 'I haven't seen the doctors. I don't know their names even.'

'Listen. The name of the doctor in charge of David's treatment is Patrick. Dr Julia Patrick. Shall I make an appointment for you?'

Rose had not even known that David's doctor was a woman. She nodded dumbly.

Mary rang that night. The appointment had been made for the next day at three o'clock. Professor Carter would also be there.

Mary said, 'Why don't you take an hour off and walk along to the infirmary? You need the air – you need a break. You could do some Christmas shopping perhaps, and then pick up the girls.'

'I don't want to be that long.'

She told David what was happening.

'I want them to postpone the next treatment, darling. Until you get a bit stronger.'

David looked as if he'd put down a heavy load. 'Oh Ros,' he said simply. 'That would be marvellous.'

It was an admission of how ill he felt. She gave him a drink and said she would call his mother.

'Darling, no. I'd like to be by myself for a while. And tell Mother, no visitors. Please.'

She said, 'Ring the bell then if you need her. She wants to be with you, David.'

'I know. I'm sorry.'

But she knew he would not ring the bell; she knew he would be asleep before she had left the house. And Maud was hurt and was determined not to show it.

'I'll leave the door open, then I shall hear the bell. Don't worry.' She smiled brightly. 'It'll be so nice for the girls to have you picking them up again. Like old times.'

Rose had to make a conscious effort to recall those old times. She remembered standing by the playground gate and watching them hurry across to her, still buttoning their coats. In a way they were lonely children because they did not need friends. There were other little girls who would wave goodbye and look enviously at the Coach; very rarely was anyone invited inside to view the dolls and the pictures. Rose wondered if they had all lived selfishly, enclosed in their small, contented world. She thought of Jon tossing about on the sea of life, looking for an anchor. Now she felt the same. There were no landmarks in this new life.

She parked at the infirmary and sat in the car trying to control her shivering. There had been no snow so far that winter, but the winds were bitter. If there was time, she would get some brochures from the travel agents today. David was right, they needed some sun.

She got out of the car awkwardly, trying to hold her flapping coat around her knees. Even the key was stiff in the car lock and she had to take her glove off to turn it. Immediately her hand went numb. She walked through the corridors of the hospital, massaging her knuckles; it gave her something to do, something on which to fix her mind.

She expected to wait, but there was nobody else in the ante-room. The paper lanterns and holly were looking dry but there were fresh flowers on the tables next to the piles of magazines. She sat on the edge of a chair, tense as a spring. her knees, thighs, even her toes, clenched against shaking.

A woman came in; a stranger. As dark as Rose herself, rail thin, bony hands, prominent veins.

She said, 'Mrs Fairbrother? I am Dr Patrick. I saw your husband on his first appointment.'

David had not mentioned her. Rose realized suddenly that he had never talked about his injections other than a brief, 'They stuck three needles in, so they must be giving me a cocktail!'

Rose stood up. 'How do you do,' she said politely.

Dr Patrick took her hand and did not let it go.

'We're glad you've come. We wanted to talk to you. John Carter and my colleague Mark Weston are in my consulting room. Will you come?'

'Yes. But—'

The woman doctor held Rose's hand firmly. 'It's not good news. You must have guessed that. Be strong. For your husband's sake, be strong.'

She went into the consulting room, led like a child by the hand. A seat was found for her. Dr Patrick stayed by her side. Professor Carter looked at his notes and another man – Rose had already forgotten his name – leaned forward.

'Mrs Fairbrother, we have Sister Gordon's reports and we have talked to her about your husband. The prolonged sickness is not caused by the drugs we are injecting. We are very much afraid that secondary cancers have already got a hold.'

Professor Carter looked up. 'Mrs Fairbrother. When I operated I removed all signs of the growth. I did not lie to you or your husband. What I did not mention is that such carcinomas spread throughout the body through the lymph glands. There is no way we can follow them.'

There was a silence, then she heard her own voice, wooden, almost scornful. 'So there was no hope. When you operated – cut him about – there was no point in it at all.'

Dr Patrick said quietly, almost in her ear, 'There was every point, my dear. The growth was large – it could not be dealt with in any other way. And we hoped that the chemotherapy would deal with the secondaries before they reached that stage.' She hesitated, then added, 'It is just possible that increased dosage might—'

Rose almost shouted 'No!' She tried to stand up and could not. 'No more treatment. He is too ill.'

'If he were admitted into the ward—'

259

'No.' She sounded slightly calmer now. 'I am looking after David now. When he was in here before he developed a bedsore. That will not happen again.'

The two men exchanged glances. Dr Patrick said, 'It is understandable that you are angry with us—'

Rose interrupted. She felt unutterably weary. It had been two weeks since she slept through a whole night. 'I am not angry with you. I am angry with myself. It was for me he agreed to the operation. I should have let him go. Peacefully. With dignity.'

'There is rarely much dignity connected with death,' someone said.

Rose said, 'I disagree. My father-in-law and my grandfather died with great dignity. And if my husband has to die I shall do all in my power . . . ' her voice wobbled. She could not believe what she had just said. She went on fiercely, 'But he's not going to die! I won't let it happen!' She turned and stared into Dr Patrick's dark eyes. 'It's ridiculous!' she laughed. 'David and I . . . we're a team. We can cope with anything when we're together!'

She stood up and wrenched herself free from Dr Patrick's long thin hand.

'Don't say anything else. I don't want to know.'

She went to the door. Someone was behind her. She said, 'Let me go! I want to be by myself!'

She walked back down the corridors with long strides, pushing her heels into the tiles as if she wanted to dent them. Outside, she no longer felt the biting wind. The car practically unlocked itself. She sat inside it for a moment, very still, telling herself she must pull herself together. But it was almost a formality; she felt perfectly together. She drove to the travel agents and picked up some gaudy brochures. She went on to the school and waited for half an hour until the bell went, without a thought forming in her head. When the girls leapt towards her, spotting the Coach before they were out of the cloakroom, she swept open the door and bowed low.

'Your pumpkin awaits, m'ladies,' she said in a deep voice.

They were thrilled. She kept up the little drama on the way home. 'The rats are working extra hard pulling us along . . . of course you cannot see them, m'ladies, they are beneath yonder bonnet!'

Ellie said, 'Daddy is better! That's why Mummy has gone loopy!'

Blue was silent until they pulled up in the drive. Then she said, 'Our mother is Funny Mrs Fairbrother and we wouldn't have no other!'

Ellie screamed with approving mirth, and Rose handed Blue the house key with great ceremony.

'To the door of your palace, m'lady!' she said sonorously.

They were just tall enough to manipulate the lock. They were growing up. But they were still only eight. How long before they forgot David?

Maud said, 'He's slept the whole time. I've just taken in some squash.' Her eyebrows were practically on her hairline, asking the obvious question.

Ellie replied to it. 'Daddy's going to get better soon!' she announced. 'That's why Mummy is completely loopy!'

Maud still looked.

Rose said, 'It's true. The wretched chemotherapy is a bit too strong for him. They're going to skip this appointment altogether and reduce the dose next time.'

She almost believed herself. She took the stairs two at a time in case David was listening.

He had pulled himself up in bed and leaned to one side to take the weight off the bedsore.

She said, 'Reprieve! You can skip this appointment and they will decrease the dosage next time!' She went over to the bed and kissed him. She knew that her eyes were shining and her colour high. 'Isn't it marvellous, darling? And they're very pleased with you. This hasn't been wasted – that's why you can wait a bit!'

He believed her. He sank back on the pillows with a sigh of relief.

'Oh Ros. You are a darling. What should I do without you?'

There were so many things she could have said to that. She had to ignore it. She kissed him and slid her hand down his spine to ease the pressure on it. Every one of his vertebrae were evident beneath her fingers. She massaged him very gently and kissed the top of his head again.

'They were very impressed that you'd lost no hair,' she murmured into it. 'Apparently it means you've got the constitution of a horse.'

He made no reply. She leaned back and saw that his eyes were closed and he was smiling blissfully.

She said, 'I'm going to turn you over and give you a rub with Mary's special cream.'

'That would be lovely,' he murmured.

She arranged the pillows and dealt with him expertly. Even so a groan escaped him as his torso collapsed to a prone position. She screwed her face up in agony for him but made no comment. The cream was practically fluid; she used her fingertips as Mary had shown her. The skin was flaking and must be irritating him. Gently she brushed at it, then rubbed.

'Oh, that is good,' he said. It was the nearest he had come to telling her of his discomforts. She wished he would complain.

Maud called and Rose said 'Come in,' and brightened her face. Maud tried not to look shocked at the sight of David's exposed and pitiful back. She said, 'How about a cup of tea for both of you?'

Rose smiled. 'Luvverly. And is there any more of that fruit jelly?'

'Oh yes. Rather.' Maud almost chortled the words. Such little things pleased all of them now.

Rose dressed the sore again, rearranged David's pyjamas, shook his pillows and settled him high on them.

He said, 'Darling, don't be upset, but I really cannot manage—'

She said swiftly, 'All right. Lemonade for you – I'll drink your tea.'

'I meant the—'

262

'So long as you have some of Mother's jelly, I'm not complaining,' she went on blandly, pouring lemonade. 'I'd like you to be strong enough to have a proper bath when Mary comes tomorrow.'

She hated to see the look of strain return to his face.

She said, 'Don't worry, darling. You'll feel better tomorrow. I promise.'

She spooned two mouthfuls of jelly into him, but he had to shake his head after that and she insisted no more, frightened he might be sick. But that night when he had fallen into one of his exhausted sleeps, she flattened her body alongside his, put her hand on his abdomen, and concentrated with burning intensity on the malaise inside him.

She spoke inside her head, levelly, unemotionally. 'I know all about free will. I know that our forefathers brought this sort of thing upon us. Nothing to do with you. But you can intervene. You can intervene through me. I'm not asking . . . I'm demanding. It's just. It's fair. Let it go. Now. Out of him. Now.'

She held her body in the awkward position for perhaps half an hour. Her head was aching, as if a nail had been driven through her forehead. She rolled on to her back. She hugged the headache to her. It was surely a sign. A sign that the illness had been taken away.

Three days later she found him in the bathroom when she took up his 'breakfast'. He had not locked the door. He was shaving.

'I'm coming down,' he announced through the lather. 'I feel much stronger. I'm coming down for breakfast.'

She was thrilled yet apprehensive.

'Can you manage in there?' He had relied on blanket baths for the last ten days. 'I'll stay and give you a hand.'

'No!' He flashed a look at her that was full of his old spirit, full of David. 'I want a bit of privacy. I won't lock the door, but don't come in. And let me put on my own socks, Ros. Please.'

She flew downstairs.

263

'He's coming down for breakfast!' she announced to a startled Maud.

Ellie said, 'Yippee!'

Blue gave her solemn smile.

Maud said, 'I'll take a tray into the sitting room. It's warmer in there.'

Rose shook her head. 'He wants to be with us. Here. He wants to get back to ordinary living.'

But she could not behave ordinarily herself; she was like a schoolgirl unable to sit still, unable to eat anything. David sat between the girls, sipping his lemonade, his gaunt face smiling at all of them. Blue leaned her head on his arm and Rose said quickly, 'Don't press on Daddy, darling,' and David said quietly, 'Let her be, Ros. I need this.'

Maud took them to school; they came back to the table half a dozen times to say goodbye. In their woollen hats and scarves and mitts they looked adorable. David couldn't get over it.

'I'd forgotten how beautiful they are. Mother too. So beautiful.'

Rose pretended to be offended, otherwise she might have cried. 'You haven't mentioned me!'

'I'm not that immodest.'

She looked at him, brows raised. 'I don't get it!'

'When I look at you, I look at me. To admire you is to admire myself.'

She did not attempt to laugh that off. She took his hand, conscious of the fleshless bones and experiencing her usual pang of terror. She said, 'Then admire yourself, David.'

He leaned forward and kissed her gently. 'Thank you, Ros.'

She was certain that at last God was on her side. Mary, the only one who knew the truth about her visit to Dr Patrick, was encouraging.

'There are natural remissions. The medical profession are still so much in the dark. He's . . . ' She glanced back over her shoulder to where David was busy finishing his dominoes. ' . . . He's marvellous,' she concluded.

That wasn't enough for Rose. 'Yes. But he looks better too, don't you think?'

There was a momentary hesitation, then Mary nodded. 'He's losing a lot of skin,' she said unexpectedly. 'Take another tube of this cream. And dress the sore twice a day now that he's up and about. Let's see if we can get rid of it completely.'

'I think the flaking skin is from his scar. It itches.'

'It always will, of course. But rub the cream into his back. That can be so soothing.'

★

Christmas Day came and went. She barely remembered it. She and Maud packed stockings for the girls, then watched them unpacked the next morning. Martin arrived and took the three of them off with him. Rose banked up the fire and pushed David's chair next to it. He managed some chopped chicken in the late afternoon but then went to bed. Surreptitiously, guiltily, Rose went to the chilly kitchen and tore the chicken to pieces and ate it dry. She was hungry for both of them, just like she'd been when she was pregnant.

He woke around midnight and reached for her hand.

'Is it snowing?' he whispered into the darkness.

'Don't know.' She made her voice drowsy, though the enormous meal she had bolted had given her indigestion and she had not slept.

'It would make it more Christmassy.'

She said, 'Impossible. It's been the most Christmassy Christmas I can remember.'

His breathing evened out and she knew he was drifting into sleep again. 'It'll be better next year,' he murmured. 'I'll make sure it is better.'

It was snowing the next morning and the snow continued throughout January. It seemed to drive the girls mad. They ran around the garden, screaming and letting their hair stream out behind them. They built snowmen and dragged each other up and down the garden path on a sledge. But David seemed to shrivel.

'Snow January, early spring,' Maud quoted. 'In a couple of weeks it'll be gone and all the snowdrops will be out.'

David looked at the finished dominoes lined up on the table.

'They're not much good. I didn't get the corners square.'

'They're lovely – what on earth are you talking about!' Maud picked one up and ran her finger over it. 'They – they're so touchable!'

'They're not square,' he repeated stubbornly.

Rose smiled. 'The girls will love them. They enjoy playing dominoes.' She assembled outdoor clothes over the back of a chair. 'I'll make another box, then you'll be better pleased.' She opened the door. 'Blue! Ellie! Time for school!'

David seemed smaller still in the sudden blast of air. She closed the door quickly, furious with herself for being so thoughtless.

'Come on, young man,' she said brightly. 'Let's put you back to bed for an hour. You can come down when the house is warmer and quieter. How's that?'

He smiled gratefully. 'Wonderful.' He got up with difficulty and went into the hall before Ellie and Blue could open the door again. Rose looked at his untouched fruit juice and Complan. His food intake was minute. She pushed the thought away quickly; his illness was in remission. Hadn't Mary said so, and wouldn't she know?

That night, the wind juddered the solid old house on its foundations. Rose turned carefully to face David and saw that his eyes were open.

'Can't you sleep, darling?' she whispered.

He said very clearly, 'Ros. Is there a computer in this house?'

She was bewildered. 'A computer? D'you mean one of those adding-up things? Didn't you have one somewhere? Why do you want it?'

266

He said, 'If there's a computer anywhere, get rid of it. It's going to take over.'

She looked at him, suddenly tense inside. She said calmly, 'There is no computer, darling. You have had a dream. It's just you, Maud, me and the children.'

For a moment he continued to stare into the darkness, then his eyes closed. After twenty more seconds of rigidity she touched him. He was asleep.

The next morning she asked him if he remembered his dream. He did not.

'That's all right then. You were saying something. I couldn't quite hear.'

He said, 'Is it snowing?'

She drew the curtains. 'No. And the wind has dropped a little too.'

'It's so cold. D'you mind if I don't get up till after the girls have gone to school?'

'Very sensible, darling. I'll get a good fire going in the sitting room, and we'll do the crossword together later. Does that sound all right?'

'Marvellous.'

But when she came up at ten o'clock he was asleep again, his cheek pillowed on his hand. Maud was in her room making her bed and Rose put her head round the door.

'Come and look at him. He's asleep.'

Maud looked; her chin began to wobble.

Rose whispered, 'Mother. I thought it would do you good to see him so comfortable.'

Maud turned away. 'He slept like that when he was a baby.' She held the newel post on the landing and looked at Rose with drowning eyes. 'Ros. He is going to be all right, isn't he?'

'Yes!' Rose answered immediately. Then knew that Maud deserved more than this. '*I* know he is going to be all right. But they – Professor Carter and Dr Patrick . . . and another doctor . . . they think . . . they said . . . ' her voice petered out.

Maud said, 'Ros. All those doctors. If they were all there in December when you went about postponing David's appointment – I mean . . . they were all there to see you?'

Rose nodded. She watched realization dawn on Maud's face. She said quickly, 'But listen, Mother. There's been a remission. Ask Mary when she comes tomorrow. You can see he's better – you can see it!'

She thought Maud might faint. The hand on the newel post whitened, then slipped off. She wanted Maud's reassurance that David looked better, but Maud had just seen him sleeping as he did when he was a baby. As if he were going back in time. To wherever he had come from.

Rose took Maud's arm and held her up.

'Mother. I felt the growth leave him. I put my hand on him and . . . and . . . willed it to leave him.' She could not mention God. Maud 'believed' – she went with Miss Westlake to chapel sometimes – but God's name was rarely spoken between them.

She leaned against the banister rail and put her head on Rose's shoulder.

'It's all right, Ros. Just a momentary . . . ' she looked up and Rose saw her own determination reflected on the older face. ' . . . Of course he'll be all right!'

They went back to the bedroom door and looked through. David had not changed his position. They went towards him and he opened his eyes and smiled anxiously.

'Have you found it?' His voice was cracked as if he had laryngitis. 'Get rid of it. It will take over. Get rid of it!'

Maud said, 'What do you mean, dear?'

Rose said, 'He's dreaming.' She leaned over the bed. 'Wake up, darling. Time to come downstairs now. There's a lovely fire in the sitting room.'

David swivelled his eyes to look at her. He did not seem able to move his head.

'Rose. I must know the truth. Is there a computer—'

'No, David. There is not,' she said firmly. 'You have been dreaming. The girls have gone to school and it's just Mother and me. We're both here.'

268

Maud gave a whimper and touched his shoulder. 'Don't worry, darling. Nothing to worry about.'

But the spectre was still with him, and could not be shaken off. He did not move but a stream of hoarse words, sometimes unintelligible, poured from him. Images from science fiction seemed to be marching through his head. Maud began to weep and Rose moved her away from the bed and took David's hand from beneath his cheek.

'Everything is all right now, David,' she said in a loud voice. 'Look at me. Listen to me. There is nothing to worry about. Nothing at all.' She repeated the words over and over again, interrupting him when he started to speak, holding both his hands in hers, willing his haunted world away.

At last he was still. The sound of Maud's quiet weeping came through to him.

'Mother. What is the matter with Mother?' He made an attempt to move his head and a spasm of pain contorted his face.

Rose said, 'You frightened us, darling. You couldn't rid yourself of a dream.'

He stared at her. His eyes were still opaque. He said in a low voice, 'Am I going mad, Ros?'

'No. It is just that. Dreams. That linger.'

She knew she was smiling widely at him as if they were sharing a private joke. She wondered if she were completely heartless.

She turned her head towards Maud. 'Mother. David's fine now. Come nearer so that you can see him.' She wanted David to be able to see his mother; to know that he was surrounded by love.

Maud got to her knees by the bed and inched forward. She did not speak.

David said, 'Mother. Rose. I want to tell you now. I am going to be better. Quite soon.'

Maud nodded. After a moment Rose said, 'Of course. We know that, David.'

There was a long moment which they all deliberately held on to, wishing it could go on into eternity. And then Maud

269

said, 'I'll make some tea.' And Rose said, 'That would be nice. We'll have it up here with David, and perhaps he'll manage some lemonade.'

He managed nothing. When Rose released his hands, one of them slid beneath his cheek again. Before they had finished their tea, he was asleep.

They phoned Mary and she arrived with a doctor. He was a locum: an Irishman with bright blue eyes and curly hair called Dr Gallagher. When he examined David his tenderness matched Mary's. He took a blood sample, finding a vein with great difficulty, apologizing for the inevitable discomfort.

'It doesn't hurt,' David murmured in his new cracked voice.

Mary smoothed his hair. 'He never complains,' she said.

Rose held her facial muscles rigid while they suggested a bedpan and a bottle would be advisable for a while.

'David needs plenty of rest,' Dr Gallagher said. 'We'll treat these symptoms as we would a bad case of influenza. Plenty of fluids, warmth, and complete bed rest.' He leaned over the bed. 'It won't last long, old man,' he said to David.

'I know,' said the abrasive voice.

On the landing, Dr Gallagher said, 'I'll let you know the results of this blood test, Mrs Fairbrother. And if I were you, I'd try to get a sleep this afternoon. You need your strength.' He handed a paper to Mary. 'In case of pain,' he said briefly.

They went downstairs and drank more tea together.

Mary said, 'I'll be in this afternoon, Ros. Maud.' She touched the back of Rose's hand. 'We shall need to turn him for the night. He hasn't the strength.'

Rose said stubbornly, 'He was up as usual yesterday.'

Mary nodded. 'Yes. He is an unusual man.'

For a split second Rose could have shouted wildly, 'Do you think I don't know that!' She could have screamed and wept and let someone take her off to hospital and look after her.

She said, 'Thank you, Mary. Thank you, doctor. You've been very kind.'

Then she saw them to the door, came back, washed up the cups and saucers and sat holding Maud's hand until it was time for lunch.

'I'll take some Complan upstairs,' she said. They both knew it was useless. Long before Dr Gallagher returned that evening and told them it would be a matter of twenty-four hours, they knew that David was dying.

Rose phoned Martin and then Jon. Martin arrived within half an hour; Jon would be there the next day.

She still did not fully believe it; she was two people, one knowing, accepting, looking back and realizing that there had never been any hope. The other stubborn and wilful and refusing to consider a world without David.

The two fused now and then, as they did that evening when Martin came downstairs after spending an hour with his brother.

Martin stood in the middle of the breakfast room where Rose was cleaning out a cupboard.

'I think I ought to take the girls home with me, Ros,' he said. 'They shouldn't be here when . . . when it happens.' His determination to keep his voice level made him sound cold and hard.

For the first time Rose thought about Ellie and Blue living out their young lives in a house of death. It was unbearable. Even worse was the idea of removing them. They belonged to David.

She stood up slowly, surrounded by the contents of the cupboard. She touched a tin with one foot and it rolled over. It was pear-halves in syrup. David's favourite fruit a year ago.

She said in a low voice, 'They ought to be here. Until the end.'

He cleared his throat. 'Ros. That time has come. It will be tonight. You know that.'

She cried out: 'I don't – I don't know that! It can't be – I wouldn't be cleaning out cupboards if David were going to die tonight!'

He pulled her into his arms and she wept uncontrollably against his chest, and then, quite suddenly, was still.

He choked, 'He'll always be with you, Ros. You know that.'

She nodded and did not look up, knowing he was weeping.

She whispered, 'The trouble is . . . the world will be a different place when he's not in it. Those tins down there . . . look at them, Martin. They are tins of fruit and vegetables and meat and soup. That's all. You don't even notice them when David is upstairs, breathing. But when he isn't, they will suddenly become obvious. Foreign matter. There will be fear . . . everywhere. Terror.' She pressed her head hard against his shirt. 'I don't know whether I can face it.'

His voice strengthened and he spoke with the utmost confidence. 'You'll face it, Ros. Just as you've faced everything else.' He made a sound that might have been a laugh. 'Even June admits that you cope with everything life throws at you.'

Her gaze did not leave the muddled array of tins. She said, 'But don't you see, with David, everything was so easy.'

He returned to his first words of comfort. 'He'll be with you, Ros.'

It was a vicious circle. She straightened on an indrawn breath.

'I must go and sit with him. He won't die when I am with him.' She believed that and it gave her strength. She said, 'All right. Take the girls back with you. Maud will pack their nighties and things.' She patted his arm. 'Thank you, Martin. But bring them back tomorrow morning. Early. You will, won't you?'

'Yes. Of course. Jon will be here then.' He flashed her a look of apology. 'Not that I . . . I meant that the girls love her and she will . . . you know.'

'I know.'

She went back upstairs. David was awake and seemed to know what was going on. His dark eyes were not clouded; she was struck again by their clarity.

He whispered, 'Martin taking the girls home?'

'How did you know? Have you been eavesdropping again?' She managed a laugh and took his hands. 'Just for tonight. Give Mother a break.'

'I'm such a damned nuisance,' he murmured. Then moved his head. 'I know it doesn't matter. Don't try to reassure me, darling.' She made to move to put on the light and he held her fingers in a surprisingly firm grip. 'Don't go, Ros.'

She stayed where she was. 'I'm not going.'

He said, 'I know I've been . . . odd. I'm all right now.'

'You're all right all the time.' She was glad it was dark; it was so hard to hold back the tears and he must not see.

'If only I could convince you that everything is going to be all right. I wish you would believe me, Ros.'

'I do believe you.'

'It doesn't matter really. You'll see.'

She said nothing to that; she closed her eyes for a moment.

He pressed her hands weakly; she opened her eyes. His were brilliant, almost glowing in the bedroom.

She said steadily, 'Are you warm enough? Shall I put the light on?'

'I don't want you to go.'

'Just to the light switch, darling.'

'No. Please stay, Ros.'

She leaned forward and put her face next to his. She had to keep swallowing; he must know. But they did not speak.

The door opened and she turned her head to see Martin and the girls framed there.

'Daddy's sleeping,' Martin hushed them. 'Just say goodnight to him quietly.'

'Goodnight, Daddy,' said Blue.

'Goodnight, Daddy,' echoed Ellie.

Martin whispered, 'Goodnight, old man. See you in the morning.'

They were gone. David's eyes were still luminous. She put her head down again. The house settled around them creakingly, as it had so often before. They heard Maud put the milk bottles out. They heard Mary's car drive up; the door slam; her voice in the hall talking to Maud. They were both coming upstairs; all three were going to turn David for the night.

Rose whispered, 'Are you in any pain, darling?'

David moved his head in negation.

She said, 'Close your eyes. The light will hurt them.'

He said nothing, but when Mary tapped, then came in and switched on the light, his eyes were obediently closed. Mary gave him her usual swift, professional appraisal as she took off her raincoat. Maud waited at the foot of the bed. She looked so old; crumpled and old.

Mary said, 'I'll get behind the bed. Can you two get either side? We'll be as gentle as we can, David.'

He smiled, his eyes still closed.

They all pulled the bed away from the wall and Mary leaned over the head and put her hands beneath David's arms. Rose and Maud slid their hands beneath his spine and linked fingers.

Mary said quietly, 'All right. Now.'

She drew David up. He seemed to rear off the pillow. His head lifted and his eyes opened. He stared past his mother at a corner of the ceiling and a great gasping groan came from his open mouth. And then his eyes closed and he rolled over on to his side.

Maud had her hand to her mouth to stop a scream. Rose said very calmly, 'Is this it?'

Mary came round the bed, sat on the pillow next to David and put her fingers to his neck.

'Yes.' She looked at Rose. 'He can hear you. Speak to him.'

Rose knelt by the bed. She smoothed the dear face and kissed the closed lids. She said, 'I knew what you meant, my darling. It was a promise you were making, wasn't it? And you've never broken a promise in your life. So of course I believe you.' A tear fell on his forehead. She kissed it away.

Mary said, 'Maud. Talk to him. He is still with us.' Her fingers were around his wrist now.

Maud said, 'David. I can't believe . . . my son . . . my son . . . '

Rose reached back with her free arm and drew Maud to her. David took a breath. It was the first one since his groan. Maud sobbed and said desperately, 'Oh David. You can do it. Stay with us.'

Rose put her mouth close to his and breathed gently into it. She said, 'Thank you, David. Thank you. Thank you. Thank you.'

She was still saying thank you when Mary interrupted her. 'He's gone now, Rose. Will you both come with me while I ring the doctor?'

Maud said chokingly, 'Can we stay?'

'Of course.'

Mary went. The two women continued to kneel by the bed, but now they held on to each other. Maud wept, bracing herself with one hand on the bed. But Rose took the hand and put it on her shoulder and held the older woman close to her. She was an awkward burden, but Rose was glad of it. She took the weight of David's mother and tearless she stared over her shoulder at the corner of the ceiling where David's last gaze had rested. She did not look back at his face. He was no longer there. She wondered with a part of her mind where he was now. In that corner of the ceiling? In his mother where he'd come from only thirty-five years ago?

When Mary came back and ushered them out of the room, Rose had to go to the bathroom. She sat on the lavatory and was shaken by a convulsion of grief so physically racking that she had to hold the washbasin to save herself from falling to the floor. And then, quite suddenly, the agony was gone. It swept through her and left her. And she was perfectly calm, staring at the wallpaper.

And she knew where David had gone.

She breathed, 'Thank you. Thank you. Thank you.' And she went on saying thank you inside her head all through the doctor's visit, the phone calls to Martin and Jon and Miss

275

Westlake and Grandmother. Then through the enormous tact of the undertakers. Then through making up two beds on the tweed sofas so that she and Maud could sleep downstairs, close to each other. And, amazingly, they did sleep. Exhausted and despairing, they held hands across the width of the hearth rug and lay wakeful for perhaps half an hour. Then quite suddenly, at the same time, the linked fingers relaxed and gradually slipped from each other. They slept.

Fifteen

Rose had very little recollection of the funeral. She told Ellie and Blue that Daddy had gone to heaven and that of course they would miss him, so it was all right to cry now and then, but not too much otherwise how could Daddy be happy. And, determined to show the girls that she meant what she said, she smiled a great deal and made sure that when she was getting meals or washing up, she sang. She sang silly, cheerful songs, like 'The sun has got his hat on' and 'Hey Mister Porter', but when she went to bed and slowed the songs down in her head, the tears would come shatteringly again. She was no longer afraid of her grief; when she was by herself she gave it full rein, and found that it would blow through her like those savage January blizzards, and leave her calm and strengthened.

Her public face made it impossible for others to give way to tears. Aileen and Jon, arriving the day after David's death, looked as though their features had been frozen. Maud's face occasionally worked uncontrollably. Martin found relief in managing everything for them; he brought papers for them to sign and escorted Rose to the Registrar's and later to the tax office, the doctor's, the infirmary. Only June, Charles and Arney abandoned themselves to grief during the funeral.

Rose, remembering Maud's collapse at Arnold Fairbrother's cremation, had decided on interment. There was comfort to be had in the age-old ritual around the graveside; David was, after all, only one step ahead of all of them there.

She begged Aileen and Jon to go back to Newcastle. Georgie was up there in the care of the ubiquitous Stan and she was suddenly anxious for him. But Aileen and Jon were there to deal with the first of the callers: the Murchisons, a distraught Mrs Whittaker, Miss Westlake; even Margaret Ellenbury. They agreed to go home on condition that Rose would bring the girls up to them at Easter. They were actually packed and ready to leave for the morning train, when another caller arrived.

Rose, thinking it was their taxi, opened the door, then was on the point of closing it immediately; the young man in the loose-fitting suit and college haircut could only be one of the new breed of Mormon missionaries.

He saw Aileen in her dark blue coat and hat and smiled delightedly.

'Say, isn't it . . . surely it's Mrs Harris?'

Aileen stared. The terrible events of the past few weeks had made her feel very old. She could feel her mind grappling with the problem of this young man's presence. Salesman? Or one of the insurance people she'd had before they knew David?

He said, 'You don't remember me. I was just a kid when we were last together.' He was enjoying the total perplexity of his audience. He turned to Rose, still holding the door. 'You must be Rose. The black hair and very blue eyes . . . they haven't changed.'

She said in the formal voice she had invented for all callers, 'I'm sorry. I don't remember you.'

He laughed. 'I'm not surprised! Eric. Eric Laben. I'm over here on business and got your address from Mrs Steedman. The people up at Churchdown told me that Mrs Rose Fairbrother looks after the house in between tenants and gave me this address. And here I am!'

Aileen glanced at Rose and noted the white, set face. Eric Laben could not have come at a worse time.

She said, 'I remember the Labens. Of course. Your grandfather came from Germany long before the war with Joe. My sister's husband. Joe Lange.' She looked again at Rose. 'Perhaps . . . will you come in?'

'That's kind of you.'

Eric Laben was beginning to realize all was not well. He stood awkwardly in the hall while Rose closed the front door.

'Mrs Steedman said I was to look you up. I couldn't go back and tell her . . . I'm on my way to Germany. Tomorrow morning.'

Rose said, 'Come into the sitting room, Mr . . . Eric.' She managed a smile over her shoulder as she led the way into the flower-filled room. Everyone trailed after her.

Aileen said, 'Well, it's really nice of you to make the effort, Eric. But who is Mrs Steedman?'

'Gee, you haven't heard then?' It was his turn to look bewildered. Flowers – all hothouse – were even on the chairs. Rose had not wanted them to freeze in the cemetery and had had them brought back the day of the funeral.

'Your sister married Senator Steedman. You wouldn't have heard of him but—'

'I've heard. I met him once.' Aileen would have liked to have caught Rose's eye. Not that the child would remember that appalling evening of Victory day. And even if she did, now was not the time to be sharing jokes. And that's what it was: that Mabe had finally got her senator.

She lifted a wreath from one of the chairs. 'Sit down, Eric.' She looked round for help. 'This is my second daughter, Joanna. Jon, Eric was Rose's friend in America.' She discovered a phrase often heard over there. 'Why don't you two get to know each other while Rose and I make some tea?'

It was the sort of thing Jon enjoyed doing, even on an occasion like this. She took off her hat and shook out her hair.

'Why not? We can catch the next train.' She held out her slim manicured fingers. 'This is wonderful, Eric. Mother and Rosie never talk about America, you know. Tell me everything!'

Aileen took Rose's arm and they went into the hall.

'Jon will explain,' she said quietly. 'Don't worry, darling. He'll be ready to leave by the time we take in the tea.'

'D'you mind if I go upstairs, Mother?' Rose responded woodenly. 'I need . . . I need . . . '

'Go on, darling.'

Aileen watched her older daughter take the stairs tread by tread, like an old lady. She could only guess at the number of times Rosie had leapt up those same stairs to see to David. Oh God, it was too awful. And this man, turning up from the past like this . . . was there no end to the awfulness?

Rose went into the bathroom and sat on the lavatory and bowed over her knees. Once again grief poured through her from her head to her toes. When she could feel it leaving her she straightened and held on to the basin with closed eyes. And, as always, she whispered, 'Thank you, David.'

Jon did not see the advent of Eric Laben as awful at all; to her he was a blessed relief from awfulness. She sat on one of the fireside stools, her new long-length dress swirling around her ankles, and asked eager questions of this stranger from her sister's past.

He decided that she must be some kind of florist and replied as diplomatically as he could.

'Well, I guess your aunt was well-off. Yeah. Certainly. But now – let's say she's better-off, huh?'

'Her new husband – he's a politician?'

'You could call him that.' Eric's tone became ironic. 'Yeah. He's retired of course. He must be in his eighties. They live in the oldest house in the village. There are a lot of villages called Georgetown in the States you know, Joanna. This one is kinda preserved for posterity. Do you have places of interest like that?'

'Oh yes. Conservation areas. Listed buildings. Our stately homes. I didn't realize America was old enough for that.'

'Sure. Georgetown in Connecticut has white wooden buildings, front steps, sidewalks and trees – it's real pretty.'

'And you live there?'

'No. I moved to New York when I was married. I'm back home now with my grandfather. You probably know that my brother and I were brought up by our grandparents, so we were very close. When my grandmother died, it seemed kinda crazy to stay in the New York apartment by myself.

So I went back to Connecticut. We live about ten miles from Georgetown. It was quite an estate before the war but Gramps has sold most of the land.'

'You – your wife – you're divorced?'

'Yeah. Didn't work out.'

'I'm divorced too. I live up in Newcastle with my little boy. And my mother.'

'Your mother was gorgeous when I knew her back in the forties. Sorta romantic too. And sad. I used to dream about rescuing her from a plane crash and looking after her!'

'Rose too?'

'Oh sure, Rose. She was just a kid – a baby. She ran around in coveralls all day with their coloured man. But on Victory night we gave a big party and that night she looked like Snow-White. She could dance too.'

Jon felt a pang of some strong emotion. A sense – familiar to her, of course – of being left out of something exciting. She hugged her knees and thought of Rose now. Might she go back to America? This man was unattached and obviously harboured romantic fantasies about her sister. But the trouble with Rose was she'd never look at another man now that David was dead.

Aileen appeared then, wheeling a tea trolley.

She said, 'Rose won't come down again, I'm afraid.' She smiled wryly. 'Have you told Eric, Jon?'

Jon bit her lip. It had been so pleasant not to think of the terrible tragedy for five minutes.

'No,' she said, without apology.

Aileen shot her a look then turned to Eric.

'Rose's husband died last week,' she said bluntly. 'The funeral was the day before yesterday – that's where all these flowers have come from.' She waved away his look of horror. 'You couldn't know. And in a way – later – she will be pleased you came. But you must forgive her for now.'

'I – I'm so very sorry, Mrs Harris—' he stammered, trying to stand up but restrained by Jon's hand on his knee.

'There's nothing you can do.' Jon reached over for a cup and saucer. 'Please drink this and have something to eat and talk to us for a while.'

Uncomfortably, he did so. And surprisingly they all enjoyed it. The twins were still with Maud at Martin's house and the next train to Newcastle was not until two o'clock. When he got up to leave Jon made sure he held her hand longer than was necessary and urged him to visit the north-east on his way back from Germany.

'I can't be away that long.' He looked at the dark eyes staring straight into his. 'Listen, Joanna, Mrs Harris. If you're visiting your aunt any time, it would be an honour to have you over. Sure, I mean it. Gramps would love it. Me too.'

Even as Aileen was saying how unlikely that event was, Jon was nodding delightedly. 'I'm sure we'll meet up again, Eric. It's in the stars! Definitely in the stars!'

Later, on the train going north, Aileen remonstrated with her.

'Why on earth you wheedled that invitation out of him, I'll never know! We shall never go to America – your aunt wouldn't have us, for one thing!'

'I gathered that from what you've told me,' Jon replied. 'That's why I thought it might be nice to have somewhere to go besides her rotten house and rotten new husband!' She giggled. 'It would put her nose out of joint if we were staying only ten miles away with the Labens, wouldn't it? How about you getting hitched to the old man and me nobbling Eric?'

'How you can be so flippant after . . . ' Aileen felt tears rising again and went on quickly, 'Anyway, I thought you loved living in Newcastle? You're always telling me how marvellously exciting it is after living in a backwater!'

Jon leaned over the table and took her mother's hand. 'Why do I do anything?' she asked rhetorically. 'I don't know. I don't want to leave Newcastle. But the top half of America is called Canada. And I simply thought . . . '

Aileen said, 'Rick. I see.' She sighed again. 'Perhaps you should write to that last address you had and tell him about David. He might come home then.'

Aileen knew nothing of Rick's and Rose's infidelity; of that Jon was certain. Just as she was certain she would not be writing to Rick to tell him that Rose was now free.

Rose was constantly amazed at how life went on. She knew it had to, but that it actually did was something else. The twins missed their father, but they knew he was in heaven because of Sunday school and Miss Westlake's assurances, so their unhappiness did not fill their lives by any means. Martin found consolation in 'looking after' the Stroud Road household with a concern that was, at times, smothering. June soon became just as trying again and even took to confiding in Rose some of Martin's irritating habits. 'He *will* leave his gardening shoes right in front of the door, my dear! In fact he does all the classic things – toothpaste cap off, lavatory seat up – you name it!'

Sometimes Rose looked at her with her intensely blue eyes, and June realized what she was saying and shut up. But not for long.

Mrs Whittaker moved down to some elderly people's flats in the city and became a regular caller. For a while she would sit quietly, talking of the past, reminiscing in a comfortable way that was soothing. But then she started complaining about the woman in the upstairs flat. Then about the rotten drainage that caused the courtyard to flood after any small shower of rain. Then about the hopelessness of the warden.

Even the Murchisons seemed to think David could be embalmed in the past and put away after just a few short months. They spoke of concerts and bingo sessions and tried to get her to come with them.

Only Maud shared her sense of total unreality. They could work together in the kitchen, discuss menus, new clothes for school, any mundane thing, yet be conscious the whole time of David's absence. The house, life itself, was suddenly very large. It was like living inside an echoing bell. Everything the same. Yet completely different. Just as Rose had known it would be.

There was consolation to be had in booking the summer visitors into the Snow-White house. The smallness of it was comforting – Rose remembered her mother's delight when they'd first dug themselves in there. Mrs Whittie's cottage next door remained empty, though it had been purchased. It made the small rank of houses even quieter. They were mostly owned by couples who commuted to the city each day. It had become a desirable area and there was no lack of tenants.

Rose enjoyed cleaning the house and looking after the garden. She would take the twins with her and they would romp on the hill and roll down the old ski slope and play hide-and-seek among the gravestones in the churchyard. There was consolation in everything she did there; no death, no fear.

At the end of that summer, when the twins were nine and beginning to talk about the grammar school with some trepidation, Grandmother summoned Rose to the house in Cheltenham.

If the Snow-White house was a time-warp for Rose, Rodney Road was a time-warp for everyone. Doreen, a shrivelled, tiny dragon these days, still wore cap and apron over a black dress and showed visitors into the morning room while Grandmother decided if she would see them. There were lace doilies under every ornament and vase, antimacassars on each chair. If it hadn't been for a series of hard-pressed dailies, the house would look like Miss Havisham's. Paradoxically Grandmother was very much on the ball when it came to business matters.

'You've done well this season, Rosamund dear,' she said, indicating an uncomfortable spoonback chair opposite her Parker-Knoll recliner. 'I did wonder after your terrible loss if you would lose interest, but the receipts are up on last year.'

'Martin advised me to increase the rents, Grandmother. Cost of living.'

'And you still had your regulars. So obviously you are keeping the place in good order.'

'Hopefully.'

Rose wondered whether Grandmother was about to give her the cottage. Martin had hinted as much and told her that the rents would be a very useful addition to her income, which, with the twins to educate, was not enormous.

Unexpectedly a little worm of enthusiasm moved in her abdomen. In spite of what she'd said to her mother not long ago, she would enjoy taking over the Snow-White house completely. Perhaps they could all go up there themselves for a fortnight next summer. She must ask Martin about it; whether it would be a 'viable proposition' as he put it.

'I have arranged for your percentage to be paid into the bank, Rose. A little bonus too.'

Rose indicated gratitude and waited while Doreen wheeled in the trolley and lit the lamp beneath the kettle. A clanking silence prevailed while the tea-things were sorted out; a silence borne well by Doreen and Grandmother, barely sustainable by Rose. Grandmother did not believe in conversation in front of domestics, and after at least fifty years Doreen was still a domestic. Rose tightened her clasped hands and tried to think how she would describe this to Maud. Thank God for Maud who was so like David and would laugh uncritically.

'I have several things to say to you, Rosamund,' Grandmother announced as soon as the heavily curtained door closed behind Doreen.

'I thought so,' Rose said dryly.

'Don't be pert, dear. I might be old but I still function fairly well.' Grandmother softened this statement with a little smile and Rose felt a pang of warmth for her. She had coped so well with losing Grandfather. An example.

'Firstly, most importantly, the education of Elizabeth and Ellen.'

'You need not worry about that, Grandmother,' Rose began but was waved into silence.

'Let me finish.' The old lady poured boiling water into the teapot, then into the cups to warm them. 'I will be responsible for that. I insist, Rosamund. It was your grandfather's wish that any issue of yours would be our ultimate responsibility. He never knew them, but he would have loved them. They are – ' she swallowed and rattled the cups busily – 'they are both the image of Jonathan.'

Rose, who looked only for David in the girls, realized suddenly that there was a resemblance to the eternally young man of the photographs. Both she and Jon had inherited their mother's dark hair, but her blue eyes must have come from her father, and she had thought the legacy stopped there. The twins were fairish like David. They had his translucent brown eyes too. But the high foreheads and long necks were a throwback to the grandfather none of them knew.

She cleared her throat. 'I hadn't thought—'

'Why should you? But you will allow me this indulgence?'

'Oh Grandmother. Of course. I'm sorry, I hadn't looked at it like that. I just didn't want you – anyone – to think we needed help.'

'I don't think that at all, Rose. I know you are quite capable of working to support your family. If you have to.'

'It's rather soon . . . I'm sure . . . Martin advises me—'

'I still have some influence with the Society of Auctioneers. I was mentioning the other day what an excellent agent you would make for holiday properties. That's your grandfather in you, of course. Capable, quiet, no fuss.'

Rose felt rather breathless. 'How kind—'

'Something for the future, perhaps. Not only monetary considerations here, Rose. When your daughters are at school, you will probably need something to occupy your mind.'

'I – yes – perhaps. When they're older.'

Grandmother poured the tea and handed cakes.

She sat back and fixed Rose with a beady blue eye.

'I've put their names down at Greystones. For 1975. They'll be eleven then. Needing security, discipline. It's a good school. It was just for boys. It now has a separate school for girls, but there are shared lessons. I thought this was a good thing – there will be so few males in the girls' lives—'

Rose interrupted firmly. 'I'm sorry, Grandmother. No boarding school. The girls stay with me.'

The carefully powdered cheeks flushed.

'Of course I knew you would feel . . . all I ask is that you think it over, Rose.'

'I don't need to think about it, Grandmother. I'm not ungrateful. I wish I could have agreed to it. For my father's sake. But David would wish us to stay together. I'm sorry.'

Rose put down her cup and picked up her handbag. She guessed the interview was over.

It was not.

Grandmother said, 'I still have some things to say, child. But before I say them, will you promise me that you will bear my proposal in mind? Elizabeth and Ellen – especially Elizabeth – are very intelligent girls and need the best we can give them. If you remain adamant, I will of course pay the fees for any school of your choice. But I have read every prospectus of every school for miles around, and though Greystones is rather progressive, I feel that it is the best. It is in the Cotswolds, which is their home and which they love. It offers all the outdoor sports – riding, swimming – everything. There are social occasions with the boys' school and although I deplore this modern permissiveness or whatever it's called – more like licence – I recognize that total seclusion makes matters worse. Weekend visits from relatives are encouraged. And it has a wonderful academic record.'

'No. I'm sorry—' Rose felt if she said those words once more she would shout. 'I cannot send the girls away.'

Grandmother replaced her cup on the tea trolley and looked at her liver-marked hands. She said quietly, 'Sometimes . . . you know only too well, Rosamund . . . we have to let our loved ones go. And if we can do that with a good heart, we keep them closer than they were before.'

She moved her shoulders and looked up. Her voice became businesslike again. 'The other thing seems trivial almost. By comparison.' She took a cake and peeled away its wrapper. 'I have purchased number two, Railway Villas. Mrs Whittaker's house.'

Rose opened her eyes wide. It was a great surprise, but good to have changed the subject.

'How exciting. Are you going to let that one too?'

'No. Not at present. There is a great deal of building work to be done on it. I foresee it taking a year at least.'

'Really? I had no idea Mrs Whittie had let the place go. Will it be noisy next summer for the visitors?'

'Oh, we cannot take in visitors next season, Rose.'

Rose was not dismayed. 'Perhaps the family – Mother and Georgie – could use it then. And I was thinking that Maud and I could take the girls there for two or three weeks. It might be a nice change if you don't object.'

'I wouldn't object. But the house will be uninhabitable for a while. You see, I am having the two houses knocked into one. There will be two bathrooms of course, an enormous kitchen, probably five bedrooms. I thought a long window all along the back of the house to give a view over the hill. It will be positively luxurious when it's finished!'

The cheeks were more flushed than ever, but this time with pleasure. She leaned back, practically waiting for applause.

Rose was horrified. Her home, her retreat, small, cosy, reclusive, was being swept away. And she had thought Grandmother might be going to make a deed of gift!

She said carefully, 'It will still be attached to the other two, of course. The rents will be kept down appropriately. I think it might be more profitable to let two separate cottages rather than one big one.'

'Rubbish!' Grandmother smiled knowingly. 'Just you wait and see, my girl. You won't recognize it when the builders have finished!'

'No,' Rose murmured. She felt unutterably depressed.

But in the months that followed she and Maud, thrown closer than ever, forged a relationship that compensated enormously for the continuing 'awfulness' of things.

Martin eventually presented them with a statement of income and outlay, and it was obvious that the first fell short of the last.

Maud started sewing again and was thrilled that her first big order would cover the cost of the telephone for half a year. That winter Rose had a letter from an old-established firm of house agents in Gloucester, asking if she would act as an agent for their Cotswold holiday cottages. She knew it must have come via Grandmother, and for a whole day she wanted to refuse it. Then she realized how little pride counted, and accepted the job gratefully. There were only seven properties involved, and they were in outlying villages where carpenters and electricians were hard to come by. But there was a good car allowance and Rose had a persuasive way with her.

They sold the Lagonda and she used the economical Coach. It made people smile and notice her. She became a well-known figure in Birdlip and Cranham, driving the decorated car with the floral curtains at each of the windows.

Surreptitiously she kept an eye on the work at the Snow-White house. By the autumn of '74 it was finished. It was marvellous. But it was no longer her old home. It was part of the awfulness.

She waited for Grandmother to summon her again and suggest advertising it; but there was no summons and when she mentioned it casually during a Sunday tea-time, Grandmother was cagey.

'I think permanent tenants again, dear. Don't you? It's rather large for you to keep an eye on things. And I certainly don't want any holidaymaker messing up all that work and worry!'

Rose felt hurt and angry.

The final awfulness happened the following year.

Rose had assumed that the twins would get through the hated eleven-plus and go to her old school in Gloucester. It gave her a nostalgic pleasure to think of them sitting at the same desks that she and Margaret Ellenbury had used not twenty years before. She remembered her favourite phrase, 'Earth's diurnal round'. It seemed appropriate again.

When the results came through and Blue had gained a place and Ellie had not, she could not believe it. Neither could they.

Blue, leggy and studious-looking, was more appalled than Ellie.

'Mummy – Gran – I can't go there on my own! I really can't! Ellie and me – we've got to go to the same school! I mean it! And if Ellie is going to—'

Ellie said tightly, 'Listen. You're clever and I'm not. You can't give up your place for my sake.'

'I'm not! You blithering idiot!' Blue was suddenly furious. 'No wonder you didn't pass! Can't you see, I'm giving it up for my sake, not yours!'

'Don't you *dare* call me a blithering idiot!' Untypically Ellie threw herself on her sister, and Blue, far more used to administering physical violence than Ellie, allowed it to happen.

Maud and Rose separated them with difficulty.

Rose said tiredly, 'There is a way out of this. Leave it for a while. We'll talk about it again in a few days.'

She told Maud that night.

'It's just my stupid pride, I suppose,' she said sadly after she'd expounded Grandmother's plans for the girls.

'Nothing to do with pride.' Maud would not let a hint of criticism be cast on her daughter-in-law, not even by Rose herself. 'It seems to me that at that time – nearly two years ago, isn't it – your one idea was to keep us together as a family. Things – circumstances – have changed now. That's all.'

Rose said, 'I don't know what to do, Maud. We shall be like two peas in a drum in this house if they go.'

'Perhaps we could find something smaller?'

'This rent is controlled while we're here. Remember what Martin said.'

'Listen. Put it out of your mind for the moment. I'll talk to Martin. How's that?'

Rose said elliptically, 'I love you. You're a wonderful woman. Did you know that?'

Maud made a face and looked exactly like David.

'Flattery,' she commented.

But before she could talk to her son, something happened that made up their minds for them. The first was a telephone call from Grandmother's friend, Emily McIntyre.

'Rosamund? Hello my dear. How are you?'

Rose felt her heart literally jump against her ribs.

'Is it Grandmother?' she asked bluntly. 'Has something happened?'

Emily laughed. 'Oh no. What a pessimist you are, my dear! Though I suppose, in the circumstances, it is hardly surprising that you would be!' She laughed again. Rose, relaxing tremblingly, mouthed into the hall mirror, 'Rhino-skin!'

'I thought I would like to keep in touch, that's all,' Emily swept on, apparently forgetting that for the past three years she had relied on her contact with Rose's grandmother to 'keep in touch'.

'Thank you, Mrs McIntyre.' Rose said politely. 'And how are you these days.'

'Not well, dear. I was saying to Edith only the other day, she has no idea how lucky she is to be able to walk.'

'I didn't realize – I'm so sorry—'

'I can barely get round Cavendish House these days,' Emily said briskly. 'And Mr McIntyre is so fussy about his food. I have to shop most days. No-one delivers any more.'

Rose bared her teeth in the mirror then said solemnly, 'It is difficult, isn't it?'

'Oh my dear, I'm glad you sympathize. Edith becomes impatient with me, I'm afraid. Of course she must be over eighty now. Only to be expected she is going to get irritable at times.'

Rose had one of her unusual pangs of sympathy with Grandmother.

Emily lowered her voice as if Grandmother might hear.

'Actually dear, that is why I wanted to speak to you personally. I know you're moving back to Churchdown and you'll have to get rid of some furniture. I wondered about that lovely little escritoire you have under your stairs. Edith told me not to mention it, but I'm certain you won't mind. I would pay you for it, of course.'

Rose's reflected face became blank.

'Moving? Back to Churchdown?'

'To the new house. The renovated house. I understood—'
Rose said, 'No. We're not moving, Mrs McIntyre.' She
looked at herself in the mirror. 'You must excuse me. I have
to go. Something on the cooker.'

She replaced the receiver and walked into the kitchen.
It was mid-afternoon and she was not cooking that day
anyway. Maud looked up from her sewing machine which
she had moved on to the kitchen table to cope with the big
loose covers she was making.

'You looked shattered, Ros. What's happened.'

Rose told her. 'Grandmother is going to give us the
cottage. Only it's not the cottage any more. I couldn't live
there now.' She laughed. 'It's a bit late, isn't it?'

Maud pushed her sewing aside and stared at Rose
through her glasses.

'Ah. It begins to make sense, Ros. I wondered if she had
an ulterior motive for buying up Mrs Whittie's place. She
must have had this in mind all the time. She realized the
Snow-White house was too small for the four of us. And
not only that . . . she didn't want you to follow too closely
in Aileen's footsteps.' She pushed her glasses further up the
bridge of her long nose. 'Don't you see, darling, she wants
a new start for you. For me too. For the girls.'

'She can keep her new start. We're doing all right as we
are.'

Maud was silent for some time. Rose filled the kettle and
put it on the stove with unnecessary force.

Maud said quietly 'We're not really all right, darling.
Are we? We can't afford this place any longer. There are
things to be done here and the firm won't do them – our
rent wouldn't cover much anyway. And we don't need all
this room – we've outgrown the house, Ros.' She took off
her glasses and held out a hand. 'Darling, stop clattering
teacups and listen. The girls love it up there. This is no
charity. Your grandmother simply wants you to have your
legacy before she's dead! It makes wonderful sense, Ros.'

Rose sat down as if surrendering. She said, 'Don't you
see, Maud? If we live up there, Ellie will go to the

292

secondary modern school. Blue will have to travel down to the Grammar on her own.'

Maud lifted her shoulders slightly.

'You promised there was a way out of that. You must have been considering your grandmother's offer of places at Greystones.'

'I . . . perhaps I was. But I strongly object to being pushed into a decision.'

Maud leaned back in her chair and smiled. 'Oh, Ros.'

'Oh . . . ' Rose smiled herself and tried to think of a word to express her sudden and probably unreasonable frustration. 'Oh botheration!' was all she could manage. But it made Maud laugh. And then Rose laughed too. And suddenly they were talking about moving and fitting furniture into the big living room with the enormous window.

They could barely wait to tell the twins that tea-time.

It was as well that the tactless Emily had forewarned Rose, because, when Grandmother expounded her plans in a businesslike manner – 'This way you will save on inheritance tax, Rosamund. The only thing is I have got to live for seven years!' – Rose was able to show unbridled delight.

She concluded, 'Oh Grandmother! Of course you'll live for ages!'

Grandmother smiled. 'Well, I've got a motive now, haven't I?' She chortled suddenly. 'I shall outlive Emily McIntyre yet! What reasons has she to hang on until 1982? None whatsoever!'

Suddenly the awfulness lifted and they made plans and accepted offers of help for the actual move and let themselves feel excited. Charles and Arney came home for the long summer vacation and were delighted to hear about Greystones.

'It's a decent enough place,' the lofty Charles informed Blue. 'You're lucky they've opened it up for girls now.'

Blue said, 'Frankly, we don't care what it's like. We shall be together and we can come home every weekend.' She looked at Ellie. 'We're happy again. Aren't we, Ellie?'

Ellie nodded. Rose and Maud, within earshot, looked at each other and nodded too. And inside her head Rose said, 'Thank you, David. Thank you.'

They were installed and arranging for Georgie to come down for the girls' eleventh birthday, when the phone call came from Jon.

Aileen had died in her sleep.

Sixteen

After the cremation Jon and Georgie went back to the Snow-White house with Rose. There seemed nothing else to do. Jon felt empty; she could almost hear herself rattling when she moved. She knew she should feel guilty; she tried to feel guilty. Perhaps guilt itself was hollow because she continued to rattle.

Rose went up to Newcastle and did 'everything'. Rose was 'marvellous'. There was not one word of personal grief, her concern was all for Jon and the children. Aileen's ashes arrived in Churchdown by post; not even Rose could bear to pack them with clothes and toys and sandwiches. She vetted the little service arranged by the Reverend Murchison so that it would not be upsetting. She drove Jon and Georgie to a local nursery and let them choose a shrub to plant nearby. She took them with her when she 'did' her holiday cottages and asked their advice about next year's renovations.

Jon wished often that she could be more like her sister. Perhaps David's death had given Rose some practice in the art of bearing pain. Perhaps it was possible to get used to pain. Perhaps there would come a time when nothing was felt . . . nothing at all. Perhaps Rose too was empty; completely and totally empty and Jon should be thankful for her own hollow inside. And then she overheard Georgie say one day, 'Nothing looks the same without Gran, does it, Aunt Rose?' And Rose replied very steadily, 'No. Weren't we lucky to have her until now?' And Jon knew that Rose wasn't empty at all.

Grandmother turned up trumps that summer. She visited them one Sunday afternoon, admired the house in her usual self-congratulatory way, then said grimly, 'I suppose your grandfather would have wanted me to do it. So I have. There's a place in the boys' school at Greystones for George if he wants it.'

Jon was still, saying nothing, waiting for Georgie. Georgie was ecstatic. It was a new beginning for him. He couldn't believe it.

'I thought . . . I thought we'd have to go back to Newcastle . . . I hate that school. And Stan—'

Jon said swiftly, 'So you'd like to go to Greystones?'

'Oh . . .' Georgie had picked up a lot of unsavoury language from the Magpies' terraces and Jon held her breath. But he managed to restrain himself. 'Cripes! It would be wonderful. Marvellous.' He looked at the woman who had always been Great-grandmother to him. 'Are you sure? It will cost a lot of money to send three of us.'

Grandmother was dourly amused. 'But it wouldn't be fair to pay for the girls and not you, would it?'

Jon wondered if she was fishing. George said innocently, 'But they live here and I don't.'

Grandmother glanced at Jon. 'Perhaps you will now.'

Jon said, 'Perhaps we will.'

Later when the children were outside, Jon felt duty-bound to try to thank the old lady. But it was hopeless. Grandmother said, 'You'll have to look lively about getting his uniform. Have the bills sent to me.' She turned on the way out to her taxi. She was leaning heavily on her stick. She said abruptly, 'I was fond of Aileen. It doesn't really matter what happened. She was a good girl and I was fond of her.'

Maud, who now had a room for her sewing, lengthened trousers for Georgie and shortened tunics for the girls. Aileen's death had shocked her to the core, and, like Rose, her remedy for everything was to keep busy. Grandmother wanted the alterations to be billed to her, but Maud would have none of it. 'It's the one way I can help,' she maintained.

'Good old Gran!'

It was Georgie who spoke. He had always called Maud 'Gran' like the twins; it was a great comfort to her.

296

Jon got a job, but her home-made beautician's certificate did not cut much ice in the big salons and she had to make do with the sort of thing Mrs Raschid had done in a tiny 'boutique' in the wrong half of Gloucester. The shop was not far from Rick's old bedsitting room in St James Street. She walked past it one day and remembered Georgie's birth.

When the children finally left them, she recognized that the emptiness had evolved into a deep unhappiness. She was worn out in the evenings, yet could not sleep. Rose drove up to Greystones on Friday afternoons to collect the children and she was always pleased to see Georgie again. But as the weeks passed, Jon could see how well he was settling in and that he needed her less and less. 'If I get chosen for the junior football team, I won't be able to come home at weekends,' he said without regret.

Not for the first time in her life, Jon felt simply redundant. She continued to send her rent money to the landlord of the flat in Newcastle. Somehow . . . absurdly . . . it gave her a little independence.

In November she had a phone call from Martin and a letter from Stan. Both were brief.

Martin offered her a job in his office at twice the money she was getting in the shop.

Stan used the word 'responsible' three times. He felt responsible in part for Aileen's death. He felt responsible for Jon because of their friendship and her work. And he felt responsible for Georgie. He concluded by asking her to write to him. He had kept her 'outlets' for her by using a temporary beautician, but could not do so for much longer.

She told Martin not to be ridiculous. She gave Stan's letter a little more consideration; in fact she read it several times. She knew it was his way of expressing his grief and sorrow; she knew that. But it was also his way of telling her to get back up there quickly. The terrible thing was, she was tempted to go. How could that be? She was with her family, giving and receiving mutual comfort after the loss of Aileen, living in their old home, seeing her son every weekend. And she wanted to go back to a small lonely flat in the north. It was ridiculous.

She wrote to Stan and told him she had a job and would be staying in Churchdown. She heard nothing.

Christmas came and went. The twins adored Greystones. Georgie was still catching up academically, but he loved the sport. He was now in the football team; he stayed at school over the weekends to practise.

In January 1976 there came another letter from Stan. He had discovered that she was still paying rent on the flat.

'So when are you coming home? It looks as though the Cod War will be settled soon and they're saying that unemployment will be worse up here than anywhere else. But money is still around, pet. Blokes come off the oil rigs with wads of notes in their pockets as thick as books. They want to buy luxuries for their wives and girlfriends. And we peddle luxuries. Everything is happening up here since this offshore oil started up. Come home. Come home and marry me.'

She talked it over with Rose but not Maud. Perhaps it was Maud who made her feel redundant?

Rose listened without speaking and when Jon came to Stan's proposal she said, 'Are you in love with him, Sis?'

'No. Of course not. And don't get me wrong. I'd never marry him. I'll never marry again. But . . . I can't explain the difference up there, Rosie. I felt I was accomplishing something at last. Off my own bat. Of course I realize now it wasn't off my own bat. But it's obvious Stan needs me for the business – if I was a liability in that field, believe you me, he wouldn't want me back.'

There was another pause. Rose said, 'Even taking that into consideration – your job I mean – I still don't see the point. You will get a better job here eventually.'

'But . . . somehow . . . there isn't a place for me here.' Jon saw her sister's face and said quickly, 'I don't mean that the way it sounds, darling. It's just . . . ' How did you tell your sister that you felt like Judas Iscariot? She tried.

'I suppose . . . in a way . . . I feel I should . . . ' She stopped, took a deep breath and blurted, 'Oh God, Rosie!

It was all my fault. Ma dying like that. Stan's fault – my fault for knowing him – letting him think he was one of the family – I have to go back – I have to – to expiate the bloody guilt or something!'

Unexpectedly tears spouted from her eyes. She covered her face with her hands. Rose sat close to her on the sofa, but she refused to use the proffered shoulder. She huddled into a corner and gasped it all out as fast as she could.

'Georgie hated the secondary school. It was rough – he thought he was a tough guy but he was with Ma and me all the time – he's as soft as – as I am!' She laughed slightly, choked, hurried on. 'He got in with the wrong set. They made him pinch stuff from Woolworths. There was a scene – oh, you can imagine. Stan took him in hand. Those were his words. Took him in hand. It meant hitting him, Rosie! Hitting Georgie! He played truant and Stan actually took off his belt and beat him!' Her tears abated and her voice steadied. She took her hands from her face and looked into the past. 'He thought – when the divorce came through – that we would marry. He tried to take us over. I should have cut free from him then. I realize that now. But the job . . . and he took me out and about with him. And he was so good to Georgie as well as . . . Anyway then some of the other lads beat Georgie up and Stan went along and sorted that out.' She laughed again. 'Georgie loved him! He really did! He never held anything against Stan. He called him a real man!' She glanced at Rose almost defiantly. 'And he is. In spite of all I just said about my independence and my job, one of the things I like about Stan is that he . . . he can cope. With anything. Anyone. He always saw to my car—' she tried again to laugh. 'And the flat. And he'd bring Ma flowers and take her out for a meal if I was working – she loved him too.'

There was a pause and Rose said quietly, 'She loved everyone.'

Jon wept again. Then she checked herself and went on. 'I'd been to Whitley Bay and the car had broken down. I phoned him. He fetched me home. We were quarrelling all the time. When we got there, Ma and Georgie were mucking about in the park. It seems they were going to the shop. Ma had told Georgie he could stay at home and help her pack to come here for the holidays. But Stan assumed he was playing truant again. He was furious with me – furious with everyone. He got out of the car, swung at Georgie and . . . knocked him out.'

Even Rose's calm was shattered by that. She drew in a sharp breath.

Jon said, 'Yes. It was pretty grim. Ma took over – we got him into the hospital. Nothing was wrong with him. I wouldn't let Stan take us home. We waited for an hour for a bus. The Volvo was just over the road. Georgie couldn't think what was the matter with us – he didn't hold anything against Stan. I was exhausted and I knew Ma was too.' She stood up suddenly and went to the big window overlooking the hill. 'Ma died that night,' she said flatly.

There was a pause, then Rose followed her and put a protective arm over her shoulders.

'Sis. Don't you see? Mother wanted to be needed. She was needed in Newcastle. She was happy. She was one of the most contented people I have ever met.'

Jon said, 'Aren't you missing the point?'

'I don't think so. Maybe if Mother had stayed here quietly, uneventfully, she would be alive. But not needed.'

'If that awful business hadn't happened—'

'It wasn't your fault, Jon. It's like me saying I caused David's cancer by making him eat his meals!'

Jon drew away slightly and looked at her sister. She said slowly, 'Do you think that?'

Rose pulled her back quickly. 'Of course not!' She rubbed at Jon's shoulder then said quietly, 'Once . . . I insisted on him drinking some lemonade. And afterwards he was sick.'

'Oh my God.' Jon turned and put her arms around Rose's waist. 'All this time. And you cannot forgive yourself.'

Rose patted Jon's shoulder. 'Of course I forgive myself. And so will you.' She reverted to Jon's problem energetically. 'There's nothing for you in Newcastle. And we're here. We can share . . . everything.'

'No.' Jon felt a sadness that went deeper than her personal unhappiness. 'No. We share our loss, Rose. We can't share our grief. Mine is different from yours.' She let her arms fall and went back to the sofa to pick up a handkerchief. She said, 'I left things in Newcastle . . . unfinished. I'm always doing that.' She blew her nose, smiling at her sister over the handkerchief. 'This time . . . this time, Rosie, I have to finish it myself.'

Rose said stubbornly, 'Darling, it *is* finished! Can't you see that? This is your home now. Something will turn up on the job front and meanwhile—'

Jon played her trump card. 'Something has already turned up, Sis. Martin phoned. He offered me a job in his office. You see, I really must go.'

Rose took a deep breath. 'Ah. I see.' She looked down at her hands. 'Poor Martin.'

Jon said dryly, 'Yes. Poor Martin.' The old Jon might have protested that some sympathy was due to her over the fiasco of the Martin episode. But the empty, hollow Jon could not have protested if she'd tried. That night she recalled the awful experience of Martin and Rick and the bell tower and knew that she could never live in Churchdown again. Rose might think she understood all about Jon. But she could not understand the rejection; Rose had never been rejected. Rose was the legitimate daughter of Aileen and Jonathan Harris, she had had grandparents, she had been wooed and won by a good man and had had her daughters properly within wedlock. Jon had had none of those advantages. Her husband had rejected her in favour of Rose.

She wrote to Stan that same night.

'Dear Stan, if you will agree to us going back to the way we were, I will come home. I cannot marry you. But I do miss you and I miss the job too. Best wishes, Jon.'

He phoned an hour after receiving the letter.

'Come back, pet. We'll be good friends. We were always good friends.'

So she went.

Seventeen

If Jon was hoping for some kind of guilt-expiation on her return, she was disappointed. The flat was as depressing as a tomb. Her mother had made it a home and Jon wanted to do the same, but it was an impossible job.

She asked Stan if he could find something else.

'Why don't we get married, pet? Then you could come to the Gateshead house.'

She almost laughed. 'Your mother wouldn't have me!' She played for time.

He was not pleased. 'All right, once the business picks up again we could afford a house down by the coast, eh? You'd like that. And I'll be a good husband.'

She looked at him silently and he shrugged.

'Sorry, pet. I promised, didn't I? All right, I'll be a good boy.'

'Oh Stan. You know how I feel.' She wondered if she too should apologize. It was all so complicated. She said again, 'I wondered if it would be easier somewhere else. The flat is so dark.'

'It's got every other thing going for it, pet. The rent is low, you've already got it how you want it, and it's handy for the West Road shop.'

He was right, of course. She could not go back to how they'd been and still expect more. But it was not how it had been before because she was now on her own. It was hard work winning back her old clientele – she had been away for six months and they had gone elsewhere. At first she had time on her hands, yet was too tired to use it.

She had long ago handed over the housekeeping to Aileen; it was something completely new to arrive home in the afternoon and have to start cooking and cleaning. And

it was new to have so much space. Aileen and Georgie
had filled the place with their presence; sometimes she
imagined she could hear them upstairs, laughing together.
She found herself with a potato knife in hand, gazing out
of the kitchen window at the long strip of garden and
wondering what her mother had thought during the many
hours she had stood here. Or pausing with vacuum nozzle
in her hand and switching on the wireless because that was
what Aileen had done.

As spring turned to summer, she was busier in the shops
and in many ways things were better. But she couldn't manage everything; the garden ran wild and there was no time
for spring-cleaning. When Stan came in in the evenings, it
would have been nice to sit out of doors as they had done
in Aileen's day. The worst thing was that the girls who had
taken the Raschids' flat and hardly ever used the kitchen,
left quite unexpectedly and were replaced by another family
from Pakistan, very different from the Raschids. They all
worked very long hours and left the sink full of greasy dishes
and passed her in the hall as if she were a leper.

She came to rely on Stan more than she intended. He
did not call in every evening, so when he did she gave
him a warm welcome. And he did not take advantage
of her obvious loneliness. All through that hot summer,
he was everything she could wish. She had not expected
him to be so undemanding, so considerate. He brought her
flowers – something he had never done before – took her
to her favourite Whitley Bay on Sunday afternoons, even
helped her choose new clothes for their summer visit to
see Georgie. She teased him and said that only guilty
men brought flowers to their lady friends, and only the
courtesans of old had allowed their men friends to choose
their clothes. He responded with a shrug. 'You know what
to do about it, pet.' She looked on his almost formal
approach as a courtship. She had been so determined not to
marry Stan, but sometimes during those months she found
herself considering it quite seriously.

They stayed at the Queens in Cheltenham for the last
week in July, and took Georgie to the lido and the cricket.

303

He was thrilled to see Stan. The girls liked him too. Nothing could have been better. If she'd been in love with him it would have been the happiest time of her life.

It was difficult to trace exactly when he changed. Perhaps she should not have stayed on for the rest of the summer vacation. He expected Georgie to come back north with them for a few weeks, but Georgie was involved in cricket now and had a friend whose father played for Gloucestershire. She had said, 'Can you cancel my other August appointments when you go back, Stan? I'll go to the Snow-White house for the rest of the holidays as Georgie wants to stay down here.'

And he hadn't objected. Not really. He'd said, 'What the hell is the Snow-White house?'

She'd been surprised. He must have heard Georgie or Aileen call it that.

'The Churchdown house.' She smiled, 'Number four with the snow-white door!'

'You're all crazy.' He did not speak fondly. 'Your mother started it of course. But you're all as bad as each other!'

She was startled, not offended. 'What on earth d'you mean? Mother was the sanest person in the world!'

'This fairytale approach to everything. You don't know much about the real world, do you?'

'You must be joking! Mother had to bring us up on her own! Rose is now having to do the same—'

'So you call your back-to-back the Snow-White house. And that little rise outside is a ski slope. And that bloody old banger is a coach!'

She said lamely, 'It's anything but a back-to-back!'

And he snapped, 'That's another thing! All that fancy work on a pair of terraced houses! Just to make some kind of dream come true! You'll never see your outlay back!'

She said wearily, 'I don't think Rose has that sort of return in mind.'

He'd dropped it then, but when she eventually went back to Newcastle there were no flowers on the table and it was obvious he had not even looked in on the flat. She did not blame him; she did not mind. Not really. But it must have been from then that things were different.

She'd been so busy all through the autumn, she hardly registered Stan at all. Certainly they rarely went dancing now, but that suited her. She was tired most evenings and when she wasn't she was trying to wash curtains in the sink or make new cushion covers. And she was discovering something that her mother and Rose had always known: ordinary domestic work could be satisfying and . . . consoling.

In November, Stan's mother was ill and she saw even less of him. She wondered apprehensively what would happen if the old girl died. Would Stan want her to live with him at South Shields? Jon dreaded another decision to be made. She finished her very late spring-clean and made an early start on her Christmas shopping and cards. She knew Mrs McKee would not want to see her, but she phoned Stan most mornings to know how his mother was. He seemed appreciative. One evening she had a strange feeling about him and rang quite late. There was no reply. She did not hang on to the phone for long in case he was trying to sleep. The next morning he confirmed that he had had an early night. 'I'm up two or three times most nights,' he explained.

She said, 'I wish I could help.'

'Pet, I'm sorry. But you know how she is.'

'Yes of course. I just meant . . . couldn't you afford a nurse for her?'

'No way.' He sounded gloomy. 'If she goes into a nursing home I'll have to sell this place.'

She was convinced old Mrs McKee had a very healthy bank balance somewhere or other, but she said no more.

That Saturday she went to the cinema, telephoned Georgie and Rose, and had her hair done at a salon near the university.

It was while she was there, anonymous under the dryer in a row of other women all shielded by their magazines, that she saw Stan at the reception desk.

She was amused at first. She guessed he was after the salon; when she realized he was after the receptionist she was piqued. But nothing more. She watched his familiar tactics from the spurious privacy of the dryer, practically lip-reading his words. When the girl fetched her coat and went out with him to the waiting Volvo, something told her this was not the first time. She stared ahead, suddenly angry. Not because he was taking out another woman, but because he was lying to her about it.

She went home and asked herself what she expected. And whether it mattered. The trouble was, Stan was like a comfortable coat: he provided warmth and smartness; he was a habit. If he wasn't coming back she would miss him. Yes. But on the other hand, if he did come back . . . what then?

He came back.

It was as if nothing had happened. She asked him about his mother and he frowned and said he did not know what he was going to do about her. She said business had been slack just when she expected it to pick up, and he said he'd look into it. Probably mid-December every damned woman in Newcastle would want her hair and face done. He got out a pile of books from his case and went through them.

'You've kept everything up together, I'll give you that,' he commented almost grudgingly. 'But dammit, the receipts *are* down. Look at this – ' He pushed over a list of takings from the four shops. 'West Road and Newgate aren't showing a profit at all. Yet Whitley Bay and Cullercotes are doing well.'

'I could have told you that.' She was rubbing hand cream between her fingers. 'There's no money for luxuries down here – too much unemployment. The people who want to spend are the oil-rig lot.'

'I told *you* that!' He pushed the papers into a jumbled heap. 'Christ. Bloody Concorde. Bloody Viking probes off to Mars. And we can't make enough money to buy a new car.'

'A new car? What's the matter with the Volvo?'

'Nothing. But if we're going to get an upmarket image we've got to look good. You'll have to get rid of that bloody

Mini. We'll invest in one good car and make sure we're going to the same places at the same time!'

Jon said, 'Well . . . yes, OK. But I'll keep the Mini even if I don't use it.'

'What's the point?' He looked at her irritably. 'For God's sake stop massaging your hands when we're talking!'

It had been so long since his outburst that day last year, she did not recognize the signs. She continued to rub the cream carefully along her knuckles. Her soft hands were her stock in trade.

'It's handy for shopping. The buses are hopeless.'

'There are local shops.'

'Which means local people. You know what they think of me.'

He said deliberately, 'They think of you as a kept woman.'

She flushed at his tone and looked up. 'Well, I'm not, am I? We both know that!'

He said, 'It depends what you mean by kept, as dear old Professor Joad would say!' He gave a wintry smile. 'I made a job for you. I showed you off to the right people so that you could get more work. I take you out and give you a good time. I'm like a bloody insurance policy to you. Except that you don't have to pay any premiums!'

She was unreasonably hurt. 'My God, Stan! I've worked my fingers literally raw to give your very ordinary little hairdressing shops a different image! Those are my – my premiums – as you so elegantly put it!'

'And who paid for the visit to Cheltenham? Let me tell you, there's no money for going down there at Christmas! In any case I can't leave Mam.'

She tried to sound calm and reasonable. 'That's perfectly all right. I'll stay with Rose and Maud.' She reached for a tissue and began to wipe her hands. She did not want a row; something told her that a row would mean the end, and as her mother had pointed out years before, Stan could be vindictive. A row might well mean no job in Newcastle. She would say nothing about the receptionist at the hairdressers. She wondered – just for a terrible instant – whether now was the time to let Stan kiss her. Pushing the thought away, she dipped into the jar of cream again and rubbed the palms of her hands together.

The action appeared to enrage him. He leaned forward and tore her hands apart. He could not retain a grip on the slippery fingers and seized her wrists instead.

He said, 'You don't listen to me, do you? You don't intend to listen to me. Ever.' He pulled her towards him. She was going to end up on her knees in front of him. A complete reversal of the scenes with Ali and Martin. Stan was going to be the one to humiliate her.

He said, 'When I think how I've run after you for the past nine years and you've dangled yourself just in front of me like a bloody carrot with a bloody donkey—'

She panted, 'Let me go, Stan! You know it's not like that – I've always been honest with you! Right from the beginning when you took Rick and Georgie to football—'

'Exactly! You got what you could out of me. Never sent me packing—'

'You enjoyed it – you said you did! You liked Rick! And Georgie!'

'Oh sure. And I liked you too!'

'We were friends. You were my employer and—'

'And I am still! And you seem to forget it! Come here—' He pulled at her wrists cruelly and she screamed in sudden panic.

'Shut up – you'll have next door round here—'

She went on screaming. 'Why don't you go down to the University Hair Salon! Pick up the girl there again, like you did last weekend? And the weekend before that. I suppose your mother isn't even ill? I suppose it's all some grand plan—'

He let her go suddenly and hit her across the face.

She fell back into the armchair, knocking the hand cream off the arm, her scream ending in a squeak of shock.

She wondered afterwards what she would have done if he'd apologized immediately. But he did not. He shovelled the books and ledgers into his expensive brief case, grabbed his overcoat from the back of another chair and left.

She stayed where she was for a long time. He had a key and might come back. But he did not. And though she was frightened and horribly isolated, she was also glad.

Aileen would not have said 'I told you so', nevertheless she was right about Stan being vindictive. Jon had appointments at the Whitley Bay hotel the next day and drove there as usual in the Mini. A tall woman, vaguely familiar, greeted her.

'Are you booked for this morning? I'm afraid Mrs Johnson has left Newcastle. But I am taking over her work. I am fully qualified.'

Jon glanced at the framed certificate on the wall. It was a replica of hers. Stan had doubtless copied it from there. In a way it was funny.

She did not bother to call at Cullercotes or the West Road shop. She drove on up the coast as far as Newbiggin and parked opposite the caravans to look at the North Sea. A pair of gannets were the only sign of life, their huge wing span evident as they swooped over the wave-tops. She spoke to them as she had spoken to the gulls eighteen months ago. 'What the hell am I going to do?'

There was no answer.

Driving home she suddenly remembered where she'd seen the new beautician before. She was the receptionist who had got into the Volvo with Stan last weekend.

Another thought followed that one without a pause.

She would go to America and stay with Eric Laben and shame Aunt Mabe into inviting her there. Just as she'd suggested to Mother four years ago. Her heart lifted irrepressibly. She was still only thirty. Anything could happen. Maybe she could be a companion to Aunt Mabe in her old age and inherit oodles of the senator's cash. Or she could marry Eric Laben. She made a face in the driving mirror – not that. But at any rate she would see where Rose and Aileen had spent five significant years. She would see where she herself had been conceived.

And then came the most stupendous thought of all. Maybe . . . perhaps . . . yes, maybe, she would find her father!

The Mini swerved slightly between the double line of fir trees. She held the wheel tightly; it was a bitter day, perhaps there was ice on the road. But she knew there wasn't. It was that last thought that had made her hands jerk involuntarily. Suddenly she knew what she was waiting for – looking for. A father.

She tightened her lips and slowed down as she came into the city. She would go home early tomorrow morning. Load the Mini up with as much as she could, give her notice to the landlord, fill the tank and just go. If the car didn't make it, too bad. But it would.

She parked carefully outside the house and took time to look around her. She might never see Topps Green again and she had been happy here, in a way. Or, as she'd said to her mother, not unhappy. Georgie had done all his growing-up here. She and Rick had thought they were going to be all right here.

She walked slowly to the door and fitted her key into the lock. At the end of the long passage Rick had hung a mirror to reflect light from the fanlight, and she surveyed herself in it. At this distance she looked the part she had played for so long: still young, but not youthful; thin and sophisticated in knee-high boots and a long tweed skirt with a fur jacket above it. Since Aileen's death she had let her short curls grow and scraped them back into a French pleat. It showed more face and enabled her to use her make-up dramatically.

She closed the front door behind her and took out combs and hairpins. Her hair fell to her shoulders. Then she went straight through to the kitchen and washed her face beneath the running cold tap. That was better. No disguises now. Rose would approve.

She smiled almost sadly. She would say nothing to Rose about looking for her father. One more secret. But Rose would not understand; she would raise objections. Jon went slowly upstairs to begin packing.

310

She had to tell Rose that she had left Newcastle for good: her Mini, piled high with all kinds of junk, gave her away. But Rose was pleased about that.

'You won't have to hurry back. George will be delighted.'

She bent down to look through the car windows at the motley collection inside.

'Mother's knitting bag! Oh Jon . . . and the little table where we used to have our tea in the winter!'

'Everything back where it belongs.' Jon smiled. 'It all came from here after all.'

'I suppose so. Oh Jon. Are you all right? Was there a row?'

'No. Yes.' Jon laughed. 'It didn't bother me. Honestly.'

'I can see that.'

Rose lugged a case off the roof rack and started up the garden path. 'Maud is out. Fitting loose covers to some chairs in the pub. I'm wrapping her presents while she's away.'

Jon followed with another case. 'It sounds exciting. You finish that while I unpack the rest. Then we can talk.'

Rose hovered for a few minutes, then disappeared into the big kitchen.

Jon went back and forth through the old sitting room which was now the hall. She was so used to talking to herself that she said aloud, 'Well, home again, Ma. Not that it's home any more, is it?' She nearly leapt out of her skin when Rose said from the kitchen doorway, 'I thought that at first. But it is, you know. It even smells the same.' She laughed. 'Sorry, Sis. I wasn't eavesdropping really. I thought you were talking to me at first.'

Jon picked up a bag she'd let fall. 'I was,' she said. Then shook her head. 'No. I was talking to Ma. I often do.'

'So do I.' Rose came and took the bag from her and put an arm around her shoulders. 'Jon . . . I know I've put up a barrier these last four years. I had to. Nobody knew how I felt. Only Maud. You do understand?'

311

Jon felt the proverbial lump in her throat. She wished she could do away with her own barrier now, at this moment. But it must remain for the rest of her life.

'Of course.' She returned her sister's hug. 'Are you telling me that you're feeling . . . I don't know . . . better?'

'I never felt bad. Not really. Just so thankful I'd known him. David. Same with Mother. We've been so *lucky*, Jon. Haven't we?'

Jon nodded, not trusting her voice.

'The barrier was because . . . I wanted to look inside. At him. That made sense. Outside, without him, didn't.'

'Oh, Rosie. Don't.'

'It's all right. I don't feel that any more. And I'm so pleased you've come home. So pleased.'

'I might not stay, darling. In fact . . . I've already made plans for after Christmas.'

'Can you tell me?'

The new frankness between them allowed Jon to say honestly, 'No. Not yet.'

'That's OK. But if I can help, let me know. And you're sure you're not upset at leaving Newcastle? And . . . Stan?'

'No. Really. No relationship can stand still, can it? Ours was either going to boil over or go cold. It went cold.'

'I'm so surprised.'

'That it went cold?'

'No. That you have come home . . . without being upset!' Rose gave a small laugh of embarrassment.

Jon said, 'I am upset usually after this sort of thing, d'you mean?' She shook her head as Rose started to protest. 'No. I know what you mean, Rosie. And though you will find this hard to believe, I truly was just friends with Stan. Since . . . Martin, I've been faithful to Rick.'

Rose looked even more embarrassed. 'I thought . . . Mother said something about Ali Raschid. I shouldn't mention it now – but we're being so frank—'

'Nothing happened. Honestly. Well . . . something happened, but it didn't get that far.' Jon laughed. 'Really, Rosie! We're in our thirties and we're talking like Victorian schoolmarms.' She stepped back, held up one hand and enunciated clearly, 'I haven't been to bed with anyone since Rick left me. OK?'

Rose kissed her suddenly. 'OK,' she said. And Jon could tell she was genuinely pleased. How strange people were.

It was such a good Christmas that Jon caught herself wondering if it was to be her last and she was going to die young. Georgie must have put two and two together over the past eighteen months, and he was delighted that Stan had disappeared from their lives.

'Don't get me wrong, Mum,' he said in his new, breaking voice. 'I got on well with Stan. Well, you remember that. And if you'd married him, I'd have been pleased. But Gran wasn't keen. And Gran said you never would marry him. So it was all rather . . . peculiar.'

Georgie was so conventional these days that anything even slightly out of the norm was 'peculiar'.

She smiled. 'Just remember, he was very good to us, darling.'

'Yes. He was. Mum . . . ?'

'What is it, honey-bun?' They were in the kitchen making mince pies. The girls were giggling in the room behind. The connecting door was open but they were behind the sofa, very obviously packing a secret present. Jon floured the rolling pin and glanced through at the enormous patio window which looked out on to the hill. And the ski slope.

Georgie lowered his voice discreetly. 'D'you think you will get married again?'

She said unequivocally, 'No.'

There was a working silence. Then he cleared his throat. 'Of course you were very young when you married Dad, weren't you?'

'Seventeen.'

'Oh.' He was obviously disappointed. 'Not that young.'

'Quite old when you think about it,' she teased.

'Don't be silly, Mum,' he requested austerely. 'I just wondered . . . I mean, we have Human Biology now.

And obviously once one reaches puberty it is possible to have children.'

'Obviously,' she said, straight-faced.

He was silent again, dabbing teaspoonfuls of mincemeat into waiting cases without much interest. Blue's voice suddenly said loudly, 'Don't you *dare* tell him, Ellen Fairbrother!' and Ellie's reply, 'Well, don't you be so – patronizing, then!'

Jon glanced at Georgie to exchange a smile and saw he was bright red. She closed the door gently.

He caught her eye. 'It's just . . . ' he swallowed on air and gasped, 'Blue and me . . . it's possible . . . we could be . . . in love.' He looked at her face and said, 'Couldn't we?'

She did not know what to say. She wanted to laugh wildly. She couldn't wait to find Rose and tell her. But she was up to her elbows in flour and Georgie was wanting an answer to his question.

'You've always fought like cat and dog,' she procrastinated.

'That was because we – you know – sort of – liked—'

'Hitting each other?' she supplied, only just managing to keep her face straight.

He said impatiently, 'Mum, we could be in love. Couldn't we?'

She cleared her throat. 'Biologically,' she pontificated, 'it is quite possible. However, we don't let ourselves be ruled by biology—'

He blurted, 'You did. You must have done. You were sixteen when . . . ' his voice, for all his bravado, squeaked to a halt.

'When you were conceived?' She leaned her white hands on the table and looked at him. His face seemed about to explode from heat. She nodded slowly. 'Yes. That is so, Georgie. I wanted Dad. Quite desperately. You probably know already how I felt.' She took a breath. 'I managed to . . . I got him. Sorry, that sounds unbearably coarse. But that's what it amounted to. I got what I wanted. And I've regretted it ever since.'

He flinched. She said quickly, 'Not you. Never you. But if I'd waited, you would still have been born, my love.

314

And if I'd waited, I might still have Dad now. Does that make sense?'

The girls must have heard too. There was a deathly hush from behind the sofa. Georgie croaked, 'I'm sorry, Mum—'

'Don't be. You've a perfect right to ask me anything you want to know. I need not have answered. But I think you're old enough to understand. To take it.' She went back to the rolling pin and added lightly, 'And perhaps to learn from it!'

The patio doors slid back and Rose and Maud came in carrying a mass of holly.

'It hurts—' Rose laughed. She opened the connecting door, went through and dropped her armful in the grate. Then she said, 'What on earth are you two doing behind that sofa?' She laughed again. 'I used to love getting behind furniture too.' She shook her head as if at an elusive memory. 'Though I can't recall just when I did it – we never had room for a sofa in the Snow-White house!'

That night, the three adults laughed sentimentally about Georgie and Blue, but Maud had reservations.

'Could be awkward later. They spend so much time together.' She could say no more in case she offended Jon. But Jon laughed.

'Don't worry. As soon as Georgie is old enough I'll take him far away!'

Rose looked up from a pile of brochures but said nothing.

Jon touched her arm. 'Don't you ever feel like travelling, Rosie? France? America? Shall we go somewhere together?'

'No.' Rose was quite definite. 'My security is here. I belong here. Besides, I couldn't afford to travel.'

It was Maud who said, 'I could lend you the money, Ros. It might do you good. You should get away now and then. You're too young to stay here with me.'

Rose shook her head. 'It's got nothing to do with age.' She put the brochures on the floor. 'I get around quite a bit looking after the cottages – that's enough travelling for me!' She looked at Jon again. 'Are you thinking of travelling abroad?'

Jon shrugged. 'Maybe.'

'Can you afford it?'

'Just about.'

Rose looked away. 'I see.'

Jon wished suddenly that she could tell her everything. So that she really did see.

When the children went back to school she wrote to Eric Laben, applied for a passport, made plans. Eventually she had to tell Rose.

'You'll stand in for me at Easter, won't you darling?' she cajoled. 'Georgie won't mind me going over there – something to boast about to his friends!'

Rose was aghast. 'Where will you stay?'

Jon told a white lie. 'Quite near Aunt Mabe's place, actually. Eric Laben has got me a room. But I'm hoping – expecting – ' she giggled – 'that Aunt Mabe will invite me to stay with her!' It would not do to let Rose know she was staying at the Laben place; Rose might well remember that it was a household of two men only.

'Jon, you're still – terrible!' But Rose smiled, if rather anxiously.

'An *enfant terrible*?'

'Well, yes. But darling, you will be careful, won't you? The Americans . . . there is something – I don't know – dangerous, about them.'

'Oh Rosie!'

'It's a long time ago – I can barely remember it – but that was the impression I got. Danger.'

Jon felt a pang for her sister. 'I'll be careful,' she promised. She did not ask again if Rosie would go with her. One of the reasons for going was to remove herself from her personal source of guilt . . . wasn't it?

The whole trip was amazing. It was agony going up to Greystones to say goodbye to Georgie. He tried to pretend he didn't mind – he was in fact pleased for her. But he was white around the mouth and repeated several times, 'You will be coming back, Mum, won't you?' It was almost worse saying goodbye to Rose at Heathrow. But then the excitement took over.

In the business of boarding, looking around at her fellow passengers, securing her seat belt and taking off, she realized how starved of excitement she had been. Her life had been too eventful in many ways, but the events had not been exciting ones. Too often they had been tragic. There had been tension and loneliness and downright fear a lot of the time; there had been nothing to look forward to unless you counted family birthdays and Christmases; the feeling of being an outsider was never far away. Somehow, now, she felt she was going back to her roots. She'd find her father and even if he was dead, it would give her a new identity. A place. Really, she was an American.

She hadn't expected Eric to meet her at Kennedy and when she saw him waving she was thrilled. Best of all, in the car outside was his grandfather, old Mr Laben. He really was old; he looked about a hundred with leathery mottled skin and a black homburg, much too big for him, which marked him out as European immediately.

He tried to clasp her hands in both of his, which was difficult as they were full of luggage.

'So like your beautiful mother,' he said. 'She would have been about your age when last I saw her.'

Eric said, 'Let's get the bags in the trunk, Grandfather. Then you can talk to Joanna non-stop!' He manhandled Jon's big case into the enormous boot and took the two smaller ones from her. She slid in by the old man.

'Say, don't you want to sit up front with me?' Eric asked, grinning fatuously at both of them.

Jon said, 'I'd like to hear what your grandfather has to say about my mother, Eric.'

'I have won fair lady!' crowed old Mr Laben delightedly. 'You must concentrate anyway on the highway, my boy!'

There was a lot of badinage like that. Ordinarily it would have bored Jon to tears, but not now. Eric manoeuvred through the streets and joined what seemed like a four-lane motorway out of New York. Between responding to this small talk and trying to catch glimpses of the city, she began to feel quite dizzy.

Eric said briefly, 'Empire State to your right. Look back and you should see the Hudson.'

'You could take Joanna to see the sights another day, Eric. Today she talks to this old man.'

'Every prospect pleases!' she came back, trying to twist around to see out of the rear window. She sat back. 'It is so good of you to meet me. I didn't expect it. I was going to get a room for tonight and come on by train tomorrow.'

'We could not let you do that.' Mr Laben shook his head ponderously. 'We did not come to see your mother off thirty years ago. The least we could do—'

'Now don't get maudlin in the back there!' Eric pulled out to the left and passed a lorry that must have been a hundred feet long.

Jon said, 'No. I want to hear everything you can remember. I've come here specially for that. I feel this is my real country. After all, I started here!'

They both laughed, not realizing how serious she was.

The house where Jon had actually been conceived was called Redgrove. It had a porticoed front and an entrance hall with twin staircases rising from it to a suspended landing. Rose had been able to describe all that. But she had always referred to the house as 'the Laben place'. And she hadn't mentioned that it was a mansion.

'Was Aunt Mabe's farm like this too?' she asked, standing, unashamedly awestruck, in front of the stairs.

'It was the home farm before everything got sold off in lots,' Eric explained. 'It's a genuine American salt box. Joe still runs a herd of Jerseys. When he retired he tried to farm the land himself, but he had to take on a couple. They're not much good.'

'He lives there alone? Didn't he remarry when Aunt Mabe divorced him?'

318

'No.'

'He must be lonely.' Her mind was already working on this new fact.

'Guess he is. But they're good friends still. He goes to dinner there every Saturday night. And most nights he comes to play backgammon with Grandfather. So you'll meet him soon.'

A middle-aged woman in jeans and checked shirt appeared then, smiling warmly.

'Maria.' Eric humped Jon's luggage again. 'This is our friend from England. Joanna—' he began on the stairs. 'Maria lives in with her husband. They do everything, even the cooking. Especially the cooking!'

Maria took a bag and followed him. Jon trailed after. It was obvious that a household of two men would need domestic help, but she hadn't imagined Maria. Vaguely she remembered Rosie mentioning a coloured man at Aunt Mabe's. A sort of butler. There was nothing formal about Maria. She was definitely one of the family.

They'd given her a lovely room on the first floor with a view looking over hills that could have been the Malverns. It had a double bed with a canopy. Eric disappeared and she and Maria talked easily together while she unpacked and Maria adjusted the curtains and turned down the bed.

'There's such a lot to do here,' Jon could see now that the house extended some way. 'I'll try not to make more work for you.'

The older woman went to the door. She was very obviously Italian. 'It is not a problem, Mrs Johnson. And Mr Laben and Mr Eric have been looking forward very much to seeing you.' She pulled her shirt lower over her jeans. 'It is good that we can give you a holiday after so much unhappiness.'

Jon stared at the closed door. Of course Eric must have told them about David's death. And they knew that last year Aileen had gone. But they could not know about Rick. Nor her real reason for coming here.

She bit her lip. How long was a 'holiday'? How was she going to go about finding out . . . anything?

She stared around the room, then at the bed. Her mother had said something about a Victory Night party here and a one-night stand. Had it been in this bed?

She stood up and went to the window, wondering in which direction was the 'salt-box' farm where Rose had played and tried to avoid Aunt Mabe. Aunt Mabe had gone now, and Uncle Joe – no blood relation of course – was there on his own.

She smiled to herself, wondering whether he needed a companion. A sort of housekeeper. Even a nurse.

Eighteen

Letters came from Jon; some for Georgie, some for Rose. They were pooled for the most part. During the Easter holidays they were read *en famille*. Their tone obviously varied considerably depending on to whom they were addressed. The letters to Georgie made life-in-America sound exciting and almost as Hollywood had depicted it for the past fifty years. Those addressed to Rose tried to make it sound quite a dull place where nothing extraordinary ever happened and where Jon was behaving in a very conventional manner.

'Listen to this!' Georgie read aloud and exuberantly, glancing at Blue now and then for any visible reaction. 'We had a super time today. Eric took me riding. Yes. On a horse – ten out of ten! I wasn't bad at all but after four hours in the saddle I didn't feel the same for a couple of days. You'd love it out here. It's like Churchdown used to be when Aunt Rose and I were children. Only it goes on and on. There are little settlements rather like our villages only more isolated. Georgetown, where your great-aunt Mabel lives, is so tidy, I can't believe it. Not a shabby house in sight. Nor a weed. Tell Aunt Rose she sends her love. But I have to tell you she is rather chilly towards me!'

Ellie said loyally, 'I don't see how anyone could be chilly to Aunt Jon.'

Georgie said acutely, 'Grandmother Harris is very chilly.'

'Well, she is to everyone.'

Blue said, 'Aunt Jon spends a lot of time with Eric Laben. Is he nice, Mummy?'

'I hardly remember him.' Rose put her most recent letter on the table with the others. 'As a matter of fact, she's not living at the Labens' house any more. She says here Aunt Mabe has insisted on her moving into Georgetown.'

'That doesn't sound chilly,' Georgie suggested doubtfully.

'I told you,' Ellie said. 'Aunt Jon has won her around.'

Rose rifled through the letters. Jon had left England in February to stay in a 'room'. The room had evidently been in the Labens' house because no mention was made of anywhere else. She must have been there at least six weeks. Now she was with Aunt Mabe. Rose had a definite feeling neither party would tolerate the other for as long as another six weeks. So it was possible Jon would be home in May. In time for her birthday.

But 3 May came and went. Jon's letters were now sent from another address – the Home Farm, Rosebridge. She was having a 'few days' with Uncle Joe who was now over eighty and needed a 'spot of loving care' as Jon put it. They heard nothing then until the middle of June when two letters arrived on the same day: one from Jon, the other from Aunt Mabe.

'Dearest Sis,' Jon wrote in her huge scrawl. 'I've been here just a month today and I can't imagine living anywhere else! Isn't it amazing! It's like coming home. As if I knew it intimately from another life. Maybe I did live here in another age. Or maybe it's familiar because you and Mother spoke of it. I'm here in the room where you slept for the first five years of your life! Can you imagine it, darling? Every morning I wake up and think – this is what Rosie saw when she was a little girl. And every night I go up the stairs very slowly, counting them like you told me you used to, because if you didn't something horrid would be waiting on the landing! Rosie, I am so excited. I am getting nearer to something which matters to me. So hard to explain, but perhaps you will understand anyway? You must have wondered about Mother – why she did what she did – and I feel as if I'm going to find out at any moment. Don't worry about me, Sis. Uncle Joe's a darling – he asked me to marry him the other day! Meanwhile I am a sort of housekeeper companion friend – call me what you like. He says I am his guest, but every two or three days he writes enormous cheques for me to pay the housekeeping expenses and he won't take any change! He has asked me to take Greta and Clark in hand – they're the hired help and they're awful – and he's asked me to do some cooking – d'you know I'm quite good at cooking and I'm really excellent at bossing Greta around! But mostly he likes me to make him laugh. And it's so easy, darling. He's so delighted with every little thing I say. I've told him about the Snow-White house and Mother and Georgie . . . d'you know, Rosie, he's my Uncle Joe too. Really – he's as much my uncle as yours, isn't he? I know Aunt Mabe is my aunt too, but I'm not very keen on her! Actually Uncle Joe told me yesterday that I reminded him of Mabel when he married her first! I looked suitably appalled and he laughed and said she wanted things to happen all the time, just like I did, and I'd better try to learn a few lessons from her! Anyway, it's a piece of cake here, darling. I am loving it. I love the farm, I love the place, I love Uncle Joe – he calls you his "chickadee". I could live here for ever!'

The other letter said, 'My dear Rose, I hate to complain, dear. It is simply not in my nature to do so. But I am afraid your half-sister has placed me in a very difficult position. It was bad enough when she accepted hospitality from the Labens – you can imagine how embarrassing it was for me that my niece was staying with someone else, and such an odd household too – no hostess unless you count Maria Rivolo whom old Rudolf Laben treats like a daughter though she barely speaks English. I thought at first Joanna was setting her cap at young Eric, who was divorced two or three years ago, but she assured me she will never marry again! I told her that she was not doing her reputation any good and begged her to come to me immediately, and eventually after she realized the true position, I am glad to say she did. But my dear child, your sister is so unlike either you or your mother. I cannot see her likeness to any member of our family and can only assume she is taking after the paternal strain. I hardly like to mention this aspect of the situation, it is long-buried, but obviously is another embarrassment for me. However, now the very worst has happened. Joanna and I had a slight disagreement and she has moved in with my ex-husband Joseph Lange, who you will doubtless remember as being rather a coarse man and well able to make the most – or the worst – of this situation. My concern is on two counts: my own reputation as a senator's wife, and Joanna's position at the farm.

I have talked to both of them, Rose, and they both seem to think it's a humorous situation. I can assure you they are the only ones who think so. So I am appealing to you. I understand that you have had to deal with Joanna's escapades several times in the past and therefore know how to make her listen to sense. I am enclosing some money which should cover your fare and any clothes you might need. Come to me, Rose dear. I have long wanted to meet you again anyway and wish it could have been in happier circumstances.'

There was a gap beneath the signature, then a scrawled postscript: 'Your half-sister informs me that you will not accept this invitation. Rose, for your mother's sake I am asking this. I would remind you that I am now seventy-seven and should not be expected to have this kind of problem foisted on me.'

Rose almost laughed aloud at this. But other aspects of it were not funny. She passed the letter over to Maud together with the enormous cheque, and watched her face as she read.

Maud showed no sign of wanting to laugh either. She glanced up almost apprehensively when she had finished.

'Oh my God. Poor old Jon. What are you going to do?'

They were sitting in the room where Maud now sewed. The windows were open on a perfect June day. The post had arrived late and Rose had taken it up with a cup of coffee.

She raised her brows now. 'Well, nothing. Jon is well able to look after herself, Maud. And as for Aunt Mabe – she had nothing to do with us for years! It's a bit of a cheek to expect me to pop over there and sort out her life! Jon is a social embarrassment, that's all. Sounds as if she's doing Uncle Joe a bit of good and no harm to herself either.' She did eventually laugh. 'Storm in a teacup.'

Maud skimmed Jon's letter and nodded doubtfully.

'Yes. I suppose so. You don't think she would marry this Uncle Joe, do you?'

'Of course not! He's in his eighties!'

'Yes. But . . . well, you know. If he promised to leave her some money or something . . . '

Rose said firmly, 'I know Jon gives the impression of being on the make all the time, Mother, but she's not really like that. She's a very generous person. She's obviously being a great help to Uncle Joe.'

Maud put the letters in a pile and picked up her thimble again. 'It doesn't sound as if she'll be back for a while anyway,' she said. 'I wonder what she's looking for over there? When she says she feels as if she's getting to the bottom of things.' Maud settled her glasses comfortably and began to tack together two pieces of brocade. There was a silence and she looked up again. 'I mean . . . I didn't mean . . . ' She removed her glasses. 'Ros, I'm sorry. I know that dear Aileen had Jon after your father was dead. It's none of my business, of course.'

Rose said warmly, 'My business is your business, Mother. You know that. And I suppose Jon's beginnings are my business.' She hesitated. 'Strangely enough, I've always tried to forget them. Jon's beginnings, I mean. I think I wanted a sister so much, I refused to admit she was a half-sister.' She fingered the letter again. 'I know Jon talked about it to Mother. Perhaps Mother told her something . . . I really don't understand that bit either.'

Maud said, 'Water under the bridge. I hope Jon won't unearth something that might upset her. Perhaps that's what your aunt fears too.'

'Perhaps.' Rose went to the window. She wondered why she did not want to talk about any of this. Perhaps because Aileen never had? After all it was no-one's business except Aileen's, and Aileen was dead. But Jon was alive. And of course it was her business. She sighed sharply and said, 'I have to go to Temple Guiting today. The tenants there are complaining about the drains. D'you want to come?'

Maud laughed. 'You don't trust your own nose?' She shook her head. 'I have to finish these cushions.' She replaced her glasses. 'Listen, Ros. If you change your mind about going to Connecticut, I can manage here perfectly well. And Martin would be up in a jiffy if there was a problem.'

'I won't be changing my mind, Mother. Besides, the children will be home in a few weeks and we both need to be around then.'

'Blue and Georgie, you mean?'

'I hadn't thought of that. But yes, I suppose so.'

Maud bit off a length of cotton. 'I had hoped Jon would be home by then to take Georgie off somewhere.'

Rose thought of her determined daughter. 'Blue would not have permitted it,' she said. And they both laughed.

But the summer holidays were no laughing matter. Ellie brought home a friend for the first time, which meant that Blue and Georgie were thrown together more than usual. Their undoubted feeling for one another erupted into perpetual bickering and quarrelling. Georgie needed chauffeuring to cricket matches at least once a week. And he had taken up jogging at school and would disappear for hours; Blue snapped his head off whenever he eventually appeared.

Georgie was essentially easy-going. He tried to explain to Blue that he did care about Steve Biko and the situation in South Africa, but until he could do something about it he intended to continue to play cricket and go jogging. Blue was in a state of simmer about every injustice in the world. She could not wait to be old enough to join in demonstrations and peace marches. Like Aileen, Rose could see that one day it might be a very good match. But until that day, Blue's bad temper made life difficult.

Meanwhile more letters came from Aunt Mabe and Jon. Jon's were small catalogues of chores she was doing on the farm. Aunt Mabe's exaggerated these chores into evidence of promiscuity.

'Eric Laben is round there most days,' she complained. 'It's probably being run like one of these appalling communes!'

And then, when the children were back at school and the summer lets were finishing, came the important letter from Jon.

'Dearest Rosie, I seem to have come to a brick wall. Eric Laben seems to think you might be able to give me a leg-over! Darling, I haven't really told you what I'm doing here, have I? I'm trying to trace my father. I know I should let sleeping dogs lie – I can hear you saying as much – if Ma had wanted me to know anything she would have told me, etcetera, etcetera. The awful thing is, I don't think Ma knew much about him. Maybe his name, and that he was married and had a son. That was enough for her and she shied off. It's not enough for me, Rosie. I have to know. Really. Please believe me – it's terribly, terribly important. Anyway, Sis. I've had to take things steadily. Aunt Mabe seems the most likely lead, and I tried to get her reminiscing – things like that. But no good. The Labens were wonderful. Old Mr Laben likes to think of himself as a bit of a detective and he told me all about the Victory Night party. But neither he nor Eric could remember who danced with Ma. Anyway then I turned to Uncle Joe. He's as keen as mustard, but no real help. Aunt Mabe's the one and she's not saying a thing. He reckons when her mouth looks like a duck's ass, she won't budge! He's a scream, Rosie, I do like him. If only he was fifty years younger, I might well marry him! But he also says you might shift her. She's certainly got a soft spot for you, darling. Don't know why? Is it because you're legitimate? And conventional? I still held out against asking you over here because I know how you hate leaving the Snow-White house. But now Eric reckons that you and Lennox Laben probably saw him. Is that possible? He says Lennox chased you all round the house or something and you ran to Ma in her room. Can you remember if she was with someone, Rosie? Because if so, that person is my father. We can't ask Lennox. He's had a breakdown and is in some mental place. Eric says he'd be unreliable anyway. But you're the most reliable person on earth, Rosie.

'Two things, darling. First, can you dig down into your head and recall anything at all about that night. And next, please, please, will you come over and be nice to Aunt Mabe and see if she knows anything.

'Darling Rosie. I'm not being entirely selfish. This place is so . . . good. The air makes you feel better. I think you should get away from home for a bit. Honestly.'

It was all so silly. Rose couldn't remember anything; she'd only been five – not even five. But she wished Jon hadn't mentioned Lennox Laben. She had shut him right away and did so again immediately she finished the letter. It crossed her mind briefly that he might have been the reason she found the start of her marriage so difficult. But even that seemed ridiculous.

She read most of the letter to Maud and was amazed at her reaction.

'I think you should go, Ros.' Maud spoke very firmly and seriously. 'It's five years since David died. I think you need to begin to look outside again.'

Rose gazed at her; she felt suddenly frightened. 'I thought I was doing that! The job with the agents – coming up here to make a fresh start—'

'Rosamund, the Snow-White house was your home—'

'But it's not the same—'

'It's even better. You said yourself you can still smell the old place.' Maud stood up and went to the window. 'In a way you're reliving your mother's life. With the girls at school it's possible to stay inside your head, and you do that a great deal.' She turned and looked at her daughter-in-law. 'I encourage that. It's wrong. You're only thirty-seven. You've got a lot of real life to live yet.'

'Mother, I thought we were happy!'

'We are. We can go on being happy. Remember Ruth and Naomi?' Rose looked bewildered and Maud smiled. 'In the Bible. Ruth stuck to her mother-in-law after her husband's death and Naomi sent her off to look for a new husband. And Ruth found Boaz.'

'You want me to go to America and find Boaz?' Rose tried to laugh.

'If that's what happens, yes.'

Rose felt as if Maud had knifed her. 'Mother!'

'And on a more practical note,' Maud swept on, 'you're needed out there. Oil on troubled waters. It's your forte.'

'I'm not going,' Rose replied with sudden little-girl stubbornness.

She did not have a passport. Nor a visa. But she did have dual nationality. There were forms to fill in and she hated doing this, having to declare herself to be a widow: it was an ugly word conjuring images of spiders and blackness. At every snag she reiterated that she was not going. But Maud or Martin would help her over the problem and it seemed, by her birthday, that she might eventually go, if only for a fortnight.

There were transatlantic phone calls and some new clothes and a new case to put them in and a St Christopher medallion from the girls and a tape for her to give to Jon from Georgie in lieu of letters, and a first-aid kit from Martin and June.

She couldn't believe it was happening. She kept saying that she would be away just a fortnight, or a month at the most, but the way the family bade her farewell it was obvious they thought she was going on an expedition to the unexplored Amazon and might never come back.

'I'll be home for half-term,' she repeated for the fourth time.

'Yes. Yes.' Ellie was sharing a phone with Blue. 'But in case not, can I bring Janet home with me again? And can we have riding lessons if Grandmother says so?'

Blue's voice overlaid the last bit. 'Listen, if you get to Washington, try to see the new President – Jimmy Carter – about Steve Biko—'

Rose said firmly, 'I shall be in Connecticut. At Georgetown. With Aunt Mabe. You've got my address and the telephone number. And I shall be back for half-term.'

'OK, Mummy. See you then,' They chorused. They saw nothing catastrophic about going to America. Even Maud seemed optimistic about it.

'You're going to have a lovely time,' she said briskly, turning away from the appeal in Rose's very blue eyes. 'Remember every little thing. I shall want to know it when you get home.'

'I'll phone you.'

'Do that.'

Maud looked so aristocratic in her ancient flannel suit and hat. Rose clung to her suddenly and gasped, 'Listen. In case . . . just in case . . . I want to thank you. I love you so much. You're part of David. And I thank him every minute of every day. So I must thank you too.'

Maud held her face steady. 'You know it's mutual, don't you? But . . . Ros . . . David would want you to go on. He'd want to go on with you. You do know that, don't you?'

Rose nodded. But it did not mean much.

She was just plain terrified all through the Heathrow business, but then came the entirely unexpected excitement of her very first flight. The plane was a Boeing and the hostess who came to her seat to explain about the seat belt and the meals had a slight American accent but was actually an English girl who had lived in New York since she was ten years old. Rose had no idea why the girl confided these facts, or even when she did so – she was too busy to stay long in one place – but by the time they were above the silvery mountain ranges of cloud Rose knew that the girl had chosen her work because it took her to her old and new country. 'You can't be in two places at once.' The hostess gave her professional smile. 'But this comes pretty near to it!'

In return Rose said, 'I was born in America, but I couldn't wait to return to England. And I've never wanted to go back.'

'You wait.' The smile became mysterious. 'You'll wonder how you could keep away for so long once you land.'

Rose, terribly English in a navy linen suit, was already homesick for Maud and the Snow-White house, but she too smiled – politely – and hoped there might be a grain of truth in what the girl said.

Several passengers looked apprehensive when the great plane came in to land at Kennedy, but Rose felt no more nervous than she had before. She went through the drill, closing her eyes and swallowing as her ears tuned in to another register; it was no worse than driving up the long hill through Cranham woods. Disembarking, hearing strange, laconic voices all around her, being herded to where the Customs awaited them – that made her heart jump into her throat. Yet, even as she looked around for Jon, she knew that the atmosphere – the air she was breathing – was deeply familiar to her subconscious. It might be different, but it was not strange, and it certainly was not alien.

Jon appeared from nowhere and rushed at her. She was wearing denim jeans and a white vest and looked like a sophisticated fifteen-year-old. Rose was so delighted to see her she allowed herself to be waltzed around publicly, almost falling over in her high heels.

'Jon, you look marvellous!' she gasped. 'Oh I'm so pleased – you look like you did at school—'

'It's the hard work!' Jon was laughing too, dark eyes looking at Rose, always impenetrable, never clear like David's.

'You even smell like you used to!' Rose discovered. 'Hay and Mother's special soap. Oh darling – it's good to see you. All this business . . . it won't make any difference, will it? We're sisters!'

Jon's eyes filled. She hugged Rose again. 'Thank you for coming,' she said in a new, quiet voice. 'I know it's been hard for you. But this isn't me yelling at you to get me out of a scrape. It's me saying let's find out about ourselves. Together. Properly.'

Rose looked at her, then nodded. 'OK. That's why I'm here.'

Jon took Rose's hand luggage and steered her into the stream of people.

'On the strength of your arrival, I've been taken back into the fold!' She grinned sideways. 'We're both staying at Aunt Mabe's. It's all so respectable. And not half as nice as Uncle Joe's. Why she preferred old Steedman to him, I'll never know!'

'What about my big case?'

'The chauffeur will get that. Yes. Chauffeur. It's so upmarket it's untrue. Mabs has sent me in the limo. Sis, it's absolutely plush. Just you wait and see!'

Rose nodded, unsurprised. She remembered the Labens' house vaguely; a hall with curving stairs and a chandelier. She could imagine what the senator's house was like.

The chauffeur was white and 'a smart-ass' according to Jon. She slid the glass partition across the interior of the car and sat on the jump seat with her back to him. 'He'll only chip in,' she said. 'That's the trouble here. Everyone minds everyone else's business.'

Rose said, 'It's not who I thought it might be. But then he would be too old now.'

'I keep forgetting you've been here before!' Jon giggled. 'Who did you think it might be?'

Rose frowned. 'I can't remember his name.' She sighed. 'He was lovely. My friend.'

'Oh Sis – don't sound so sad. This is a marvellous place to be! If you've come out to rescue me, you'll be eternally grateful! Send for the girls and Georgie and we'll all live out here!'

'You're as mad as ever!' Rose smiled.

They were driving through the outskirts of New York to get to the north turnpike. There was a park and a few trees; red and yellow leaves; it was fall. She thought of it as fall, not autumn. It reminded her of another fall: when she and David had stood behind the summerhouse in Stroud Road and known that their time together was coming to an end.

She felt suddenly faint in the air-conditioned car. 'Can you put down the window or something? Look at the trees. Look at that salt-box farm. Oh Jon.'

Jon pressed a button and both windows descended; a rush of air blew their hair. She said above the wind, 'Are you all right, Sis? I'm sorry. Is all this going to upset you? Was it very awful?'

'It wasn't that. It was . . . I suddenly remembered . . . *felt* . . . David.' Rose took a deep breath, then leaned back against the upholstery and closed her eyes.

'Oh God.' Jon moved across to sit by Rose. 'I'm sorry, Sis. You never talk about him.' She took Rose's hand. 'I hoped – so much – it wasn't hurting any more.'

'It doesn't. I've always been . . . just thankful.' Rose concentrated hard on not passing out. She said, 'Just then. It came to me. That's all.'

Jon was concerned. 'Darling. Some time you have to let it out. If it's to be now, then . . . let it be now.'

Rose opened her eyes and smiled. 'Honestly. I'm all right.' The limousine was going fast through countryside that looked English. She said steadily, 'Don't worry, Jon. Just . . . not quite orientated yet.'

Jon said hopefully, 'It could be jet lag, actually. It does funny things.'

Rose nodded and smiled and at last sat up straight again. She said determinedly, 'Now. Let's talk.' She still held Jon's hand and she lifted it up and down to emphasize her next words. 'You do realize that as far as memories go, I'm hopeless. I can remember Aunt Mabe being horrid to poor Mother and me wanting to get back to England and have you and nobody would know anything was wrong. At least, I suppose that's what I thought.' She smiled. 'Mother and I never talked about it, ever. We wiped it out of the memory banks!' She laughed. 'But I probably can talk Aunt Mabe round to spilling any beans. If she has any to spill.'

Jon said gloomily, 'She says she hasn't.' She pressed a button and the nearside window closed. 'What about you and this ghastly Lennox Laben? Did you find Ma that night?'

Rose said, 'I don't think I did. It's all such a muddle.'

Jon patted her hand reassuringly. 'Don't worry about it now. Maybe when you've had a talk with Mabs, things will come back. OK? Let's just enjoy being together for now.'

Rose smiled. 'Sounds great,' she said.

The sisters were silent as the car sped on. Jon closed the other window and opened a cabinet. Glasses, bottles, tiny packs of sandwiches were revealed. She raised her eyes at Rose who shook her head.

Jon said, 'I'll wait too. Dinner will be enormous in your honour. I hope you realize Mabs is acting as if the Queen is coming to tea!'

'What's it like there? When you say plush—'

'I mean grand. Porticoed front. It's called Court House. And it used to be a courthouse. Before the senator converted it, of course. Right in the middle of this little town. Georgetown. There are tons of Georgetowns in the States, but this one is lifted straight from colonial days. You'll love it.'

'Is it near the old farm?'

'Oh yes. And Uncle Joe goes to dinner once a month. He's coming tonight, of course.'

Rose said faintly, 'How . . . odd.'

'It doesn't seem odd really. They're all quite friendly. The Labens too. Of course they're all about a hundred and fifty.'

'Not quite.'

'Nearly. The senator looks as though he was embalmed last week.'

Rose started to giggle in spite of herself, and Jon said, 'That's better.'

Rose did feel much better. She sat forward and stared through the window again. They had been travelling for an hour on the turnpike and she wondered if she were imagining that she recognized the low line of hills on the horizon. A name came into her mind: Miss Millward. Who on earth was Miss Millward?

She said, 'There used to be cows and horses at the farm. Pigs and hens too.'

'Just cows now. A pedigree herd – Jerseys. We could keep hens actually. I could cope with hens if Clark objected.'

'Clark!' mocked Rose.

'And Greta. Yes. Never mind the cows, they milk Joe all the time!'

Rose said, 'Aunt Mabe is worried about you being with Uncle Joe.'

'Yes. I know that. It embarrasses her to death. I tried a spot of blackmail on her actually.'

'Jon! What on earth do you mean?'

'Told her I'd behave myself if she helped me find my father.'

'What did she say?'

'Oh, she just clams up. At the moment the thought of all that business coming up again embarrasses her more than her crazy niece shacking up with her ex-husband!'

Rose tried to look shocked and failed. But she did say, 'Listen, Jon. It might seem funny now, but you know how tongues wag. And if you want to stay here . . . '

'Don't worry. I'm the soul of discretion.'

Rose rolled her eyes towards the roof of the car. She could see Aunt Mabe's point of view only too well.

Jon said, 'D'you know one of the good things to come out of all this digging and delving? It makes me appreciate Grandmother much more. I can understand now why she was so anti Ma and me. If Aunt Mabe can be so touchy, it must have been worse for Grandmother. She must have seen me as an act of unfaithfulness towards her son. Yet she has still sent Georgie to Greystones.'

Rose nodded slowly. 'I used to wonder why I was so obviously the favourite. It was awkward at times—'

'When you had to try to get a flat for Rick and me?'

'Not that so much. The little things.' Rose nodded again. 'Yes, you're right. Maybe I shouldn't have stuck my head in the sand all these years.'

Jon squeezed her sister's hand. 'Good-oh!' she said. 'We're going to get to it together, Sis. I feel . . . wonderful!'

'Yes.' Rose smiled. 'I don't feel so bad myself.'

They drove around the front of the house and through an archway into a stableyard that could have come from hundreds of stately homes in England except that everything was white. Even the disused pump in the middle of the bricked yard. But the flowers were left untamed and

335

obviously had no idea it was fall. Geraniums, asters and enormous chrysanthemums jostled up the walls and around the pump, and purple lobelia sprouted along the edges of the bricks. Rose had already done a great deal of exclaiming as they sped through the village, and her entranced silence spoke louder than words as they climbed slowly out of the car and stood by the pump.

Jon said, 'This is Jason, Rosie. Jason, will you take Mrs Fairbrother's bags up to the stable room next to mine? We'll go straight in and meet the oldies.'

Jason was young, blonde, Germanic. He said, 'Welcome aboard, Mrs Fairbrother. I shoulda stopped to let you out at the front, I guess, but I knew you'd like this.'

Rose was touched. 'Oh I do. Thank you very much. It's so like home. And the flowers—!'

'Completely sheltered. Plenty of sun. They'll go on till November.' He gathered up the bags. 'See you at dinner.'

Jon took Rose's arm. 'You're next to me in one of the stable rooms,' she said, pointing back at the smart conversion behind them. 'Sounds a bit off, but really it's marvellous. Gets us away from the oldies.'

'And Jason will eat with us?' Rose asked, thinking that things had changed since she was here last.

'Lord no, Mabs believes in keeping the servants in their place! He'll wait on table!'

They went through a kitchen that was all stainless steel and white surfaces. Jon called, 'Hi there, Cookie! Taking my sister to see Mabs, then we'll be back to talk to you!'

A thin-faced woman appeared around an enormous fridge. She did not return Jon's casual greeting and made no attempt to smile at Rose. She was as warmly brown as Fack had been, but no archetypal retainer was this. Rose almost stopped short in her tracks as the thought came into her head. Fack. That had been his name. She wanted to remember him properly; she had loved him and he had loved her. Later, she would recall everything about him, not now.

They crossed a parquet-tiled floor, cool and smelling of furniture polish. There were shallow stairs to the left, a white-painted door with brilliant brass handle on the right.

Jon opened it. A voice said, 'There you are! I saw Jason take the car on round the back yard. Typical when we're all waiting at the front!'

Rose stretched her face into an automatic smile. The voice was familiar. So much was familiar, half-remembered, felt in the bone. This woman had been one of the first people she'd known.

Aunt Mabe was sitting in a spoonback chair almost surrounded by low tables holding her immediate needs. Rose had time to take in an array of medicine bottles, tissues, cologne, a tapestry ring with spilling silks, a tall glass. Then Aunt Mabe held out her arms and she crouched to be enfolded. There was a momentary close-up of pleated skin and faintly bleeding lipstick, before she put her head awkwardly against the wiry white hair.

'My dear, dear, child. I thought we would not see you again.' There were tears in the voice. 'Rose. Aileen's child – my child too. Oh my dear, my dear, it's been too long.'

Rose was surprised. They had never been close.

'Lovely to see you,' she mumbled inadequately into the scented lace about the bony shoulder.

'So much grief . . . such tragedy . . . ' Aunt Mabe was definitely weeping now. 'If I could have helped . . . been there . . . no-one understands more than I do . . . '

Rose began, firmly, to withdraw.

'Please don't worry about me, Aunt Mabe. I am surrounded by . . . Jon . . . the children . . . Mother—'

The head jerked back. 'Your mother? Rose – dear child—'

Rose said quickly, 'David's mother. Maud Fairbrother. We are very close.'

She sensed this did not please her aunt. Rose was supposed to be lonely, distraught, stricken.

Aunt Mabe murmured something but her mood had been interrupted. She allowed Rose to stand up though she retained one hand in hers. She put on a determined smile and said, 'You had better meet the senator, dear child. You'll remember him of course, but you have changed a great deal so he cannot possibly have any recollection of you!'

Non-recognition was mutual. The tiny wizened figure in the enormous armchair on the other side of the flower-filled fireplace was completely unfamiliar to Rose. She wondered what to call it. Jon, with a grin in her voice, said swiftly, 'Rose, Senator. Senator, Rose.'

The figure began to struggle. Rose rushed forward. 'Please don't get up – er – Senator. So kind of you to have me. At such short notice.' She took the outstretched claw in her hand, frightened it might turn to dust. She did some quick sums: Aunt Mabe was eighty and surely the senator had been much older than Aunt Mabe at that awful party? She smiled and nodded at the old man as he gave what sounded like a prepared speech of welcome. She could remember so little of it. Dear Fack. And a cake. And Aunt Mabe dancing with the senator.

Someone wheeled in a trolley of bone china tea-things. Aunt Mabe officiated. There was a spirit lamp and a tiny silver kettle. 'I still adore my English tea-time,' she said, sadly nostalgic.

Jon said briskly, 'You should have come to England now and then, Mabs. Kept in touch. Those muffins we had yesterday weren't the real thing at all. Ours are chewy and give you chronic indigestion half an hour after eating.'

Aunt Mabe shook her head. 'Joanna does enjoy teasing me,' she said, even more sadly.

'I like to keep everyone happy. Don't I, Senator?' Jon put a familiar hand on the trousered knee. The senator actually laughed. Aunt Mabe's mouth puckered and tightened.

Rose said, 'You would have been welcome. Perhaps you could come next summer?'

'Maybe, maybe.' Aunt Mabe passed tea-cups. Jon moved one of the tables for the senator. Rose sat down and let impressions begin to settle. Jon had called it plush. It described it exactly. They had kept the painted wooden walls of the original room, the floorboards too. But the Victorian furniture had been recently reupholstered; the paintings on the walls were originals, the rugs were Oriental, the curtains too. Nothing had been sacrificed to comfort. It was very plush indeed.

Aunt Mabe wanted to know about Aileen. Joanna had not brought so much as a picture of her poor dear mother. Luckily Rose had packed a lot of photographs. The last one taken of Aileen was outside the Snow-White house before the conversion. It looked suddenly small, almost mean.

Aunt Mabe was genuinely moved.

'Look at this, honey! Wasn't she just the most beautiful little creature you ever saw?' She glanced up. 'Not like either of you two girls,' she added, without intentional cattiness. 'But it looks as if your daughters have taken after her, Rose. Wouldn't that be just wonderful?'

Rose, who always sought to see David in the girls, smiled noncommittally.

Jon said, 'Georgie is entirely like his father. Red hair, blue eyes, charm. The lot. No mistaking it. Let's hope the same can be said about me.'

Aunt Mabe sighed and looked at Rose. 'So she's told you, has she? Have you ever heard anything so ridiculous? It was VJ night, for God's sake! Aileen was drunk and came right out of her shell. There were at least half a dozen men crazy about her that night. No-one except Aileen knows which one she went upstairs with!' Aunt Mabe blew out her withered cheeks. 'And she'd never say – she did not want to see him again, she told us! Not even Joe could persuade her and she was always fond of him. Why didn't you ask her about it before she died?'

Jon said, 'She wouldn't talk about it much. And—' she swallowed visibly. 'We didn't know she was going to die. It was so sudden.' She stood up and went to the window. One of the panes was bottle glass and she circled it with her finger.

Rose stood up too. 'Jon—'

Jon thrust her hand behind her commandingly. 'I'm all right. Stay put. It's just that . . . nobody seems to realize how important it is to me to find my father. Even if he's dead!'

The senator cleared his throat. 'Only too happy and delighted to stand in for—'

Jon said curtly, 'No. Sorry. Not good enough.'

Aunt Mabe sighed and again turned to Rose. 'She seems to think we must know the man! How could we possibly, Rose? Tell her it's just a ridiculous schoolgirl quest that can never come to anything.'

Rose said, 'Well, I can't agree completely. I mean, I've blocked the whole thing out of my mind for so long now, but bits are coming back. Maybe I will remember this man. I mean, there must have been a guest list—'

'Rose, I cannot possibly ask poor old Rudolf Laben for a 1945 guest list!'

Jon said shortly, 'I already did. If there was one, he couldn't find it.'

Aunt Mabe said, 'And if he had and you'd found every serviceman on that list, you still wouldn't know—'

Rose said slowly, 'I might.' She half closed her eyes. She could almost see the hated Lennox. She remembered running, filled with panic, opening a door . . . She went on, 'You see I was in the bedroom that night, Aunt Mabe. I saw Mother in bed with a man. He was dark-haired. He had brown eyes too. I think . . . given time . . . I might recognize him.'

Aunt Mabe made a sound of distaste and began, 'You? In the same room with – ? Oh my God—'

But Jon shrieked and ran at her sister. And the senator smiled as if glad that something interesting might be about to happen.

Dinner that night was what Aunt Mabe called informal. With twelve people around the long table in the actual courtroom of the house, Rose found it impossible to feel anything but very formal indeed. Aunt Mabe explained that in the public gallery above the ancient room, they would have a small orchestra playing when they gave a proper dinner party. And the witness box would be full of flowers instead of bottles as now. They would also have outside help with the cooking and serving. Tonight the sour-faced Cookie produced iced soup and Maryland chicken. Jason brought it in on a trolley and everyone helped themselves while he did the drinks. The room, three storeys high with enormous skylights in the roof, seemed to absorb the conversation like a sponge. As it grew dark, Jason brought in candles, and moths nose-dived through the skylights and clustered suicidally around the spears of flame. Jon jumped up and turned the handles to close the lights.

Rose began to feel very tired, isolated, lonely. Last night she had been with Maud in the Snow-White house. What had possessed her to come here?

Yet Uncle Joe, on her left, looked and sounded exactly the same as she remembered. Especially when he said, 'Well, my little chickadee – d'you remember how I used to call you my little chickadee?'

She nodded and tried to smile. The long stretch of time between then and now shrank slightly.

'I thought you would. We were good friends. And how are you these days, my little chickadee? Mabs tells me that life has not been kind to you?'

Rose was surprised. 'Oh, but it has. I've had a wonderful life. Wonderful.' She tightened her eye muscles against tears.

'You've *had* a wonderful life? It's in the past – is that it?'

She had always known he was a kind man; she had not thought he was terribly sensitive. Her smile was rueful but warmer.

'Listen,' he said urgently. 'I know you've come to try to stop Joanna finding her father – Mabs can't stand it. Or her. But she's a great girl, Rose. You can be proud of her. She's told me about . . . things. Her husband. The others. She's headstrong and unlucky, but you can still be proud of her!'

Rose blinked and smiled. 'Thank you, Uncle Joe. People don't always realize . . . '

'I don't want her to go back, Rose. I want you both to come and stay with me. For as long as you like.'

'Thank you.' She meant it. 'But I've got two daughters back home. And a wonderful mother-in-law.'

'Bring 'em over. Bring 'em all over. Send the girls to a good American school. Let 'em marry good American boys.'

'I don't think Aunt Mabe would like that.'

341

He grinned. 'That would make it better! I bet it sticks in her craw the way you call her Aunt Mabe, doesn't it? I notice Joanna calls her Mabs.'

'I hadn't thought – I really don't know—'

'Listen. I had a great idea. Wanted Jon to marry her old Uncle Joe.' He drained his glass and laughed. 'That would put Mabs's nose around the back of her head! I told Jon – I shan't last long and then you'll have the farm and the money—' he laughed again.

Rose said slowly, 'I thought you and Aunt Mabe were supposed to be friendly? It sounds to me as if you minded losing her. Quite a lot.'

' 'Course I minded. But I knew it had to happen. Funnily enough that day of the party – VJ day. I knew then. She made a dead set at him. And anything Mabs wants she usually gets.' He looked suddenly sad. 'Except a family. And she blamed that on me.'

'Oh . . . I'm sorry.'

'Don't be. Poor old Steedman held out for years. I thought I might keep her by default as it were!'

Rose said, 'Uncle Joe, seriously now, are you helping Jon – offering hospitality – just to get at Aunt Mabe?'

He shook his head vigorously. 'That's just the icing on the cake! I want to find Jon's father for a lot of reasons. Curiosity. And something to do with making it up to little Aileen.'

Rose stared at the candles. The icing on the cake. There was another memory there somewhere. She blinked.

He went on, 'It's so long ago. Mabs tried to make it into something . . . dirty. But Aileen wasn't like that. It had to be something quite special.' He looked across at Jon who was talking animatedly. 'Well look – it *was* something special, dammitall. She's the result. If we give her a father, Rose – even a dead father – we can give her dignity. Give Aileen dignity.' He too blinked. 'Am I making sense?'

She nodded, quite unable to speak.

He seemed to lose some of his assurance. He coughed and said, 'We're talking thirty-two years. It's a helluva long time.'

She nodded again. A cake. And Fack . . . dear Fack. She said huskily, 'What happened to Fack, Uncle Joe?'

'Fack?'

'Aunt Mabe's butler. Sort of. General factotum.'

'God. You mean Tom. Died. Broken heart I reckon, his son was rotten.'

Another memory stirred but she was so tired she could not follow it up. Uncle Joe glanced at her and patted her hand.

A blue-rinsed head leaned forward from beyond Uncle Joe.

'So you're from the wild north of England?'

Rose smiled and explained that it was Joanna who lived in Northumberland; she lived in Gloucestershire.

'And where might that be?' The blue-rinse lady sounded indulgent.

Rose felt herself regress. 'Sort of . . . on the left and up a bit.'

Everyone laughed. The other guests had to be told what Rose had said.

She felt very tired indeed.

Until they met for dinner each evening, life at Court House was like life in a hotel. People came and went; breakfast and lunch were self-service affairs in the kitchen; the tea trolley was wheeled into the front sitting room every day at four o'clock but Aunt Mabe was not always there and the senator – who always was – did not drink tea. Dinner could be *en famille* or it could suddenly include up to four guests. Any more and Cookie had to be forewarned. As it was, her life was hard. Rose understood after the third day why she looked so gloomy.

Aunt Mabe did a lot of calling; she still used cards which were printed in copperplate by an ancient press in the village. In her way she was like Aileen; she wanted time to stand still – even go backwards. Rose quickly understood too, why Aunt Mabe had to get rid of Jon as quickly as possible. Jon was very much of the seventies – worse than

343

that, she came from the permissive sixties of England. The English sixties legend had already started here and Rose failed to convince Aunt Mabe that the groups of long-haired hippies who drifted amiably through the village occasionally were all that most of England had ever seen in the apocryphal sixties.

'I daresay it was all drugs and psychedelics in San Francisco and London and some other places,' she protested on the second evening. 'But in Georgetown and Churchdown life went on without pot or – or – anything.' She touched Aunt Mabe's hand comfortingly. 'Our life in Churchdown was centred around the seasons – like yours here. D'you remember that bit from Wordsworth about life's diurnal round—'

'Jon is the exception,' Aunt Mabe said firmly. 'She's disruptive. You can't deny it, Rose.'

Rose said quietly, 'Jon has had a difficult time, Aunt Mabe. And I don't want to discuss her like this when she isn't around. If you don't mind.'

'Well, all I can say is, if you can remember anything about Aileen's dratted boyfriend, for goodness sake try to find him and put an end to all this!' She saw Rose's face and added quickly, 'You're both very welcome – you know that – but the sooner Jon stops asking questions, the better! Everyone is wondering what on earth is behind it!' She dabbed at her face with a napkin. 'And please call me Mabs, dear. Everyone else does. Mabe sounds . . . common.'

Like Aileen before her, Rose felt the poor relation. She tackled Jon later that night while they strolled across the courtyard to their rooms.

'Listen, Jon. I don't know where to begin, but begin we must. Would Eric Laben see his brother for us?'

Jon stopped by the white-painted pump and looked up at the sky. It was deep purple, milky with stars.

She said, 'Rosie. It's so great to have you here. I wish – I wish—'

'What?'

'Nothing.' Jon shook her head. 'Just that I was a better person.' She went on walking. 'I got in touch

344

with a detective agency today. Barnes Bros. I chose them because it rolls off the tongue, don't you think. Try it. Barnes Bros.'

'Well . . . it sounds OK. But you've got nothing for them to go on.'

'Only what you can remember.' Jon sighed deeply. 'I just wish you weren't so bloody good at burying it all in your subconscious. I thought – after a couple of days here – you might come up with something else. But this is the fourth day and . . . zilch.'

Rose said nothing for some time. She stared at the sky and wondered if David was up there somewhere. He wasn't.

She smiled blindly into the darkness. 'Listen. We'll go to the farm tomorrow. See Uncle Joe. I'll talk to him about Fack. I might remember something else.'

They went over to the salt-box farm the next day. Jason was taking Aunt Mabe – Mabs as Rose must now call her – to visit an ageing actress and the senator was prevailed upon to hand over the keys to the 'runabout' which turned out to be a large Oldsmobile. Jon drove, assuring Rose that Jason had let her take the wheel on several occasions. It was true she managed the enormous car very well; they arrived an hour after their phone call and found Uncle Joe in the cowsheds, pretending to take an interest in the milk yield.

It all came flooding back to Rose. The rooms were smaller, of course, but after the Snow-White house they still seemed large. The atmosphere of a working farm was more definite now; the couple who looked after the animals were allowed to eat in the kitchen; their boots were in the back porch, their voices could be heard in the dining room. Soon it would be their farm and Uncle Joe would be relegated to one room. Rose could understand why Jon had been so welcome: Greta and Clark practically sprang to attention when she arrived.

They drank coffee and Uncle Joe took them around the farm.

Rose said, 'What happened to Fack, Uncle Joe?'

'Fack? You mean old Tom?' He grinned. 'I'd forgotten all about him till you mentioned him at dinner the other night. He was very fond of you.' He shook his head. 'He wasn't as old as me. But he had family troubles. Sort of broke him up.'

'He was . . . my friend.' Rose turned away from the cows. That hadn't been Fack's domain. She said, 'Did you talk to Mr Laben? About the party at his house on VJ night?'

'Matter of fact I did.' Uncle Joe put one arm around Jon's shoulders, the other around Rose's. 'You don't know what all this means to us old codgers. A chance to talk about old times and not be accused of senility! Chance to play at detectives too—'

Jon said firmly, 'Did you get any names, Uncle Joe?'

'Nope.' The old man leaned heavily. 'They didn't know half the folks there anyway. If anyone turned up in a uniform, they were in. Simple as that.'

Jon drooped visibly.

'I thought . . . hoped . . . you might come up with something.'

'Well I didn't say I didn't!' The arms became heavier. 'I got something all right. You'd best come and look at it.'

They trailed into the house again, skirting a clump of manure on the way. Rose remembered how quickly such evidence had been cleared up in the old days.

Uncle Joe was breathing stertorously by the time they'd got back to the sitting room. They parked him in a chair; he was grinning foolishly.

'Behind the clock. The big envelope. Found it in the desk. Right at the back.' He nodded in the direction of the original mantelpiece. Jon whipped over and fetched the envelope. Rose said, 'Are you all right, Uncle Joe?'

'Of course he is! He's just laughing – he's got something special up his sleeve,' Jon said impatiently.

'I'm all right, chickadee.' The old man fumbled out a photograph and passed it to Jon. Rose looked over her shoulder. There were the chandelier and the curving stairs. Beneath the stairs' graceful arch were assembled about fifty people. She spotted her long dress between two pairs of

346

trousered legs. Eric. And someone else. Lennox Laben. Rose shuddered and moved down the line to where her mother, very young, very fragile, sat between Aunt Mabe and someone else. A man. Naval uniform. Dark.

She said in a low voice, 'Oh my God. That's him. Jon. That's the man . . . it's blurred, I know, but of course he'd be a naval man. Father was in the navy – she'd have been attracted by that immediately. I'm sure . . . that's your father.'

Jon gave a little squeak. And so did Uncle Joe.

They looked at him. He had slumped forward in his chair and his head was resting on the arm. His lips were the colour of ripe plums and his skin was waxy. It was quite obvious that Uncle Joe had had a heart attack.

Nineteen

Uncle Joe did not die. He did not even go to hospital. By the time the medics arrived, Rose and Jon with the help of Greta and Clark had got him on to the day bed in the window. He was conscious again and assuring them that he was all right. He was still grinning inanely and Rose was not at all certain it was not just a muscular spasm. He must surely know that he had got what he wanted. Rose and Jon could not leave him now; not even Aunt Mabe would expect that. And with the two of them here, everyone's reputation was pristine. It couldn't have worked out better if he'd planned it.

Rose soon discovered for herself how much Jon had been needed here, and what a blessing it must be for Uncle Joe to have her back. Greta and Clark were a far cry from the couple of Rose's day who had been real farmers and had originally owned the place. Greta and Clark were instantly worried about their future.

'I ain't no nurse,' Greta stated as she lugged Uncle Joe's legs on to the bed. 'And Clark ain't no doctor neither.'

Rose said, 'That's just as well.' She and Jon between them propped the lolling head. They had already loosened the clothing and knew that the old man was going to be all right this time. 'Jon. Give Clark the car keys so that he can move the car from the door to make room for the ambulance.'

But Uncle Joe refused to go to hospital.

'Send the quack over,' he whispered faintly. 'If I'm going to die I want it to be here. At the farm.'

So the ambulance was sent away and the doctor came and after half an hour with the old man, talked to the girls in the kitchen. Greta and Clark had miraculously disappeared to their own quarters above the garage and the girls had

348

emptied ashtrays, picked up papers, filled the dishwasher and made tea.

The doctor nodded. 'Yes, he can have a cup in a moment.' He sat at the newly scrubbed table. 'Do you girls know anything about nursing a heart patient?'

Unexpectedly Jon said, 'Yes. Rest. Quiet. Light frequent meals. Cheerful company . . . '

The doctor smiled. 'It's about all you can do. Your uncle is over eighty. He wants to stay here. What do you say?'

Jon said, 'Of course. We'd like to look after him.' She did not look at Rose. 'No problem,' she said airily.

'Oh, there will be.' The doctor's smile widened. 'Your uncle will make sure of that. But at least we can see how it goes for a while.'

He stood up and held out his hand. 'Jeff Blatt. I'm new here. I've attended Mr Lange twice before. And I've got the Labens on my list too.'

Jon took the hand and smiled warmly. 'We have every confidence . . . '

Rose let her hand be shaken too.

'I'll get a prescription filled and bring it round this evening,' he said. 'One under the tongue if the patient feels any pain.'

'Yes. We know.' Jon went to the door with him and held on to the jamb, waving for some time. 'Just to make a lasting impression,' she murmured through her teeth. 'And do stop looking so worried, Rosie! He's going to be all right. And I've committed you to nothing – I can stay here and you can go back to Court House.'

'I'm not worried about *that*! In a way it's a relief to get away from Aunt Mabe – we're so obviously not welcome there. But this . . . this could have repercussions.'

Jon closed the door at last and went to the table. 'Take it a day at a time, Rosie. Come on, let's pour tea all round and take it in to Uncle Joe. Poor old lamb. He's done us a good turn and he's not quite up to it all. We must include him in everything. Get that photograph and talk about it – let him see how pleased we are.'

Rose looked at the sugar bowl with disgust and fetched

349

a clean one. There were traycloths in the drawer; she laid a tray as she'd done so often for David.

They took it in. Uncle Joe was still grinning. Rose arranged tables and chairs. When she looked up Jon was holding his cup for him and saying soothingly, 'Let me do it, Joe. Sip gently. Don't talk. You've had enough excitement for one day.' She got some of the warm sweet liquid down him, wiped his chin, smiled warmly into his eyes. 'Now. Can you listen – are you interested?'

He nodded slowly but emphatically. Jon echoed the nod.

'Then I'll tell you what we thought we'd do. And if you don't like it, you can say so. How's that?'

The grin stayed idiotically in place but he said, 'Fine.'

Rose sat back in her chair. From the kitchen came the hum of the dishwasher. She tried to let it seep into her mind relaxingly. No point in getting upset, after all. Uncle Joe was nothing like David; he wasn't going to die. And if he did she wouldn't have to get behind any barriers as she had after David, then again after Aileen's sudden death. Uncle Joe was nothing to her; not really. And they were better living in the salt-box farm looking after him, than as unpaying, unwanted guests at Court House. But somehow, quite suddenly, home seemed a very long way away.

Jon said, 'Greta and Clark have slipped back into their old ways in the two weeks since I left here, Joe. Do you know that?' He nodded once. She went on smoothly, 'We can get it straight. We can manage them. And Dr Blatt. And you. What do you say to that?' His grin widened. He nodded again, then glanced at Rose. Jon said, 'Now. About the photograph. It's the one thing we needed, Joe. You did wonders to find that. I've already contacted an enquiry agency, but, as Rose pointed out, I couldn't give them a thing to go on. Now, it's different.' She looked again at Rose and raised her brows. 'Does this sound all right to you, Sis?'

There were no decent alternatives; Rose knew she did not want to go back to Court House on her own. She nodded.

Jon went on hopefully, 'And it sort of frees you to do your remembering. Doesn't it?'

Rose said hesitantly, 'I suppose it does. Though I think I've done it all, Jon.'

Jon said firmly, 'I don't. When you looked at that photograph, I could practically hear the wheels in your head clicking, darling. And if you recognized my father, then you might recognize someone else too. A name. Something.'

Rose couldn't think straight any more. She remembered this 'American feeling' from long ago; a feeling of being rushed and hustled into things. Where was Fack now to come and whisk her away to the safety of her own room?

Jon took her silence for agreement, and drank her tea like whisky with a quick flick of her head. She turned back to Uncle Joe. 'All settled. You don't have to worry about a thing.'

He leaned back against the pillow. Jon moved to the other end of the room and began rearranging books in a bookcase. Rose gathered together the tea-things. Uncle Joe had stopped smiling and was asleep.

They looked at him. Jon whispered, 'I wonder . . . is there such a thing as a self-induced heart attack?'

Rose shook her head, but Jon put a finger to her lips and led the way back to the kitchen.

She leaned on the table, laughing silently. 'I thought I was so clever. An opportunist if ever there was one. But d'you know, Rosie, I think the old man had it all worked out before he produced the bloody photograph! That cunning old son of a gun!'

'Dr Blatt—' Rose began.

'Oh I don't say he faked the whole thing. He's probably felt awful for ages. Should have seen a doctor before.' Jon straightened and looked around the kitchen. 'D'you know, Sis, I like this place so much. As long as Joe doesn't die on us things couldn't be better, could they? I'll soon lick the place into shape again. You can have a complete rest, darling. I promise. It won't be too bad, will it?' She stared at Rose pleadingly and Rose had to smile ruefully.

*

The sudden change in arrangements suited Aunt Mabe very well indeed, and she arrived in the car with Jason that evening, bearing their clothes and armfuls of flowers for Joe and a carton of *pâté de foie gras* for their meal.

Already Jon had separated Greta and Clark long enough for Greta to clean two spare bedrooms and make up their beds. She now organized her into arranging the flowers all over the house. 'And tomorrow we'll start on polishing the silver and brass,' she announced. 'You and your husband can eat breakfast in the kitchen after the first milking. Then your other meals can be taken in your flat.'

'If we're cooking for Mr Lange, it seems mighty stupid to carry the food over the yard—'

'You won't be cooking for Mr Lange,' Jon said kindly. 'I shall be doing that.'

'Cooking all the time? For the three of you?' Greta sniffed loudly. 'I know you did little bits and pieces before, but you'll find it's a full-time job—'

Jon smiled and nodded and said, 'Now. If you'd just take this stuff into the laundry and put it in the machine, we can manage for the night.' She smiled. 'See you bright and early tomorrow then. Thank you, Greta. And thank Clark for his help too, won't you?'

Aunt Mabe, overhearing the last, said admiringly, 'You sound so . . . English, Joanna. I didn't realize—'

Jon said, 'It's how the Indians talked to me in the beauty salon, Mabs.' She sniffed at an enormous jug of chrysanthemums. 'Mmm, from the stable yard, yes? Rosie and I will go to sleep to the same smell as last night.' She smiled. 'A lot can happen in twenty-four hours, Mabs.'

'Yes.' The elderly woman sat down heavily at the kitchen table. 'I want to thank you girls. If anything had happened to Joe this afternoon . . . I'd have missed him.'

Jon raised her brows at Rose. And Rose lifted her shoulders helplessly. It was somehow tiring to realize that even at eighty years old the emotional battle still went on.

She studied the photograph without any more results, and they posted it off to 'Barnes Bros'. But that evening she

352

said suddenly, 'Miss Millward. Of course. She taught me how to dance!' And Jon looked triumphantly at Uncle Joe. 'It's coming back, Joe! Bit by bit, it's coming back!'

Rose went to see old Rudolf Laben.

'I realize Lennox is ill, Mr Laben. But would it be possible for me to visit him? He was older than me, you see. And he must have been with me that night when . . . he must have been with me that night.'

Mr Laben said, 'If it is possible to manage without Lennox . . . ' He turned to the window. 'It would not be a good idea to see him, Rosamund. In any case, I do not think he could help you.'

Rose stared at the bowed back. So Lennox had been as nasty as she had remembered – she was perfectly right to shy away from that particular memory. Strangely, the sudden justification of her old fear allowed her to let Lennox into her head. Yes. He had ripped her beautiful Snow-White dress. And then he'd chased her. Lots of corridors.

She said suddenly, 'May I go upstairs and look around, Mr Laben?'

'Of course, my child. Maria will take you—'

'No. I need to be on my own.'

Rose walked around the house. She had remembered it as enormous, a kind of Hampton Court maze. It was not enormous. She walked up another flight of stairs at the end of a corridor. Yes, this was where she and Mother had slept that night. And where Lennox had found her. She walked around the room, then to the door. She had run down to the next floor in search of Mother. And three doors along that landing, she had opened the door. Lennox had been behind her. She stood in the middle of the room. No. It had not been Lennox. Not Lennox at all. Someone had caught Lennox and given him a good hiding and then followed her.

She stood at the foot of the bed and remembered Mother's face in the crook of a male arm. She turned slowly and said aloud, 'It wasn't Lennox. It wasn't him at all. It was another boy. It was the boy who came out of the cake!'

She ran downstairs, suddenly unbearably excited.

Mr Laben said blankly, 'The cake? What do you mean, child?'

'I was looking for Mother. Lennox was after me. I went into her bedroom and I thought he followed me. But it was the other boy. He'd got rid of Lennox somehow and he'd come to take me back to the party. And then – later – he came out of the cake. And Fack said he went away. To school.'

Mr Laben too was staring. He said quietly, 'My God. I'd forgotten. What a scene that was. He was the son of your aunt's general factotum. Tom. His name was . . . give me a second – his name was Abraham. That was it. Abraham. He was sent to reform school. I don't know what happened to him. I think Tom died before he came out.'

'Abr'am. That was it. Abr'am.' Rose felt her eyes fill with tears. 'Fack's son. He rescued me. And I'd forgotten him.' She turned to the door almost violently. Through its fanlight she could see the hall and the tip of the chandelier. She said, 'I must find him. I must find Abr'am.'

Behind her Mr Laben said enthusiastically, 'You might have it now, Rosamund! This boy – he was about twelve – yes? He might well know the identity of Joanna's father!'

'I have to find him anyway. I have to apologize.'

'For what? My dear girl—'

'For forgetting him!' Rose turned back into the room. 'Mr Laben, try to remember his full name. And where he was sent to school. Isn't there anything else you remember about him?'

'Maybe your aunt . . . it's so long ago, my child. And in those days coloured servants—'

'I didn't know he was coloured. I didn't know Fack was coloured.'

'But surely – Rose dear – you might have forgotten a lot of things—'

'Not that. I saw it, of course. But he was just a person. Just Fack. And his son . . . he was wonderful.' Rose swallowed. She knew she was making a perfect idiot of herself. 'He was like a knight on a white charger!' she said defiantly.

And Mr Laben shook his head despairingly. The mother had been a romantic too. He remembered that all right.

Aunt Mabe swore she had forgotten Fack's surname, even if she had ever known it. Rose was sure she was hiding it deliberately when she threw up her hands in horror at Rose's latest search.

'My dear, I know it's 1977 and we're all equal in the sight of God! Yes, I know all that – and that he was your friend! But can't you see that I simply cannot associate myself with . . . the senator would never stand for it!'

But Uncle Joe murmured, 'Sure I remember, honey. Was it Brown? No, that was a book, I guess.'

Jon could be brutal when it suited her. 'Don't go to sleep now, Joe!' she said sharply. 'There must be some record left somewhere.'

'Wages.' Joe smiled at his two interrogators. 'The desk. In my office.'

The contents of the desk were chaotic. Joe had obviously rifled it to find the photograph. Rose and Jon spent a whole evening going through everything. Jon commented, 'I can see why Mabs left him for the senator. He's got the farm and these shares. Otherwise . . . '

'Here it is.' Rose hardly heard her sister. She was as determined now as Jon had been. 'Thomas William McKenzie.' She looked up blankly. 'A Scotsman? Surely not?'

'Did he wear a kilt?' Jon asked straight-faced.

'Shut up, Jon. He was special. Really special.' She sat back on her heels. 'Thomas McKenzie. I don't see where that gets us.'

By way of answer, Jon reached in her handbag, found a notebook and flipped through it, picked up the phone and dialled. After a long wait she wrinkled her nose. 'One of these new answering machines,' she said. Then, in an affected English accent, 'Mrs Johnson here. Something new has cropped up. I need to know the whereabouts of . . . Abraham McKenzie. Born . . . ' She lifted her brows at Rose who shrugged then said, 'About 1930, I would imagine.' Jon relayed this, then added, 'Coloured. Admitted to a reform school about 1945.' She looked at Rose again who again shrugged. 'That's about it. I can be contacted now on Georgetown 48509. Thank you.' She replaced the receiver. 'He'll ring tomorrow morning. Bet you anything. Good old Barnes Bros.'

Rose doubted whether the response would be as quick as that, but sure enough the next morning when she answered the telephone at eight o'clock, a voice announced, 'William Barnes here. Am I talking to Mrs Johnson?'

'Mrs Johnson's sister here.' Rose felt a lift of spirits. 'Surely you haven't got some results yet?'

'I think I'd better talk to Mrs Johnson,' said the voice repressively.

Rose fetched Jon and almost danced by her side. It was impossible to work out what was happening from Jon's repeated, 'Yes. Yes. I would imagine so. Yes. At one o'clock sharp. Yes.'

At last she replaced the receiver.

'Well.' She looked at Rose. 'Looks as if you've hooked a big fish here, Rosie. Apparently we should already know Abe McKenzie. He's been on British television as well as over here in the States.'

'A television star?' Rose felt a terrible pang of disappointment.

'Hardly. A politician, I suppose you'd say. He was one of the lawyers that put together the Civil Rights Act and the Voting Rights. Whatever they are.'

Rose had to confess ignorance on both counts. She frowned. 'The year we were married . . . d'you remember the Washington march? Before Martin Luther King was assassinated?'

'Was it then? I've heard of that, yes.'

'I think – I'm almost certain that straight after that – must have been when the twins were born – there was some important law passed.' She shook her head helplessly. 'I'm afraid . . .'

Jon said, 'Anyway, if it's the same Abe McKenzie, he's got an office in New York and dear old Barnes Bros will be

356

delighted to take us there any time we want – his chance to meet the man, I suppose.'

'It can't be the same one,' Rose said, wanting to be convinced.

Jon said, 'Well, this Abe McKenzie had a father called Thomas William. And he was sent to reform school at the age of fourteen. And he put himself through college and law school. He was the youngest to qualify in his class. He went straight to Memphis to offer his services to—'

Rose said, 'When can Barnes Bros take me to New York?'

'You heard what I said, surely. One o'clock sharp.'

Rose nodded. 'We'll have an early lunch. Tell Uncle Joe.'

'He'll love it,' Jon said and moved to the cooker.

Rose sat in the front of the large convertible car. The hood was down and it was difficult to talk into the wind. Barnes Bros turned out to be a middle-aged man who introduced himself as 'William Barnes at your service. Retired State Police. Private investigator fourteen years. No complaints.' Rose was content to leave it at that. She was not uncaring about William Barnes's possible wife and children, but just at the moment her single-mindedness needed no intrusions.

They did not take the same road that Jason had taken only ten days before. They approached the city from the north, descending on it from hills west of the Connecticut river. Rose enjoyed the unusual view of the skyscrapers against the ocean, but already she was wishing she had phoned ahead to make an appointment. Already she was wondering why she had come: was it to thank him for what he had done thirty-two years before? Was it to applaud his achievements? Was it to ask if he could remember a certain face in a certain bed? In spite of the fresh autumnal wind, she felt her face flame. She should have used the telephone. Much less embarrassing. But she had chosen to come in person.

William Barnes bawled something at her and she leaned to the left to hear him.

'Will get the top fixed while you're seeing Abe McKenzie!'

She had thought the open top was a matter of choice and shouted back, 'It's fine!'

For the first time he smiled. She wondered if her hair was that much of a mess.

They drove through Queens, then Brooklyn, and into Yonkers. Apartment blocks made the grid system very obvious. They passed a small park bereft of grass, and took a turning to the left. Mr Barnes pulled in to the kerb and consulted a map. 'Wrong turn,' he commented briefly and reversed smartly into an entry. They whirled back the way they had come and turned right. Unexpectedly the apartment blocks gave way to a row of brownstone houses facing a clump of trees which must belong to the park. Railings enclosed small basement areas; there were window boxes here and there spilling withered nasturtiums.

They pulled over to the railings and Mr Barnes recited the numbers slowly, 'Two-four-eight. Four-nine. Five zero.' He hauled on the hand brake. 'This is it, Mrs Fairbrother. Reckon he doesn't go in for much show.'

It certainly was an unpretentious office for someone who had helped write American history. The house was narrower than its neighbours and at some time an extra storey had been added, giving it a surprised look. Four sash windows, one above the other, surmounted the front door. Pictures of Martin Luther King were pasted in each one.

Rose hesitated and Mr Barnes got out and came around to her side. He opened her door.

'I'll hang about in case you can't get to see him yet,' he said tactfully. 'If you're not out in ten minutes, I'll go to a garage and get the soft top fixed.'

'Please not on my account.' But Rose was smoothing her hair selfconsciously and he just smiled.

She was wearing the linen suit she'd arrived in and when a girl emerged from the basement in jeans and a tee shirt, she felt ridiculously overdressed. The girl carried a box file; she smiled briefly at Rose, then jogged down the street.

Rose swallowed and climbed the steps to the door. She read the inscriptions on the brass plate there: Donovan

358

and McKenzie. Lawyers. She was suddenly reminded of St John's Lane and the Providential offices there. She closed her eyes and knocked. Her eyes were still closed when the door opened.

'Can I help you?'

The voice had the traditional Southern lilt. Rose opened her eyes and saw a young woman, taller than herself, polished ebony cheekbones, a cloud of black hair, perfect teeth.

She said, 'I hoped to have a word – briefly of course – with Mr McKenzie.'

The girl's smile widened. 'No-one has more than that on a Friday afternoon!' She held the door for Rose. 'Abe will be out of here in one hour – unless Jimmy Carter calls personally, of course! Meanwhile you're in luck because no-one is with him.' She ushered Rose into a long passage which seemed to go to the other side of the house. A banister curved down to the basement; a stained glass window was above it. Halfway down the passage another banister led upwards. The girl walked towards it.

'You're English,' she said over her shoulder. 'You haven't got an appointment. You seemed to be sleepwalking.' She reached a landing and turned. 'You're from a British magazine and you want to feature Abe McKenzie in your women's page!'

Rose hung on to the newel post and caught her breath. 'Well, I'm English, yes. And I haven't got an appointment.' She smiled suddenly, liking this girl very much. 'But . . . I haven't got a job. And I don't want to interview Mr McKenzie. I met him years ago. On VJ night. And I wanted to ask him one question. It will take – literally – five minutes. Less if he doesn't know the answer!'

'Hey. I love a mystery.' The girl held out her hand. 'Eugenie Porter. What is your name?'

'Rose Fairbrother. I was Rose Harris . . . before.'

Eugenie nodded, smiled again as if she knew Rose needed reassurance and opened another door.

'Boss. A lady to see you. She wants no more than five minutes of your time. Personal matter. Name, Rose

Fairbrother – used to be Rose Harris when you knew her.'

A male voice said, 'Rose Harris? Never heard of her. And it's three o'clock.'

Eugenie inserted all of herself into the doorway and spoke again in a low voice. The male one said something; it sounded resigned. Eugenie emerged.

'Go right in,' she said.

Rose went. If she had expected an instant of epiphany she was disappointed. But she had not known what to expect. The man sitting behind the huge deal table looked older than the forty-six years he must surely be. He looked older than Fack had looked. He was enormously solid and thickset and his wiry thatch of hair was almost white. And his dark eyes, glancing up at her from the papers before him, held only perfunctory politeness. Nothing more.

She moved further into the room. It had been a large square bedroom at one time. The ceiling had plaster mouldings and a long pendant centre light. They were the sole remnants of its past; the Venetian blinds at the sash window, the metal shelving around the walls, the office chairs and carpet were all of the seventies.

She stood beneath the light. She did not know what to say; she had relied entirely on recognition. If she did not know him, then obviously he would not know her. She had been four at the time of their meeting.

He said brusquely, 'How can I help you, Mrs Harris?'

She said, 'Mrs Fairbrother. Rosamund Harris was my maiden name.'

He frowned. 'You're English.'

'Yes. But I was born here. In America. During the war. At my aunt's house in Connecticut. Mrs Mabel Lange.'

He leaned back in his chair. He had been making notes with a pencil. He held it now at both ends, balanced delicately above the papers. 'Ah,' he repeated.

'Yes. I knew your father. He was my friend.'

He said a curious thing then. He balanced the pencil on his thumbs and asked lightly, 'And were you his friend too?'

She was taken aback by this lateral move. She looked at him, startled. 'I – I think so. I don't know. I was a child. What do you mean?'

He shrugged. 'I wondered - when you went home to England – whether you enquired for him in your letters to your aunt? You know the kind of thing friends do.'

She flushed. His impatience had gone; in its place was enmity. It was almost tangible.

She said simply, 'I did not write to Aunt Mabe. I don't think my mother did either. You see, we were sent home in disgrace.'

He was very still, looking at her without staring. Suddenly the pencil fell from his thumbs to the papers before him. He stood up with surprising briskness for such a big man, and lugged one of the plastic chairs to the side of his desk.

'Sit down, Mrs Fairbrother.'

She obeyed him. Her legs were trembling and she was very hot. The linen suit had been too thin in the car and was now much too thick. She had worn entirely the wrong thing.

He went to the window and made a gap in the slats of the blind and peered through it.

'Incredible weather for October. There's no air-conditioning in here. D'you want the window open?'

'No. I'm fine.'

He turned and came back to the desk. He was smiling but still without friendliness.

He said, 'My father spoke of you often. He wondered how you were.'

She faltered, 'I'm sorry. It all seemed like another life once we were back in England.'

'Of course. It was.'

A little spurt of defensiveness made her say, 'He could have written to me.'

The big man turned away, the smile gone. He picked up the pencil and looked at it.

'He couldn't write,' he said evenly.

'But . . . it was the middle of the century! You talk as if
– he was properly employed by my aunt! He did accounts
– things like that!'

'Yes. He was intelligent all right.' He began to doodle
on a scrap of paper. 'He was born in 1898. OK. So
he wasn't a slave. Shall we say he still had a slave
complex?'

The defensiveness went. She thought of Fack. He had
been wise. And dignified. And resourceful. He had made
Aunt Mabe look small and undignified. And he had always
been Rose's refuge.

She said quietly, 'Fack was no slave. He was a wonderful
man. I shall never forget him.'

'But you did.' The voice rose from its level tone and was
sharply accusatory.

She could easily have let anger rise to meet his; but it
was as if Fack was in the room. She almost looked round
at the door to see if he had appeared, as he so often did
when voices were raised. She smiled.

'Not really. And he would have understood.'

The smile must have come through in her voice, and it
made things worse. The pencil broke on the paper.

'I thought we were talking about justice,' he said, staring
at what he had drawn.

She was surprised. 'Were we? Surely if we're talking
abstracts – and I honestly did not realize we were – then
we were discussing friendship.'

He was silent for a long time. Then he threw down the
pencil and swivelled his chair to face her.

'Perhaps we were. Now. What can I do for you, Mrs
Fairbrother? Did you want to know where my father is
buried?'

She flushed again. 'No. I came for something very . . .
mundane.' She wished she could leave without asking
anything else of this strangely aggressive man. 'Something
about that . . . night. The night of the party.'

'Ah.' He was bland now. 'I too am very forgetful about
that night. It wasn't happy for me. I tend to block the
whole thing out.'

She could not meet his steady gaze. She remembered now when she had encountered it first. Beneath a sofa. And though she might have been only four years old, she hadn't let him down then.

She said firmly, 'You will have heard the story, of course. My mother met someone that night. My sister, Joanna, was born back in England. Fack must have known, though my aunt kept it from everyone else apparently.'

'Why do you call him Fack? His name was Tom. Like in *Uncle Tom's Cabin*.'

'He was the General Factotum in the house. He ran everything. He was important. I would have called him by his full name if I could.' She lifted her eyes and stared straight into his. 'It was like giving him a title.'

This time it was his gaze that dropped. But he did not apologize. 'Go on,' he commanded curtly.

'My sister is . . . I suppose the psychologists would call her insecure. She married unwisely and much too young – she was pregnant. So she now has a son of fourteen. And she is thirty-one.'

'She married an American?'

'No. A Welshman. Eric Johnson. He's emigrated to Canada now.'

'Go on,' he repeated.

'After the marriage, there was another man.' She flushed again.

He said quickly, 'She was looking for a father figure.'

Again Rose was surprised. 'Yes. I think she was. How did you know?'

He shrugged. 'It's a fairly well-known syndrome. What about you?'

'Me?'

'Yes. You were brought up in a fatherless household too.'

'But I had a father. Photographs. Things like that. And his parents . . . I had them too. And Jon didn't. She must have known, even as a small child, that they disapproved of her. And when she was old enough, she knew why.'

'So you married. And presumably happily.'

She drew in her breath so that her voice emerged stifled. 'Yes. Yes, I did.'

'Is he with you, this husband of yours?'

'No.' She forced herself to breathe properly. 'He died. Five years ago.' She went on fast. 'It's all right. I've learned . . . you know. All that sort of thing. And there hasn't been much time . . . I've got two daughters. Twins. They were thirteen this summer. And there's Georgie – my nephew – Jon's son, that is. And I've got the best mother-in-law anyone . . . ' her voice petered out as she realized she was gabbling. She made a strange sound that could have been a laugh, and said, 'Sorry.'

He did not attempt to reassure her. He said, 'What about your mother? Aileen.'

So he remembered that much. She almost gave the odd laugh again, but managed to control it.

'She died just after David. She had a bad heart. I think she must always have had it. But Jon blames herself for that too . . . ' She shifted in her chair and reached for her matter-of-fact voice. 'Look. The thing is, whether you remember that night or not, you were there. Actually in the room with me and my mother and . . . Jon's father.'

He too shifted in the swivel chair. It turned slightly and he reached for the broken pencil. He said, 'I was?'

She was impatient. 'Yes. I hadn't said anything to Fack about you being under the sofa with cake crumbs all over you. So you thought you should repay me. And you got rid of that awful Lennox boy and followed me into my mother's bedroom. And when you saw what was happening you got me out again.'

'I did?'

She said flatly, 'Yes. You did.'

'Let me see. That was 1945. And now we're 1977. Thirty-two years, d'you make that? Thirty-two years ago. When I was helping out my father. Not even a hired waiter. And you expect me to remember a face I might have seen for two seconds? Do you remember it?'

She said, 'I was four and you were fourteen. I didn't know what was happening. I think you probably did.'

His full mouth twitched at the obvious sarcasm. He threw down the pencil and turned to her with upturned palms. He said frankly, 'Listen. I vaguely remember the whole chaotic business. But what happened afterwards has somewhat overshadowed the events beforehand. I'm sure you understand.'

She looked him straight in the eye. Then she said, 'I think I preferred you when you were rude. At least you were then being honest.'

His eyes narrowed. 'There were a lot of people there that night. White people. They all looked the same to me.'

She said, 'To me too.' She actually smiled. 'But maybe when you're a child, all grown-ups just look like grown-ups.'

He leaned back in his chair. 'An interesting theory. In this case it doesn't help.'

'You were almost adult. Fourteen.' She moved her shoulder bag to her lap and opened it. 'I've got an old photograph here. Mr Laben took it, I believe. Everyone at the party should be there. Do you remember any of the people?'

He took it almost unwillingly. Then he put it on his desk and turned his chair to face it. She started to count inside her head. She had got to twenty – counting slowly – when he reached into his coat pocket and fitted some thick spectacles on his nose. She went on counting. She was silently saying 'thirty-five and a half' when he spoke.

'Absolutely fascinating. Another age. You look like Snow-White.'

Again the surprise. She blurted, 'We called our house the Snow-White house. We still live there.'

He made no comment and continued to stare at the photograph as if to imprint it on his brain.

At last he handed it back. His thumb was on the chin of the naval man standing by Aileen.

He said, 'That's the one.'

She stared at it. So she had been right. Jon's father.

She said, 'You don't leave much manoeuvring space for doubt, do you?'

'No.'

She smiled but went on staring at the man who was Jon's father.

She said, 'Jon came to America to look for him. She was an embarrassment to my aunt – she's so direct – frank – hard to describe her. My aunt sent me what amounted to an SOS. And Maud – my mother-in-law – thought it would be good for me to get away. Right away.' She glanced up, still smiling. 'All I want to do is go back home. Like my mother. Hide in the Snow-White house with my children. So I have to find this man.' She stood up. 'Thank you for your help. Probably the private investigator will now be able to —'

He said, 'Leave the photograph. I'll find him for you.'

She was so surprised this time, she almost collapsed back into her chair again.

'But I thought . . . you just wanted to get rid of me . . . '

'You're not going to leave until you find him, it seems. I can do that quicker than any agency.'

She blinked at the near-insult.

'Well. I . . . ' She held the photograph out to him waveringly, and he took it and went to the window again. She was dismissed.

She took the chair back to the wall and passed his desk. He had been doodling a cake. With a huge wedge missing.

She went to the door.

He said over his shoulder, 'As a matter of fact I never forgot you. And I knew you the moment you came in. Your eyes haven't changed. They are still very blue – doesn't go with the black hair.'

She said brilliantly, 'Oh.'

He said, 'Leave a number with Eugenie, will you? I'll call as soon as I have something.'

'Um . . . yes. All right.'

And she left.

Eugenie was apologetic.

'Was he rude? He's always rude at first. Seems to think it gets down to realities or something. Confrontation therapy. That kind of thing.'

'Yes. I think he was rude. But he's going to help me.' Rose smiled brilliantly at the attractive young secretary. She felt marvellous all of a sudden. As if she'd shed a huge load.

Eugenie said, 'He's a wonderful man. A truly wonderful human being.'

It was such an Americanism. A wonderful human being. All human beings were wonderful; things of wonder, walking miracles.

She crossed the pavement to where Mr Barnes was holding open the door of the convertible. The roof was up. So the wind wasn't going to chill her to the bone and mess up her hair any more. Bit late in the day, but that was the way it was. Things were going to be all right now. She was very conscious that two storeys above her, Abe McKenzie was watching her get into the car.

Twenty

Rose was by now completely fascinated and intrigued.

The link with her early years had been fully established at last; the fact that the boy who had rescued her from Lennox Laben was now an eminent lawyer with a chip on his shoulder made the whole thing seem like pages from a novel. She could think about it as if she weren't involved; she could smile at the twists and turns of life and fate. It was perfectly natural and 'all right' to be curious about him and about what had happened in the last thirty-two years; about how he had become the man he was.

But as well as the sense of reading a book, there was something else. She was part of her surroundings now, no longer just a visitor. The burnt-sugar smell of New York, the perspective of the buildings viewed from ground level, and then from the Connecticut hills above; the way the sun set in layered clouds that night and appeared to roll around the city like a blanket – she was terribly aware of everything. Her perceptions were at their height. Halfway home she asked William Barnes to stop the car and roll back the roof again.

'It's mighty windy tonight, ma'am,' he demurred.

'I know.' She tried to explain. 'The wind takes you into it all somehow. Don't you think?'

'Oh sure. It's just that most women – pardon me, ladies – are worried about their hair-dos.'

'Oh that's all right. I haven't got one.' She considered saying 'and I ain't no lady', then decided against it. He might think she had been drinking. Strangely, she did feel slightly squiffy.

Jon had got things well organized at the farm. Uncle Joe was asleep but earlier she had got Clark and Dr Blatt to move the day bed into the window so that Uncle Joe could watch the farm work outside. That had been her excuse to demand a pristine yard; Clark had spent the whole afternoon hosing it down. She wasn't popular but there had been no strikes or resignations so far.

'It will let him know he's still boss,' she said to Rose over their late supper. 'And it might help Clark to raise his own standards too. They're very low.' She spoke lugubriously and Rose laughed.

'You've got everybody's interests at heart, Jon,' she said.

Jon grinned but said seriously, 'You can joke about it, Rosie! But I could get stuck in here. I really could.'

Rose spoke seriously too. 'Does that mean you won't worry if we never find your father? Or if – when we've found him – he doesn't want to know?'

Jon thought about it, frowning now. 'I'm not sure. You sound so hopeful tonight, Rosie. It has become a distinct possibility instead of . . . well, a pipe-dream perhaps. It makes me realize that the man in the photograph might well be horrified at the mere thought of having a thirty-one-year-old daughter and a fourteen-year-old grandson!'

Rose leaned across the table. 'You mean it might be better to cherish the pipe-dream?'

'I don't know. I just don't know. Not until it happens . . . how could I? I just wish I could establish myself – I don't want him thinking I'm some pauper.' She shook her head at Rose's face. 'Not literally – I don't mean that. But I haven't done anything with my life!' She shook her head again at Rose's incredulous expression. 'All right, I've done plenty. Too much. But I haven't got anywhere.' She looked into her coffee cup. 'I thought he – the man – my father – would make me feel that. But I realize – from his point of view – it's not so good.'

Rose put her hand on Jon's wrist. She felt optimistic, almost ebullient. She said, 'Listen, Sis. Of course you don't know what to think or feel. Just live from day to day and don't worry about it. Time for decision if and when this Abe McKenzie turns something up.'

'And you think he will.'

Rose smiled. 'If there's anything to be turned up, he will turn it!'

'He's quite a character, isn't he? Did he say anything about how he came to jump out of that cake? It sounds like a fairy story!'

'He says he blocked it from his memory. But he'd doodled a replica of the cake on his notepad!'

Jon said sadly, 'It's a pity he's coloured.'

Rose was astonished. She withdrew her hand and sat up straight in her chair. 'What on earth d'you mean?'

'Well . . . ' Jon did not meet her eyes. 'You know. It's five years since David died and . . . '

'My God, Jon!' Rose stood up. 'I thought you had more sense than that!' She shoved her chair under the table and picked up her handbag. 'For one thing I haven't noticed his colour. And for another . . . I'll never look at another man! How could I after David!' She was so angry she thought she might even hit Jon.

Jon stammered, 'Rosie. I'm sorry—'

'Don't even bother to apologize – it's meaningless when we don't speak the same language!'

She was gone from the room. She did not offer to clear the table. Half an hour later Jon tapped on her door but she pretended to be asleep. Her heightened perceptions were all now concentrated in an unreasoning anger and she could not relax. Towards dawn her fevered brain seized on something else: she might not have noticed Abe McKenzie's colour, but he had noticed hers. The aggression had been at least partially because she was white.

She began to cry. She muffled the sounds by holding the pillow around her face until she almost suffocated herself. Feverish and uncomfortable, she dropped into a light sleep as Clark went out to start the milking.

When she got downstairs the next morning the kitchen was as clean and tidy as a new pin, breakfast was laid and Eric Laben was sitting at the table.

'Jon's taken in Joe's breakfast,' he announced, standing up courteously. 'She said you and Joe had such rotten nights we must let you sleep on.'

Rose's head was thumping as if she really had a hangover. She collapsed into a chair and pushed her hands into her hair. 'Joe too?' she said. 'I'm sorry. How is he?'

Eric poured her coffee and passed it across. 'Not good, I'm afraid. He wants to see his lawyer and the doctor today.'

Rose looked up. 'I thought the doctor came yesterday?'

'He did. He was here when I called in the morning.'

Jon came into the kitchen. She glanced quickly at Rose then went to the sink.

'There was a call for you, Sis. Someone called Eugenie. From New York.'

'Eugenie? Was there a message?'

'Just to call her back. Number's on the pad.'

'Thanks.' Rose finished the coffee and took the cup to the sink. She said in a low voice, 'Sorry.'

Jon said, 'Nothing to be sorry about.'

'Yes there is. I know you meant well but—'

Jon said, 'Make your call, Rosie. If they've got something it will mean you can go back home.' She went to the door, touching Eric's head in passing. 'Come on. I want you to prop Joe up while I rub his back.' She held the door while he went through to the hall, then she looked back. 'But it was true, what I said. Five years, Rosie. And you're not like Mother.'

Rose did not ask what she meant. She swilled her cup, went to the phone in Joe's study and dialled the number on the pad.

Eugenie answered immediately.

'Hoped it was you. May I call you Rosamund? We're on to something this end, Rosamund. The boss didn't go to the lake last night. He looked up an old buddy who works in the Pentagon. Showed him the photograph. Came up with a possible name and wondered if it might ring a bell for you.'

'You mean Mr McKenzie—'

371

'For God's sakes! Abe! Everyone calls him Abe!'

' – gave up his weekend to go looking for this man? I feel terrible!'

'Well, don't. Rosamund, you don't know our future president very well, do you? He does what he wants, or what he thinks will help the cause.'

'The cause?'

'Equality. Racial equality. The thing we're supposed to have but haven't quite.'

Rose gulped for air. 'And you said future president?'

'He wants to be the first coloured president of the US of A. Thought you'd have done your homework on that one!'

'I haven't done any homework. I knew nothing about Mr . . . about Abe. Except that when he was fourteen years old he jumped out of a cake.'

'He . . . what?'

'You must ask him about that one.' She wanted to laugh again. Her head was better. She felt wonderful. He might even do it . . . become the first coloured president. He might even do it.

She said, 'D'you want me to come to New York again, Eugenie?'

'Oh no. He just left a message to give you this name over the phone and have you mull it over for a coupla days.'

Rose was ridiculously disappointed. She had already considered ringing Aunt Mabe to ask if Jason would drive her to the city.

Eugenie went on, 'He retired as a Commander about five years ago. Name, Philip Duddington. Married. One son killed in Vietnam. Wife died in '74. He's taken an advisory job in the Pentagon. Naval defence. Which is how Abe traced him, of course.'

'But he had no idea . . . he could have left the navy after the war. Anything.'

'The boss forgets nothing, Rosamund. He would have known most of the people on that photograph by name. Place cards, things like that.'

'But he was fourteen!'

'He was born cunning.' She paused. 'He's a very complicated person, Rosamund.'

'Yes. Yes, I got that impression yesterday.' Rose cupped the phone in her right hand and pushed her hair back from her ears. 'Duddington. Philip Duddington. No. It doesn't mean a thing.'

'OK. Not to worry. He thought it wouldn't mean anything to you. Just a chance. He'll be in touch next week.'

'Well. Thank you, Eugenie. And please thank . . . him . . . for me too.'

'Certainly will. Bye now.'

She was gone. And Rose continued to hold the phone and to frown unseeingly out of the window.

The day passed busily but also leadenly. Rose was amazed at Jon's enthusiasm for Joe's welfare, the smooth running of the farm, the meals. Joe mentioned a fruitcake made by his mother when he was a boy. Jon got up early as usual on Sunday morning and made a fruitcake. It was delicious.

'A fluke,' she said modestly.

Joe smiled happily through crumbs. 'You missed your vocation, Jon.'

Jon returned the smile wryly. 'Yes. I think I have, Joe. That's my trouble.'

She was more sentient too and knew that Rose was finding it hard to mark time at the farm.

'Go into Georgetown. Visit with Mabs – she'd like that.'

Rose said, 'You sound American, Jon. "Visit with Mabs". You love it here, don't you?'

'Yes. Before you arrived, Jason took me to New York. We went up the Empire State and the World Trade Center and along Battery Park and Civic Center. Rose, it's marvellous. When you go up to see Abe McKenzie next week, make certain you see something of the place.'

'But you like it here too. You haven't been off the farm since we arrived last Tuesday.'

'Well. It's the old story, isn't it? Great to be needed.' She laughed. 'I was so busy being an exciting lover for Rick, I never got round to being a wife.' She shrugged. 'Mother cooked and did most of the cleaning. I was still a spoiled kid.' She laughed again, almost embarrassed. 'Anyway,' she added flippantly, 'don't forget I was conceived just down the road – I'm more American than you are!'

Rose did not reply. She watched as Jon laid a tray for Uncle Joe's lunch. It was the sort of job she would normally have been doing. But nothing was normal in America. Nothing was ordinary.

She went to visit Mabs on Monday. And on Tuesday she rang Maud for news of the girls and Georgie. Maud sounded as near as Eugenie had done.

'Are you all right?' The voice was surprisingly deep and aristocratic. Rose was reminded of when she had known Maud first; in her rather odd hats and straight suits. Fourteen years ago.

'Mother, I'm fine. Everything is happening all the time here. I haven't had time to be homesick or anxious. I feel awful I haven't phoned for a week.'

'How could you with all this business of your uncle's heart attack? What about Jon?'

'She copes better than I do. She's got the farm – everything and everyone – under control.'

'She's more like you than she realizes.'

'And you? What about you?'

'I'm coping. But I'll admit to you Rose, I'm damned lonely.'

'Oh Mother.' Rose held the receiver hard against her ear. 'It won't be long now. I can't go into it all on the phone, but we're almost sorted out.'

'I didn't mean . . . Ros, don't rush on my account, please. I was the one who practically pushed you into going!' She breathed a little laugh into the phone and it whispered in Rose's ear, sadly. 'I just wanted you to know that you are well and truly missed!'

Rose thought of the hall at the Snow-White house where the phone was. It would be midday there now, probably chilly.

'What's the weather like?' she asked foolishly.

'Raining. Grey.'

Rose looked out at the blood-red autumn sun above the barn. She said, 'I'll be home soon. In time for Guy Fawkes night.'

'Ridiculous child,' Maud replied.

Rose replaced the receiver, smiling. No-one thought of her as a child over here; not even Aunt Mabe. She trailed into the kitchen where the last crumbs of the fruitcake littered the tea trolley. Jon was in the garden watering a small herb bed she had discovered beneath the study window. Dr Blatt was with Uncle Joe; and the lawyer. She wondered whether Joe might have some quixotic idea of changing his will in favour of his two nieces-by-marriage. She hoped not. It would be the last straw for Aunt Mabe.

The phone rang on Wednesday morning, and it was Eugenie.

'Rosamund? Nice to hear you. The boss would like a word.'

'Oh.' Rose covered the phone with her hand and said to Jon, 'New York. News.' Inexplicably, Jon smiled, nodded, and left the room.

Eugenie said, 'You're through now, Abe. And I've put Grunbaum's into this morning's slot and cancelled everything else. OK?'

Abe's voice said, 'Fine.' And Rose pulled the chair from beneath the desk and sat down quickly.

'Hello – are you there, Mrs Fairbrother?'

'Yes.' She covered the phone again and cleared her throat. 'Yes, I'm here. I want to thank you for acting so quickly last week—'

'It's about that,' he interrupted brusquely. 'Can you pack an overnight bag and come into the city for a few days? I think I'd like you to meet Commander Duddington before we go any further.'

'Um – well – yes. I suppose so. I'll have to see what Jon thinks, of course.'

'I'll be along to collect you just after lunch. I need to meet your sister, obviously. We shall have to tackle this thing gently, Mrs Fairbrother.'

Gently? The word hardly applied to Abe McKenzie.

She said, 'Well. All right. Why don't you come to lunch? We can hold it for you. And perhaps you can recommend a small hotel—'

'I've booked you into the Pierre. It's got a bit of a view over Central Park. I think you'll like it.'

'But I might not have been able to get away!' she bleated.

'In that case, it would have meant you did not want to find your sister's father after all.' He waited and when she said nothing he asked quietly, 'Have you seen anything of New York?'

'No.'

'I thought not. In that case, your stay here will have two purposes.' There was a noise in the background. He said quickly, 'My client has arrived, Mrs Fairbrother. I'll be with you about one-thirty. Thank you for the invitation to lunch. I'd like that.'

Rose replaced the receiver very carefully. Last Friday she had not known how she felt. She still did not know. But she was glad to be in touch with Abe McKenzie again.

Uncle Joe liked him instantly. He recalled the cake incident with hearty guffaws which did not do him much good. He lay back on the pillows, panting and pasty.

Abe said, 'Take it easy, Mr Lange. It wasn't funny at the time.'

'No. It was outrageous!' Uncle Joe spluttered again. 'I remember your father admitting to the Juvenile Judge that he had no control over you! What father ever had control over his fourteen-year-old son, I'd like to know!' He sobered. 'Poor old Tom. You hurt him that day, boy.'

Abe glanced at Rose and smiled slightly. He said nothing.

It was Jon who spoke. 'I think Mr McKenzie is rather too mature to be called boy, Joe!' She laughed, pretending not to recognize the significance of the term. 'And lunch is ready in the kitchen. So if you want to talk to Joe about anything, Mr McKenzie, perhaps you'd better do it before he falls asleep!'

Abe's smile deepened. Rose was glad that he liked Jon. Glad, and surprised.

'Commander Duddington is a medium-sized fish in the Pentagon. He is chairman of a number of committees. He can sway opinion. He's got an excellent record.' Abe put his fingertips together; Rose could imagine him doing so in court. 'First, we must be certain he is the man. Secondly we have to find out whether he wishes to acknowledge his daughter, or not. He has a position to keep up. A daughter at this stage could be . . . tricky.' He looked at Uncle Joe. 'Your sister-in-law might have mentioned a name at some time. Could it have been Philip?'

Uncle Joe narrowed his eyes. 'I don't rec'llect her mentioning any name. In fact she made damn sure no names were mentioned. Mabs said once that if she knew who the man was she'd make me horsewhip him. So I guess little Aileen decided to keep her lip buttoned.'

Jon said in a small voice, 'Poor Ma. She put up with a lot just to protect him.'

Abe said crisply, 'Or maybe to protect you. We don't know much about him. It'll be up to Mrs Fairbrother to find out.'

Rose said, 'Yes. What did you have in mind exactly?'

'He's got an office in Manhattan. And he's due there to pick up some papers on his way to Washington where he will stay with his sister. I think you should go about this straightforwardly. Look him up – I'll arrange that for you. Tell him who you are and that you remember him from the party. That your mother spoke of him and you always wanted to meet him. Take it from there.'

'Won't you be with me?'

'Nope. I'm a lawyer and he knows that. I'd make him feel defensive before we'd begun. This is to be entirely informal. You're looking up old acquaintances from your childhood. It'll be up to you where you take it after you register his reaction.'

She swallowed. 'It's good of you to take a continued interest. But I feel now that we should relieve you—'

'You're doing me a favour. I'd like to know more about Mr Duddington. Perhaps later, if you can establish anything, I can be introduced.'

Rose looked at him sharply. She suddenly had a feeling that Abe McKenzie was not being altruistic at all.

He had an open car.

'I noticed that the car you came in before was open. I guessed you like them,' he said, stowing her case in the back.

'I do.'

She smiled. William Barnes's car had been open when they arrived; not when they left. So Abe McKenzie had seen her right from the beginning. His surprise had been entirely feigned. She was still exhilarated, but her uncertainty diminished. This was a battle. She had no idea what she was fighting or why, but at least she knew who her opponent was. She looked at him as he glanced to his left to manoeuvre on to the turnpike. He was thickset in neck and shoulders, but he had the fine long nose of his father and the full sensitive mouth too. Suddenly she thought of something Maud had said and she smiled into the wind.

He glanced round and saw her.

'Something funny?' he called.

'A joke. My mother-in-law . . . just a joke. About a man called Boaz.'

He was silent while they overtook an enormous family saloon. Then he said, 'I reminded you of this guy, Boaz?'

'Well. No. Not really.'

He said abruptly, 'Your mother left you comfortably provided for? And your mother-in-law shares expenses?'

She said levelly, 'No to the first, yes to the second.' She looked at him steadily. 'You need not worry about your expenses, Mr McKenzie. I can pay you.'

'I know that. Your paternal grandmother has money.'

Her eyes widened; she was furious. 'How do you know? That's my personal—'

'William Barnes.'

'William . . . the detective agency?'

'Private investigator.'

'But he doesn't know. Unless Jon . . . and anyway it was *confidential*!'

'Like the Philip Duddington business, in fact.'

She was silent and furious.

He said, 'Look. It wasn't all Barnes. I was talking to your uncle while you got lunch. I talked to Jon when you were fetching your case . . . I need to know as much as possible—'

'Why?' she burst out. 'I'm – we're grateful for what you've done. But now your part is over. Even if you eventually meet this man it is quite unnecessary to know everything about our family life—'

'Mrs Fairbrother.' His voice was quiet but stern. 'I have a reputation to maintain. Not for its own sake. Or my sake. But because what I do reflects on the organizations I represent. I have pulled strings to find out about Philip Duddington, and I've done it for you. For old times' sake if you like. For my father. So I need to know that you are . . . worthwhile.'

'Have I passed the test?' she asked with deliberate sarcasm.

He took a wide bend and suddenly there below them was the sea and a diminutive city. He said quietly. 'Yes. Oh yes. You've passed the test.'

They drove down Fifth Avenue and parked under the awning of the Pierre. It was a luxury hotel. The bell captain opened the door for Rose and she smoothed her hair, suddenly feeling shabby. Abe handed over his keys, the car was driven away and they went up to the best hotel room Rose had ever seen. Pictures on the walls; a wonderful writing table in the window overlooking Central Park; her own bathroom and television and coffee machine and . . . everything.

She said, 'It's marvellous. I see why you needed to know about my circumstances. Supposing I hadn't been able to afford it?'

She sensed his sudden anger.

'The firm are paying your expenses, Mrs Fairbrother. You are our client. I told you, I needed to investigate your background to be certain of your integrity.'

She said lightly, 'I wish I had similar guarantees.' She went to the window. 'When will you let me have my bill?'

'I told you—'

She rounded on him. 'You said I was your client. Therefore I shall expect a bill, Mr McKenzie. As you discovered, I have – er – access to funds and can pay my way – in fact I insist on it!'

He stared at her. His eyes were unfathomable. He had never let anyone into his soul as David had.

He said, 'So be it.'

She let her breath go, and then smiled. 'Thank you.' She walked around the room. 'I shall enjoy this. I think I'll have my dinner up here and fiddle with the television. It'll be like playing house!'

'Ah. I wondered – I asked Eugenie if she'd come and look after you this evening. I have to be somewhere else, otherwise . . . '

She looked at him, surprised. He actually sounded diffident.

'That's all right. I'd love to see Eugenie if she can spare the time. But if not—'

'It's all arranged.'

'Oh.' She glinted at him humorously and said, 'I see.'

Unexpectedly he laughed. Then he held out his hand.

'D'you know, you haven't changed. Goodnight, Mrs Fairbrother.'

She took his hand and shook it solemnly. 'Goodnight, Mr McKenzie,' she said formally.

Dinner was wonderful and she pumped Eugenie unashamedly about Abe McKenzie. And though Eugenie seemed frank to a degree, Rose knew that she was only giving out the information that Abe authorized. Indeed, when their crêpes suzettes were flambant, the attractive secretary admitted as much.

'Well, let's see. You now know that Abe came out of the reformatory in '47 when he was sixteen years old. He never says why he was there in the first place. He got a bad name for himself somehow and the cops must have pinned something on him. He's pretty bitter about it. Anyway, he put himself through college and was halfway through law school when his father died. He then joined the Communist party and was gaoled for subversive activities – handing round leaflets in the campus it was – during the McCarthy witchhunt. He was in the State Pen where they've got a good library. He didn't waste that year. He went back to law school and was the top student of his year. He was just twenty-four. Life had been a bummer so far. The Commies preached equality but didn't practise it. His father – he worshipped his father – had been a servant all his life and had died before he was fifty. His mother had died before he knew her. But he had his brains and he had a driving ambition. For success, yes. But for something else, and he didn't know what till he met the doctor.' Eugenie looked absent-mindedly at the few crumbs left on her plate. 'He was an inspiration, was Martin Luther King. For everyone. Whites too – only Abe doesn't really believe that.' She sighed. 'Abe met him when he'd established himself with Evan Donovan. He was doing all right – civil cases, nothing political, but Donovan trusted him and let him buy into the firm as soon as he had some cash. He still wasn't satisfied – still didn't know quite what he was after in life. Then he met Dr King and that was it. He knew what he wanted then.' She glanced up and smiled. 'He talks about "the cause" like the old Crusaders must have talked. It's his religion. Especially since Dr King was assassinated.' She sighed deeply. 'I can remember the Washington March, you know. My parents wouldn't let me join it – we lived down in Tennessee. But the newsreels covered it pretty well. Abe was there. Right up in front. Ready to come between the doctor and any bullets. He wanted to die for Luther King. After the assassination, when he knew he had to live for the cause, not die for it, he became morose and withdrawn for a long time.'

The wine waiter approached and filled their glasses and she sat back, remembering.

'I'd just joined the practice then. I was eighteen and raring to go. I thought I would marry Abe and make a new life for him – be his inspiration – all that kind of crap.' She laughed. 'I'm still a very single lady!'

Rose said inadequately, 'You must know him very well.'

Eugenie shrugged. 'I've made him my business. But of course I don't know the real man. I doubt if anybody does. You can assemble facts and they don't amount to anything unless you've got a special key which puts them in the proper context.' She smiled. 'I've talked too much. You wanted to know about him and Abe didn't tell me to button my lip, so . . . you got it!'

She laughed and Rose said, 'In other words, he wanted me to know about him. I wonder why.'

Eugenie looked surprised. 'You're bright too, aren't you? Well . . . you deserve an honest reply to that one. He wants you to know your place in all this. For old times' sake he's taken on this job. But that's what it is, a job.' She folded her napkin with exaggerated care. 'Abe has a weakness, Rosamund. He thinks he wants equality for all men. But he's just slightly biased. And he doesn't know it.' She smiled wryly. 'Underneath his logic and balanced judgement and all the rest, he's still angry. With life, he thinks. But I think it's with the whites.'

Rose said, 'Perhaps you can't blame him.'

Eugenie leaned forward and said intensely, 'Don't you see, it won't work like that! One race above another – whether white or black – that's not what Dr King wanted!' She stared at Rose's blue eyes for a long moment, then subsided in her chair. 'Sorry. I don't usually think about it. Time to take that into consideration when Abe's in the White House! But it's cropped up again lately because of you.' She laughed. 'He wanted to help you, Rosamund. But he came as near as dammit to chucking you out the day you arrived. Because you're white.'

Rose too folded her napkin. She said quietly, 'I know.'

'You do?'

'Yes.' She smiled at the attractive girl opposite her. 'He helped me before, you see. He didn't want to do it, but he owed me one. So he did. This time, he doesn't owe me a thing. So of course it's more difficult for him.'

Eugenie surveyed her, surprised. 'Hey. You know him pretty well, Rosamund Fairbrother!'

Rose shook her head. 'No. But I know that much.'

Eugenie said, 'Let's have coffee and call it a day, huh? You look bushed, and we've got a heavy programme tomorrow.'

'We have?'

'Sure. I'm picking you up at ten and we're going to Forty-Second street to get some literature from the Convention and Visitors' Bureau. That will give us a sort of tourist's route. I think it takes in the Woolworth Building and St Paul's Chapel and the Custom House . . . all the things you have to see. We come back here to pick up any messages around fourish. And take it from there.'

Rose was ridiculously disappointed. She had imagined that Abe would take her around.

She said, 'What about your work?'

Eugenie smiled. 'This is my work. Don't you think I'm lucky?'

'But there must be things you have to do. And I'm quite capable of taking myself around the sights.' Rose hated the idea of Abe relegating her to client-level, though he had been at pains to tell her that was all she was.

'Listen,' Eugenie spoke with mock sternness. 'When the boss gives me an assignment, I don't quibble.' She laughed. 'Make the most of it, Rosamund. Because when he tracks down your Philip Duddington, you're going to be in the front line, I guess!'

Rose accepted a cup of coffee from the waiter and wondered what Maud was doing. And how Blue and Ellie were getting on at school. And whether Georgie was behaving himself. And what on earth she was doing sitting in the dining room of the Pierre Hotel next to Central Park, digging up the past.

Twenty-one

Rose slept badly again that night. There were no tears, but there was bewilderment and something which could have been fear. The suspicion that Abe McKenzie was using this whole situation to further some personal end was growing stronger. Had Eugenie actually used the word 'cunning' when describing his cleverness? Even if she had not, she had painted a picture of an opportunist. And the sudden appearance of herself as a reminder of his own past must surely be some kind of opportunity. And she hated it that he 'noticed' her colour. It wasn't like that for her; never had been.

She got up at dawn and stood by the window, watching the joggers below her. The trees were shedding their leaves now and in spite of the hermetically sealed windows, she imagined she could hear the runners' feet rustling through them. As the sun came out of the water, she made herself some tea and tried to write to the girls. It was a feeble attempt. She found some postcards in a rack, and chose half a dozen and sealed them into the airmail envelope. It was seven o'clock. She went back to the window and stared down again. Over to the right some horses and riders were trotting sedately. She said aloud, 'You're in a state and you don't know why. America doesn't agree with you after all. The sooner you're back home and into your little groove, the better. So all you can do is to go along with this peculiar scheme and hope it works out.' Yet even as she spoke the words she knew she felt more tinglingly alive than she'd done for years. Perhaps that was the trouble. Perhaps that was what frightened her.

She went into her en suite bathroom, showered, dressed. She looked at herself in the tall pier glass. There she was, no longer Snow-White, dark hair liberally threaded with grey, eyes dark with sleeplessness. She would be forty soon. She was still surrounded by a large and loving family. She was coping. She spoke aloud again, this time to her mother.

'Did you feel like this, Mother? You had Jon and me and the security and quietness you wanted. But did you too feel – just sometimes – utterly useless?'

The reflection in the pier glass stared back at her and there were no answers. She tightened her muscles and looked at herself as other women did; checking her clothes. Then she took off the navy linen suit and pushed her long legs into jeans.

Eugenie was a great companion; no doubt about that. At the Visitors' Bureau they were given maps and directions for a 'Heritage Trail'.

'How d'you feel about walking, Rosamund? This is all in lower Manhattan.'

'I'd love it,' Rose said enthusiastically. 'Only one gripe about the Pierre, and it applies to all hotels here. The air conditioning means you can't open a window.'

'Yeah. But you'd be thankful for it in August and January,' Eugenie smiled. 'We haven't got it at the office and believe me, it's a factor to battle against!'

Rose said only half-jokingly, 'And you've got plenty of those, I imagine.'

Eugenie nodded.

They used the Lexington Avenue subway and came out at Brooklyn Bridge and straight across the road to view the Civic Center. By the time they reached Fraunces Tavern, it was midday and they stopped for lunch. Eugenie rang the Pierre to see if there was a message from Abe. There was nothing. So in the afternoon they continued to Hanover Square and finished up looking over old sailing ships at South Street Seaport.

It was six o'clock when they got back to the hotel and Rose was worried that Eugenie was 'working overtime'.

'Honey, when you work for Abe McKenzie, there's no such thing as overtime. It's a twenty-four-hour job. And anyway – ' Eugenie flashed her marvellous smile – 'this sort of work I like!'

But when she rang the office from the little phone booth in the foyer, Rose could see her frowning and obviously arguing with her employer. She emerged looking very apologetic.

'Rosamund, I know I just said I was committed to twenty-four hours a day for Abe, but the fact of the matter is, I do have a date for tonight – old friends from Tennessee. I just can't put them off. And I thought Abe would kinda take over. But he's up to his eyes too. Will you mind being alone tonight?'

Rose fought a feeling of being let down.

'For goodness sake, Eugenie! I'm thirty-seven years old. And I've been on my feet most of the day! I'm exhausted – dinner in that gorgeous room and an early night – yes please!'

But when she got up to her gorgeous room, it did indeed seem solitary and cut off. The vague hum of hotel life was all around her, making her feel more than ever left out and let down.

She made tea. She wasn't hungry. She might be tired but she couldn't rest. She fiddled with the television; took a bath and put on her dressing-gown. It was seven-thirty.

Suddenly, she made up her mind. She took off dressing-gown and nightie, and dressed herself again in jeans and tee shirt. She put Jon's jacket over the shirt, grabbed her bag and went down again.

The girl at the desk was professionally friendly.

'Chinatown? Sure, there are some good restaurants there, Mrs Fairbrother. We recommend the Shanghai.' She maintained her smile. 'When Mr McKenzie arrives I'll call you a cab.'

Rose looked at her in surprise. The personal service here was almost too good: not only her name recalled, but Abe's too.

She said, 'Mr McKenzie? Oh no, he's not coming here. Call me a cab now, would you?'

The girl nodded and Rose drifted towards the doors and waited beneath the awning until the cab drew up and the porter opened the door ceremoniously.

'Where to, ma'am?' he asked.

'Chinatown, please.'

But the cab driver wanted an address.

'I'm not sure yet,' Rose said. 'Can you just drive around a little?'

He said gloomily, 'You're British. You want to eat out Chinese. OK.'

He drove. Rose thought determinedly that she must remember everything to tell Blue and Ellie and Maud. She saw Brooklyn Bridge lit up to her left.

'This is Canal Street,' called the driver over his shoulder. 'Now see – the first of the special phone booths.'

Rose stared curiously at the pagoda-shaped telephone box.

'This is Bayard Street. How about the Flaming Dragon?'

'I'd like somewhere small and quiet. What about the Shanghai? The hotel recommended that one.'

'Sure.' He turned the cab expertly and drove down more narrow picturesque streets. She had an impression of silk banners and dragons; paper lanterns, lotus flowers.

The driver drew to a halt outside a small shopfront.

'This is it, lady.' He turned. 'Listen, I don't hold with ladies going to these places on their own. Might be OK to run around London after dark, but it sure ain't here. I'm going to wait ten minutes before I drive off. It's OK, nothing on the clock.'

She was overwhelmed and tipped him heavily. But she did feel a definite qualm as she went through the door into the tiny room beyond. She was used to Westernized Chinese restaurants and this one gave no concessions at all to its host country. A waiter who looked horribly like Charlie Chan took her to a table where two other people were already eating. They did not look up as she joined them. They were both grey-haired, both dressed in black cotton even to small round hats on their wispy hair. The waiter went away and returned with an exquisite bone china handleless cup sitting on its saucer, half full of what Rose was almost certain was clear lemon-coloured tea. She smiled her thanks and he inclined his head and produced a menu written in Chinese characters. Before she could demonstrate her incomprehension, he slid away again. Embarrassed, she took a tiny sip of her tea. It was delicious. She studied the menu anxiously for clues and remembered with gratitude the cab driver waiting outside.

A hand appeared at the top of the menu. She looked up, startled. One of the other occupants of the table was smiling reassuringly. He had paused in the continuous job of transferring rice from plate to mouth with chopsticks.

'Over. Over,' he said. Rose might have wondered if it were some kind of incantation, but for the hand on the menu. She turned it over obediently; there, beautifully printed, was a list of foods in English.

'Oh thank you,' she beamed, forgetting the cab driver instantly. 'I thought I would have to go hungry!'

'Go? Oh no. You stay. You are very welcome.'

She saw now that the two men were quite elderly; they both smiled at her and their teeth were yellow and worn like those of old horses.

'Thank you.' Then, because they continued to nod and smile expectantly, she said – almost laughing at her own absurdity – 'Um . . . do you come here often?'

The other one spoke with no accent at all, not even American.

'This is our first time. We are on what you would call a mission.'

'A mission?'

'We are priests. But we do not wear robes because we live with our people here and work – write letters, deal with lawyers – and in the evenings we eat at the Shanghai!'

Rose nodded. 'Yes, we would call that a mission. How long will you stay?'

'One year in your time. Next Chinese New Year, we go home.'

'I didn't realize . . . how fascinating,' Rose said, thoroughly relaxed now.

388

She ordered chicken with rice and almonds and looked around her. She had been well advised by her hotel; the tiny restaurant seemed to be full of older people. She unwrapped her chopsticks and wondered whether she would be able to cope with them. One of the priests leaned over and fitted them between her fingers and encouraged her to practise. Somehow it all reminded her of Mrs Raschid and the kitchen in Newcastle. She felt a warmth for these two men who had welcomed her so unstintingly. Just like Mrs Raschid. Just like Fack. But not like Abe McKenzie.

As if she had conjured him up with her thoughts his voice spoke behind her.

'There you are! I've tracked you down at last!'

She looked up, staggered.

'What on earth are you doing here? Eugenie told me—'

'Quite. May I sit here?' He had not waited for the waiter. She looked across at her two companions who nodded genially. Abe had already seated himself next to her. He was smiling and sounded almost jolly; but she knew that he was angry. She had no idea how or why she knew this, but she was certain.

'How did you find me?' she asked, still amazed by his sudden appearance.

He turned his smile on her; she wondered how black eyes could be so cold.

'I arrived at the Pierre just after you'd left. Surely the girl on the desk told you I'd phoned?'

'No.' Rose frowned; she had said something which might have been construed that way. 'At least, I don't think so.'

'You don't *think* so!' He lost his smile for a second and regained it with a slight edge. 'Either she did or she didn't, Mrs Fairbrother!'

'Well . . . never mind. Go on.'

'She told me you'd taken a cab to Chinatown and probably come here. I took another one and cruised until I saw yours parked outside this place. Spoke to the driver . . . not too difficult, you see.'

'Well . . . ' she was at a loss. 'In a moment the waiter will bring you tea and a menu. I take it you will let me buy you—'

He said in a very low voice, 'We can't stay here. Where's your coat?'

'I didn't have one. Just Jon's denim jacket—'

'Where is it?'

'I don't know. I'm not leaving, Abe. I've ordered chicken and almond rice.'

He said grimly, 'We'll go back to the hotel. I want to talk to you.'

'I'm not leaving.' She was seething now, but played his game and kept smiling. 'Would you like to meet my new acquaintances? They are Buddhist priests on a mission to New York. Isn't it interesting?' She leaned over the table. 'This is my lawyer. Mr Abraham McKenzie.'

'Ah.' They both inclined their heads with apparent delight. The more fluent of the two spoke up. 'We deal often with the legal system here, sir. It is excellent. Considerate and just.'

'Er . . . good.' Abe shifted his considerable bulk in the chair as the waiter approached with the cup and saucer. 'I don't think—'

'It's delicious,' Rose assured him. 'And so real and . . . unaffected . . . don't you think?'

He accepted tea and menu with good grace. He glanced at her. 'OK, you win. I'm sorry.' It was said so simply she forgot her anger. He leaned across the table too and began to talk to the two older men. She watched him. He was courteous and friendly and she could see why he was such a success professionally. She could have sworn he was being completely sincere, if she hadn't known about him.

Their food arrived at the same time; Abe was good with chopsticks and she managed somehow. It was delicious; the chicken had that indefinable sweet flavour which the sauces gave it and the almonds were toasted to perfection.

The priests stood up to leave. There was much bowing and smiling. They hoped their various paths would cross again. Rose wished they would stay; suddenly she did not want to be alone with Abe McKenzie.

'Would you like something else?' he asked, moving slightly away from her into the vacated space.

She was not hungry, but at least in this small intimate place they could not have an argument.

'I'd like another cup of that delicious tea,' she said, sounding like Aunt Mabe going over the top.

He ordered it and it arrived with a plate of tiny biscuits.

'Chinese fortune cookies,' he said. 'Without the fortunes, thank God. Something you wouldn't know about, Rose. They weren't around much in the nineteen-forties.'

She was shocked to hear him use her name; not Rosamund. Rose. Fack had probably called her Rose.

She said, 'We have them at home. They didn't catch on.'

He picked one up and nibbled at it. He said, 'Rose, did you get my message and go out to avoid me?'

The unexpectedness of such a direct attack almost made her spill her tea. She sat up straight.

'Good God! I'm not one of your Southern belles motivated by pique, Abe! Of course I had no idea you were coming to the hotel. Why on earth would I—'

He stopped her with a hand on her forearm. His hands were very warm, very dry.

'I'm sorry. Sorry. Sorry. I didn't think I'd misjudged you. You're straight. Just for a moment, I forgot that.'

She stared at him for a moment, still angry. Then he smiled at her and she subsided.

'All right. Apology accepted.' He removed his hand and she tucked her arm into her side. She wanted to tell him that his mental clock had stopped in the nineteenth century, but she did not. 'Something important came up, did it?'

He did not answer immediately. Then he looked away and picked up another cookie.

'Yes. I'm afraid our Commander Duddington is going straight to Washington. His secretary is taking his papers to him there. So you won't be seeing him in his Manhattan office.'

'Oh . . . ' she did not quite know how she felt about that. 'Well, I wouldn't have missed today for anything. Eugenie has been marvellous.'

He nodded. 'She's a good girl. I knew you'd enjoy each other's company.'

'Can't we . . . I mean, surely we're not giving up?'

His smile was wonderful to see. 'Well done, Rose. The bulldog bit.' He picked up another cookie. 'He'll be in Washington tomorrow. I thought we could meet him there if you weren't too tired.' He grinned again. 'Eugenie says she walked you off your feet today.'

'Not at all. It was all most enjoyable.' She too picked up a cookie. They were getting on so well that she risked taking a leaf from his book. She held the cookie above her tea and said, 'I take it before you asked me, you booked a flight? What time is it?' Calmly she dunked the cookie and put it into her mouth. It went to nothing and she swallowed and looked at him.

He was not at all put out. He showed his wonderful teeth in a smile. 'Touché. I gather Eugenie has been telling you how I work? I thought we'd go by train. You'll see more of the landscape then. Seven a.m. tomorrow morning from Penn station. I'll pick you up at six-thirty. Is that OK?'

'Fine.' She held the tea-cup between the fingertips of both hands and rested her elbows on the table. 'And don't worry about what Eugenie told me. I heard exactly what you wanted me to hear. No more. No less.'

He simply refused to be discomfited.

'Good. Eugenie is an excellent assistant.'

'And, of course, in love with you.'

At last she had got to him. His dark face took on a purplish tinge.

'What utter nonsense! And how typically female! No such thing as simple loyalty in your book, Mrs Fairbrother? A woman has to be in love before she can commit herself to such an old-fashioned notion?' He stood up. 'It is strange how the Aryan races have this notion of enslavement. It is ineradicable.' He picked up his jacket from the back of his chair. 'I'll have a cab waiting outside for you when you're ready. You won't mind going back to the hotel alone as you are obviously so independent and capable.'

He left her still holding her tea. She should have felt enormous triumph at having punctured his outer skin. But she did not. She felt rather cold and bereft.

It was a three-hour trip to Washington. In the cab across Manhattan, in the bustle of Pennsylvania station and the business of settling themselves in the club car of the seven a.m. Amtrak Metroliner, it was only possible to exchange mere formalities. Then Abe asked her if she would like breakfast. She longed to say no, but the sharp autumnal air of early morning and the sight of the breakfasts around her were all too much.

'Those buttery-looking things,' she said in a low voice.

'Waffles,' he supplied. 'Some of those? And coffee?'

'Tea if possible.'

'Sure.' He grinned, suddenly companionable. 'Forgive and forget?'

She shook her head. 'Forgive, yes. But never forget. Forgiveness is easy if you suffer from amnesia.'

He put back his leonine head and laughed. 'Rose, you are the most down-to-earth woman I have ever met.' He sobered slightly but still grinning, he added, 'As long as we don't have to go back to being Mrs Fairbrother and Mr McKenzie. Both those names are a mouthful.'

She nodded. 'Funny. I thought – before I met you – that I might be able to call you Fack. But you're not like your father.'

'No.' He swivelled his chair away from the slanting sun. 'No. Tom was a saint. I'm no saint.'

'Eugenie says you want to be the first black president of the United States.' She looked at him and saw he was not smiling. She said quickly, 'Abe, I'm sorry about that Eugenie gibe last night. It was a nasty thing to say. Until you pointed it out, I didn't realize—'

'I knew that. I chose to take exception to it.' He made way for the waiter to serve breakfast, then sat forward to pour tea. 'Listen, there are certain things – subjects – which rile me. It's my weakness and I accept that. Shall we agree to give them a miss?'

She glanced at him, surprised. He could be so frank – had been so frank just now – then suddenly he was shutting her out again. Was it Eugenie? Was he in love with her?

She said, 'I'm sorry—'

'Don't apologize. It's me.'

But she had meant that she was sorry they could not discuss everything under the sun.

She smiled. 'Never mind the blame. Tell me what is happening today. And what is this gorgeous gooey stuff around the waffles?'

'Maple syrup. And how do you like your tea?'

'Milk, no sugar. I say, isn't this fun?'

'Yes.' He smiled at her again. 'How long since you've said that?'

She thought back. 'I must have said it often. Picnics on the hill with the twins and Georgie.' Her eyes stared beyond him. 'I remember saying it once in Lynmouth. A long time ago.' She came back to the present. 'Maybe I haven't said those precise words lately. Not since David died. I suppose I take my responsibilities a little too heavily.'

He nodded. 'Me too. We see life as a battle to be fought, instead of a piece of cake to enjoy.'

She laughed. 'That's it! And Jon – my sister – she comes into the latter category!'

'Yes. She's very lucky, isn't she?'

'I never thought of it like that. Yes. In a way she is. But it hasn't made her happy so far.'

'She's eaten the cake too fast? Given herself indigestion?'

Rose laughed. 'That could be it. She's certainly happy now. She loves it here. And the work on the farm – organizing everything – looking after Uncle Joe – it seems to be her forte.'

'Everyone needs to be needed. Nobody has relied on her before, perhaps?'

'No. She was the baby for so long. She almost played the baby for Rick, too. When people wanted to lean on her, she shied away.' She was thinking of Martin and Ali.

He said, 'Of course. Her role had already been defined for her. Now that she is so near to finding a father, she doesn't have to make that particular role for herself any longer.'

'You've lost me.' Rose laughed. 'I'm not very bright, I'm afraid.'

He looked at her. 'You don't have to act that role for me either, Rose. You are very bright.'

'No.' She flushed. 'I meant . . . I'm so ordinary. All that complicated introspective stuff – it's not for me.'

He smiled, but did not follow that up. Instead he said, 'What about Jon's husband?'

Rose looked out of the window. 'She loved him. She might still love him.' She frowned at a wide expanse of lake. She said, discovering it for the first time, 'I spoiled that.'

He watched her, silently. She turned from the lake and said, 'Water under the bridge. You haven't told me yet where I'm to meet Philip Duddington.'

He waited a moment longer, then poured more tea and said, 'Rose, I have something to confess.' He passed her cup and looked at her with his veiled black eyes. 'I should have told you immediately, but . . . I wasn't sure I wanted to help at first. The fact is, when I saw that photograph I knew the man. I've met him about three times. At conventions to do with civil rights – things like that. I knew I was in the ideal position to introduce you to him. This afternoon there is a reception at the South African Embassy. It is a goodwill thing to soften us up over the sanctions. I was invited several months ago, and declined the invitation. I would like to increase embargoes, not lift them. But yesterday I heard that Philip Duddington will be there. He is representing naval defence.' He shook his head. 'I cannot see the link either, but he will be there. And I am now going. With my guest.' He inclined his head to her courteously. 'But until you have actually met him, it would be better if he did not know that. It might er – prejudice – your case.' He grinned at the deliberate jargon. Then went on, 'It seems to me, Rose, that we can be frank about this meeting – up to a point. You are here, looking up old friends. Your aunt, the Labens, me – you knew my father well – etcetera. Your mother spoke of him often. This was a wonderful chance to meet him. Got the picture?'

'Yes.' She was enormously relieved that he had come out into the open and admitted he knew Philip Duddington. She had suspected as much. And of course, if they were opposed politically, it was obviously better to keep her connection with him quiet.

He went on, 'Whether you will tell him about your sister is something for you to decide, Rose. I cannot help you. You'll have to rely on your instinct at the time. If he suggests another meeting, it would be ideal – give you more chance to weigh up the situation. But if not – you'll have to stake all on one throw, or decide to call it a day.'

'That sounds the very best we can do.' She was stupidly happy. She grinned. 'I had a feeling you knew more than you were telling me.' She leaned across the table. 'Abe . . . thank you for helping. It must seem so trivial to you. But . . . I can't explain all the intricacies, but it is important to our family. Very important.'

'Nothing has been done yet, Rose,' he said warningly. 'He's not the easiest of men. I know him only officially of course, but—'

'Don't worry. You've done your part. I just want you to know how grateful I am – Jon is too.'

He said brusquely, 'Drink your tea before it gets cold. And look at the trees. Washington is supposed to be the leafiest place in the world, did you know? They'll be blowing about the streets . . . everywhere.'

He was changing the subject. She admired him more than ever. She looked at the passing view. It was all . . . marvellous.

Abe hired a self-drive car at Union station and zipped her around on a lightning tour of the city before lunch. They drove from the Lincoln Memorial past the Washington Monument to the Capitol, and behind that to view the Supreme Court and Library of Congress. She particularly wanted to see the Vietnam War Memorial and she wandered around the stone walls of that on foot, looking at the lists of names and feeling a sense of kinship with this enormous and generous nation of her birth. It occurred to her that to share a grief is a privilege as great, if not greater, as sharing a happiness.

He seemed to sense her mood and drove her over the bridge to the Arlington cemetery. And then to the other Georgetown where he had booked two rooms in the kind of small hotel that proliferated in London. A mid-terrace house, without the porticoed front of so many of these old residences, it could have been a private home.

'Now this—' Rose swept her arm around the tree-lined crescent – 'this is lovely. It's a bit like Bath at home. Or Cheltenham. Or—'

'It's probably not much younger than they are,' Abe interrupted, laughing. 'The first senators used to put up in Georgetown and travel in to Washington by stagecoach each day.'

She looked at him, suddenly serious. He had the American pride and joy in his country; he was loving showing her around, getting as much pleasure from it as she was. Eugenie had warned her that he was a complex character; and she knew that. But at the moment, he was simply an American.

He stopped laughing and looked at her.

'What's up?' he asked bluntly.

She laughed, and shrugged. 'I don't know. I think I saw the boy who was covered in cake crumbs. The boy who jumped out of the cake claiming an American victory for everyone.'

He said, 'I am still that boy, Rose.'

She said, 'No. Not all the time. You are a man of politics some of the time.'

'Politics are simply a word to describe a social system, Rose.'

'And in order to obtain a system of their choice, politicians twist and turn and compromise—'

He laughed, but unamusedly. 'You're against compromise?'

'You see how you pounced on that one word?' She walked across the wide pavement to the bole of an enormous plane

397

tree blotched yellow with age. She put a hand on the rough trunk as if it could connect her with the past. 'That boy . . . he knew nothing of compromise. He was . . . splendid!'

She expected him to fire back at her and was angry with herself for letting the short exchange happen in the first place. But as usual he confounded her. He joined her and touched the sleeve of her suit gently.

'Come on. Let's book in and get ready for this reception.' His smile was heartbreakingly sweet. 'And Rose . . . I know what you mean, and you're right of course. I tell myself – when I'm wheeling and dealing – that the ends justify the means. But I know they don't always. So . . . remind me of that boy now and then.' He opened the door and stood aside to let her into the small lobby. He added almost shyly, 'I never thought of him as being . . . splendid . . . before.'

She had not known what to pack. It seemed to her that American women either wore jeans and shirts or were very formal; there seemed nothing in between. She was mostly in between. She eventually chose a dress she had worn to the school open day last summer. It was sober as befitted a 'parent' on these occasions, a soft grey silk shirtwaister, but it was beautifully cut and the skirt had reminded her of her wedding dress. It swathed her still-slim hips and then swirled just below her knees in a way that she liked. After she had showered and changed she stood foolishly in front of the mirror, twisting back and forth so that the skirt lifted to Marilyn Monroe levels. Then she moved to the bed and sat down to put on her earrings, half ashamed of herself. She knew that the excitement and bubbling happiness inside her had nothing at all to do with meeting Philip Duddington. That whole business now seemed very secondary. The main action was entirely elsewhere . . . it had to do with feeling young again – really young. Maybe as young as four years old.

Whatever it was, it gave her confidence. The embassy was splendid and ornate in the old colonial style. It reminded

her of the Labens' big, chandeliered hall, on a gigantic
scale. She was introduced to the ambassador who looked
like wartime pictures of General Smuts; then Abe was
introducing her to a tall woman in long gloves and saying,
'Mrs Fairbrother would like to meet Pip Duddington
eventually. D'you think you could introduce her to Mrs
Corcoran?' And the tall woman took her by the elbow and
steered her away from Abe without a word. As if it were
somehow rehearsed.

They threaded their way through knots of people and
came to an elderly lady in cashmere and pearls talking to
a waiter about obtaining China tea.

'Ah. Dorothy.' The woman in gloves leaned down and
pecked exactly like a hen pecking corn. 'My dear, this is
Mrs Fairbrother from England. She particularly wants to
meet Commander Duddington.'

'Pip? How marvellous! He will be delighted!' She took
Rose's arm. 'Off you go, Helen. Do your duty elsewhere.
Mrs . . . er . . . and I will get acquainted.'

She steered Rose towards a table.

'My dear, I just love London. Even when it rains – in
fact especially when it rains! I can remember it before you
stopped having coal fires and had pea-souper fogs. That
was something. Like being in a Sherlock Holmes book. I
just loved taking a taxi along the Embankment to the next
party and hearing the fog hooters—'

Rose looked round for rescue. Abe had disappeared. So
had the gloved lady.

She said, 'I don't know London terribly well, actually.
I live in Gloucestershire. But I was born in this country
during the war.'

'How *marvellous*! I thought you must have met Pip when
he was Naval Attaché in London. But you knew him here?'

They reached the table and sat down in two armchairs.

'Yes. Um . . . Actually not personally.'

'Mutual friends.' Mrs Corcoran shot out a hand and
detained a waiter. Again she mentioned tea. 'Drinks at this
hour are not for me. Will you take Lapsang? Or Ceylon?'

'Ceylon would be lovely.'

'Now. Mrs . . . I've forgotten what Helen said your name was.'

'Fairbrother. Rosamund Fairbrother.'

'And you have friends who know Pip?'

'My mother knew him. A long time ago.'

'And your maiden name was?'

'Harris.'

'Harris. Harris. Do I know your family?'

Rose swallowed; she felt very hot indeed. 'My aunt is Mrs Steedman.' Rose interrupted herself. 'I'm afraid I didn't catch your name.'

'Dorothy Corcoran. I am Pip's sister. And d'you know, I have met your aunt. Once. I believe she married Senator Steedman quite late in life?'

'Yes. She was married to Uncle – Mr Joseph Lange before. I lived with them in Connecticut as a child.'

'My dear, how marvellous.' Mrs Corcoran passed tea. Her eyes were very sharp. She looked Rose over in a series of short glances.

Rose smiled. 'Am I being screened, Mrs Corcoran? I thought I'd like to meet your brother, however briefly. I've managed to make contact with most of the people my mother and I knew over here. But it was all a very long time ago. Victory night, to be exact.'

Mrs Corcoran screeched a laugh. 'Screened. Say, isn't that marvellous? Screened – I must remember that.' She sipped her tea and stopped laughing. 'Your mother knew Pip?'

'I believe so.'

Mrs Corcoran drank her tea in sudden and unnerving silence. All around them people stood in groups talking animatedly; they were isolated around their table.

The elderly woman put her cup down with a click and held up a finger. A waiter appeared.

'Will you fetch Commander Duddington and more tea? In that order.' She smiled at Rose. 'It will do Pip good to be reminded of those days. He enjoyed the war.' She leaned forward. 'His wife died recently, Mrs Fairbrother. He is . . . vulnerable.'

Rose nodded, accepting the vetting process. 'I understand.'

Mrs Corcoran said, 'Ah. Here he is now. Pip dear. A young lady from England to meet you. Mrs Fairbrother.'

Rose stood and turned. The man was still straight as a die; he wore uniform with a lot of gold braid. His hair was thin, his ears prominent, his eyes pouched, but with a staggering sense of shock she recognized something about him.

His sister spoke against the hum of general conversation. 'You might remember her better as Rose Harris, Pip. Quite a small girl, I should imagine. Victory day, 1945.'

He smiled formally and then reached for Rose's hand.

'A great pleasure. Anyone from those days . . . you must have been evacuated here. Am I right, Mrs . . . ?'

'Fairbrother,' Rose supplied. 'And, well, yes, in a way.'

He released her hand and moved around the table. They sat down.

Mrs Corcoran said, 'I've ordered more tea. I'm glad I came now. This is the best thing that has happened at one of these receptions for many a long year!'

The other two laughed. Suddenly Rose knew she had to be perfectly open about this meeting. She said, 'It was so lucky Mr McKenzie knew you. And so kind of him to bring me here to meet you.'

'Abe McKenzie?' Philip Duddington's heavy-lidded eyes looked directly at her.

'Yes.' She smiled. 'It's all right, I know that you are political adversaries. But my wanting to see you has nothing to do with politics. Mr McKenzie was – is – the son of my aunt's old general factotum, so I got in touch with him hoping he would help me to find you. And he knew you! Wasn't it lucky?'

'Yes. You could say that.'

There was a long pause; what Jon would have called a pregnant pause. Rose could feel brother and sister sharing their tension.

Then Philip Duddington said, 'There was a victory party that night. At the house of—'

'Rudolf Laben.'

'That was it. Yes. I've never forgotten that party. Was Mr Laben a relative of yours, Mrs Fairbrother?'

Rose said, 'No. My aunt was a friend of the Labens. I played with the boys sometimes. Fack – Tom – must have looked after me as a child. I was very fond of him. When I came to the States last month, I wanted to look up as many people . . . Tom was dead, and I was put in touch with his son.'

Mrs Corcoran said casually, 'Mrs Fairbrother and I have had a little chat, Pip. I have met her aunt. She is married to Senator Steedman.'

'Ah.' The commander seemed to relax slightly. He smiled at Rose again. 'So. We haven't met since those days?'

The tea arrived. Rose shook her head and through the throng caught a glimpse of Abe standing in a group of men around the ambassador. He did not look her way.

'I thought not. I would have remembered you, I am sure.'

Mrs Corcoran said, 'How long are you staying in Washington, Mrs Fairbrother?'

'Well. Now I've met your brother, I shall go back to Connecticut tomorrow. And probably fly home in a week or so. My uncle is ill and I would like to see him improved before I return.'

'You came to Washington just to meet me?' Rose could understand why her mother had been so instantly attracted to this man; the hooded eyes twinkled above the tea-cup and there was a warmth about him that promised protection. What she could not understand was why Aileen had never contacted him when she knew she was pregnant.

She nodded, smiling back. 'Yes. I've always known of your existence. And I wanted to meet you.'

He said carefully, 'How do you mean – known of my existence?'

She told her first lie. 'My mother spoke of you, Commander.'

Full realization dawned. 'Of course! That's it! You were – are – the daughter of little Aileen Harris. Yes?'

She did not have to feign astonishment. 'You remember her name? You remember her?'

402

He replied – formally gallant – 'How could I forget her?'

She said, 'But . . . but she never got in touch with you, did she? And it's thirty-two years ago!'

He laughed. 'Perhaps that's it. The one woman who never made demands.' He sat back, staring into the past. 'I went back on duty two days later. And my wife . . . she was very demanding. I was no good at writing letters in those days. But after Christmas I went to see Aileen. The Labens told me she'd gone back to England. And that was that.' He looked up. 'Aileen. How is she? My God – surely I'm not going to have another chance?'

Rose swallowed. 'I'm sorry. She died. Two years ago.'

He looked genuinely sad. Mrs Corcoran, apparently only listening with half an ear, said acutely, 'She must have been still young?'

'Yes. She was in her mid-fifties. She had a bad heart. We think now that she knew about it for years and that was why she led such a quiet life.' She glanced at the commander. 'We went back to England to virtual retirement. But don't get the wrong idea. We were very happy. She was particularly so. My mother-in-law said once that she was a complete and contented person.'

Mrs Corcoran said, 'And your husband, Mrs Fairbrother? He is not with you on this . . . pilgrimage?'

Rose looked at the older woman. 'He died before my mother.' She cleared her throat and filled in the few remaining details. 'I have twin daughters. They are thirteen. At boarding school back home. My aunt asked me to come out . . . and I felt perhaps . . . I should.'

'So it *is* a kind of pilgrimage?' Mrs Corcoran smiled. 'Look. This is hopeless, trying to converse against this crowd. Why don't you dine with us this evening? Pip is staying with me and we planned to be quiet – just the two of us. It would be delightful if you would join us, Mrs Fairbrother.'

The commander leaned forward. 'I endorse that heartily!' He forced a roguish smile. 'In other words, may I second the motion?'

Rose had hoped to see some more of Washington with Abe, but she could not hold out against this man. Suddenly she realized why he was so winning. His eyes, darting at her with a kind of diffidence, were full of charm, and so like Jon's. She needed no more proof that this man was Jon's father. She smiled and nodded.

'Thank you so much. I should enjoy that.'

Abe was delighted too. Unflatteringly so.

'Don't hurry back. Did they ask you to stay overnight?'

'Of course not! He's lost his wife and she thinks it will be an interesting evening for him, and that is all.'

'Dorothy Corcoran is the most suspicious old biddy this side of the Ohio river! I thought the connection with me would put the can on the whole thing!'

'Well, you told me to play you down, so I did.'

'Son of ole black Joe?' he mocked.

She said crossly, 'Shut up, Abe! He's nice. I can see why Mother . . . and he's like Jon – or rather she's like him.'

'So you're convinced he's the one?'

'Yes. But I'm not sure how he will take the news.'

'I can tell you. He'll haul up the gangplank and repel boarders. He'll deny it. Before you mention your sister, you must get him to admit he slept with your mother.'

She was appalled. 'How can I possibly do that! Honestly, Abe! Jon has agreed that if he doesn't want to meet her, that's his choice! I wouldn't dream of taking that attitude – it's as if I'm trying to trap him!'

He said nothing. They were in her room which overlooked the genteel sweep of houses opposite. He went to the window and gazed down.

She said slowly, 'You *want* me to trap him. There is something behind all this. Something more than Jon's happiness.'

He said stubbornly, 'I just think he should be made to admit parentage. Even if he then backs away from actually meeting—'

'Why? I can see it's important for Jon. Why is it import-ant for you?'

He turned and came towards her. 'Rose. It's something to do with us. I don't quite know . . . I don't understand it. Yet. But it's . . . winding up the past. Closing a chapter? Opening a new one?' He spread his hands. 'I can't explain. I might be able to later. But now . . . it's too soon.'

She stared at him. Suddenly she felt an overwhelming tenderness pour through her; it was a physical sensation; it made her want to sit down before her legs gave way. She turned from him blindly, and went to the closet for a cardigan. She was cold. She knew exactly what was happening even if Abe did not. And he must never know. It must never be allowed to happen.

She said steadily, 'It's finishing a chapter. Making certain it is finished. For always.'

She slid her arms into the cardigan with difficulty but did not move away from the closet.

Behind her Abe said jovially, 'Well. What are you going to wear tonight?'

There was only one dress that was long. She picked it out and laid it very casually across the bed.

'Hobson's choice,' she said lightly. And he laughed at the Anglicism, perhaps not even understanding it. The moment had passed. She looked at the dress; it was one of Jon's, a pale green top shading into a darker green skirt. 'It'll have to do,' she added in a deliberately gloomy voice. And he laughed again.

The trouble was, she liked the elderly brother and sister more and more as the evening went on. Mrs Corcoran's home was surprisingly unpretentious, very much like the small hotel in Georgetown. The butler reminded her of Fack and obviously ran everything, including Mrs Corcoran's wardrobe. That lady said during the simple meal, 'You know, Jameson, this dress grows smaller when I eat!' And he responded seriously, 'I did advise you to wear the blue, madam.'

Philip Duddington met Rose's eye at this and they smiled simultaneously.

When the coffee came they moved to the easy chairs by the open fire. The flames were flecked with blue and Rose said unthinkingly, 'Frost tonight.'

'Really?' Mrs Corcoran widened her eyes. 'Are you a meteorologist too?'

Rose laughed. 'It's what we said as children. When the fire burned blue.'

'You make your childhood sound like something out of a book, my dear. You mentioned a brass-railed nursery fireguard when you described that delightful cottage – what did you call it – Snow-White's cottage? We had those as children, many years before your infancy.'

'We tried to make that kind of a world. It must have been so shattering for my mother. The loss of her parents. Then her husband. Then . . . we returned home.' Rose shook her head. 'She literally burrowed back and made that kind of world for us.'

There was a pause. Mrs Corcoran poured more coffee and glanced at her brother.

He cleared his throat. 'Rose . . . may I call you Rose?' He inclined his head when she agreed and added, 'Please call me Philip if you feel able.' She nodded too though she was not sure whether she could do so. He said slowly, 'You have implied several times, Rose, that you had brothers or sisters in this little world your mother made for you. Is that so?'

She swallowed. 'Yes. A sister. Joanna. I named her actually. Because I intended to shorten her name to Jon. My father was called Jonathan and he was known as Jon.'

There was another long silence. Rose drank some coffee and knew she could not prevaricate as Abe had wanted. Philip Duddington could deny it if he so wished. She would have to tell him about Jon anyway.

She too cleared her throat. 'My father's ship had been torpedoed during the War of the Atlantic. He had already been dead for some time, of course. But I must have subconsciously known about the disgrace my mother was in. That was my way of . . . stopping any gossip, I suppose.'

Mrs Corcoran jumped the next question and said straightly, 'Did your aunt make her leave when it was discovered she was pregnant?'

'I don't think so. She would have wanted Mother to go away, of course. She knew the senator then – her reputation was important to her. But my mother chose to go back to England because of me. I knew we'd be all right there. Safe.'

Mrs Corcoran said, 'Thank the Lord for small mercies! I would certainly have had to cut her off my Christmas list if she had done any such thing!'

Rose almost laughed. She could imagine Mabs's fury at being punished for something which had happened thirty-two years ago and was not her fault anyway.

Philip Duddington said, 'Your sister – Joanna – you are saying she is my child, Rose. Is that it?'

Rose spoke as calmly as she could. 'I think so. Mother never actually said. But the likeness is there.'

He said, 'Oh God.'

Mrs Corcoran leaned forward as if to touch him but he shrank away. She said, 'Wait a moment, Pip. Don't say anything.' She turned to Rose. 'How did you know? Your mother could have known any number of men—'

Philip said hoarsely, 'Dorothy! Be quiet! Rose, my sister did not mean—'

Rose said calmly, 'There was just one man. If you'd known her, you wouldn't have even asked that question.' She put her cup down. 'I'm sorry. I've upset both of you. I'll tell you what happened, then I'll leave and you can put the whole thing away from you. My sister has somehow . . . lost her way. She wanted very much to find her father. She came to stay with my aunt, but of course no-one knew anything. So they sent for me. Because . . . as you know . . . I was there. The Labens had a photograph. You were on it. I recognized you. I'd . . . come upon you. That night.'

He said in a low voice, 'I remember. I'm sorry.'

'I was only four. It meant nothing to me. I couldn't remember much at all. But there was someone else there with me. Abe McKenzie. The son of my aunt's general factotum. He was fourteen at the time. I talked to him and he remembered and said he would introduce us. And he did. That is all there is to it. Obviously if you do not wish to meet Jon, then she will come back home with me. No harm done.'

Mrs Corcoran breathed, 'Abe McKenzie. Of course.'

Philip Duddington said heavily, 'What do you know about Abe McKenzie, Rose?'

She said, 'He is a lawyer. In New York. He is dedicated to the cause of civil rights. He was one of Martin Luther King's protégés.'

'Did you know he is being considered as one of the judges for the Supreme Court?'

'No.' She felt a sense of doom.

'They are chosen by the President. But . . . there are naturally advisors. I am one of the advisors. I have been against Abe McKenzie because I consider him to be – in his way – racist.'

Rose looked at him, her eyes very wide. The sense of doom deepened and became an ache through her whole body.

She said very quietly, 'Look. I'll go away. Forget you ever saw me—'

He leaned forward and put a hand on her arm. Mrs Corcoran said, 'Well.' She reached for the coffee pot. 'At least we know you are not implicated, Rose. I may still call you Rose?'

Rose felt her eyes begin to sting dangerously.

'I *am* implicated in a way. I thought – wondered – suspected – right from the beginning that Mr McKenzie had an ulterior motive—'

Philip Duddington said quietly, 'You had nothing to do with it, Rose. That is what matters to us. And you must understand that you cannot drop out of my life now. I have to see my daughter.'

Mrs Corcoran passed a cup. The coffee was strong and black. Rose sipped gratefully.

He went on. 'Abe McKenzie is of course hoping that I will want this kept under wraps. The scandal, etcetera.'

Rose said, 'Oh my God—'

He went on, 'With or without Abe McKenzie, I would have wanted to see my daughter. That is absolutely certain, Rose.' He sat back in his chair. 'Whether I would have wanted to do it quietly is now an academic question.' He too took a cup of coffee and sipped it thoughtfully. 'The problem to deal with, at the moment, is whether I resign as an advisor first or after the publicity . . . first, I think.'

Rose was appalled. 'Surely that won't be necessary?' She closed her eyes. 'I don't think I can take this—'

Mrs Corcoran said swiftly, 'Pip was going to step down anyway, my dear. He is overdue for complete retirement. This will merely—'

'But the – the disgrace—'

'Can be minimized,' Mrs Corcoran continued smoothly. 'In fact, it may well be turned inside out. A question of honour, as it were.'

Philip smiled briefly. 'Dorothy, you are wonderful. That aspect does not bother me in any way. I assure you both of that very sincerely. I've done the work that has come my way as best I can. That is all that matters.' He sipped again and sighed. 'I am afraid what does worry me is that Abe McKenzie may well get into the Supreme Court on the eddies of everything else.' He tightened his mouth grimly. 'He won't get in by blackmailing me, that is certain!'

Rose fought a feeling of complete disorientation. She was caught up in something way beyond her experience and it was terrifying. The core of her revulsion was the knowledge that all along Abe McKenzie had been using her. The trip on the Amtrak, the tour around Washington, the moment in the hotel at Georgetown . . . She felt sick.

Mrs Corcoran said firmly, 'Listen, that is a separate problem. Really, nothing to do with Rose. And I have a feeling this young lady would like to get right away from Washington very quickly!' She smiled. 'So how about if we talk about . . . Joanna? Was that your sister's name, Rose?'

Rose swallowed. It was difficult to bring her mind back to Jon and her obsession with finding a father.

'Yes. Joanna,' she said in a small voice.

'Tell us about her,' invited the older woman.

Philip Duddington sat forward. 'Yes.' He flashed her that warm smile. 'Tell us about my daughter, Rose. Please.'

So she began to talk about Jon. The naughty little girl who had wanted excitement; then love and security. And had been unsuccessful. And as they questioned her, she found she was understanding Jon better than she had ever done before. Because she too, had fallen in love with a man who did not return her love.

Twenty-two

Rose remembered very little of the rest of that evening. Mrs Corcoran gave her a card on which was printed her address and telephone number and it was arranged that when she got back to the farm she would give it to Jon and ask her to telephone or write and arrange a meeting. Anywhere, any time. Philip Duddington would have come back with her there and then, if his sister had not cautioned diffidence.

'Both of you – Joanna especially – are over-anxious about this whole thing. Take it step by step. Let Joanna choose the time and place. And you – Pip – remember that this girl has lived a whole lifetime without you. She has been married and has a son.'

'I was married. And had a son,' he reminded her.

'Yes. But she has been aware that she has a father – however much of an unknown quantity he might be. You have known of her existence for a few hours only.' Dorothy Corcoran looked to Rose for support and Rose nodded fervently. She wanted to get away. From all of them. She wanted to be by herself.

A taxi took her back to the Georgetown hotel at midnight. She was terrified Abe might have waited up for her, but there was a note on her door which said, 'Hope all OK. Sleep well.' She screwed it up and threw it in the frilled bin by the dressing table. It was tempting to leave immediately, but the practical difficulties were too enormous and she wouldn't give him the satisfaction of knowing the extent of her pain. So she went to bed. She thought she would lie awake again, but before she had even started to tell her brain to relax, she was asleep. She had slept like this after David's death and thought it was total exhaustion. When she woke the next morning she wondered whether, in fact, her mind was unable to cope with the grief and had shut itself off. There was no refreshment from her sleep, simply unconsciousness for a few hours.

Abe knew something was very wrong, but to his credit he used none of his tactics to discover what it was. He enquired whether she was meeting Duddington again and when she shook her head, he offered her another day to see Mount Vernon or even Richmond.

She said quietly, 'I'd like to get back to the Pierre, pick up my stuff and go back to Jon. If that's all right with you.'

He said sympathetically, 'Complete failure last night?'

Rose looked at her coffee cup. That was what it had been, in a way. A complete failure of her instincts, her own feelings. She glanced up and said brightly, 'Not at all. But the next move is ours. I need to get back and talk to Jon.'

He stared at her, his dark eyes suddenly understanding. He said in a low voice, 'You've heard about Sara. Someone has told you about Sara and Tom.'

She could not meet his gaze. She stared down at the waffles oozing maple syrup and felt her spine rigid against the ladder-back chair.

He said quietly, 'I told Eugenie not to mention them. But I might have guessed someone would tell you. I met Sara on the march that time, Rose. She'd gone for the fun, the excitement. But I didn't know that. I was lonely, idealistic. We got married just before Tom's birth. He's twelve now.'

Her hands were flat on the thick linen tablecloth; it wrinkled beneath the waffles and she straightened it compulsively.

He said urgently, 'Rose. Listen. Sara and I share a roof. For Tom's sake. That is all.'

She said very levelly, 'This has nothing to do with me. It is not of interest—'

He interrupted her. 'Don't go away from me like this, Rose!'

'I can hardly—'

'You're running away! Your mother ran away when she knew that Duddington was married and had a child. You are doing the same thing!'

She repeated woodenly, 'I have to talk to Jon.'

'I'll drive you down to the farm this afternoon.'

She smoothed the starched cloth and picked up her fork. She said, 'That's all right. You've done enough. I'll make my own arrangements.'

He looked at her. His face gave nothing away. 'I see,' he said slowly.

They barely exchanged courtesies on the train. There were magazines on the tables and she read one of them from cover to cover and could not remember a word afterwards. He got a cab at Pennsylvania station and dropped her off at the Pierre without suggesting another meeting of any kind. He did not even shake hands when she left him. The bell captain carried her stuff through the foyer and into the elevator and she just managed to find money for the tip before the tears ran down her face. She stood in the centre of the room and wrapped her arms around her body in an effort to control the inward agony. She told herself it was damaged pride, a feeling of betrayal . . . it was both those things. But it was something else. Another loss. Another bereavement.

She looked at her watch; it would be evening in England. She sat on the bed, reached for the phone, crouched right over it and asked the operator to get her the Churchdown number. Maud replied at the first ring.

'How are the girls?' Rose asked.

'Fine. I knew you were going to ring. I was waiting. What's happened?'

'I've met him. He's very nice indeed. He wants to see Jon.'

'Wonderful. When are you coming home?'

'After that first meeting? I don't know.'

'What's the matter?'

'Nothing. I'm tired. Sightseeing, meeting strangers. You know.'

'I know something's wrong. Is it Boaz?'

'Boaz?'

'Yes. Boaz. Has he turned out to be Jon's father or something?'

'Oh . . . Boaz! Oh Mother, you're so . . . sane.'

'Tell me.'

She was going to lie or fob Maud off. Then she said, 'Yes. It's Boaz. And no, he's not Philip Duddington. He's someone else. And he's used me for his own ends so I'm feeling a bit let down.' She tried to lighten her voice. 'It'll be great to get home.'

'D'you want me to come out?'

'Oh Mother . . . ' Rose began to cry quite audibly. 'I'd love it more than anything. But I'll be back before you could buy a plane ticket. And there has to be someone there for the girls. And Georgie. I'll tell Jon what is happening and I'll book a flight. Tomorrow. The next day. I must have been mad to come.'

Maud's voice came sternly over the line. 'Oh no. I wanted this to happen. I had a feeling it might. Darling, don't you see – it doesn't really matter about him letting you down. It's what has happened to you – that's what matters. You've had to accept David's death. You've had to accept that there is a future for you. A personal future. Nothing to do with me or your girls. Can't you see that?'

'Not at the moment.' But she could almost have smiled, if her mouth hadn't been shaking all over the place. 'Let's talk about it when I get home. I'm going to order a cab or something to get back to Jon now. I'll ring again tomorrow. How's that?'

'Wonderful. Unless something happens about Boaz. Then stay as long as you can. For always.'

Rose said, 'Darling, you are marvellous. But even without . . . what happened . . . it wouldn't have done. He wants to be president of the United States. And I want to be an ordinary woman.'

Maud was still laughing almost hysterically when they were cut off.

It was dark when the hired car drew up outside the farm. Jeff Blatt's car was also there, and every window in the place was alight. Rose thrust a handful of notes at her driver and let him lug her case to the front door. She did not suspect anything was wrong; she had phoned Jon to say she was on her way and she supposed this was Jon's way of welcoming her back. But immediately she went into the square hall, she knew that Uncle Joe had gone. Her experience of death told her that he was not there. It was strange, uncanny even; but not upsetting.

Jon heard the door and came out of the kitchen. She was huge-eyed, white-faced, her dark hair had been permed since Rose had seen her last and it stood out, a frizzy aureole. She was wearing a bright red dress.

She said tensely, 'He died about an hour ago. You just missed him. Oh Rose, I'm so sorry.'

Rose hugged her. She felt the tremor in the shoulders; Jon had looked on the old man as so specially hers.

She said, 'It doesn't matter, darling. You were the one who looked after him. I'm glad you were here. Wonderful for him, and an honour for you.'

Jon looked at her with swimming eyes. 'Oh Rosie, you couldn't have said anything better! It *was* an honour! Clark and Greta were in town getting groceries, and I rang the doc, but he wasn't actually there when Joe . . . ' her face crumpled. 'It was an honour! I didn't realize . . . is this how it was for you with David?'

Rose smoothed the wild hair and thought about it. 'Yes. Yes, it was,' she said. And for the first time that day, she smiled.

Jon wept anew. 'So there is something positive to come out of all of it, after all!' She sniffed against Rose's shoulder. 'He didn't want the drapes drawn. He said that. And he didn't want us in black or anything. So I backcombed my hair and put on this thing and drew back all the drapes and lit the lamps—'

Rose said quietly, 'It's as if you are both welcoming me back, Jon. It's lovely.'

The door to the drawing room opened and Jeff Blatt came out. He looked relieved to see Rose and immediately handed her the death certificate.

'You'll be all right now, Mrs Johnson.' He was already fastening his bag. 'I can let you have a sedative if you—'

Jon said, 'Of course I don't need anything like that! Joe . . . it was a good end. And he knew he was going to die. A couple of days ago – just after you'd left, Rosie – he said he wouldn't see you again.'

Rose murmured, 'I had no idea it was so close.'

The doctor said, 'I'll be off now. The funeral directors will take everything out of your hands.'

Jon said, 'I've rung them. And Mabs. She said as you were coming home she would leave it till tomorrow.'

Rose went to the door and stood there while the young man drove away. Jon had already gone back into the kitchen.

She called, 'I'm cooking something, Rosie. You must be hungry.'

Rose walked across the hall. Jon was putting an empty frying pan on to the cooker.

Rose said, 'Sit down, Jon. I'll make us some tea and we can eat later – after the undertakers have been. You need to relax.'

Jon suddenly left the cooker and flung herself on Rose.

'Darling – I think he's left me the farm! I didn't want anything! I didn't do it for that! You know I didn't – you do know that, don't you?'

Rose stroked the rough, wiry hair. 'Of course I know that, Jon. He was part of your American family. You loved him for that – and because he was a lovable man too.'

Jon nodded vigorously. 'But Jeff Blatt . . . he knows. He was there that day with the lawyer. And he thinks I'm a gold-digger! And Aunt Mabe will think so too. And maybe the Labens!' She wailed piteously. 'This is what you were thinking of when you said it might be a tricky situation – wasn't it, Rosie?'

'Well . . . maybe I was. But Jon, he's got no-one else to leave his place to. You need not feel guilty. It must have been wonderful for him to realize that right at the end of his life there was someone who cared about the place—'

416

'Oh I do – I do, Rosie! I'll live here and work it properly again – I'll have poultry like you said you used to have! And maybe, later, horses. If I can get some decent help. But no-one will have much to do with me, darling.' Her voice broke again. 'And I'll be so lonely!'

'Jon . . . Jon.' Rose managed to settle her in a chair. 'Listen. Half of this is your natural grief. And it's good to let it out. But try to see things properly. If you're serious about working the farm, Georgie will help you—'

'Not for two or three years at least!' Jon rubbed her face with the palm of one hand; mascara streaked it like war paint. 'Don't you see, it's the usual pattern for me! I can't get away from it, Rosie. I get what I want, but it turns sour on me immediately!' She looked up. 'D'you know, I've never had friends. Not proper loyal friends. And when I came here first, they were all there – ready-made as it were. The Labens and Maria and Uncle Joe – even Aunt Mabe cared a bit about me!' She hiccoughed a sob. 'And now . . . they'll drop away. You'll see. I sensed what Dr Blatt thought. And even dear old Joe whispered something about Mabs's mouth going like a duck's ass.' She tried to smile and failed.

Rose said, 'Sit there while I make some tea. And just believe me when I tell you that everything is going to be fine.'

She filled the kettle and fetched cups. Jon stayed, slumped on the chair like a rag doll. She looked terrible. She looked up and whispered suddenly, 'You don't mind, do you, Rosie? He said you'd understand because you'd got everything you wanted anyway. He thought I needed it.'

Rose gave an exclamation of distress and came back to the chair in a hurry.

Jon wept anew. 'I love this place, Rosie! I could live here and farm it properly and collect Toby jugs or Wedgwood . . . everything would be perfect! If only he'd left something to you and Mabs as well, it would have been all right!'

Rose crouched by her and said sternly, 'Shut up, Jon. You're tired and overwrought. It's a wonderful thing that Uncle Joe did. He knew what he was doing all right – no-one else will care for the farm like you will. If you don't enjoy it, he'll . . . turn in his grave!'

Jon managed a wavering smile and scrubbed at her eyes again.

'Oh Rosie, I'm glad you're back! When you left I thought how clever I was to cope on my own. I really thought I was becoming self-sufficient at last. But I'm not.'

'Well, I don't think you're going to be lonely, darling. Not now. You see, I think your father is going to want to spend a lot of time with you.'

'My father! Oh my God – I'd forgotten why you went to Washington! Rosie – what happened – you talked to him – he wants to see me – oh my God!'

Rose laughed and went back to the cooker to make the tea.

'Let's have a hot drink first, Sis. You don't realize it, darling, but you're in shock. You've dealt with a death in the last hour. Lit up the house – dressed yourself up. Just let's have a cup of tea quietly.' She put cups on a tray and said seriously, 'I think you're quite wrong about that "pattern" you mentioned. I think everything is going to be right for you now, darling. Joe loved you – and in a funny way he left you the farm for Mother's sake. He wanted to make it up to her in some way. He said that was why it was important to find your father – to give Aileen some dignity as well as you. They all loved Mother, you know. That's what makes them so special. And that's why you fit in here, Jon. They want to like you too.' She passed tea. 'They'll want you to make a success of this place. Don't worry about it.'

Jon said impatiently, 'Yes. But what happened with Philip Duddington?'

Rose said, 'I'll have to tell you in a moment – I can hear a car. Probably the undertakers. Drink your tea and I'll see to them.' She stood up. 'You've done wonders, Jon.'

'I had a good teacher!' Jon gave another watery smile and pecked at Rose's cheek. 'We'll have supper and you can tell me about New York and Washington and help me to get over the horrors!'

*

It was late when they sat down to eat. The undertakers had had to drink coffee and go through their reassuring patter. They would take care of everything. From black-edged cards to newspaper notices. Rose watched them drive slowly away with Uncle Joe on board and thought bleakly that when it came to the end, undertakers were the most important people on earth.

She told Jon very briefly that Philip Duddington was in fact her father and was most anxious to get in touch with her. Jon was suddenly apprehensive.

'But he's so . . . important, Rosie! Surely he'll have to keep me a secret? I mean, it won't do his reputation much good.'

Rose was suddenly agonizingly tired. 'I don't think he cares much about reputation any more, Jon. He's lost his wife and his son, and he heard the day before yesterday he'd got someone. Family. He feels the same way as you do.'

'Oh Rosie.' Jon had washed her face and combed her hair flat again. She looked almost normal.

'The thing is, darling – if you do want to live here – and you might change your mind later – Aunt Mabe won't "drop" you. Not by a mile. If she does, Mrs Corcoran – Pip's sister – will drop her! And that would be the absolute end for Aunt Mabe.' Rose tried to laugh, but it did not work.

She leaned forward emphatically. 'The main thing is, Jon, he's very, very nice. And I think he loved Mother – he tried to get in touch with her later, but she'd gone back home and he took that as a turn-down from her and did not pester her again.' She stood up and pushed back her hair. 'I'm really done. I'll have to go to bed. I'll tell you all the details tomorrow. But I must say, darling, that if he'd turned out to be a roadsweeper, he'd have still been a father in a million.'

'OK.' Jon managed a wry smile. 'It's all marvellous, Rosie. But just at the moment, all I want to do is to come back home with you and see Georgie.'

'I know.'

Rose barely had the strength to get undressed and wondered how she would cope with the next week of arranging a meeting, helping to make that meeting work . . . Uncle Joe's funeral . . . Aunt Mabe . . . it was all too much. And she wanted to be home, so very much.

But it was amazing – as she had discovered before – how relatively simple it was to live hour by hour, day by day. Over the next week she told Jon almost everything that had happened to her during the last four days. She was surprised to find she could do so without mentioning Abe's name more than two or three times. She helped her to sort Uncle Joe's things and deal with Aunt Mabe. She phoned Maud and Mrs Corcoran and made the funeral arrangements. She felt as if she might be caught up in a black comedy, she was so expert at all the arrangements. She hardly thought of Abe. Or so she told herself.

After the funeral they went back to Court House in Georgetown. The Labens were there and other friends and acquaintances of Joe's whom Rose and Jon had never met. The news had been well and truly bruited that Jon was now the owner of the farm and it was interesting to see everyone's reactions. As yet nobody knew that Jon was the daughter of Philip Duddington, yet they all accepted her as the new owner of the farm without reservations. Aunt Mabe introduced her to some friends of Joe's as 'our niece who came over from England specially to nurse poor Joe'. Jon caught Rose's eye through the discreetly milling throng and closed one eye. Rose shook her head, but was glad to see that Jon had regained her wayward spirit. Suddenly Jon had a place in the community. People were going to watch with interest as she took on the farm and dealt with Greta and Clark with true English aplomb.

She said herself over a plate of profiteroles, 'I feel . . . different, Rosie. I won't have to lean on Duddy as much as I thought. I didn't want that. I wanted us to meet on some kind of equal footing.'

Rose nodded but queried, 'Duddy?'

'Well, I can't call him Dad or Pop. And Pip is too much like *Great Expectations*. So I thought . . . Duddy. It's such a funny name – might as well make the most of it!'

Rose grinned. 'But you're sure about staying? You could sell for a lot of money, you know.'

'Joe wanted me to stay.' She waved across heads at Eric Laben. 'Not only that, it gives my life some point. I don't want money. I want to care for someone or something.'

'You're wonderful.'

'No I'm not. You're wonderful. But you can't see it, which also makes you an idiot.' Jon smiled brightly as she spoke and moved away to ask Jason for more sherry.

When everyone had gone, Aunt Mabe made for the small sitting room, the senator close behind.

'Come on, girls. You've told us nothing about your New York quest, Rose. I know this business has taken all the – the – fun out of it. But Joe would have loved to hear what happened. So let's have a talk – it will be the next best thing.'

Rose could practically see Jon melting towards her aunt. They sat as they had done on the day of her arrival, the teapot on the spirit lamp, the senator apparently comatose in his chair. But then Jon's defensiveness had been tangible; now her aggression had all gone. Rose had never seen her so relaxed.

Rose kept her own feelings well out of it and recounted her four days away in some detail. Aunt Mabe was entranced to hear she knew Mrs Corcoran. Even the senator sat up at that.

Finally Aunt Mabe said, 'Well . . . you girls have certainly stirred up a hornet's nest since you arrived! I thought you were meant to be such quiet little things!' She smiled forgivingly. 'We could do with you, here. No doubt about that. I know we can't keep you, Rose. Your whole idea has been to get back to England as soon as possible. But Jon. What do you think?'

Jon spoke frankly. 'I've been talking to Rosie. I love the place. And I'm fairly sure Georgie would love it too. I'd like to work it properly again. It . . . it would give me something to do. Something worthwhile. But if . . . this man, my father . . . doesn't like me . . . it might change things. I just don't know yet.'

421

Mabs pursed her lips. 'You mustn't think like that, Jon. You're a woman in your own right now. Before . . . maybe you were depending on the outcome of the meeting rather too much. Wanting something from it. But now . . . ' she drew a judicious breath. 'It seems to me you're in an excellent position.'

Jon looked at her for a long moment, then said slowly, 'Funny. That's how I feel too. Maybe we are alike in some ways. Joe said we were.'

Unexpectedly a flush coloured Aunt Mabe's withered cheek.

'Did he?'

'Oh yes . . .' Jon risked teasing her. 'And that you could make your mouth look like a duck's ass.'

Aunt Mabe flushed more deeply, then laughed. 'The old . . . son of a gun,' she said.

Then she added, 'And if Rose can stay on until after the commander's first visit – act as a kind of go-between, Rose – I'm sure it will work out all right.'

It had not occurred to Jon that Rose might return home before then. She looked anxiously at her sister.

'You will stay, won't you, Rosie?'

Rose nodded. She had been away less than a month, after all. It just seemed like a lifetime.

When Rose eventually telephoned Washington, Philip Duddington was not there, but Mrs Corcoran was as civil as she had been before. She sent her regards to Mabs and commiserations to all of them.

'Pip was terribly disappointed to have to delay his trip to Connecticut, but I thought it was a good thing on the whole. Time for him to consider . . . everything.'

'Has he changed his mind about . . . anything?' Rose asked, equally cautious.

'No. But he has been to see Mr McKenzie. I gather it was all-cards-on-the-table for both of them.' She paused then said, 'Pip has a great respect for Abe McKenzie, Rose. He might not think he is ready for the Supreme Court, but the man isn't quite fifty yet. He's got time on his side.'

'I understand, Mrs Corcoran.' Her heart sank. Abe had won. Philip Duddington had capitulated to pressure and in a year or so – when no-one could make any awkward connections – Abe would get what he wanted.

Mrs Corcoran said, 'I'll ring you again about dates and times, my dear. Pip is busy winding things up here, but there won't be a long delay. He is very keen indeed to meet your sister.'

Rose said dully, 'I'm so glad.'

As she replaced the receiver, Jon was at her side.

'Is something up? You sound awful.'

'Nothing's up at all. It was Mrs Corcoran. She sends love, sympathy. You know. And she'll give us a date and time when she's seen her brother.'

Jon said reflectively, 'I shall call him Duddy immediately, and to his face. If he takes it the right way I shall know . . . all kinds of things. And after all it's affectionate, yet it need not imply a thing to outsiders if he doesn't want it that way.'

'Will you mind? If he doesn't?'

Jon looked through the window at the evening ritual of getting the cows in. She said, 'Thanks to Joe, no, I don't think I'll mind. Joe has given me a kind of self-esteem. Along with all of this—' she swept her hand around the room, half-embarrassed.

Rose said, 'I loved him as a kid. I didn't know what chickadee meant, but I liked it.'

Jon went to the window and waved at Clark. 'Just to let him know I'm around – d'you know he enjoys whacking the cows to get them inside. And there's no need for it. They want to come and be milked.' She turned and saw Rose grinning. 'Yes, OK. I'm going to be a real dragon, I know that!' She shook her head. 'Joe thought of us as the children he hadn't had. I'm so glad we arrived on the scene before he died, aren't you?'

Rose nodded emphatically. 'You did the right thing coming out here, Jon. In all kinds of ways.' She turned away. 'But I wish I hadn't come, all the same.'

Jon was genuinely distressed. 'Darling, none of it could have happened without you! You had to come! Oh Rosie . . . has it been that bad?'

Rose forced herself to turn again and smile reassuringly. 'I'm just homesick.'

But Jon said, 'This is your home too, Rosie. You know that.'

But if Rose was certain of one thing, it was that her home was not here. And never could be.

*

Philip rang that night and talked to Jon. Rose, packing Uncle Joe's clothes, watched her sister's face with affectionate amusement. The tough exterior melted as it had done for Joe and for Aunt Mabe after the funeral. She coloured faintly after the first five seconds on the phone, then she smiled and finally laughed explosively with a mixture of relief and pleasure.

'Of course I want to see you!' she exclaimed at last. 'That was why I came to America!' He must have said something about all the years before, because she replied, 'Well, it was up to Mother, wasn't it? If she did not want to tell you—' There was another pause; her smile came and went. Then she said, 'It won't be a shock for me. But you've only just learned of my existence.' She laughed again and glanced in Rose's direction. 'We do look a bit alike, of course. But I have brown eyes and Rose . . . well, you know about Rose.' She nodded several times, then she said soberly, 'Listen, Rose has told me about . . . you know . . . Abe McKenzie. I know you more or less have to acknowledge me in order to stop him from blackmailing you—' She stopped talking and listened. 'Well, that was how it sounded,' she put in. She listened again and said, 'If you're sure . . . that's a weight off my mind . . . but in any case, I expect Rose told you when she phoned before, I shall be staying here, I think. Working the farm. So . . . ' She smiled. 'Yes. That would be nice. Another reason for staying here. Thank you . . . Duddy. I'm going to call you Duddy. Is that OK?' She laughed joyously at his reply and said, 'Hey, you sound nice!'

424

She put down the phone and looked at Rose. 'He's everything you said. He said I should stay here as I have a ready-made family already indigenous . . . well, that was what he said. What does indigenous mean, Rosie?'

'Oh shut up! So you're going to meet him?'

'He's coming here. Tomorrow.'

'With Mrs Corcoran?' Rose asked apprehensively thinking of the state of the yard outside.

'No. He wants to get to know me himself first.' She made for the kitchen. 'I'll make scones, I think. And Rosie . . . ' She paused in the doorway. 'Abe McKenzie isn't going to try to use this business for his own ends after all. In fact he's told Duddy that he's not interested in getting into the Supreme Court at all.'

Rose stared after her, her face without expression.

*

She saw the car long before it arrived and knew that it was being driven by Abe. She was in her bedroom shaking a bedcover from the sash window and the car came off the road and took to the lane as if it knew its own way to the salt-box farm. Neither Philip Duddington nor a chauffeur could have been so confident of the way. It swept past the gates that guarded the drive to the Labens' colonial mansion and slowed for a couple of chickens that ran out of one of the smallholdings opposite. Then it bucketed over the cattle grid and into the yard and Rose, peering down, saw Abe's hands on the steering wheel before the passenger door opened and the long lean figure of 'Duddy' stepped out.

She waited there, like an audience of one in the gods, while Jon came out of the door and stood facing the man who was her father. Then he held out his hands and Jon put hers into them, and quite suddenly he gathered her close and she gave a little sob and they were rocking together as if about to waltz across the yard.

Rose could not hear what was said, but after some talk from both of them, Jon's father turned and drew Abe forward and Jon shook hands. Then she led the way indoors. And Abe looked up and saw Rose and just stood there, hands hanging loose by his sides, somehow terribly vulnerable, like a man awaiting condemnation.

She withdrew into the bedroom and stood for a long moment surveying her unmade bed. She did not want to meet him again; it was too difficult – he was too difficult. He was a man with a cause and an overweening personal ambition. She could not cope with such a man. But Jon's voice was calling from below, telling her that 'Duddy' had arrived and they were all going to have sherry before lunch. She had put on a very English jumper and skirt that morning. Her reflection stared at her from the mirror; she looked somehow condescending. She pulled off the skirt and pulled on her jeans. Then she got out of the jumper too and shrugged into a checked shirt. Then she combed her hair upside down so that it was full around her face. And then she went downstairs.

Greta, persuaded into a respectable overall, was doing vegetables in the kitchen and jerked her head at the trolley loaded with coffee things. Rose wheeled it into the sitting room, glad to have something to do. She wondered about lunch. Jon and she had planned a very English menu, roast beef, Yorkshire puddings, Brussels sprouts and potatoes followed by cabinet pudding. But supposing Abe did not like stodgy food?

The sitting room seemed to bubble with Jon's and Philip's excitement. Everything gave them pleasure: he loved being called Duddy. She adored him using her full name, Joanna. They had just discovered that they both liked Laurence Olivier, *Gone with the Wind*, sweet corn and winter sports.

'D'you remember my first skating lesson, Rose?' Jon's face was alight now as it had been then. 'And the toboggan run on Churchdown hill?'

'Say, we could go to Sun Valley this winter, if you like,' he said. 'I haven't been there in years!'

Rose poured coffee and kept her eyes away from Abe, though she knew every time he moved. He was sitting in the window where Uncle Joe's bed had been. He was wearing denims and a sweatshirt. She was glad she'd changed.

Philip said, 'Dorothy sends her love, Rose. She would like it if you and Joanna could visit her before Christmas.'

Rose passed him coffee and smiled. 'That is most kind of her. I'm afraid I shall be going home soon. But perhaps Jon—'

But Jon too was unwilling. 'I think I'll have to stay on here for a while, Duddy. I have to get the hang of things. I thought maybe my son could come out when Rosie goes back. I'd love you to meet him.'

They talked about Georgie. Jon had photographs and showed them around. Abe took his turn; he stared at them intently.

'Your daughters are very beautiful, Rose. They are close to their cousin?'

Rose looked at him properly for the first time since his arrival. The trouble with Abe McKenzie was that he was so very sentient.

She said, 'Yes.'

He passed the family snaps back to Jon. She took them and smiled at him.

'Thank you, Abe. I may call you Abe? Thank you for everything you've done to bring this about. I realize you and Rosie were friends before I was born, but that was no reason to go to so much trouble—'

He interrupted gravely, 'It's been no trouble. It's been a pleasure. I want to make that clear. It's been a pleasure.' He smiled at Jon. 'I do everything else for other reasons. It is good for me to do something for pleasure now and again.'

Philip said uncomfortably, 'That brings me to my piece. Rose, I was entirely wrong about this man. He had no intention of using his inside knowledge to gain anything at all for his advantage. I apologize unequivocally for thinking so, and for passing on my suspicions to you.' He nodded at Abe. 'That was why we came together today. He thought I might need some backup and I thought this apology was due in front of you girls.'

'That's very generous of you, sir.' Abe too nodded as if they were making an agreement. 'There is no need for any embarrassment, I assure you. As Rose pointed out at some stage, the world of politics is a pretty dark labyrinth.'

Rose wanted to say 'Did I?' but she could not allow herself to enter into a direct exchange with Abe. Instead she murmured something about lunch and beat a retreat into the kitchen.

It all went very well. The two men loved the English food, though the beef had probably been done to death by their standards. Jon showed 'Duddy' how she had liked to fill her Yorkshire puddings with gravy when she was small. And Philip suddenly started talking about his dead son, who would have been older than Jon had he lived.

'He was the reason your mother never contacted me,' he said unexpectedly. 'I know that now. I'd told her that my wife and I . . . We'd married too young. But Aileen came across a photograph of Richard, and she would never have risked splitting father and child.' He smiled. 'I knew your mother for just a few hours, Jon, but in many ways I feel I knew her completely. Am I right about Richard?'

Jon said, 'Yes.' Her own smile was inverted. 'You know, Duddy, if I hadn't met you I wouldn't have known that. It's so obvious now. But I wouldn't have known it.' She looked across the table at Rose. 'She was just . . . great. Wasn't she?'

Rose nodded.

After lunch they went over to Aunt Mabe's for Philip to pay his respects. The senator, totally ignored as a rule, came into his own and they talked earnestly together while Aunt Mabe tried to pretend Abe wasn't there, in spite of Jon telling her it was all his doing.

'My dear.' She spoke seriously. 'You will be made. Socially, I mean. Winters in Washington – parties—'

Jon said firmly, 'I don't want that, Mabs. I want to stay at the farm and make it a proper home.'

'But . . . Washington, Joanna! High society!'

'I shall have all the society I need. Georgie. You and the senator. And maybe Rose and Maud will bring the girls for Christmas.'

Rose said nothing.

Mabs said, 'Such a pity about your husband, dear. You do need a man about the place. The hired couple – they're hopeless.'

Jon grinned. 'They're getting better all the time. I'm licking them into shape!'

Abe said quietly, 'I think the commander – and his sister – would enjoy life down here.'

Jon brightened. 'They can come for Christmas too!'

Mabs beamed and wondered aloud if she could hire enough staff for a Christmas party – guests of honour to be Philip and Mrs Corcoran.

Abe said in a low voice, 'Rose, when are you going home?'

She turned slightly from Aunt Mabe. 'I'll telephone tomorrow. The soonest available flight, I think.'

'Will Jon be all right?'

Rose said hardily, 'I don't know. But I must see my family again.'

'I'll make your reservations. Or rather Eugenie will. She'll phone you. Don't worry, she's an expert.'

'I think I'd prefer to do it myself. Then I shall know exactly—'

'The day after tomorrow. How would that be?' He lowered his voice further. 'Let me do this last thing, Rose. Please.'

She shrugged. 'As you please. It can go on my bill, which I take it you will send to England.'

His eyes flickered and she knew he was annoyed. 'There will be no charge for services rendered,' he said woodenly.

She said coolly, 'It will be impossible to split your actual services from the hotel bills and train tickets—'

'There will be no charge for anything,' he repeated.

She stared at him angrily. He was putting her in a very invidious position. But she refused to argue. 'You are paying dearly for your pleasure, Mr McKenzie,' she said.

And he said with equal deliberation, 'I don't care, Rose Harris.'

They returned to the farm and the two men left immediately for New York. Philip was to return in a few days;

he had business to clear up before his final retirement. He promised he would bring his sister and stay for a week at least.

Abe held out his hand.

'I do not think we'll be meeting again, Joanna . . . Rose. I'm glad I met you. It seems to have tied some strings for me.'

'For us too.' Jon pumped his hand warmly. 'Maybe we shall meet again, anyway.'

'It's a big country.' He smiled at her and turned to Rose. She held his hand as loosely as she dared. It was very warm and very large. 'Goodbye, Rose,' he said. 'And thank you.'

She could not believe he was going to go out of her life like that. She smiled formally and nodded her farewells and stood with Jon at the door to wave until they were out of sight. He was gone. It was terrible. Appalling.

Jon went inside and produced two pairs of rubber boots.

'We're going to hose down the yard,' she announced.

'Why?' Rose asked blankly.

'So that you won't have to cry. Or scream. Or anything else.'

She donned one pair of boots and waited impatiently while Rose pulled on the other. Then she marched into the barn and emerged with the end of the hose already gushing water. She thrust a broom at her sister and directed the water at the trodden manure of the day. As in a trance, Rose began to sweep.

Jon said, 'You're going to hate me for saying this, Rose. Until I saw you with Abe today, I didn't think it would do. Not because he was coloured – don't think that. But he's from a different world. A world you would have hated.'

Rose swept as if her life depended on it. The drain cover blocked and she scrubbed at it vigorously.

Jon said, 'Now . . . I see that whatever differences there are don't matter. You love him, Rosie. He loves you too, you know.'

'No!' She looked up momentarily, then down. 'No. He doesn't love me and I don't love him. There's an attraction. That's all.'

'Like between you and Rick, that time?'

It was as if the world stopped. Rose held her broom handle into her chest, leaning on it hard. Jon directed the water into the air where it sprayed almost noiselessly on to the bank of the vegetable garden. It was getting dark. Shockingly, again Rose was reminded of a night in the Stroud Road garden; this time when she and Maud had made a bonfire pile while they waited for news of David.

She did not attempt to deny anything. The guilt rose in her throat like bile.

She said, 'Have you always known?'

'No. He told me before he went to Newcastle. That's why I asked you to go and see him for me. I knew it would be hell for you. I hated you.'

Rose looked up. 'Jon . . . I'm sorry . . . '

'That's why you've done so much for me, isn't it? Guilt?'

'*No!* If I've done anything for you, it's not been because of that.' She was suddenly certain of that one thing at least. 'Jon, let's stop doing this – let's go indoors—'

'No.' Jon directed the water on to the concrete yard again. Mud splattered at Rose's feet. 'I've never been able to talk about it before. I might not now unless we keep going with something.' She looked up. 'Sweep, Rosie. Use some energy for God's sake. Otherwise . . . you might try to kill me.'

'What do you mean?' Rose sent a rivulet of water down the drain and then another. She said, 'Jon, I don't think I can bear this. Why do you bring it up now – how can we – how can we – bear each other now that you've spoken? We've become so close – you've ruined all that.' She gave a mighty sweep with the broom, then leaned on it. 'Oh God. You've blamed me all these years – it was my fault! Oh God—'

Jon said sharply, 'Shut up. You don't know what happened. You don't understand. I've brought it up now because of Abe. Because you're so blind. Because you

431

won't let yourself admit you love Abe – because you think it's disloyal to David. You're frightened of feeling guilty again. Like you did after Rick.'

'Jon—' she almost screamed her sister's name in protest. But Jon directed the spray of water towards the vegetables and replied quietly enough.

'Listen, Rose. If it means that you never have anything to do with me again, I still have to tell you everything. Perhaps – later – you'll understand me better then. Why I was so . . . angry . . . so miserable. Will you just listen? Please?'

Rose stared at the water around her feet and began to sweep again.

Jon said very clearly, 'When you married David, it wasn't right, was it? You'd got Rick on your mind – he fell for you. Not me. And you felt something for him too. But you were right, it was only physical and once you'd got it out of your system, you and David were fine. Right?'

Rose stared at her. Her hands around the broom were soaking and numb with cold. She whispered, 'How did you know all that?'

'I could see it. Every day, every minute you and David were together, it was obvious.' Suddenly Jon's expression was pitiful. 'It made me . . . vindictive. When my own marriage was on the rocks – when Rick had gone up to Newcastle and left me – David visited me in hospital. And I told him. Oh God, Rosie, I told David that you and Rick had been lovers. And I've had to live with that ever since!'

Rose stopped sweeping and looked at her sister.

Jon sobbed suddenly. 'That's why I hardly ever came to see you! Until David was ill, we were like strangers! And the funny thing was – ' her sob changed into a laugh – 'you didn't even realize we were strangers!'

Rose thought she was going to faint. She stared and stared.

Jon spoke with a kind of desperation. 'Listen, I need not have told you this. Rosie – I could have kept it to myself till I died. But you've got to wake up to the fact that Abe isn't another Rick. You are in love with Abe. If you like – you and David are in love with Abe. David is you now. You're not the same Rose as before. You're not Rose Harris. You're Rose Fairbrother. And Rose Fairbrother is in love with Abe McKenzie. And I think you should admit it, even if it can't come to anything. Admit that you still have feelings! Admit that you're not trying to follow in Mother's footsteps and living just for your children!'

Rose continued to stare. Jon dropped the hose and it emptied itself over a row of cabbages. Neither woman moved. Jon said at last, 'Rose, for God's sake, say something. Do something. Hit me with that broom – anything—'

'How can I? You behaved naturally.' Rose blinked hard. 'David never spoke a word of this to me.'

'Of course not. There was no need. He knew—'

'But at the end . . . he could have said something.'

'He had forgotten probably—'

'Don't be absurd!' For the first time Rose's flat tone changed to one of anger.

'It was gone and buried. I promised I would never mention it. He said he never would.'

'If only he had said he could forgive me—'

'Don't be an idiot, Rosie! As he saw it, there was nothing to forgive. You had done something against your nature for his sake!'

'Christ, you make adultery sound like buying a birthday present!' Rose's voice lifted in agony and Jon came towards her, arms outstretched.

'Rosie – Rosie—'

'Get away!' Rose almost screamed the command. 'Can't you see I am going mad! I cannot explain to him – ask him to understand – nothing! He's dead! David is dead! I shall never see him again!'

She crouched suddenly in the wet mud. The broom clattered on to the concrete of the yard.

Jon tried to gather her up but she struck out against any help. She rocked on her heels, arms around her knees, head on her arms. She made a peculiar keening sound.

Jon came as close as she could and said urgently, 'Rosie. Listen to me. You do not need to ask anything of your husband. Or to explain anything at all. Don't *you* understand, my dear, he understood everything. Always. Don't you see that was why I seduced poor Martin? I wanted someone like David. I wanted someone who would always forgive and always understand. That's why I've wasted so much time looking. That's why I wanted to find my father.'

The keening stopped and after a while the rocking abated. Jon put a tentative arm across Rose's shoulders and was not repulsed.

It was almost dark now and the lights were switched on in the flat above the garage. Greta's voice yelled raucously across the yard, 'Everythin' all right, miss? Had a bit of a fall, have you?'

'Nothing to worry about, Greta,' Jon called back and again, urgently to Rose, 'darling, come on inside now, please. You're going to catch cold crouching in the mud like this.'

Obediently Rose stood up and made for the house, head down, shoulders bowed. Jon picked up the broom and threw it into the barn. She fiddled with the tap and then ran after Rose and got to the door ahead of her. She was panting, her eyes suddenly bright in the light from the kitchen.

Rose lifted her head and looked at her and said, 'It's all right. I'm all right. Don't panic.'

'You're not all right.' Jon pulled out a chair and held it for her sister. 'I've as good as stuck a knife in you. How could you be all right?'

Rose sat down heavily. She could not seem to straighten her back.

'I don't know what to think. How to feel. We had seven perfect years after that. We were so close. And all the time . . . he knew.'

Jon did the usual things. Filled the kettle and plugged it in. Thrust cups on to a tray.

'I've tried to tell you that it didn't matter to him—'

Rose said, 'It would have mattered. He must have gone through hell. It would have mattered.'

434

'All right. But he under*stood*. He didn't let it spoil . . . anything! Surely you're not going to let it do that for you?'

Rose said in a strange, thoughtful voice, 'It was practically a deception. He deceived me.'

Jon came round the chair and knelt by it.

'Darling, please don't talk like that. You sound quite mad. If you have to accuse someone, let it be me. I was the one who told him, remember!'

'Of course you told him. When you knew – when Rick told you – you had to retaliate – you had to hurt me.'

Jon rocked back on her heels. 'But you wouldn't have done such a thing, Rosie!'

'No. Perhaps not. That doesn't make me particularly admirable. Oh God. How I hate myself!'

'Why? Because you slept with Rick once?'

'I suppose so.' Rose touched Jon's shoulder. 'Darling, if it helps you, it was so meaningless. It had nothing to do with love. Nothing at all.'

'I know. And . . . after I'd talked to David, I think I knew that. Oh Rosie, don't let it come between us. Please. I wish I'd never told you. But—'

Rose said steadily, 'I'm glad you did.'

She wondered if she meant it. They drank tea together; it was true they were very close now. They continued to talk through most of that night. Rose felt again and again that her mind must slip over the edge of sanity and into madness and each time, Jon pulled her up and forced her to face just the facts and not their myriad implications.

Towards dawn Rose said, 'I must sleep, Jon. I feel so sick and ill.'

'Not alone. I'm staying with you.'

'Please. I want to be by myself.'

Jon bit her lip but could say no more. She watched from the hall as Rose climbed the stairs slowly, pulling herself up by the banisters. At the top Rose turned and looked down. She swayed slightly and Jon came to the foot of the stairs.

'It's all right. I'm not going to fall.' Rose smiled. 'Listen, Sis. You're making a fresh start here. And I've got to do the same. And I'm going to try to do that. Remember – whatever I do, it's because I'm trying to make a fresh start.'

Jon nodded without real comprehension. She waited until the bedroom door closed after her sister, then went outside to have a word with Clark. Work. That had been Rose's answer in the past. It made sense.

Twenty-three

Maud could not get over her.

'I expected you to be so unhappy, Ros! My dear, you're positively blooming!'

Rose said sedately, 'Yes. I feel extremely well, Mother.' She knew that she would have to tell Maud about Abe at some stage, but it could not be yet.

Because of the time difference, she had arrived at Heathrow in the early hours of the morning and slept away almost twenty-four hours. She felt no sense of jet lag. At six o'clock, two mornings after saying goodbye to Abe and Eugenie, she was in the kitchen of the Snow-White house, making tea as if she'd never been away. It was November. Six weeks ago she had left so fearfully. Now she was quite different; she consciously did a spot check of her own body and mind. There was no fear, no tension anywhere. And she was different in another way too. For five years she had been a widow. She was a widow no longer.

She poured tea for Maud and smiled. 'How would you like to go out there with Georgie, darling? Just to see what it's like. I've given you a garbled version of the farm and Jon's hopes for it, but until you've actually seen it you can't really picture it.'

Maud said, 'Perhaps next year, Ros. I'll save up for it.'

'I can afford to get you a ticket, Mother. My own trip cost next to nothing.'

Maid said very directly, 'Would I meet Boaz?'

Rose's smile deepened. 'No. I don't think so.'

Maud shook her head. 'In any case, Ros, I think Georgie and Jon should be by themselves for a bit.'

'Perhaps.' Rose thought about the future. 'Blue will be lost. We'll try to take the girls out and about a bit at Christmas, shall we?'

'That sounds nice.' Maud sipped her tea and looked a million questions but said nothing.

Rose said, 'It's all right, Mother. It happened. I fell in love again – quite differently because of David, of course. But it was the real thing. Is the real thing. And I'm not unhappy about it. Perhaps I shall be later on. But it couldn't be anything permanent, so I – I seized the moment I suppose. Twenty-four hours. Rather like my mother.'

'Oh Ros. I'm glad.'

'Are you? Really?'

'Of course. D'you think your mother ever regretted it?'

'I don't know. Her life would have been much easier without Philip Duddington.'

'I'm not saying that. What I'm saying is that having met Philip Duddington, if she'd turned away from him, don't you think she would have regretted it always?'

Rose thought hard, frowning over her tea cup as if she could see the past in the steam.

'Yes,' she said slowly. 'Yes, perhaps so. Certainly I would not have forgiven myself for turning away from Abe McKenzie. I'm proud of what happened. I'm proud that I initiated it.'

Maud sighed. 'I'm glad,' she said simply. 'You've opted for life, Ros. I'm so glad.'

Rose finished her tea and looked through the patio windows.

'Let's throw on some clothes and go outside! The garden is full of the most marvellous pearly cobwebs! Let's go and look at them!'

Maud smiled happily. 'You go and look at them, Ros. I'll look at the newspaper instead!'

Rose waited no longer. The garden reminded her of icing on a cake. An enormous cake, big enough to contain a person. A very special person.

438

Georgie was so excited he could barely wait for the end of term. He packed and unpacked half a dozen times and seemed unaware of Blue watching silently and moodily.

'Did Mum say she was going to have horses on the farm?' he asked Rose. 'I've had riding lessons this term and I'm not bad.'

Blue snorted and Ellie said, 'You were good. They wanted you to enter the end-of-term competition.'

'I couldn't. Football.' Georgie paused. 'I shall miss football.'

Blue burst out, 'You talk as if you're going for good! I thought it was just for the Christmas hols?'

'It is.' He looked at her. 'You know I wouldn't go for good. Not without you.'

She kicked a chair. 'You sound pleased enough to be going without me now.'

'Well. I haven't seen Mum for ages. And . . . well, you know . . . the farm . . . I mean . . . it's such a surprise! Like a present.'

'It is a present. That's what a legacy is, idiot. A present,' Blue told him scathingly.

'Yes, but it's a present I haven't seen yet.' He took a shirt out of his case and packed another one. 'Besides, Mum must be lonely now that Aunt Rose has left.'

She voiced her fear. 'You won't change your mind and stay out there, will you?'

'Don't be crazy. I've got to get some O levels and I don't sit them for two years.' He closed his case and sat on it. 'But the Head was talking to me about it last week. I don't think I stand a chance of university here. But in the States they give scholarships for sports things. I could get a football scholarship.'

'I wouldn't see you for three years!'

He looked crucified. 'But you'll be at university, Blue. And if I don't go too – if I just get a job with Martin or something, you'll sort of leave me behind.'

Ellie said, 'Well, I won't get to university and she'd better not leave me behind!'

439

Blue laughed unwillingly and they went downstairs together.

Before they took Georgie to Heathrow, Rose told them almost everything about her stay in America. It took the best part of an evening; there were incredulous interruptions and once or twice sheer disbelief crept in.

'But that means Aunt Jon isn't your proper sister, Mummy!' Blue objected when Rose had recounted the events of VJ night and got them back to Churchdown and the birth of the baby.

She said, 'In some ways it made us closer than sisters, Blue. Perhaps as close as you are, as twins. I helped my mother to bring up Jon. I loved her as a daughter as well as a sister.'

Georgie said slowly, 'It explains a lot of things.'

'Yes. I thought so too. When I remembered all of this.'

'How do you mean – remembered? You must have always known,' Ellie said.

Rose tried to explain how it had been. It sounded far-fetched and unreal. But Georgie nodded. 'I do that. Shut things away. I think it's a good idea, actually.'

'Sometimes.'

Rose took a deep breath and started to tell them about Abe. Maud leaned forward and put coal on the fire.

George said, 'He sounds great, Rosie. Helping you like that. Is he really going to be president, d'you think?'

'He says not. His son, perhaps.'

She went on to tell of Uncle Joe's death and Jon's closeness to him. And her inheritance.

'She loves it, Georgie. She could sell it of course – come back here – buy a place for you both. But she would like to stay out there and work it properly.'

'Yeah. I got that much from her phone calls.'

'How d'you feel about that?'

'Well. OK I think. I wish she wasn't on her own, but I suppose this father of hers will come to stay now and then.'

'Your grandfather, Georgie.'

440

'My gosh! My grandfather! I hadn't thought . . . it's a bit of a turn-up for the books, isn't it? I've never had a grandfather.'

'Nor an aunt quite like Aunt Mabe. You're in for an interesting holiday.'

He said haltingly, 'The only thing is, Aunt Rose, I'm going to miss this family. And the Snow-White house. And if there's any snow I won't be able to use the ski slope this year.'

She knew what he was saying and she smiled directly at Blue as she replied. 'We'll all be waiting for you, Georgie. Especially the ski slope.'

It wasn't as bad as they'd thought without Georgie. Ellie's friend Janet had had to cry off this holiday, and Ellie and Blue did everything together just as they'd done in the old days.

On Christmas morning they went to church and old Mr Murchison came back with them for his Christmas lunch. It was a time for reminiscing and they all spoke of Aileen.

It was the old priest who threw another ray of light across the enigma.

'You know, she was retiring – that much was obvious – but she was never, ever, melancholy or depressed. D'you agree with that, Rose?'

Rose nodded. 'I used to think it was Jon that made life so exciting through my childhood. But it was Mother as well. She made life's diurnal round seem at once inevitable and full of possibilities.'

Ellie said flatly, 'Oh yes. Gran was *fun!* We could have told you that, couldn't we, Blue?'

'It was the way quite ordinary things were important,' Blue said with her usual perspicacity. 'Tea-time round the fire, pasting up the photograph album—'

Maud chipped in, 'Even I know what you mean and I knew her for just a short time. Ritual. She made ritual important.'

'Life's diurnal round,' Rose murmured like a Greek chorus of one.

'And she was so adaptable,' Maud went on. 'I don't think I could have pulled up my roots and gone to Newcastle and made a home up there in a flat.'

'And she was thrilled to bits about Grandmother Harris's alterations to the Snow-White house,' Blue added.

Ellie said, 'It's a pity you're not more like her, Mummy. All that fuss about going to America!'

Rose laughed. 'Yes. But then, I'm just an ordinary sort of woman.'

And Maud laughed too. And then Blue and then Ellie.

Mr Murchison looked round, smiling. 'Have I missed the joke?'

Rose put her hand on his arm. 'We're being silly. Have another cup of tea before you go. Then we'll walk back up the hill with you.'

'That would be nice.' The old priest looked round. 'The best Christmas since my dear wife departed,' he said.

Rose nodded emphatically. It was the same for her. Just the same.

Georgie came back full of it. Aunt Mabe had managed the Christmas party she'd set her heart on. There'd been a quartet in the 'minstrel's gallery' at Court House, and after an enormous meal, Jason and his helpers had cleared away the tables and there had been dancing – sedate dancing, but dancing nevertheless. Because Georgie had had ballroom-dancing lessons at school, he had been much in demand.

'Only with all the old women!' he added hastily as he saw Blue's expression.

He took her hand. 'You'll love it out there, Blue. The farm is great. Mr Laben says Mum can have some more land if she needs it. She's already got some hens and she sells all this natural stuff in Georgetown. They're all potty on natural foods out there.'

'What about your grandfather?' Blue asked.

'I like him,' George spoke definitely. 'But he wants to do everything for us and Mum says that's not on. We've got to look after ourselves properly now. But he's only saying all this because we're the only family he's got. His son was killed in Vietnam. It's like a new world for him, finding Mum.'

'And you,' Blue said.

'Well, yes. But I'm not bright like his son was. I'm more like . . . Dad.' He glanced at Rose. 'I think he might be disappointed if I turn out to be a farmer, don't you, Aunt Rose?'

Rose thought about it. 'I don't think he would. He doesn't need either of you to fit into a special slot – he just wants you *there*.' She hugged him suddenly. 'You know more about him than I do, Georgie. I met him about three times. But I liked him – and Gran liked him very much. Is that enough for you?'

Georgie nodded, grinning. Rose made a point of mentioning Aileen and Philip now, and he recognized this and appreciated it. She wanted that long-ago affair to become important and very special. Never sordid.

In the New Year came a letter from Eugenie.

'My dear Rose, Abe has asked me to write to you, so it's obvious you two don't correspond. Why the hell not? I don't understand any of it. And he's not as unhappy as I thought he'd be. He seems to have loads of energy and he's driving me mad. But what's new? Do hope you're OK too. I think about the two of you all the time. That drives me mad too.

'Anyway, Rose, he's asked me to write to tell you he's found your brother-in-law. It wasn't too difficult. He works for the Canadian Pulp Manufacturing Company and he tracked him down in Calgary just like you said he would, and had a chat with him. Yes, he went personally, please note! I gather it was tricky. Mr Johnson was unco-operative to say the least. Of course he did not know who the hell Abe was, and when Abe told him he was your American lawyer, he buttoned up worse than ever. Anyway, Abe got across all the salient points – the death of your husband and mother, your sister's . . . what shall I call it, pilgrimage? And the main one, that she is now farming in Connecticut. Naturally he was stunned. I can imagine Abe firing off these shots,

443

can't you? Confrontation therapy again. They got through all right and he started listening properly. Just how Abe put it to him that your sister was ready for a reconciliation, I don't know. You'd said to leave you out of that bit because you didn't want to put any more personal pressure on him, but he must have guessed that if you'd sent your lawyer after him you were keen on the idea. Anyway, Abe left it at that. It's up to Mr Johnson now.

'I'm going to tell you something. He told me not to, but I'm going to anyway. Sarah and Tom have left. A week ago when I started this letter. It's knocked him sideways. Not Sarah, Tom. They've gone off with Sarah's boyfriend who Tom likes a lot, so it's possible Abe won't see much of the boy. It's all very well to have legal access but if he's living on the West Coast and Abe is here on the East, it's not so easy to arrange.

'I thought you should know, Rose. You did say, if I could comfort him, that was OK with you. But I can't. Not now. Because of you – because, somehow, you've made him more self-sufficient than ever. And I'm glad of that in a funny way. I mean it. Whatever you did for Abe, I thank you.'

Rose read the letter several times, then gazed unseeingly out of the patio windows at the familiar view of the hill. She wondered if this changed anything for her; for Abe. And eventually she decided not.

But that afternoon there was a sale at a big house in Miserden. She was in any case going to look at another summer cottage there, and she took Maud with her.

'We'll look in on the sale. It might be over by the time we get there. But they tend to work from the ground floor up. And when I looked in last week, there was something I wanted from the top floor.'

'Servants' bedrooms?' Maud queried.

'No,' Rose said. 'Not exactly.'

Maud tucked herself expertly into the Coach and slammed the door. 'What was it exactly?'

'Well, there were some gorgeous curtains. Probably pre-war but with heaps of wear in them. And a fireguard.'

'A fireguard?' Maud locked in the newly-fitted safety belt and looked her surprise.

'Yes. We used to have one just like it.' Rose manoeuvred out of the lane on to the main road. 'A brass rail around the top. You know.'

Maud said slowly, 'A nursery fireguard.'

'Yes.' Rose switched on the wipers. It was raining and one or two blobs of snow stuck to the windscreen too.

Maud said, 'And the curtain material?'

'Aeroplanes. Old-fashioned biplanes. You know the kind of thing. They'll all go cheap. No-one will hang on until the end in this weather. Anyway no-one will be interested in such old things.'

Maud was silent for some time, then she said, 'Probably the moth will be in the curtains.'

'I wanted you to come so that you could check on them.'

Another long silence while they ground up Crickley Hill. Then Maud said, 'David used to have curtains with planes on them.'

Rose took her left hand off the wheel and touched Maud's knee. Maud gave a sob and said, 'Are you sure?'

'Yes.' Rose nodded. 'I went to see the doctor last week. The baby will be born next July.'

'I – I don't know what to say, Ros.'

'Are you angry? Disgusted—'

'*No!* Never! But . . . I am frightened for you.'

'That must be why I'm not. You're carrying the fear for me.' Rose smiled into the mirror. 'You know how much I shall need you now?'

Maud spoke with a catch in her voice. 'It's what everyone of my age wants to hear, Ros. Oh my dear—'

Rose drew into a lay-by, pulled on the handbrake and turned to her mother-in-law. 'Listen, Mother. I am so happy – please don't worry about me. I know now exactly how my mother felt all those years ago. Why everything was exciting for her.'

Maud said pitifully, 'But Jon was—'

'Jon was white. This baby will be in between. That's what makes it so wonderful, Mother. Don't you see that?'

445

'Yes. In a way. What about Ellie and Blue?'

'We'll see.' Rose hugged Maud and turned to the wheel again. 'Let's go and buy stuff for our new nursery, shall we?'

By the time they reached Miserden Hall it was blowing a blizzard and hardly any people milled around the auctioneer on the upstairs landing. Maud and Rose slipped past him and climbed the stairs to the attic rooms. The curtains were in an untidy pile in an old wicker basket. Maud shook them out one by one.

'They're beautiful,' she breathed. 'Not a sign of moth anywhere.'

Rose said, 'And here's the guard.' She unearthed it from a jumble of cot-pieces.

Maud gathered up the swags of material. 'I can make curtains and covers from these,' she said. 'Which room did you have in mind? The one that looks on to the church?'

'Yes.' Rose smiled at her mother-in-law. 'And I can polish this up beautifully – look at the brass – no pitting at all!'

They examined their finds gloatingly. And suddenly Maud said, 'Ros. This is the most exciting thing that has happened since you and David moved in with me. I feel as if I'm having yet another nibble at life!'

And they laughed together.

It was a year since Jon had arrived in America. She remembered it as an afterthought when she waved goodbye to Clark and Greta. They had given her a week's notice the previous Wednesday and were parting without acrimony on either side, though Jon had had no luck in recruiting other help.

She watched the taxi bump over the cattle grid in the biggest rainstorm of the year, and went straight round to the barn to feed the chickens. The rain dripped off the brim of her sou'wester and found its way somehow inside the collar of her mackintosh and down the tops of her boots. The chicken run was a sea of mud and she did not dare let the birds into the pasture with the cows, because Rudolf Laben had warned her of the foxes only yesterday.

Everything was muddy. She had been using the milking parlour off and on since Christmas, anticipating trouble from Greta and Clark, and she went inside now to start the morning scrub-down. She surveyed the floor without pleasure. Then said aloud, 'It's a challenge, woman! Go to it! And if you do a good job, I'll let you sit down with a cup of coffee for ten whole minutes!'

She went to it. But she couldn't pretend she wasn't aching in every limb and tired out. It was heaven to kick off her boots outside the kitchen door and go into the warmth of the house. Clark had done no outside work at all today; why should he, after all? She had been up at five to do the milking and collect the eggs. There had been no time for breakfast either. That was something Clark never missed. She sighed. She wouldn't mind a job as paid help on a farm; it was easier than owning one.

But she didn't regret Clark and Greta. She had certainly made them work harder than they'd ever done before, but they had been incapable of working on their own initiative and she'd had to watch them all the time. There was no commitment and very little interest from either of them. Eric Laben was more real use than they were, turning up at weekends and helping her to plant the spring and summer vegetables. Duddy would have come down and helped too except that Aunt Dorothy had been taken ill in Washington and he was looking after her. And anyway Jon still wanted – more than anything – to be independent. Mabs had telephoned and said, 'Any reply to the ad? No? Listen, I'll tell Jason to come and give a hand for a few days.' And old Rudolf Laben had said that Maria's husband Leo would be glad to help when he could. It was not what she wanted and she had said no gratefully and 'prettily' – as Mabs would say – and prayed that someone would turn up in answer to the attractive-sounding ad she'd put in all the local papers.

She spread her hands and looked at her nails. They were a disgrace. She would wash her hair this afternoon – that would tidy them up – two jobs in one. She smiled, thinking of the way she'd rubbed cream into her hands so carefully not very long ago. And her hair, fastened with a rubber band in a pony-tail, was now innocent of all colouring. She caught sight of it in the hall mirror through the kitchen door, and grimaced. She was going grey.

She did not hear car wheels on the grid, so that the doorbell startled her unduly. She stared down the hall again: a male shape was outlined at the front door. It must be Eric, he would have walked over from Rosebridge. On the other hand, he'd have come around the back to look for her in the yard.

It was the first time she'd been in the house alone since Uncle Joe died. She glanced around the kitchen. All the tools were outside. She picked up the rolling pin and went down the hall.

'Who is it?' she called.

A voice said, 'Me.'

She stared, incredulous. It couldn't be. Yet it was. She opened the door cautiously. Rick was there, encased in waterproofs, rain dripping from eyebrows and nose. Even his blue eyes looked drowned.

She said, '*Rick!* What the hell—' She clutched the rolling pin across her midriff. 'Oh my God, is it Georgie?'

'No.' He spoke quickly, trying to reassure her. 'Everything is OK, Jon. I came to see you . . . just to see you. No strings. Nothing.' He dashed the water from his face and tried to grin at the rolling pin. 'Looks as if you were expecting me!'

'No. I—' She glanced at the rolling pin. 'I'm sorry, Rick. It's so totally unexpected.'

'Could I . . . come in? I've walked from Georgetown and it's further than I thought.'

'Oh my God,' she said again. 'Oh Rick. Of course.' She led the way to the kitchen and put the rolling pin on the table. 'I'm really sorry. I'm on my own here, you see. And I didn't hear a car. And it seemed better to be prepared.'

He did not sit down. He stood in the corner by the door and dripped on to the mat.

'I understood you'd got help here,' he said.

448

'Take off your mack. I'll make some more coffee. Sit down, Rick. Please.'

'I can't stay. I've got two weeks' holiday and I wanted to know . . . things. Georgie . . . You.'

'Just sit down. If it's only for ten minutes.' She filled the kettle and laughed. 'Not that we can say everything in ten minutes. Stay to lunch, Rick. I've got some photographs of Georgie. But it'll take me time to find them.'

'I . . . all right. Thanks.' He shrugged out of his outdoor things while she made the coffee. He wore enormous seaman's socks under his boots. They made damp patches on the tiles.

She said, 'I think there are some socks of Uncle Joe's upstairs. I'll see in a minute.'

'These are oiled. They're OK. Really.'

He had acquired a slight accent. And his hair was dark with rain so that she could see he too was going grey. She thought, suddenly frightened, 'It's nine years since he went . . . nine years.'

He repeated, 'I thought you had help here, Jon. A married couple who saw to the outside work.'

'They left. It's no rest-cure here. They were used to letting things slide downhill with Uncle Joe. I wanted to get the place on its feet. So they left.'

'And you're running everything?'

She grinned. 'Only from today. And I've advertised. Trouble is, I'm very low on actual cash, so I can't offer the going rate. But there's a flat over the garage – it's not bad.'

'I thought – maybe – Stan.' He looked at her. 'Or someone.'

'No. No-one.'

She refused to tell him how celibate she'd been since he'd gone.

She said, 'So you know about this place. And presumably Uncle Joe. What else?'

'I think I know everything. I've thought so much about Aileen. She was a remarkable woman. I wish I'd been able to see her again – tell her so.'

449

'Yes.' Jon also refused to be sentimental. She poured coffee and pushed his mug in front of him. 'But if she'd been alive I wouldn't have come over and Rose wouldn't have found out about my father. You know about my father?'

'Yes. Chap called Philip Duddington. Delighted you turned up, I gather?'

'And . . . ' she sipped carefully. 'You know about Rose?'

He was a long time replying. He looked into his mug, then stirred in sugar. At last he said, 'It was Mr McKenzie who came to see me.'

'Abe?' Again she was incredulous. There had been no message from that quarter since Rose left. She wouldn't have known anything of those last twenty-four hours if Rose hadn't written to tell her. She breathed deeply, twice. 'Did he tell you . . . I mean, what did he tell you? About Rose?'

'That they were in love. That she'd felt free to love him because of something you'd said. That you must be a terrific person to have said it. Things like that.'

She breathed again. 'And . . . how did you feel about it?'

'Awful at first. To think David had died and I hadn't known. And that she had loved this chap . . . he seemed so *old*.'

'He's ten years older than she is. She knew him when she was a kid.'

'Yes. I heard.' He stirred thoughtfully. 'I thought I'd got your family out of my system, Jon.'

'And you haven't?'

'I don't know. I hoped I'd know when you opened that door just now. But I didn't.' He looked up with a hint of his old mischievous smile. 'What about you? How do you feel about me now? Have you got rid of me?'

She smiled ruefully. 'I don't know either. It was such a shock. Seeing you standing there. Hearing that Abe came to see you like that. I don't know how I feel.' She stood up and took her mug to the sink. 'I was glad when you went, Rick. I was so tired of it all . . . of myself. I'd been obsessed with you for so long. It had eaten me up almost.' She turned

450

on the faucet and held her mug beneath the water. 'And afterwards . . . I said to Ma once, I wasn't exactly happy. But I wasn't unhappy. She kept Stan at bay, and we had a good, satisfying domestic life. Georgie loved her so much. It was all right. Then, when David was ill, Rosie and I seemed to come together again. She didn't know of course that I'd . . . well, never mind.'

He said, 'You told David about Rose and me. Did you?'

'Oh God. You always knew me so damned well, Rick. How did you work that out?'

'I suppose I guessed from the moment I told you on the hill that you would have to hurt Rose in some way. And that was the obvious way.' He drank some coffee. 'Then – when she was here with you, you told her what you'd done, did you?'

'Yes. That's what Abe meant.' Jon turned her mug upside down on the draining board and gazed through the window. 'It was something to do with David forgiving her – not even that – ignoring it. He arranged for her to go up to Newcastle afterwards and talk to you. Almost as if he wanted her to realize, later on, that he trusted her completely.' She shook her head. 'I don't know. At first I thought she'd go mad. I've never seen grief affect anyone like it did Rose that night. We didn't go to bed till dawn. It was as if she cried out the five years she'd been without him. And then . . . then she went to Abe.'

He finished his coffee. 'Thank you for telling me.' He stood up. 'If you could look out those photographs and give me Georgie's school address, I'll be on my way.'

She looked round at him wearily. 'Oh sit down, Rick. I'm not about to seduce you or anything! Sit down and you can look at the snaps while I cook some lunch. Then I'll run you back to Georgetown.'

He actually laughed. 'I keep seeing glimpses of the Jon I knew. All this—' he swept an arm around the kitchen – 'having a new family – everything – hasn't really changed you, Jon. What do they make of you out here?'

She looked at him. 'As a matter of fact, Rick, they respect me. And . . . what's more, I respect myself.'

He looked back at her, then sat down again.

'I'd like to stay to lunch. Thank you,' he said.

He told her about himself. He had done exactly what he'd set out to do, worked hard with his hands and won back his own self-respect.

'Perhaps we were bad for each other?' she suggested as they washed up the lunch things and settled down with the photograph album.

'I was bad for you. I was a con man when you met me. Nothing more or less. You were only a kid.'

'I think I was bad for you too. I was clinging, possessive . . . awful.'

'Perhaps, if we'd waited – if I'd gone away for a few years and come back when you were in your twenties – perhaps it would have worked then?'

'Who knows?'

'Quite.'

He couldn't believe Georgie had grown so tall.

'He looks great.'

'That's Greystones. Grandmother, I suppose. He was fast becoming a delinquent in Newcastle. It was awful for him.'

'Following in my footsteps. That's how it was at home. Why I moved down to Gloucester and tried to be something I wasn't.'

She said, 'Georgie wants to farm.'

'Can you hang on that long?'

'How do you mean?'

'Well, if you don't get any help, how will you survive?'

'I'll get some help.'

He dropped the subject then, but just before the February day drew to a close, he asked her to show him around the farm. They donned boots and waterproofs and trooped around the barns and sheds.

He said, 'I don't know a thing about farming, but it looks pretty good to me. Everything's well maintained. The sheds are weatherproof.'

'I shall be bringing the cows in soon. You can see the milking parlour in action if you like.'

'You're going to do that by yourself?'

'I've been doing it for a week now – I needed to get the hang of it before Clark left.'

'You're quite a girl, Jon. I'd forgotten.'

She shrugged, sniffing rain from the tip of her nose. 'You didn't know. I didn't know.'

They walked up the bank towards the gate and he held it open for her. Then he said, 'Look, Jon. I didn't come to see you straightaway after McKenzie's visit. I thought he'd report to you, then if I appeared the next day you might think . . . ' He strode over a puddle to stand by her side. 'I didn't want you to think I was trying to move in. You know, you being a property-owner and all.'

She grinned. 'Well. You know how it really is now.'

'Yes. Listen. Jon. I could hang on for the rest of my holidays. Live in the flat. Give you a hand. If you like.'

She didn't jump at it. There was so much to think about and no time to think. She said, 'What if . . . if I started . . . being obsessive again?'

He laughed. 'You know me too well now. I don't think you could ever feel so intensely about me now.'

'No,' she agreed almost sadly. 'Those days are gone for both of us. But . . . I haven't even looked at the flat. They might have left it like a tip. Probably have.'

'It won't worry me. You should see some of the places I've slept in over the past few years.'

She hesitated. 'I'd rather you did stay in the flat, actually. That sounds mean, inhospitable. But I'm still having to work at . . . you know, the self-respect thing. I'd feel . . . better.'

He nodded. 'I know. It's all so quick. So sudden.'

They walked towards the pasture to get the cows. He said, 'I'm not trying to teach you anything, Jon, but the Welsh farmers used to keep their cattle in shed during the worst of the winter. There's not enough grass here for them – you have to supplement, don't you?'

'Yes. I thought you knew nothing about farming?'

'I don't. But you were either on the farm or down the mines back home. So some of my mates had to be farmers.'

She opened a gate and the cows meandered towards her.

'It would certainly cut down on the work. Maybe – for a while—' she turned and the cows followed her back to the farm. Rick followed behind, shutting gates, smacking rumps, as if he'd been doing it all his life. She wanted – just as she'd wanted when she was little – to go into the corner of the milking parlour and giggle till she wept.

Twenty-four

Georgie was the first to know about Rick moving into the farm.

The girls came home alone for half-term because he was going on a football tour, and the news, coming third-hand as it were, was garbled to say the least.

'It's not a secret. Exactly,' Ellie said as soon as they got into the Coach.

'Aunt Jon doesn't want anyone getting the wrong idea, that's all,' Blue added. 'In case it doesn't work.'

'You see,' Ellie explained carefully, 'they're not married. And they're not going to get married.'

Blue smiled. 'That's what Georgie says Aunt Jon says,' she enlarged unhelpfully.

Rose did not display the pleased amazement they had anticipated. It was as if she'd known for some time. But she couldn't have because it had only just happened.

'I'm glad. Whatever the arrangement, it's worth a try,' she said.

Blue gazed soulfully out of the window. 'It's so obvious they're in love. But of course they won't admit it. Not yet.'

Ellie said severely, 'Georgie said not to jump our guns. Uncle Rick is just working at the farm for the moment. Because Aunt Jon can't get any proper help.'

'He'll be worth a dozen helps,' Blue stated categorically. 'He's like Georgie. An outdoor type. And strong as an ox.'

'How do you know? You can't even remember him!' Ellie protested.

'Yes I can. But even if I couldn't, it stands to reason, doesn't it? He's supposed to look like Georgie. And Georgie is good at all sports and things. And he's been working as a lumberjack for years, so he's used to a really hard life.'

Rose said, 'But Georgie is right. We mustn't imagine they'll live happily ever after just like that.'

'Mummy, don't be so pessimistic!' Blue said.

Rose laughed. 'You're supposed to be the realist. Just be pleased they're living under the same roof, and Aunt Jon has someone to help her.'

Ellie said precisely, 'They're not exactly under the same roof. Uncle Rick is living in the flat over the garage.'

'Oh. Is he?' Rose raised her brows, not disappointed at all. She was glad in a way they hadn't fallen into each other's arms.

Ellie said, 'Where's Gran?'

'Making curtains and things.' Rose glanced in the mirror and turned off the main road.

'Who for?'

Blue corrected maddeningly, 'For whom.'

'Who for?' repeated Ellie.

'The small room over the bathroom. Where I've got all my paperwork for the cottages.'

'Posh. Is it going to be a proper office?'

'Not exactly.' Rose smiled briefly and nodded her head at the hedgerows. 'Winter thorn, look. And there's some pussy willow around the house.'

Ellie closed her eyes dramatically. 'Spring,' she breathed. 'Don't you just love it?'

Blue said, 'Mother. Could we find enough money to go to America this summer? Please?'

Rose caught her daughter's eye in the driving mirror. The significance of being called 'Mother' instead of 'Mummy' did not escape her.

She said unequivocally, 'No.'

Blue said, 'Oh . . . botheration!'

They settled in quickly as usual. Maud was thoroughly hugged; a phone call from Arney scornfully dealt with.

'He wanted to come up tomorrow, Mummy,' Ellie said. 'I told him we've got three days at home, and we need every one of them!' She made a sound of disgust. 'He's much too old for me! He's nearly seventeen!'

Rose looked at Maud wide-eyed.

'Did you know about this?'

Maud shook her head, laughing helplessly.

'How am I supposed to keep up with what is going on in this house? I'm seventy years old! Nobody makes any allowances for my advancing years!'

She was hugged again. 'Aren't you glad about that?' Blue said. 'Anyway,' she collapsed on to the sofa, 'nothing *is* going on here! Nothing at all. Georgie will be off to America for the summer – Arney will probably come up and make sheep's eyes at Ellie who can't stand him. You won't let me go on any demos or marches. And we can't afford to go to see Aunt Jon and Uncle Rick! Really exciting negatives, wouldn't you say?'

She surveyed her mother and grandmother in some disgust; they seemed to be in the grip of hysteria.

It was Ellie – usually the less sentient – who said, 'What's going on? You're both different somehow. Mummy was different at Christmas after America, but I thought she would have got over that by now. But she's still peculiar. And now Gran.' She looked over at Blue, still supine on the sofa. 'I know. Aunt Jon and Uncle Rick are going to get married and we're going to the wedding! That's why Mummy didn't answer properly when you asked her about going over—'

'I answered properly,' Rose spluttered. 'I said no!'

'Yes, but you usually say that you're sorry and then you explain that in two or three years you will have saved enough to take us over. You never just say no!'

Blue sat up. 'Are they getting married, Mother? Could we go to the wedding?'

Rose controlled herself. 'As far as I know, they are not getting married. And even if they do, we still cannot afford to go over there.' She looked over to Maud. 'Something *has* happened, darlings. I hardly know how to tell you, but it looks as if I'd better do so now.' She sighed suddenly. 'The reason I gave you such a straight no in the car, Blue, was because I won't be able to save any money for the next few years. Not at all.'

Blue's face held steady; she was determined not to show disappointment. 'Grandmother has stopped paying our fees,' she said flatly. 'And you're going to have to work like hell to keep us at Greystones. Well, that's not on. We'll leave. We'll get jobs.'

'Of course we will, Mummy! You idiot. Surely you know we'll help. Whatever happens.'

Maud stood up suddenly, hugged both girls, and sat herself on the arm of Rose's chair. She said, 'We're relying on that, Ellie. We're relying on both of you to help.'

Rose shook her head. 'No. Don't let them feel bound by any loyalties, Mother. Please.' She looked at the girls. 'Grandmother won't stop your fees, my dears. She's a fair woman. She won't punish me through you. That I do know.'

Both girls were apprehensive now. Blue said, 'What has happened?' They too moved closer together.

Now that the moment was on her, Rose did not know how to begin. She had determined to tell the girls about the baby during this holiday and it was a bonus that Georgie was not at home. But they weren't even fourteen yet; and they were David's daughters.

She cleared her throat. 'When I was in America . . . I mentioned to you about Abraham McKenzie, didn't I?'

Ellie said impatiently, 'Yes – yes. The lawyer chap who found Aunt Jon's father—'

But Blue interrupted. 'You knew him when you were a little girl. He was the son of the man who looked after you. Fack, you called the man.'

Rose looked at her daughters. Their eyes were clear tea-brown. It was as if she were talking to David. And she would know instantly if they were disgusted, or betrayed.

'What else did I tell you?'

Blue said slowly, 'He was ten years older than you. Fourteen. And he jumped out of the Victory cake and waved a flag and said they'd fought together and they

458

must . . . ' She stopped speaking, then added, 'He sounded rather splendid.'

Ellie nodded. 'He saved you from someone called Lennox.'

Rose said, 'He's still splendid. He's still in the rescuing business.'

There was a silence. Then Blue said, 'You're in love with him. You're going to get married. You think we'll mind.'

Ellie burst in again. 'Mummy, you really are mad! Did you think we'd mind? Really? It's wonderful – marvellous!'

Rose held out a restraining hand. 'That's not it. We can't get married. There are too many things against us getting married. But yes, I am in love with him.'

'Oh . . . ' Blue forgot that she was growing up. 'Oh, Mummy! How awful. You're unhappy too! Couldn't you possibly marry him? He'd love the Snow-White house! He's had a hard life, hasn't he? Reform school, didn't you say? We'd look after him—'

Rose said quietly, 'I'm going to have his baby, my darlings. In July.'

The girls were stopped in their tracks. There was a waiting pause. Rose felt Maud's arm around her shoulders, gripping hard. She refused to apologize or soften the plain words. But she waited as if they were her judges, about to pronounce a sentence.

Ellie spoke first, hesitantly. 'She – he – it – will be our half-sister or brother? Like Aunt Jon is to you?'

'Exactly the same as Aunt Jon is to me. Yes.'

'And you had to look after her too. I mean—' Ellie glanced rather wildly at Blue and back to her mother. 'I mean, Gran wouldn't marry . . . '

Rose inclined her head. 'I looked after her. Yes.'

Ellie said, 'And you're just the same as real sisters.'

'Yes. I think we are. Closer in some ways.'

Ellie nodded. She seemed to have said her piece. Still Rose waited. Condemnation would come from Blue.

Blue spoke up at last.

'It is just the same as Granny and Aunt Jon, isn't it? Like a pattern. But, you could make it different, Mummy. Whatever you say, you could marry him.'

'Is that what you want me to do?' Rose asked.

'It's not me – I mean, it's OK for us. And we would be OK for the baby – just like it was for Jon. Only better, because no-one minds single-parent families any more. We do them in Sociology and they're perfectly all right.'

Rose said dryly, 'Oh good.'

'But she – he – will be coloured. So it would be better really if he had us for the white bit and his father for the coloured bit.'

Blue had put it so succinctly that neither Rose nor Maud so much as smiled.

Rose said slowly, 'You're willing to be his white family, then?'

'Course!' Blue looked at Ellie as if her mother had said something particularly stupid. 'We've got no option, have we?'

'Well, yes. You could have nothing to do with the baby.'

Ellie exploded. 'What are you talking about? It's our baby! You should understand that, Mummy – after having Aunt Jon! It'll be lovely for us! We can take her out on the hill and show her everything – we shall love it.'

'Only you're worried about the colour?'

Blue stood up suddenly. 'I'm not,' she declared, as if taking on the world. 'I won't let anyone say a word about colour! I don't care about not going on demos or marches, or anything like that! This is our cause – our very own cause!' She jumped on to the sofa and raised her fist. 'Fairbrothers unite!'

Ellie said, 'Here we go again.' She rolled her eyes in exasperation. 'And it'll be me who does the knitting – she still drops every other stitch!'

Rose did not know whether to laugh or cry. She could see into the depths of both pairs of eyes: there was no condemnation; no disgust; just excitement.

Maud stood up.

'Get off the furniture, Blue. And let's have a cup of tea. Then perhaps you'd like to see the new nursery?'

Blue leapt to the carpet like a gazelle.

'Ah! It's not going to be an office at all! All mysteries solved!' She swung around the room. 'I felt so mizz coming home without Georgie. And now . . . everything is marvellous. And new. Is this how babies make you feel? No wonder people go all soppy about them!'

Ellie sat on the floor and wound her arms around her mother's knees.

'Don't be scared, Mummy. If Gran could do it, so can you.'

Rose gathered them both to her.

Jon was disappointed Georgie was not coming to them for Easter.

She gave Rick the letter to read while he ate his breakfast. It was a glorious morning and he had been up for three hours already; he ate well.

'Maybe the boy feels awkward about me being here?' Rick sensed her disappointment keenly. 'Look, would it help if I went away for a couple of weeks? I ought to go back to Calgary anyway. Get the rest of my stuff. Explain to the company what happened.'

Jon smiled. 'Seems awful you haven't had a minute to do all that.' She picked up the letter and held it as if she could touch Georgie through the scrawled words. 'What a bargain you had, Rick! Longer hours, less money, no overtime.'

He said steadily, 'We're doing all right, Jon. No regrets?'

'Of course not! It's been a wonderful bargain from my angle!'

'But . . . you know what I mean.'

'Yes. I know. And it *would* be awkward for Georgie. You're his father and you're living in the hired help's room.' She poured more coffee. 'Everyone thinks it's a scream – you realize that, do you?'

'When you say everyone—'

'I mean the neighbours. The Labens. Mabs and her doting senator. Everyone who likes a bit of gossip.'

'Well, that's OK by me. I like to think I'm brightening people's lives.'

She was silent, re-reading Georgie's letter, sipping coffee. He finished his eggs and pushed his plate away.

'Jessie is going to calve today,' he said. 'I've got a feeling about her.'

'How do you mean? Shall we need the vet?'

'No. I don't think so.'

'We can afford it.'

'Everything is perfectly OK with her. I'll get her into the barn this morning and keep an eye.'

'Oh Rick . . . thanks.' She looked up from the letter. 'Don't go back to Canada. Not yet. It's too soon.'

He was silent, looking at her. Then he said, 'OK. But maybe in the summer vacation . . . you'd have him to give you a hand with things. And it might be better for him to get used to you again before I appear on the scene.'

She said, 'Rick. I think it would be all right – better anyway – if – when Georgie is here . . . could we . . . could you . . . move into the house?'

He went on looking at her. 'Is that what you want?'

'Only if it's what you want.'

'It's what I want.'

She was tense and still. 'Just an arrangement? For Georgie's sake?'

'I suppose so. But an arrangement for our sakes too – or at any rate for my sake.'

'It would be more . . . sensible.'

He said, 'It's got nothing at all to do with being sensible, Jon. It's got nothing to do with Georgie either. This is you and me we're talking about. How do you feel about having me around? It's been six weeks now. We haven't had a row. Things have gone really well – I think.'

'Yes. Of course they have. It's been . . . great, Rick.'

'For me too. I feel as if I'm investing in this land.'

'Yes. Well, then . . . '

'But . . . Jon, I don't really want to go on living in the flat over the garage. I think about you in the evenings. And the mornings. I'm sorry – I don't want to wreck what we've got. But . . . I'd like to try for something more.'

She spoke so quietly he could only just hear her. 'That's the first time . . . '

'The first time? What do you mean, Jon?'

'The first time you've . . . asked me. Before, it was me asking you. Through Rose usually.'

He put his hand on the table near hers. 'I wanted to ask you before this. But . . . you know – turning up out of the blue with hardly any money – trying to get my legs under the table again. It seems I'm always doing that.'

She said, 'It's not quite like that, is it? If it hadn't been for you turning up, I might have had to sell.'

'I don't think you'd have done that.'

'I wasn't going to ask Duddy for help. If I was to keep my self-respect I had to be certain I was financially independent!' She looked at him and gulped. 'You've enabled me to do that, Rick. So don't talk about getting your legs under the table! That's a horrid phrase.'

'Prevalent in Wales.' He looked at her. 'Oh Jon. We've wasted such a lot of time.'

'Perhaps we had to waste it. To know what we really wanted?'

'Perhaps.' He smiled gently. 'We were all flames, no real warmth. Now . . . I think we've got some warmth. Do you?'

She reached across the table and put her hand over his. Rough skin met rough skin. She laughed briefly. 'Work-hands, my darling. We've changed so much.'

He said, 'So, it's all right? You'll have me back?'

She nodded. 'And you? Will you have me back? Another arrangement to see how it works?'

'I'd like to get married again, Jon.' He smiled. 'I won't rush things. I'll bring you flowers. I'll court you properly this time. We'll do everything properly.'

She held his hand hard. 'Oh, it will be lovely, Rick.' She looked down. 'There's only one thing . . . Rose. Do you still . . . how do you feel about Rose? Please be honest, Rick.'

He said, 'That time she came up to Newcastle . . . it was over then. I'd put her on a pedestal, Jon. She was like someone from another age. Can you understand that?'

'I think so.'

'I was glad when you told me she loved Abe McKenzie. It made her human again. But I'd got over Rose long before that.'

She smiled. 'I do understand what you mean. I was like that about you. I was obsessed with you somehow.' She stood up and began taking things to the sink. And she said thoughtfully, 'Before, I was just in love with you, Rick. Now I like you as well. And that is terribly important.'

He stood up. He made no attempt to take her in his arms. But he asked instead, 'Have you got a minute?'

'Yes. I've fed the poultry.'

'Right. It's a decent morning and there are some daffs beyond the orchard. Come and let me pick you a bunch.' He grinned, and some of the old glint was still there. 'Your first bunch of flowers, Jon. From a very great admirer.'

She laughed. 'Let me get my coat.'

And they walked into the morning together.

They were still cautious at first. And then Philip came down for the Easter weekend and Mabs and Richard Steedman came over for dinner. It was their attitude that seemed to confirm and reinforce the relationship.

Mabs said, 'Well, it was obvious from the first . . . I mean, Rick wouldn't have offered to help you, and you wouldn't have accepted his help if there'd been nothing between you.'

'I was pretty desperate, Mabs.' Jon had cooked a moussaka and they had all dined rather too well, which made this frankness easy. 'Greta and Clark had left and no-one had replied to my ads.'

Rick smiled. 'But *I* wasn't desperate. Abe McKenzie had told me you were settling in this country, and I wanted to know where Georgie was. I fully intended going back to Georgetown that afternoon and getting a bus to Kennedy.'

Jon hadn't thought of that. 'So you wanted to stay? You must have thought we stood a chance?'

'Of course. And after the first week I was certain it would be all right.' He sighed. 'If only you'd been an insurance agent, Jon, it might have worked the first time!'

She laughed. Rick told Mabs some of his experiences at Providential. Mabs said, 'You must have been quite a character, Rick.' She pulled her mouth down. 'A confidence man, I'd say.'

Rick nodded ruefully. 'In a way. I conned Jon.'

'No. I think I always knew what you were up to. Trouble was, I thought it was great!' Jon thought back. 'The only person you really conned was Ma. She thought the world of you. She'd be so pleased we're back together.'

Unexpectedly Philip Duddington said, 'Aileen probably wasn't conned at all. I bet she knew exactly what was going on. But she could see through Rick's outer bit, and knew that underneath he was the right one for Jon. Simple as that.'

'I hope you're right, sir.' Rick lifted his glass. 'She was the mother I never had.' He looked around the table. His red hair curled around his ears because Jon had taken over with the scissors and could not bear to cut it too short. His eyes were clear and very bright. Jon thought with a little thrill: he's happy . . . I've made him happy.

He said, 'Let's toast Aileen, shall we?'

'To Aileen,' they said in unison, and Mabs wiped her eyes ostentatiously.

And then the phone rang.

Jon went into the hall to answer it. She checked her watch: eleven-thirty at home, so it wouldn't be Rose. But it was.

'Rosie! How lovely! We're all here – just toasted Ma. Are you all right? Rather late for you to be . . . '

She stopped speaking and listened. From the dining room everyone else listened.

Jon said, 'My God! What on earth will you *do!*'

Another pause, then she said, 'How can you be so calm – what? You're not calm, you're ecstatically happy?'

Rick came into the hall and hovered uncertainly.

Jon said, 'I can't believe this. The girls are ecstatic too? And Maud? But darling – you can't – you really can't go through with it – have you thought it through?' She stared at Rick above the mouthpiece. 'What? You understand how Mother felt? Excited? Not a bit cowed or worried? Well, yes, but it was a bit different, wasn't it? No-one really realized what was happening. And it wasn't as if . . . ' She listened and her face coloured slightly. 'No, darling. I am not prejudiced. I love Abe almost as much as you do! It's just so . . . *difficult!*'

Rick mouthed something to her and she shook her head abstractedly.

'Listen, Rosie. I'll phone Abe. I'll phone him now – I don't care. He's got a right to know. What? You don't mean that, Rose. You couldn't . . . all right, all right, all right. I won't phone him. I promise I won't tell him. Oh my God. I wish I was with you. Phone me tomorrow. Give me time to think. Will you phone me tomorrow – promise? All right. Yes, all right. Yes. Goodnight then, darling.'

She replaced the receiver with great care and looked at Rick. 'She's having Abe's baby,' she said flatly. 'And she's delighted about it.'

May and June flew by. The girls came home most weekends and sometimes Georgie came with them, sometimes Ellie's friend Janet. Everyone appeared to accept Rose's pregnancy without question. Even June talked about it naturally, though through pursed lips. Grandmother sighed with resignation. 'Bred in the bone, I suppose,' was the worst she could do. After that presents arrived regularly from her.

Maud said, 'Well. My fears are proving groundless, Ros dear. People never fail to amaze me.'

'It's the Boaz syndrome,' Rose said seriously, looking at her mother-in-law with very bright eyes. 'They know it's no accident. They think you sent me off to find him. They think I'm quite a girl!'

Maud laughed and hugged her. 'Well. I could have told them that.'

She went into hospital at the beginning of July to rest before the Caesarean. 'The best of having to have an op this time is that it can be planned properly,' she said to the girls when they visited. 'You two threw all our plans to the winds!'

Blue was suddenly scared. 'We've been so excited about it, Mummy. We forgot it was . . . dangerous,' she said.

'It's not dangerous.' Rose smiled warmly. 'You paved the way for this one. Not a bit dangerous.'

She was so relaxed she fell asleep after the premed injection. She never knew what kind of reception her baby had from theatre staff. When she took him into her arms, still feeling drowsy from the anaesthetic, she made no reference to his colour.

'Good Lord,' she said, sleepily awestruck. 'It – it's a boy!'

And the doctor said jovially, 'It really did have to be one or the other, Mrs Fairbrother.'

'Yes, but . . . ' she began to laugh. He was so different from Blue and Ellie. They'd been tiny scraps of humanity; this one was plump and robust. His eyes were startlingly blue in his coffee-coloured face. His voice was enormous. She spluttered, 'I hadn't remembered that he'd be a complete personality. Immediately!'

They swaddled him and put him in her outstretched arms. The nurse supported his head and talked to her while they 'tidied her up' as they put it.

'He's lovely. Really lovely. And so strong too.' She was full of congratulations. 'Have you thought of any boys' names?'

'Not really. But I'll have to call him Boaz.'

'Boaz?' The nurse tried to keep the horror out of her voice. 'That's very . . . unusual, surely?'

'Yes. I suppose it is. But his ancestor was a good man to follow.'

Rose looked at the tiny face. There had been no birth pangs for this baby; his skin was smooth and his cheeks filled out. She said very gently, 'Hello, Boaz. I'm your mother. I'm so pleased to see you.'

And quite suddenly, he stopped crying.

Everyone loved him, but Georgie and the twins were besotted. They would take it in turns to hang over his cot, exclaiming at every clench of the fist, every flutter of the ridiculous lashes. Georgie acquired a camera and took reels of film.

'For Mum,' he explained. 'It'll be ages before she sees him. I'll take snaps of him at every one of his stages so that she doesn't miss anything.'

'You're going out for the summer then?' Rose said.

'Oh yes. It's OK now. Dad and Mum are back together. Properly. I shan't muck it up like I did last time.'

'Georgie – it was nothing to do with you! You must never think that!'

'No.' Vaguely Georgie remembered Aileen talking to him about his mother. 'No. But I didn't want to interrupt anything. You know.'

Rose kissed him. 'You'll make a really nice husband one day,' she said.

After he had gone the weather was warm. It was Jubilee year and the street parties had been held in wind and rain; now the summer blossomed at last. They opened the new windows wide and ate their meals in the garden within reach of the pram. And they were all out there one day when the door bell rang.

Rose said, 'Blue, be an angel. If I have to get up once more I shall melt!'

Blue, dangling a daisy chain above Bo's sleeping face, crooned, 'Won't be a minute, baby,' and trailed through the house. She saw through the hall window that a taxi was at the gate. For a wonderful moment she thought it was Georgie, home unexpectedly, and she opened the door wide. A tall, burly man stood there. His hair was startlingly white against his dark face, and though she knew immediately who he was, she was shocked because she hadn't visualized him as being so old.

His voice was deep; gravelly almost. 'Hello. You must be one of the twins.'

She hung on to the door. She did not know if this was danger. She croaked, 'You're – you're Bo's father. Aren't you?'

He said, 'Bo?'

'Boaz. Our baby.' She began to close the door. 'You can't have him.'

He said, 'Wait!' Then hazarded a guess. 'Blue – it is Blue, isn't it? – I haven't come to take anything. If you think I should go away, then I'll go. But . . . as you pointed out . . . Bo is my son as well as your brother.'

She hesitated, holding the door between her elbows. It was so unusual for anyone to get her name right, not even Miss Westlake knew unless they wore different clothes.

She said, 'We're happy. We don't need you, you know.'

She watched him get shorter somehow. 'I accept that. Of course. And I'm glad – very glad. But I've come a long way—'

'You could have let us know. Phoned . . . written.' There was something so appealing about him. He wasn't a bit like her father – she had wondered if her mother had found a stand-in for him. He was a powerful man; yet he was so terribly vulnerable. He looked as if he needed someone like her mother. And other people too . . . like Ellie and herself and Maud. She straightened her back. 'You've got your own family, after all!'

He spread his hands. She was fascinated to see the palms were so light. So it was a deep suntan. Environmental.

He said very simply, 'You are my family.'

She knew he was getting under her defences. She said quickly, 'Sorry. You can't come any further.'

'You want me to go?'

'Yes.' she said firmly. And he turned and went back down the garden path to the taxi, and after a second's hesitation she closed the door.

She whipped to the hall window. He looked so old. Why hadn't Mother told them he was an old man who needed looking after? But of course she should have known. Mother must be nearly forty, which made him nearly fifty!

She said, 'Damn!' And opened the door again.

'Hey!' She couldn't even remember his name. He turned and looked. She said, 'What do you think about Steve Biko?'

He said, 'What do you think I think?'

It had been a silly question of course, but all the same he'd given the right answer.

She said, 'Hang on. Sit on the grass or something. You can't come in yet but I'll ask the others what they think.' She shut the door again. She just wished Georgie was here; there were no undercurrents with Georgie. He'd sort it all out in five minutes. And then she thought: suppose it was Georgie knocking on that door and wanting to see me . . .

Boaz slept through the bombshell, completely indifferent. Maud's eyebrows climbed up to the brim of her ancient straw hat and stayed there while she looked at Rose. Rose sat up very straight and for some reason put her hands over her ears. And Ellie, amazingly, screamed and giggled and rolled on to her back.

Blue said angrily, 'What's the matter with you – idiot!'

Ellie controlled herself long enough to gasp, 'It's so romantic! Like Uncle Rick and Aunt Jon! He's come to – to claim Mummy!'

Rose and Maud transferred their gaze to her in astonishment. Rose stammered, 'Is that how you see it?'

Maud said, 'Where is he, for goodness sake?'

Blue said, 'I sent him away. Then I couldn't. So he's sitting on the front lawn waiting to see what you say.'

Rose sprang to her feet, hands still at head level.

'He shouldn't have come. We agreed . . . Jon must have told him, but he still shouldn't have come!'

Maud said, 'He wants to see Bo. That's all.'

'Yes.' Rose let her hands fall. 'Of course.'

Ellie said, 'Bet it's not. Bet he wants to get married and take you over to America—'

'We'd see Aunt Jon then. And Georgie!' Blue chipped in, suddenly very interested.

Maud held out her hands in a calming way. 'Steady on, girls. Mr McKenzie is already married and has a son of his own.'

'Actually . . . ' Rose brought her hands to waist level and rubbed them against her cotton skirt; it was very hot. 'He's not. I didn't tell you. Sarah left him and took Tom with her. Just after Christmas.'

'Ah.' Maud put her own hands in her lap and waited.

Blue stood on one leg. 'Mother, you'll have to see him. You can't leave him out there much longer. He's old. He might faint.'

Ellie sat up. 'I don't mind getting old after all. It's quite exciting really, isn't it?'

Blue said briefly, 'Shut up.'

Rose said, 'You must stay here. Nobody is to leave.' She turned to Blue. 'Bring him through, darling. Let him see Bo.'

Blue did not wait for any afterthoughts; she ran through the big living room and into the hall and pulled open the door. He was standing exactly where she'd left him. He looked terrible.

'You could have sat down on the grass,' she said almost accusingly.

He smiled briefly and shook his head. 'Actually, I couldn't.'

She assumed he must have rheumatism. Gran found it quite hard to sit on the ground and needed a hand up each time she did so.

'Come on then. You can see Bo. He's asleep though and you mustn't wake him. We want him to have his feed as late as possible so that he'll sleep through the night.' She glanced at him over her shoulder. 'He's very young to go right through the night, you know.'

'Yes. Yes, he certainly is.'

She stood aside at the patio windows and let him go through ahead of her. He did not seem to notice the view and made no comment about the house either. Of course he'd never seen it when it was small; but it was a point in his disfavour. That and his age. On the other hand, there was Steve Biko.

He did not look at the pram or Maud or Ellie. He said, 'Hello, Rose.'

And she said, 'Hello Abe.'

Then there was a silence.

When it had stretched to screaming point, Maud said, 'Why don't you two have a walk on the hill? Get the preliminaries over. Then you can come and be introduced and have some tea, Mr McKenzie.'

He said hoarsely, 'I'm sorry.' And at the same time, Rose said, 'You promised to stay here!'

Maud said soothingly, 'We'll stay here. You two go for a walk.'

Rose hesitated, then seemed to see the sense of the suggestion. She turned abruptly and walked to the gate at the bottom of the garden. Abe followed her.

Maud looked at her granddaughters. 'Well!' she said.

And this time even Blue giggled helplessly.

Abe said, 'You should have told me, Rose. I had a right to know.'

'Yes.' It was difficult threading their way through the molehills, but she had somehow lost the footpath. She had known this hill since she was five years old, yet she was lost.

She stopped suddenly and sat on one of the larger tumps.

'Abe, how could I tell you? We'd decided to live our own lives, at least until our children were grown. Wouldn't it have seemed I was changing my mind if I'd written to tell you?'

'But . . . it was so stupendous, Rose. We love each other – we've made a baby together – and I didn't know!'

'You didn't tell me about Sarah and Tom. So I thought that was how you wanted it.'

'How did you know about Sarah and Tom?'

'Eugenie told me. When she wrote about you seeing Rick. And thank you for that, Abe. It seems as if they're working something out.'

He sat down heavily on a neighbouring molehill and surveyed her with that same intense, waiting gaze.

He said briefly, 'Good. And by the way it was your brother-in-law who wrote to tell me about the baby.'

'Really?' She smiled, genuinely pleased for an instant, then said, 'Well, I can see why he did. But I wish he hadn't.'

He said, 'Rose. If I'd told you about Sarah and Tom, would it have made any difference? Would you have told me about Boaz then?'

She looked at her hands. 'I don't know.' She glanced up. 'It's still so difficult, Abe. Oh, I feel just the same. When you walked through the doors just now . . . oh, I feel just the same. But you've still got your . . . ' she paused and smiled at him, 'your cause.'

He too smiled and made as if to reach across from one molehill to the other. Then he sat back.

'Darling Rose. I could hold you now, kiss you, convince you that love is all that matters, and you'd never really believe me. But it is.' He closed his eyes for a moment, then went on, 'D'you remember the end of *War and Peace* when Pierre finally realizes that the whole world is there, in his children's sleeping faces? Wars and strivings and the cruelty of man to man – I've been trying to do something about it most of my life, Rose. But the salvation is right with us. We don't need to go out looking for it.'

'Abe – my dearest Abe – it's different for us. We'd have to go out and fight for our domestic happiness!'

'Oh, I'm not saying anything would be easy. But you don't lack courage, Rose. You never did. You covered for me when you found me under the sofa that time. And you didn't just scream when Lennox chased you. And last autumn when you broke through convention and every damn thing and came and got me . . . that took courage.'

473

She said nothing. He took another breath and tried again. 'Is it your daughters? Blue seems to me to be very adaptable.'

She smiled fleetingly again. 'Yes. You could say that. And Maud too . . . she's ready for anything. I just cannot bring myself to crash into your life in America and ruin all your ambitions—'

He said, 'Rose, there has already been gossip in the press about us. And I'm not going to keep you a secret. Whether you come back with me or not. I'm going to talk about you with pride, my darling. And Boaz too.'

She was silent again, gazing around her as if she were indeed making her farewells at that moment.

Then she spoke almost shyly. 'He's . . . rather special, Abe. I know all mothers think the same. But really . . . he's only eight weeks old and he sleeps all through the night. And already he smiles at us. He knows each one of us individually. He's so content. As if he's happy to be with us.'

He looked away from her suddenly and down at his feet; his face worked uncontrollably for a moment.

She was still staring down at Gloucester. She said, 'And I want you to notice his eyes, Abe. They're still blue. I realize they will probably change, but it makes him . . . unusual.'

He said huskily, 'I love you so much, Rose. I think I always have. Without knowing you . . . in my bones somewhere has been this feeling of Rose.'

'Oh . . . Abe. Don't.' She choked a laugh. 'I don't mean don't tell me you love me. What I mean is . . . you don't have to. Because I know.' She reached across at last and took his hands in hers. 'You see, I feel the same. It's no good, Abe. I can't manage without you. We wouldn't have been brought together like this if we weren't to stay together. It doesn't need courage at all. It's the natural thing to do.'

He held on to her hands like a drowning man and she looked into his eyes and left her molehill to hold his head against her shoulder.

'It's all right, Abe. Don't . . . my dear, please don't. It's all right. We're together.'

He put his arms around her waist and held her so tightly to him that she could hardly breathe. She remembered David . . . the park . . . she kissed his wiry hair and smoothed it. She had been frightened then; frightened to go forward and take what was being given her so generously. She was no longer frightened.

She waited until he lifted his head, then she kissed him. Then she said, 'Come and see our baby, Abe. Come and meet your family. And have some tea. And talk.'

And after a while they stood up. Rose found the path and they wandered back like so many lovers before them, hand in hand.

Ellie and Blue were waiting like twin Sister Annes at the gate. They disappeared as soon as they saw their mother, and Abe's first official view of his future stepdaughters was of them carrying trays sedately out of the house as if they'd been at it for the past hour.

Maud, followed, carrying a gigantic teapot. She looked at them and beamed.

'So it's all right?' She put the pot on the picnic table and advanced with outstretched hand. 'I'm delighted to meet you at last, Mr McKenzie—'

'Please. Abe,' he insisted, taking her hand.

Rose said, 'Mother. Abe is going to be your son. D'you think you could kiss him?'

And Maud drew back, opened her arms and flung them around Abe's wide shoulders. It was the signal for mayhem. Blue and Ellie joined in the ensuing scrum, screaming their delight.

'We'll live in America, won't we Abe?' ' . . . at least some of the time?' 'Can we come when Georgie is there?' 'And Abe, can Gran have a room for her sewing – she's brilliant at sewing.'

Maud tried to hush them, but to no avail. Abe would not even let her go. His long arms seemed capable of encircling them all. He said, 'Make all the requests you like. You know darn well what my answers are!'

475

It was Maud who said gently, 'You'd better come and look at Boaz now, Abe. He woke up while you two were taking your walk, and he'll need a feed very soon, then he'll want to go to bed.' She glinted up at him. 'He really is such a good baby. I know all grandmothers are prejudiced, but speaking entirely objectively, this one is special.'

So Abe went to the pram and looked inside. Startlingly blue eyes stared straight back at him; Rose had prepared him but even so he drew in his breath sharply. And then, the most amazing thing happened. The baby held up tiny clenched fists and smiled. Almost as if he recognized his father.

Abe said quietly, 'I need not have worried, Rose, need I?'

'How do you mean?' She held his hand which was draped around her neck. It tightened on hers.

'You would have come to look for me quite soon, my darling. Because it's so obvious that Boaz McKenzie is going to be the first coloured president of the United States!'

The girls exploded with more laughter. And Maud smiled as she moved towards the tea-things. But Rose looked at the man who had emerged from the Victory cake so many years ago, then back at the tiny boy child in the pram.

And she wondered.

THE END

BY SUN AND CANDLELIGHT
by Susan Sallis

They discovered the empty cottage in 1940 – when they were still at school, four teenage friends from wildly different backgrounds and with the war casting its shadow over their lives.

It was to the cottage that Monica came, pregnant, alone, frightened, and it was there that their story really began. For Bessie, born secretly and shamefully to one of them, raised by another, and loved by them all, came to represent what was the very best in their lives.

A huge and powerful novel – of four friends and the lifetime bonds that held them together.

0 552 13545 3

SUMMER VISITORS
by Susan Sallis

Madge was four years old when she first saw the Cornish sea and fell in love with it, and it was there that her family grew and suffered and loved. It was there she and her mother went to recover from a heartrending family tragedy – there she was forced reluctantly into marriage – there she fell into a wild and passionate wartime love.

And it was there she saw her children grow and love and cope with the secret legacies the years had left them, until finally they became more than just Summer Visitors.

The magnificent story of a family and the woman who held them together.

0 552 13346 9

SUSAN SALLIS OMNIBUS –
TWO NOVELLAS BY SUSAN SALLIS

FOUR WEEKS IN VENICE

Abigail Langley was determined that before illness finally restricted her way of life, her daughters would have one marvellous holiday to remember for the rest of their lives. Selling her only asset – grandmother's emeralds – she took Susan and Christine for four wonderful, luxurious weeks in Venice. And, secretly, Abigail was hoping that her girls would meet 'eligible suitors' – the way girls did in the old days – suitors who would remove most of the economic worries in their lives. But it was Abigail who found a suitor – a most unsuitable American who nicknamed her 'Duchess' – and as the Langley family succumbed to the spell of Venice, so their lives took a totally and most unexpected change.

RICHMOND HERITAGE

Mary Richmond's marriage had been crumbling for years. Her husband's whole life was totally concerned with Milton Mains, the family farm in the Devon hills. And as Mary was excluded more and more from her husband's life, so she began to think her marriage was over. Then came the bombshell. Her father-in-law died, leaving huge death duties. Milton Mains had to be sold, a smaller place purchased. Mary knew she couldn't desert Jim now, for the new farm meant grinding work – shared work – for both of them.

0 552 136131

A SCATTERING OF DAISIES

THE DAFFODILS OF NEWENT

BLUEBELL WINDOWS

ROSEMARY FOR REMEMBRANCE

by Susan Sallis

Will Rising had dragged himelf from humble beginnings to his own small tailoring business in Gloucester – and on the way he'd fallen violently in love with Florence, refined, delicate, and wanting something better for her children.

March was the eldest girl, the least loved, the plain, unattractive one who, as the family grew, became more and more the household drudge. But March, a strange, intelligent, unhappy child, had inherited some of her mother's dreams. March Rising was determined to break out of the round of poverty and hard work, to find wealth, and love, and happiness.

The story of the Rising girls continues in The Daffodils of Newent and Bluebell Windows, finally reaching its conclusion in Rosemary for Remembrance.

A Scattering of Daisies   0 552 12375 7
The Daffodils of Newent   0 552 12579 2
Bluebell Windows   0 552 12880 5
Rosemary for Remembrance   0 552 13136 9

A SELECTION OF FINE TITLES
AVAILABLE FROM CORGI BOOKS

THE PRICES SHOWN BELOW WERE CORRECT AT THE TIME OF
GOING TO PRESS. HOWEVER TRANSWORLD PUBLISHERS RESERVE
THE RIGHT TO SHOW NEW RETAIL PRICES ON COVERS WHICH MAY
DIFFER FROM THOSE PREVIOUSLY ADVERTISED IN THE TEXT OR
ELSEWHERE.

☐	13718 9	LIVERPOOL LOU	Lyn Andrews	£3.99
☐	13600 X	THE SISTERS O'DONNELL	Lyn Andrews	£3.99
☐	13482 1	THE WHITE EMPRESS	Lyn Andrews	£3.99
☐	13230 6	AN EQUAL CHANCE	Brenda Clarke	£3.99
☐	13556 9	SISTERS AND LOVERS	Brenda Clarke	£3.99
☐	12887 2	SHAKE DOWN THE STARS	Frances Donnelly	£3.99
☐	12387 0	COPPER KINGDOM	Iris Gower	£3.99
☐	12637 3	PROUD MARY	Iris Gower	£3.99
☐	12638 1	SPINNER'S WHARF	Iris Gower	£3.99
☐	13138 5	MORGAN'S WOMAN	Iris Gower	£3.99
☐	13315 9	FIDDLER'S FERRY	Iris Gower	£3.99
☐	13316 7	BLACK GOLD	Iris Gower	£3.99
☐	13631 X	THE LOVES OF CATRIN	Iris Gower	£3.99
☐	12607 1	DOCTOR ROSE	Elvi Rhodes	£2.99
☐	13185 7	THE GOLDEN GIRLS	Elvi Rhodes	£3.99
☐	13481 3	THE HOUSE OF BONNEAU	Elvi Rhodes	£3.99
☐	13309 4	MADELEINE	Elvi Rhodes	£3.99
☐	12367 6	OPAL	Elvi Rhodes	£2.99
☐	12803 1	RUTH APPLEBY	Elvi Rhodes	£4.99
☐	13738 3	SUMMER PROMISE AND OTHER STORIES	Elvi Rhodes	£3.99
☐	13413 9	THE QUIET WAR OF REBECCA SHELDON	Kathleen Rowntree	£3.99
☐	13557 7	BRIEF SHINING	Kathleen Rowntree	£3.99
☐	12375 7	A SCATTERING OF DAISIES	Susan Sallis	£3.99
☐	12579 2	THE DAFFODILS OF NEWENT	Susan Sallis	£3.99
☐	12880 5	BLUEBELL WINDOWS	Susan Sallis	£3.99
☐	13613 1	RICHMOND HERITAGE/FOUR WEEKS IN VENICE	Susan Sallis	£3.99
☐	13136 9	ROSEMARY FOR REMEMBRANCE	Susan Sallis	£3.99
☐	13346 9	SUMMER VISITORS	Susan Sallis	£3.99
☐	13545 3	BY SUN AND CANDLELIGHT	Susan Sallis	£3.99
☐	13299 3	DOWN LAMBETH WAY	Mary Jane Staples	£3.99
☐	13573 9	KING OF CAMBERWELL	Mary Jane Staples	£3.99
☐	13444 9	OUR EMILY	Mary Jane Staples	£3.99
☐	13845 2	RISING SUMMER	Mary Jane Staples	£3.99
☐	13635 2	TWO FOR THREE FARTHINGS	Mary Jane Staples	£3.99
☐	13730 8	THE LODGER	Mary Jane Staples	£3.99

*All Corgi/Bantam books are available at your bookshops or newsagents, or can be ordered from the
following address:*

Corgi/Bantam Books,
Cash Sales Department,
P.O. Box 11, Falmouth, Cornwall TR10 9EN

Please send a cheque or postal order (no currency) and allow 80p for postage and packing for the first
book plus 20p for each additional book ordered up to a maximum charge of £2.00 in UK.

B.F.P.O. customers please allow 80p for the first book and 20p for each additional book.

Overseas customers, including Eire, please allow £1.50 for postage and packing for the first book,
£1.00 for the second book, and 30p for each subsequent title ordered.